Advance Praise for Allegra Hyde's

Eleutheria

"*Eleutheria* is gripping, surprising, and full of the poetry of planet Earth. This book is a marvel." —CJ Hauser, author of *The Crane Wife: A Memoir in Essays*

"*Eleutheria*'s timeliness alone is enough to justify a wide and appreciative audience, yet Hyde's exceptional artistic gifts— especially the complex characters and charged language— make this novel's urgent concerns all the more powerful." —Ron Rash, author of *In the Valley*

"My god, can Allegra Hyde write! *Eleutheria* is a thrilling and utterly transporting novel about survival and hope and the tenacity of love in a dying world. Hyde's characters are unforgettable, her sentences crystalline. I was surprised and delighted and moved at every turn." —Kirstin Valdez Quade, author of *The Five Wounds*

"With her captivating novel, Allegra Hyde leads us on a willful, sinuous search for answers in an upended world. *Eleutheria* is a rallying cry for our collective change of direction." —Pitchaya Sudbanthad, author of *Bangkok Wakes to Rain*

"*Eleutheria* is utopian writing at its best and boldest. . . . Every sentence Allegra Hyde writes is alive with grace and power and enviable moral clarity." —Matt Bell, author of *Appleseed*

"Incisive, darkly funny, and farseeing. . . . A stunning debut."
—Vanessa Hua, author of *Forbidden City* and *A River of Stars*

"Clear-eyed, buoyant, and far-reaching. . . . I read *Eleutheria* in one breathless day and was sorry to leave this world, where our mistakes and tragedies are shown to be as fully human as our most generous dreams."
—Adrienne Celt, author of *End of the World House*

"Allegra Hyde's visionary first novel is like a terrarium, a small new world made by someone who cares deeply about our survival. . . . But far from being a closed system, everything inside this book—both the ecological disasters and their elegant solutions—is an invitation, radiant with possibility, asking us with love and urgency to change."
—Jennifer Tseng, author of *Mayumi and the Sea of Happiness*

"A twisty, startling tale of climate change and utopia more than worthy of all its ambition. I wept when it was over, for Willa, but also for this mess we're in—a mess Hyde illuminates with beautiful, affecting prose, bizarre characters who are so completely themselves, and plot twists that shock even as their root is in the inevitability of generations of selfishness. This is a haunting book about reckless, heartbreaking hope."
—Lydia Conklin, author of *Rainbow Rainbow*

"Vivid. Wry. Exceptionally clear-sighted."
—Morgan Thomas, author of *Manywhere*

ALLEGRA HYDE

Eleutheria

Allegra Hyde's debut story collection, *Of This New World*, won the John Simmons Short Fiction Award through the Iowa Short Fiction Award series. Her stories and essays have appeared in *The Pushcart Prize*, *Best of the Net*, *The Best Small Fictions*, and *The Best American Travel Writing*. Originally from New Hampshire, she currently lives in Ohio and teaches at Oberlin College.

Eleutheria

Eleutheria

Allegra Hyde

VINTAGE BOOKS

A DIVISION OF PENGUIN RANDOM HOUSE LLC

NEW YORK

A VINTAGE BOOKS ORIGINAL, MARCH 2022

Library of Congress Cataloging-in-Publication Data
Names: Hyde, Allegra, author.
Title: Eleutheria / Allegra Hyde.
Description: First Vintage Books edition. | New York : Vintage
    Books, 2022.
Identifiers: LCCN 2021032415 | ISBN 9780593315248 (trade
    paperback) | ISBN 9780593315255 (ebook)
Classification: LCC PS3608.Y365 E44 2022 | DDC 813/.6—dc23
LC record available at https://lccn.loc.gov/2021032415

Vintage Books Trade Paperback ISBN: 978-0-593-31524-8
eBook ISBN: 978-0-593-31525-5

Book design by Nicholas Alguire

www.vintagebooks.com

Printed in the United States of America
10 9 8 7 6 5 4 3 2 1

For my parents

That their jurisdiction shall reach only to men as men, and shall take care that justice, peace, and sobriety, may be maintained among them. And that the flourishing state of the republic may be by all just means promoted.

—*Articles and Orders of the Company of Eleutherian Adventurers,* 1647

The space between the idea of something and its reality is always wide and deep and dark.

—Jamaica Kincaid, 1991

Eleutheria

MY FATHER HAD A THEORY for why people went to the ocean in the summer, spent their savings, their vacation days, to plant themselves on a patch of sand within sight of the water.

Even if they don't know it, my father said, what they want is to be close to death.

That's what going to the ocean was, according to him: a chance to strip down and expose yourself to danger. To risk sunburn and dehydration and errant strikes of lightning, the foot-slice of seashells, sand-submerged needles. At the beach, you could wade out into waves that might pull you into a riptide or the jaws of a shark. Or even if you only dipped your toes in the water, you'd still know you were stepping into something so vast it could engulf you, swallow you whole.

It's not that people want to die, said my father, it's just that when they go to the beach a part of them knows, deep down, that they could. So afterward, when they return to their three-hour commutes and their cubicles, they return with a secret sense of survival. They feel woken up. More alert.

My mother snorted when she heard this. She, like my father and I, was crouched in the dark gut of our emergency bunker—yet unfinished, but stocked with canned goods, blankets, a stack of semiautomatic rifles. We were practicing what to do in the event of an electromagnetic attack.

Going to the beach, said my mother, won't save you when S-H-T-F.

My parents didn't think we needed the beach because, unlike the masses, we were already alert to the horrors and dangers of the modern world. Unlike the masses, we were already prepared.

So, I didn't go to a beach until I was nearly eighteen, and then it was only a shabby artificial one near Logan Airport. I didn't go to a beach until after my parents couldn't survive themselves.

And when I went with Sylvia, that felt different—not like pressing in close to death, but already existing in an afterlife.

Really, my father's theory didn't mean much to me until these last eight months, the ones I've had to think through what happened on the island, what happened at Camp Hope. All this time I've had to wonder what it was we were really doing—what it was I did—and now, of course, I have hardly any time at all.

Maybe I should have been thinking of my father right from the beginning. Maybe I should have thought about where I was really going when I first careened over the archipelago in a turboprop gunshot from Florida, and those islands looked to be all beach, the Bahamas scattered along the turquoise lip of the Caribbean, their coastlines sandbar-swirled, coral-dazed, the islands so low in the water they seemed poised to hold their breath. A little more sea-level rise and they'd be washed away. Already their edges were eroding, ocean swells grabbing at coastal roads, at the underbellies of beach houses not yet leveled by hurricanes. The worst of the storms had turned whole resorts to matchsticks, their swimming pools gone green from neglect, pagodas engulfed by vegetation, hibiscus blooming in marbled bathrooms, quail doves shitting on embroidered towels—another empire born and bowed—and yet when I looked down from the turboprop, pressed my face to its oval window, I felt only possibility. I felt more than alive.

My whole life I've run away from my parents' way of thinking; that's what I wish people understood. Despite everything that has happened—the way everything looks—I only ever wanted to make the world better. I only ever wanted to help.

You should know, too, that I recognized Eleutheria from the air. I knew the island even before the turboprop circled toward a ragged stretch of tarmac. The island bathed in the water like a fishhook: a skinny hundred miles that curved at one end, its shorelines barbed by peninsulas, baited with the green sway of sea grapes, beaches as pink and fine as spun sugar.

I felt Eleutheria catch my heart—and pull.

1

My name, my full name, is Willa Marks. There's nothing in the middle. My parents must have had their reasons for the omission, though I've always considered it a sign of honesty. A middle name can lurk in a person like a bomb: a secret identity poised to pop off. I'm simply me.

What I'm trying to say is that I'm going to tell you the truth. I don't have time to tell you anything else. And it's important for you to hear the truth because what has been said about Camp Hope, about me, is a shadow of what really happened.

Let me start with the easy parts.

I was twenty-two when I boarded a plane and flew to Eleutheria.

I was drunk on ideas.

I was so drunk, in fact, that when the turboprop shuddered into a nosedive—cabin lights flickering, pilot crackling over the intercom—my limbs remained limp. While the other passengers hunched in their seats, prayers on their lips, I kept my eyes open, savoring the rush of arrival, the jarring smack of it reverberating through me.

The turboprop did not land elegantly, but it landed intact. Even so, had the plane crashed onto the island, I'd still have walked out of the wreckage, beatific. I'd been awake the length of a day, a night, and that had not yet become a problem. I was the kind of person who took exhaustion in stride, let it warp my surroundings into dreamscapes. And so far, everything had gone right.

Out the airplane window: palm trees, a heat-seared tarmac, men in orange vests strolling from the steel maw of a rusted aircraft hangar. Around me, a dozen other passengers unbuckled their seat belts. Some smiled relievedly, others wiped away tears. A woman's purse had spilled into the aisle and I helped her collect her things, though I curbed my impulse to ask if she was from Eleutheria. To get caught in conversation might break whatever spell had whisked me from Boston to the Bahamas, a spell meant to carry me on to Camp Hope. I wanted to arrive unimpeded, unburdened, slick as a fish released into the sea. If I could have, I would have traveled to the island naked. As it was, my backpack contained only a change of clothes, a passport, sixty-five U.S. dollars, and my well-thumbed copy of *Living the Solution: The Official Camp Hope Guide to Transforming Ourselves and Saving the Planet.*

I had the envelope as well—the one from Sylvia—but I tried not to think about it.

What I thought about was Camp Hope. Specifically, about arriving at Camp Hope and making my life mean something. Had you watched me exit the airplane, my preoccupation would have been obvious. You would have seen a young woman who tripped over her own boots—a size too large—as she entered the hangar. You might have noticed one of my overall cuffs was rolled up higher than the other, that my backpack zipper gaped partially open. Back in Boston, I would have been a person your eyes glazed over on the street: shiftless, among the masses of the newly unemployed. I had an oval face, brittle yellow hair that went dark at the roots, a stub of a nose. I was thin, but not jagged. Scrappy, though in an untested way: like a runaway who has only just left the house, or an actor playing a role. Familiar enough to forget.

In the echoing dimensions of the hangar, however, I stood out. I'd traveled to the island alone and there was no one there to meet me. I had little luggage. I was white and the only person queued in the International Arrivals line. A weary customs agent took my passport, studied it, shrugged. There were no biometric scanners here. Not in this makeshift terminal, arrivals separated from departures by a plastic partition. The original building, like so much else on the island, had been ravaged by hurricanes. Under different circumstances, I might have been made teary-eyed by the scene of my fellow passengers embracing loved ones, opening luggage to reveal supplies from elsewhere—bags of dried rice, baby clothes, phone chargers—but I fixed my attention on the airport exit: a square of sunshine on the far side of the hangar.

I have what you could call a tendency toward fixation. This tendency has been described as childish by some. People have told me, in general, that I have a childlike demeanor. My short stature is partly to blame. Also, my smattering of freckles—though these would multiply, day by day, colonizing my complexion the longer I remained on Eleutheria. I did not have any muscle tone, though that would change as well. I had little coordination. I have only ever been graceful in photos. Pinned under someone else's gaze, I look best in stillness.

I was not still. Walking with rollicking, over-long strides, I burst out of the hangar into dazzling sunshine. A parking lot shimmered, woozy with heat, its perimeter rimmed by a chain-link fence. In the distance, a narrow highway disappeared into a low swath of scrubland.

My skin burned hot; I had *Living the Solution* churning inside me and with it the heat of my own ambition. I tended to flush in odd ways—in my fingertips, mostly—though if you'd been watching, this would have been invisible. You would have seen only a pale girl striking out across a parking lot. A lost girl, harmless—or even in harm's way—easily manipulated. A rube. It was true, my official education extended only through high school, homeschooled at that. But I was not entirely inexperienced. At twenty-two, I'd had my own unusual education. I considered myself intellectually advanced in one significant way: I was too wise for cynicism. I had outsmarted doubt.

No one at Camp Hope knew I was coming. No one would know who I was when I arrived. I maintained, nevertheless, a propulsive confidence. Reaching the edge of the parking lot, I started down the side of the highway, soaking in sunshine, electrifying my body, intending only to move closer to my destination—a place in my head, rather than direct view—so that, if you'd been watching, you might have seen my eyes go unfocused, my chin lift, my chest tugged forward by an invisible string.

Someone *was* watching. A pickup truck trailed me out of the parking lot and onto the highway. There were four men in the truck: two in the front and two in the back. The pair in the back wore sun-faded T-shirts that billowed in the breeze, their arms stretched along the edges of the truck bed. The man in the passenger seat wore an orange vest, as if he'd just stepped off the airport tarmac. The driver was obscured.

I kept walking and the truck kept rolling, until the man in the orange vest called: You a surfer? Or—

A fugitive? interrupted a man in the back.

There was laughter, but I didn't care—I didn't even break stride. In my mind's eye, my destination glittered: an eco-paradise, a pragmatic arcadia, an answer to the problem that had haunted me my whole life.

Are you lost? said the man in the orange vest.

Though I'd barely spoken for a day and a half, my answer burst forth, bell-like and bright: I'm going to Camp Hope.

The truck stopped rolling. The men's laughter ceased. I continued on, unperturbed, reciting lines from *Living the Solution* beneath my breath, swinging my arms as I walked the ragged edge of the highway.

Ten minutes later, the truck again rumbled alongside me. All the men had gotten out except the driver. He leaned across the passenger seat, his face visible for the first time. He was handsome in a plaintive way, his eyes half-closed, his jawline shadowed by a beard, his dreadlocks pulled behind his head. He asked if I was really going to Camp Hope.

Sure am, I said.

Camp Hope is far, far from here, he said.

I can manage, I said—though in truth it was hotter than seemed possible for the month of May. Only squat palms and brambly foliage stretched before me, with no sign of a settlement or even the sea, save for the wheeling arc of a gull overhead.

Also, said the driver, you're walking the wrong way.

He told me to let him give me a ride. He said he didn't mind, speaking in a tenor of nonchalance I should have perhaps recognized as forced. He was, in fact, keenly interested in what I had to say and where I was going. Deron was his name. For a long time I was angry at him, given what would happen later on, though my feelings have since changed. I hope Deron is well and happy wherever he is now, even if—in his own way and for his own reasons—he did make everything more complicated.

The truck roared down the highway, wind slicing into the cabin through the open windows. I might have remained quiet, watched the landscape blur past, convinced an invisible current was carrying me closer to Camp Hope—but of course, that was not what was happening. That was not happening at all.

The truck cabin was cramped and Deron was tall, yet he maintained a casual posture, except where his hand clenched the stick shift. The grip meant little to me; I hadn't spent much time in trucks and didn't know anything about driving them. What I noticed was that Deron had used an elastic tie with pink plastic beads—the kind little girls wear—to gather his hair. This made me like him. When he asked my name, I told him.

I'm Willa, I said. Willa Marks.

Out the windows: scrubland sprawled in every direction, except for a tumbledown gas station, plywood fixed over one window like a pirate eye patch. Further on, a worn sign indicated an upcoming settlement.

Willa Marks, said Deron, you don't look like the Camp Hope type.

I'm exactly the type, I said.

Deron nodded with exaggerated slowness. The truck rumbled into a small community comprised of cinder-block homes painted pastel pinks, yellows, teals with white trim. A group of men watched the truck pass from the shade of a garage. A lone woman, scowling, sat beside a spread of cucumbers, tomatoes, and papayas. Farther on, a pair of children dangled from a swing set. Chickens skittered into the brush.

Deron repeated my name to himself, as if trying to remember where we had met, and for the first time on my journey, I felt uneasy. I did not like hearing my name said aloud, chanted like a password to a history I'd forgotten.

Willa, Willa, Willa. What does that mean—*Willaaaa*?

I shrugged. My mother once told me she named me Willa because there was a willow in her front yard growing up: a tree everyone thinks of as peaceful, with its long droopy branches, thin leaves. Really, it's a ferocious tree, with roots spreading underground, fingering the foundations of houses, bubbling up the asphalt of driveways. I never quite believed my mother, though. If she had admired the tree so much, why hadn't she named me *Willow*? Now she was too dead to ask.

Why don't I look like the Camp Hope type? I said.

A smile hitched one side of Deron's mouth. As if he hadn't heard my question, he said he had an interest in names. He asked if I knew the meaning of the island's name—*Eleutheria*—his accent smoothing off vowels at the beginning and the end of the word, the way ocean water smooths down glass, making me feel a little seasick, storm-tossed too. He started talking about the island's history. There'd been a shipwreck, religious colonists. My attention drifted. Out the truck window, confectionary-colored houses gave way to abandoned buildings, vines snaking their walls. Beyond them lay piles of twisted metal, roofs displaced from their frames. A rowboat's rotting stern crested a wave of fruit pods in the branches of a tamarind tree. This part of the island had been hard-hit by hurricanes.

Isn't that interesting? said Deron—his smile turning too friendly—How you can end up so far from where you originally intended to go?

Sure.

My unease intensified. I did not know if we were actually driving to Camp Hope. I had no map, only the promise of a place spelled out in *Living the Solution*: the book's hard corner pressing through the fabric of the backpack in my lap. Perhaps I had trusted too quickly; it wouldn't have been the first time. And for all the merits of *Living the Solution*, the book wouldn't help me if I was about to be abducted.

They're expecting me, I said. If I don't show up at Camp Hope, they'll wonder where I am.

Deron steered around a section of washed-out road. He asked why, if the Camp Hope people were expecting me, no one had picked me up.

Got in on an early flight, I said.

No other flights coming in today.

I'm a day early.

A truck passed from the other direction and Deron lifted two fingers from the wheel to wave. The coast surged into view: the water crystalline, tourmaline-tinged, lapping a stretch of bone-white beach. Deron said that since I'd gotten in early, I should see other parts of the island. Better parts. Better people. He could take me to the new hotel.

Bahamian-owned, Bahamian-operated, he said. We're trying to rebuild—

I'm not a tourist, I said.

Call yourself whatever you like, said Deron. It might be worth taking your time, before diving headfirst into something you don't understand.

I understand Camp Hope perfectly well.

The truck rounded another bend; we entered a settlement overlooking a harbor. On a stretch of sand, the metal carcass of a backhoe hulked like a beached whale. The corner of *Living the Solution* pressed deeper into my ribs. That book—it had offered me an option when there seemed to be no others. It described how, despite the odds, a small group of people could change the world for the better. If I tried hard enough, believed hard enough, my life could be more than a series of disappointments, failures, half tries, and hurt.

When Deron started talking about the new hotel again, I interrupted.

Look, I said. All I care about is Camp Hope. And getting there. It's going to launch any day now and I have to be there. I have to help.

Deron flexed his stick-shift hand, resqueezed.

Any day? he said. Like tomorrow?

The truck turned onto a side road camouflaged by overgrown brush. Branches slapped the windshield. I had no idea when Camp Hope would officially launch into the public eye. *Living the Solution* had not included a precise timetable. All I knew was that the launch was likely soon; it had to be. I said

this to Deron, describing the planet's track toward climatological disaster—how Camp Hope was humanity's best shot for
changing course—my voice raw by the time the truck lurched
to a halt, just short of a clearing.

Please, Deron, I said.

He lifted his chin toward the windshield. Past the clearing
stood a vast wall: twenty feet high and draped with cascading
bougainvillea. An emerald city. A green mirage.

Camp Hope.

I grabbed my backpack and leapt out of the truck. A huge
pair of double-doors were set in the bougainvillea wall, their
brass handles sparkling in the sun. I might have run straight to
them if I hadn't felt guilty for doubting Deron.

You're coming too? I said, as he eased himself from the
driver's seat.

Deron tugged at his hair tie, cleared his throat. He said: I
wanted to give you my number, in case—

He beckoned for my hand.

I held it out, trying to be patient as he turned my palm to
the sky, pulled a pen from his pocket, and pressed the inked
tip to my skin. That close, I could see the stubble around his
jaw. He was younger than I'd initially thought; he smelled
faintly of paint solvents and I noticed, for the first time, the
blues flecked on his T-shirt were the same blues around the
island—turquoise, indigo, aquamarine—as if the sea and sky
had splashed on him and stuck. A current of anxiety hummed
beneath his casual manner, though if it had always been there,
or just appeared, I could not be sure.

He finished writing his number but did not release my
hand. I discovered I did not want him to. Hand in hand, I
remained anchored to someone known, however slightly.

You should call me, he said. If you ever have something you want to discuss about Camp Hope. Such as the launch, and what it means for the rest of the island. Or, Willa, if you need to talk—

My heartbeat quickened; I pulled my hand back against my own body. Intimacy, I reminded myself, slowed down progress. I knew that from experience. I also knew that one of Camp Hope's many revolutionary elements was its approach to two-person relationships: there were none. Love was a distraction—an ethical pollutant—in relationships both romantic and platonic. The same went for family ties, which could poison a person's moral compass. And morality meant everything at Camp Hope; morality would win our environmental struggle.

I sprang away from Deron, flinging a goodbye over my shoulder as I hurried toward the doors set in the bougainvillea wall.

I did not need a partner. I did not need a family. I did not even need a friend.

By design, Camp Hope did not yet have a web presence—or a public presence of any kind. Everything I knew about it came from *Living the Solution:* a book I had encountered under unusual circumstances and, technically, not been meant to see.

There was, however, an abundance of information about the book's author: Roy H. Adams. A military man, for years he had basked in the computer screen glow of command centers, in the adulation of joystick warriors, his approval one link in the kill chain that turned foreign villages to dust. In photos online, he stood in front of American flags, his hair razor cut, his square jaw set, his eyes flinty. He looked like a man who expected his steaks rare and his golf courses pesticide-drenched; a man who believed he was entitled to all that he touched.

And yet, that same Adams had written, in *Living the Solution*, about giving up his military career, his marriage as well. Such sacrifices, he explained, *were a small price to pay in the WAR against climate change, a WAR for humanity's very SURVIVAL.*

We'd been losing that war. There'd been decades of environmental marches and bumper stickers, special light bulbs and bike racks, sit-ins and die-ins and speeches, NGOs and IGOs and NPDESs and panicked scientific studies—and for what? Torrential rain spurred landslides in China, smothered whole cities. Spore-laced dust storms forced mass evacuations in Australia. There were the ongoing food shortages—a drought squeezing Brazilian soy, a wheat blight hitting Russia—along with the desperation brewing on the force of that hunger. *Boat people*, pundits called the hundreds of thousands of refugees floating from coast to coast. Begging for the right to dock. Begging for scraps. Dying. Bodies washing up along the Bay of Bengal. On the flooded plazas of Barcelona. Americans looked on with ephemeral pity, the tragedy ever seeming elsewhere—acute or temporal—even as wildfires seared the west and toxic algae bloomed in the Great Lakes. We were moored in apathy, in the comfort of willful blindness. Even as CO_2 levels ticked upward and glaciers sweated smaller and entire ecosystems expired. The average environmentalist, according to Adams, only whimpered, equivocated, begged for corporate salvation, gave into the ease of greenwashing, the capitalist diversion epitomized in reusable shopping bags:

keep on spending. In America, we still had our guns, our flags, our stranglehold on exceptionalism. We still had the distraction of virtual realities, the Hollywood phantasmagoria, the pharmaceutical raft of painlessness. We still had the audacity to call climate change a problem for another time—another country—as if we weren't already proverbial frogs, our skin sloughing off in hot water.

Our challenge boils down to one thing, Roy Adams had written, *the distance between what people want and what people need.*

Camp Hope was a prototype. A nucleus. A revolution waiting to hatch. It modeled what could be: made progress into paradise, showed how environmental living could be desired rather than feared. And while it's true land was cheap in the Bahamas—the post-hurricane government desperate for income, any whisper of industry—Adams had also chosen to build Camp Hope in Eleutheria because the location sent a message: he wasn't afraid of hurricanes or sea-level rise or anyone else's opinions.

I couldn't wait to tell him I wasn't afraid either. Because in truth, it was Adams I wanted to see as much as Camp Hope. It was Adams—as a repentant man, a reformed man, a visionary—who made me believe humanity could be galvanized, the planet saved. Because if Adams could change, anyone could.

Including me.

The doors to Camp Hope opened with ease, well greased, silent. I had to shield my eyes as I stepped inside: the compound's low breezy bungalows and pavilions and laboratories all painted in a wash so white, the buildings gleamed with snow-blinding brightness.

But this was Eleutheria: an island blessed by equatorial warmth. Between the buildings were garden plots flush with melon leaves. Feathery carrot tops. Rows of purple beans. An orchard offered trees loaded with avocados and sugar apples. Hibiscus blossomed everywhere, at once jewel-like and giant. This was Camp Hope: the text of *Living the Solution* rippled into reality. Solar arrays glinted from rooftops. Carbon capture units hummed near the shore. A wind turbine twirled overhead. All of it, all of Camp Hope, spread out as immaculate and people-less as a museum diorama.

I giggled—astonished and perplexed—and as my voice exited my mouth it diffused into the landscape.

Hello? I called, but that sound also dissipated.

Sunlight dappled a pathway of crushed shells. I meandered along it, ducking under trellised passion fruit vines, through open-air hydroponics labs, into sleeping quarters filled with bunks made bandage-tight. From an observation deck, I watched an egret slide over a curving stretch of sand, settle on a gnarled clump of mangroves. At the center of the grounds, a geodesic dome humped from the earth, its glassy surface composed of honeycomb panels.

One of the panels flickered. I rushed forward—bracing for my first encounter with a Camp Hope crewmember—but met only the reflected slouch of my overalls, my knot of hair, my own wide eyes.

Behind the glass, rows of tables sat empty.

I licked salt from my upper lip, the sun squeezing sweat from my pores. Everything was right and yet nothing was right. On a rigid laundry line, dish towels fluttered in the breeze, as if trying to tug themselves free. I let one flutter against my face. I turned in slow circles, wandered onward. Time elongated, minutes expanding, doubling back. I became unsure of which pathways I'd taken, the hibiscus blossoms I'd already passed. Though the Camp Hope compound was contained on a stubby peninsula—covering a square mile at most—it seemed city-sized, sprawling.

I leaned against a raised garden bed to catch my breath. My elbow upset a watering can perched on the ledge, sending the container crashing onto the gravel below. Water glugged out and disappeared.

My throat tightened; I called another hello into the grounds—still serene, fragrant with flowers and ripening fruit. The wind turbine pinwheeled overhead. The ocean sparkled in the distance. That Camp Hope's crewmembers could have given up—abandoned everything—seemed impossible. That Roy Adams could have, even more so. I entertained the idea of foul play: there were corporations, governments with something to lose if Camp Hope succeeded. Yet the grounds showed no sign of a struggle.

I wondered if the crewmembers were hiding.

I wondered if they were invisible, Camp Hope's advanced eco-technology having spurred unprecedented genetic mutations.

I wondered if they'd all been sucked into the sky by a green god who welcomed them into a chlorophylled paradise.

The sun pressed down like a hot thumb, crushing these ideas. I slumped into the leafy shade of an elephant ear and unpeeled my backpack straps. Sweat swept my forehead, stung my eyes. I had forgotten to pack a water bottle. In my rush to leave for Eleutheria, I had forgotten to pack a lot of things.

I had Deron's phone number inked on my palm, but no

phone with which to call him. This omission had been deliberate. According to *Living the Solution*, Camp Hope was equipped with a central communications hub, but crewmembers otherwise abstained from the Internet and its environmental cost: the mineral mines and server farms, the unquenchable thirst for electricity.

The absence of personal phones and computers would also help keep Camp Hope a secret until its launch.

I reached into my backpack, my fingers skimming the pages of *Living the Solution*. The book had compelled me away from everything I'd known—compelled me in a way that made it hard to go back. Even if I wanted to, I didn't have the funds for a return ticket.

I pushed my hand deeper into the backpack, past the wad of crumpled bills, my spare underwear, my passport. I touched the envelope from Sylvia.

Cream-colored, made from smooth, expensive paper, the envelope refused to reveal its contents even when held to the light. Sylvia had sealed the envelope with crimson wax, stamped an insignia with one of her rings—a flourish at once preposterous and elegant. Wasn't that her way? She must have enclosed a letter; she was the kind of person who wrote letters—her script sinewy, spring-loaded—though it was also likely she had enclosed money. I knew she had: a crisp set of hundred-dollar bills, sharp enough to draw blood.

I pressed the envelope between my sweaty palms, held my palms to my forehead, closed my eyes. To open the envelope would mean admitting Sylvia had been right. I could hear her telling me so: *You try hard to be good, but there's no such thing as good*. Her voice, it reached through my rib cage, squeezed the air from my lungs: *There is only scarcity and plenty, our fear of—*

The island wouldn't let my eyes stay closed. Sunlight tunneled under my lids, pried them open, filled my vision with a quivering orange brightness—like live stained glass.

I moved to rub my eyes; the color shattered into the air.

Monarch butterflies. As a child, I'd seen them perched on the milkweed growing along the back roads of New Hampshire. I'd thought the species had gone extinct. Yet here they were, whirling upward. I stuffed the unopened envelope into my backpack and scrambled to my feet. Sylvia would have called it juvenile, taking inspiration from butterflies. I remembered I no longer cared. At that same moment, I heard voices—real voices—drifting across the grounds, sweet as light through a church window: a promise made good.

The Camp Hope boathouse was a leggy, square structure with a breezy deck. From this deck, a wharf extended into a turquoise cove, and beyond that cove, the ocean stretched to the horizon: the edge of cloudless sky.

At the boathouse, I found the crewmembers.

They numbered seventy in total. Men and women of many complexions, mostly young—all youthfully athletic—with their hair cut short or drawn into neat ponytails. They wore neoprene wet suits, the letters CH emblazoned on their chests. Some stood knee-deep in the cove, ushering a flotilla of kayaks onto the sloping sand. Others carried the kayaks to storage racks in the boathouse. Still more passed snorkeling gear and scientific instruments toward stations for cleaning.

I marveled at them. These were modern pilgrims: environmental devotees, who'd heard the call for revolution. The crewmembers were among the best and brightest, the most physically exquisite people in the world. They were here on Eleutheria because they believed in Roy Adams's commitment to reforming society by living it anew.

While I was disappointed not to see Adams himself, the crewmembers' operation otherwise enthralled me: balletic in its ease and synchrony. I might have gone on watching, enjoying the sheer perfection of their movements, had I not been noticed.

Three women rose from beside a pile of snorkeling gear. They approached with a bounce in their steps, a light in their eyes, their ponytails swishing. Even now, it's easy to picture them. They bore down on me like the future.

Those women; those newborn women, their skin soft with baby-fat radiance. Women with big straight teeth and strong hands agile enough for knot tying, dexterous enough to play cello. Women who were well hydrated. Women who ate ice cream, but only twice a week. Women with a smug wholesomeness: who knew a lot, but not too much. Women who were swift decision-makers. Women who slept through the night. Women who swam laps at dawn. Women who were pretty without makeup, but not so pretty it caused problems. Women who knew what they were doing and had come to do it.

Women who looked me up and down.

It's an intruder, said one.

It's only a girl, said a second.

Shall I find Lorenzo? said the third, smirking at the others as if to reject the idea.

I'm here to join Camp Hope, I tried to say—but my mouth had gone dry, my tongue immobile and fat.

The trio squinted at me, whispered to one another. The word *girl* buzzed between them, which seemed strange since we were all about the same age.

The girl can't stay, said one.

The girl can't leave either, said another. She's seen the grounds.

It had never occurred to me that I might face resistance to joining Camp Hope. The main challenge, I'd always assumed, would be getting there. When I'd imagined arriving at the compound, my mind shot forward—past the logistics of initiation—to the good and important work I'd do as an official crewmember.

My dizziness made the surrounding landscape spin. I became aware of my scuffed-up overalls and matted hair, my odor. The intense heat and the long journey had caught up to me. Exhaustion plucked at my attention—though also a sense of recognition. I knew these young women: these fellow girls.

The trio started asking questions, their voices overlapping, interjecting: When had I arrived on the island? How did I get here? How had I found Camp Hope? How long had I been in the compound? Had I touched anything? Had I taken photos? What was the matter—was I going to faint? Would I like something to eat? Would I like something to drink? Did I know even minor dehydration could reduce cognitive function 15 percent? Had I really come all the way to the island planning to just *enlist*? Didn't I realize there were procedures for recruitment? That a person couldn't just show up? That the crewmembers had been carefully selected for their specific talents, skills, and traits?

The trio asked and asked, often without waiting for an answer, as if the articulation of a question was the point of the exchange. Occasionally, they glanced over at the other crewmembers—continuing to put away the kayaks—as if verifying the distinctiveness of their status. They relished this small performance of knowledge.

It was then, even through my exhaustion, I realized how I knew the trio—or knew their type. They were quintessentially collegiate, as if plucked from a manicured quad between classes and dropped in the Bahamas. They were like the young women who had once hovered around Sylvia.

Liberal Arts Girls, I labeled them in my head, putting an emphasis on *girls*.

You do realize, said one—the tallest among them, whose name I'd later learn was Corrine—that under no circumstances could a person walk in and "join" Camp Hope.

You also can't leave, said the second tallest—Dorothy. For security reasons.

We're about to launch, said the shortest—Eisa—with a flick of her ponytail. Isn't that thrilling?

The young women who'd hung around Sylvia intimidated me at first. They had read Foucault, and could differentiate Doric and Ionic columns, and they knew what happened to Prussia. They wore sweaters without crumbs embedded in the fibers. They never burped. And yet they'd sought out Sylvia because they'd wanted her approval, not because they'd wanted to truly know her. Let alone love her. Those young women were all so competent, yet their competence was built on the head-pats of supervisors. For all their book knowledge and their museum visits and their semesters in Rome, they were hoop-jumpers. Box-checkers. Résumé-builders. They were so well rounded they had no edges. They were just ethical enough.

Liberal Arts Girls, I thought again and smiled, even as Corrine said something about putting me in a containment cell. I understood why this trio was here: Camp Hope had been designed as a perfect composite of function and form. This trio had been recruited to fulfill a specific role and to cultivate a specific desire among external viewers. When Camp Hope launched, these young women would look good among the other crewmembers, all of whom had their own roles, talents, desirable qualities. But I had not come all the way to Camp Hope to be sidelined. Liberal Arts Girls could be tamed, you only needed a hoop.

Well done, I said—interrupting Dorothy's recitation of international trespassing laws—you've nearly passed the Intruder Alert Test.

Excuse me?

I licked my lips, my thoughts racing forward, the premise unspooling: There's only one more step, I said. You'll need to take me to Roy Adams.

What are you talking about? said Corrine.

Your response to the test was excellent, I continued. Especially given the lack of forewarning. But the lack of forewarning was the whole point. All that needs to happen now is for me to speak to Adams so I can confirm your proficiency.

The Liberal Arts Girls narrowed their eyes.

This test is being timed, I said.

How are we supposed to believe that? said Dorothy. No one said anything about an Intruder Alert Test.

Maybe we should get Lorenzo? said Eisa.

Out in the cove, crewmembers continued their graceful

machinations as they stowed the last of the kayaks, though I had the feeling they were listening—that the whole island was listening. All the palm trees and seagulls and hermit crabs and starfish had perked up, trying to catch what came next.

I reached into my backpack and pulled out *Living the Solution*.

The Liberal Arts Girls drew in a collective breath. Corrine started to ask how I'd gotten a personal copy, only to be overtaken by Dorothy, who murmured that the book hadn't yet been sent to anyone outside Camp Hope, before her words were overwhelmed by Eisa, who twirled her ponytail with a finger and said: It all makes sense now.

The Liberal Arts Girls moved quickly after that. The trio was nothing if not efficient, task-oriented, rhetorically effective when it came to explaining the situation to the others. Roy Adams, it turned out, was snorkeling around one of Eleutheria's most magnificent reefs. If I was supposed to see him, I could travel to his location.

So, I was installed in a kayak, handed a paddle, and pointed down the coast.

Once you're around that peninsula, said Corrine, head north. Just keep an eye out for the coral outcroppings.

Put in a good word for us, said Dorothy.

Eisa squeezed my shoulder, pushed.

What to say of the journey that followed?

I remember it only in pieces. I know beyond the shelter of the cove a stiff breeze sprang up. Once around the peninsula, larger waves jostled the kayak's sides. My paddle strokes—arrhythmic, unbalanced—launched saltwater into my mouth, sprayed every inch of my skin. I hacked forward anyway. I no longer felt thirsty. I no longer felt tired. I did not feel much of anything except the distance closing between me and Roy Adams. We were two planets, orbits aligning by degrees. We were two people who'd soon be able to sit down and talk. I'd explain why I'd come to Camp Hope, my commitment to helping. I'd officially join the movement that would make the world new.

I paddled harder, breath seesawing from my lungs. I felt giddy. Sun-drunk and helium-hearted. The sea and sky tilt-a-whirled, and more monarchs fluttered past, though they may have been the wink of sunbeams on water, my own eroding consciousness. Below the waves, purple forms bloomed with metropolitan ambition. I was no longer sure where the sea began and my paddle ended, what was large and what was small. I stirred up cyclones with every stroke. I summoned in breakers. I jolted as the kayak's yellow bow struck an under-water obstacle, sending me splashing out, crawling out, my feet kicking coral, my clothes so heavy, so wet, they felt like a skin I no longer needed to wear.

I was not surprised when a monstrous figure rose dripping from the water.

Its horn broke the surface first: blunt-tipped and tubular and channeling a hideous rasping breath. The crest of its head followed. Then a glassy cyclopean eye. And, finally, a massive man-torso.

Did Sylvia send you? I wanted to scream—and maybe I did—though I can't be sure, because the world had faded into elsewhere. I was gone.

THEY WERE ELSEWHERE, they were gone—far from everything they'd ever known. Whisked south across the Sargasso Sea, they sailed with full hearts, on fair winds, until, the island in their scope, the sky began to change.

And yet, who could look away from that emerald streak of earth?

They were Puritans, numbering seventy in total. A company of sallow-cheeked men, unflinching women, who'd heard the call for reinvention. Their captain, a man of nearly sixty, stout but stubborn, had promised them an island—uninhabited—fertile enough for their ambitions. He'd offered up a ship: cedar-hulled, canvas-rigged, built in the Bermudian way. While back in England, Royalists and Parliamentarians were at each other's throats, on this distant isle they could reform their old society by living it anew.

As if living was so simple.

The sky blazed crimson before clouding dark, like an octopus dazzling in the breath before ink. The sea grew anxious, then spiteful, clawing the ship with monstrous waves that drenched the forecastle, rivered down into the hold. Too late they stowed their mainsail. All those sallow-cheeked men, unflinching women, they gripped the starboard rails transfixed by what awaited—their future, greening the horizon—even as the sea roiled and rain slashed the air and lightning skewered their mast like the finger touch of God.

In a storm, sound loses meaning. It gets swallowed by a starless chaos, lost in a sea spray fusillade. Still the Puritans called out, joining their screams with the shriek of wind and splintering wood as their ship ran aground on a reef.

The Devil's Backbone they named the reef later—they who outswam the drowning tug of hosiery and buckled boots, the swift darkness in a throatful of brine, who awoke, the next morning, to the chatter of birds and the scuttle of crabs and dripping green leaves, big as dinner plates. The Puritans-turned-settlers who believed the worst had passed.

The only thing to do was pray, and so they prayed in the manner they preferred: unimpeded by kings, hierarchies, taxes. They clasped their hands so tight their knuckles whitened to the pale of parchment paper. They called for bounty with lips storm-cut and bleeding, their words iron-tinged with hope.

Their prayers were answered with a cave: a home, high-ceilinged, acoustics of the finest church. At the cave's threshold sat a boulder with pulpit-like dimensions—a shape too perfect for coincidence—it seemed to signal blessed times ahead. The island might yet fulfill its new name, a christening that transcended the egotism of common conquering, or even scriptural recommendations.

Eleutheria, their captain called the island. A Grecian word for freedom.

Though the sea had stolen all the settlers' worldly goods—their canvas sheets and sewing kits, their steeled handsaws and fishing tackle and matchlock muskets and every grain of meal—they believed they'd kept their morals. They could recite their prayers by heart. Survival seemed a given, with their godly project before them. Survival seemed their right.

2

I need to talk about survival—about surviving.

Because while I didn't look backward for most of my life, I can do so now. And because long before arriving on Eleutheria, before even learning the island existed, I was a child of New Hampshire, raised among water tanks and spare batteries and six-pound cans of black beans, in a swampy swath of woods sixty miles from Canada.

I was raised to survive—which is to say: I was raised to know better.

I was raised to know your vision narrows when heatstroke sets in. That you can drink your urine three times before it goes toxic. That a half mile of distance can save you in a nuclear blast. That damp cotton can kill you when the weather turns cold. That you can disinfect a wound using mouthwash. That one of the best fire starters is dryer lint. That knives make the most valuable tools, assuming they feature a bone-breaker edge.

Which is to say: I should have known not to kayak out to

that reef with so few supplies, on so little rest. I should have known not to go to Eleutheria in the first place. And before all that, I should have known not to fall in love with the wrong person, for the wrong reasons—to get so caught up in someone I lost track of myself.

Yet, I made every mistake my parents warned me against.

What's strange, though, is that they're dead and I'm living. Despite everything, I'm still here.

I was my parents' only child. More children, in their eyes, only presented more risks, and the world to them was already brimming with risks. Superviruses. Solar flares. Deep state drone strikes. Fearfulness offered a means of defense, but also a dogma. A calling. A gift. Fear brought my parents closer, their marriage built on shared visions of apocalypse. More than once, as a child, I tiptoed past their bedroom and heard grim whispers growled in breathless succession, their fear a form of foreplay, annihilation both inevitable and ecstatic.

Which is to say: my parents are one of the reasons I've never understood love like other people do.

Let me explain—

I was five years old when my mother first put a gun in my hands. A .22 with a smooth wooden stock, the gun butted against my shoulder while its long metal nose rested on a pile of cordwood. My mother's housecoat brushed against me, wafting disinfectant and tobacco. She muffed my ears in ear protectors, stepped back for an inspection. The cigarette in her fingers fumed like a tiny smoke signal.

Don't be scared, she said—then yelled so I could hear through the ear protectors—Match the little groove with the little dot. Hit the safety with your thumb. Pointer finger on the trigger. Don't be scared, baby. Don't be scared.

Out beyond the scope: a forest, feathery with ferns, dim even in daytime. Between the forest and me, a scarecrow—a straw-stuffed man—dressed in one of my father's flannel shirts. His arms stretched wide on plywood armature. His rubber-glove hands hung limp.

Shoot him, yelled my mother, her housecoat vibrating. Shoot the bad man dead.

My finger skimmed the trigger. The straw daddy smiled, his crooked face penned onto a pillowcase. My real daddy grimaced. A big man with a soft jaw and spindly legs, he slapped at a mosquito on his cheek—slapped himself awake. Bug blood smeared through the bristles of his beard.

Aim right here, my father said, pointing to his breast pocket: his own heart.

The gunshot cracked loud. My parents both flinched—my mother's cigarette launched spinning into grass. She swept the butt off the ground, still burning, and hurried to the straw-man. My father followed, slapping at mosquitoes that were real and imagined. They both knelt down. My mother stroked the pillowcase face.

If she teared up because I had hit the strawman—or because I hadn't—I don't know. My father wrapped his arms around my mother's housecoat, his limbs inner-tube thick. She wriggled, but he hugged tighter, pressing a bristled cheek against her smooth one.

I lifted the gun. It was heavy, hard to drag off the pile of cordwood, the barrel hot. I cradled the gun carefully into the grass. *Take a nap,* I told it. *Take a nice long rest.*

My parents were no longer beside the strawman. They had vanished, or else retreated back to our cabin. Inside my ear protectors, the world was quiet. I tiptoed past the strawman into the twilit maw of oak and poplar and birch, the mustiness of leaf litter rising to meet me. Sunbeams stabbed down from the canopy. Ferns skimmed my waist. I picked my way over rotted logs, my toes oozing in the mud slicks left by vernal pools.

Out in the woods, the bullet had *thunked* into the ram-rod trunk of a sugar maple. Sap seeped forth like sugar-sweet blood. I walked until I found that tree. I pressed my finger to its hurt place. I licked its wound.

Love, for me, has meant a bullet in a tree trunk: a slow-seeping sweetness. It has meant annihilation and paradise—two sides of the same coin. It has meant getting what you want, when what you want is also the worst thing for you. It has meant my parents, who, for all the terrors they impressed upon me, also made me believe in impossible odds.

When my parents met in the early nineties, they had nothing in common beyond the fact that they both lived in a rust-wrecked suburb of Boston. My mother had a developing taste for heroin and a declining hold on her job at a retirement home. She scraped together enough money to split rent with some colleagues, to party on Lansdowne Street. She didn't like her roommates, but as she once told me: living with them beat the hell out of staying with her own "demented relations."

She'd spent the first years of her life in foster care; her adoptive family, a set of stern Catholics, expected a gratitude she wasn't ready to give.

My father had no job at all, just a room in his father's house: a squeaky-floored colonial, crowded with brothers and inbred pit bulls. Having flunked out of tech school after one semester, he considered himself an autodidact, a connoisseur of the arcane. Minutia masked the embarrassment of his own laziness; he was an early adopter of the World Wide Web. Stoppering up his family's landline, he dialed into the gold rush of information, plunged face-first into the shifting sands of chatroom commentary, and dredged up conspiracy theories with a prospector's vigor.

It's hard to explain, my father said to me once—in a rare moment of nostalgia—how alive I felt in those days.

It's harder, though, to picture my parents meeting, much less falling in love. From what I've pieced together, my mother always had boyfriends, the way some people have freckles or back pain. My father owned an iguana.

It's hard to imagine, yet also inevitable, so I imagine their meeting like this: around 1:00 A.M., my father slouches at a desk in his bedroom, his face glowed by a PC—too absorbed to notice the party his brothers are throwing downstairs—when my mother reels into his room and flops onto his lap. She has wandered upstairs, too drunk to find a bathroom; the green twitch of the computer caught her attention. *What are you looking at?* she sputters into my father's ear, his facial scruff tickling her neck. In his panic, my father tells her the truth: *They're saying the moon landing was faked.* My mother releases a forceful burp and my father—not wanting this sharp-elbowed, carbonated woman to leave—lists other conspiracies, adding embellishments to keep her eyes from drooping closed. *Get real,* my mother says. *You're full of it.* My father shakes his head. *I'm the most honest man you'll ever meet.* His own bravado startles him. He tells her a web address to visit, if she can get online; if she wants to know more, she could also meet him tomorrow night at Sonny's, a twenty-four-hour gas station. *Can't meet here,* he says, trying to sound mysterious.

My mother vomits into his waste bin.

The next night, though, she pulls her beat-up hatchback into Sonny's. She's still wearing her uniform from the retirement home, a cigarette smoldering on her knuckle like a red-hot engagement ring. My father has already arrived. He's driving a car he had to borrow, though he won't tell her this—not yet. First, they have to roll up beside one another, drivers' windows aligning. My mother half-spits, half-exhales into my father's car as she says, *Tell me more about the government mind control.* There is a rage in her eyes that could be mistaken for beauty. She flicks her cigarette, one hot spark leaping to my father's bare arm. He grits his teeth, squeezes his toes; the pain feels good, though he's not sure why. He can't tell if she's mocking him, if this is all a big joke. He doesn't know yet that my mother has always felt cheated by higher powers, that she already believes there's a conspiracy keeping her from her real life.

Are you sure, says my father, *you're ready for this?*

She's sure. My parents are the worst possible partners for each other, but from that point on they are always together.

When my father, unexpectedly, received a small inheritance, it was my mother who suggested they buy a camper, flee Boston. They did not trust the coasts, not even then. Not with the Pilgrim Nuclear Power Plant—out of date and ill-managed—a sitting duck in Plymouth. Not with the advent of the hockey stick graph: harbinger of a modern Biblical flood. Not with a drug-deepened paranoia clouding their minds. My parents were equal opportunity when it came to information on the end of the world. The Judgment Day hellscapes of red-faced televangelists blended into the sea-level warnings of weary environmentalists, then later into the stern anxiety of newscasters discussing Y2K. So my parents fled north, parking overnight outside Walmarts, before seeking shelter in White Mountain campgrounds. They stocked up on instant potatoes, canned tuna, Kool-Aid—*just in case*, they joked, until it wasn't a joke. Because somewhere in the tectonic friction of one century and the next, all of America sweating with the terror of a computer glitch, the potential mischief of zeros and ones, I was made.

I was dutiful as a girl, ever seeking to please my parents. This was, in part, because I hardly knew anyone else. My childhood involved a slow pulling away from other people as my parents became increasingly paranoid, eventually retreating to an old hunting cabin in the woods—though our isolation did not happen all at once, or even in a linear manner. There were times I was taken to supermarkets with my mother like any other child. I attended elementary school with a windswept contingent of ski slope workers' kids—though none of my classmates spoke to me unless necessary. More than once, the MRE my mother had packed for my lunch was sabotaged as a prank.

Going unnoticed, I learned, was an essential survival tactic. It was also what my parents often expected of me. During their Narcotics Anonymous meetings, I was instructed to keep quiet in the back of the room. At these meetings, I lurked among the stacks of folding chairs, eating packets of hot chocolate without water, scooping out the sugar crystals with a wet pinky, sucking. Most of the attendees, I decided, had surprised expressions—slackened jaws, bulging eyeballs—as if shell-shocked by their own life.

I can't say if my parents were surprised by the direction their lives took. I do know they quit drugs when I was conceived, which suggests a vision of normalcy. Of course, nothing went as planned: my arrival wedged disappointment into our family before it had even taken shape. My mother had wanted me out of The System. She wanted a home birth. She wanted me undocumented. There was freedom, she said, in living beyond the bureaucratic treadmill. No taxes, for instance. And I would never get drafted. Before I was born, she worried about the vaccines hospital staff might inject into my tiny body. She feared that they—whoever *they* were—would steal my DNA or switch me with another child or implant a tracking device under my skin. My father agreed with the plan for a home birth, until, ten hours into labor—my mother bleeding and screaming in the bathtub—it became clear she might not survive without professional assistance. So I came into this world under a hospital's fluorescent glare. I received a birth certificate and everything. My mother never forgave my father for this; when they fought, she brought up his decision as a mistake, insisting he overreacted about the blood and the screaming. I don't know if she ever forgave me either. My botched birth suggested an irreparable co-option by mainstream society. I could have been a pure thing, completely theirs. Instead, I already belonged to something else.

older, and my family's contact with the world grew more restricted, I spent entire afternoons building terrariums—filling mason jars with plant specimens I'd gathered from the woods.

We had an abundance of jars from my parents' ill-fated foray into homesteading. For all their interest in survivalism, my mother and father were inept when it came to the demands of such a lifestyle. Halfway through canning her first batch of tomatoes on our stove, my mother gave up, red-faced from steam and frustration. The same went for my father's attempt at DIY kerosene lamps. My terrariums, though, I made by instinct. I dropped stones into a mason jar, enjoying the meteoric clink they made against the glass. Then I added a layer of sand, a layer of soil—my fingernails collecting crescent moons of dirt. I installed plants, having scoured the forest to find the right specimens: a three-inch pine sapling with needles soft to the touch, its root like a long thin whisker; a hardy sprig of wintergreen, red berry attached; an emerald lump of moss. I splashed in water. I stretched cling wrap over the mouth of the jar, secured the translucent lid with rubber bands. Once sealed, the terrarium became a universe belonging only to itself. The taut plastic trapped moisture, cycled condensation in miniature monsoons. I placed the jars along the cabin's windowsills for observation. Sometimes insects would hatch, flit around, die, their bodies reabsorbed by the appetite of an enclosed ecosystem. Sometimes moss swampishly crawled up the glass. I liked setting different scenarios in motion, observing varying ratios of soil and water and light. The same ingredients in different quantities produced wildly different results—a basic principle, but one that allowed me, as a young girl, to imagine my reality was one among many. There existed other versions of me.

For a while, I assumed I would grow up to be a scientist. I imagined my terrariums becoming grand experiments. I saw myself handling fizzing beakers while dressed in a lab coat white as a tooth. In my online homeschool courses, however, I earned only average scores in the science portions. And my mother was skeptical of the profession.

The periodic table, she said, won't save you when—

My mother air-spelled the initials for *Shit Hits The Fan*. Though she and my father often described, in lurid detail, scenarios for societal collapse, they made a point not to curse in front of me.

Were my parents logical? They were not. They worried about intercontinental air pollutants, but smoked nonstop.

I had my terrariums, though. They offered the promise of an escape, even if that promise was never fulfilled. Lined up along windowsills, the glass jars were destinations I could observe but not enter. To enter was to bring ruin. Peeling back the cling wrap would contaminate a perfect reality with outside air and outside water and outside life forms. It would break the spell. I could only admire, imagine, protect. I was both creator and exile. I was happy enough.

———

Yet my terrariums could not save me from what happened a few weeks shy of my eighteenth birthday, on a sunny September afternoon. I was down in the survival bunker, working on a complicated terrarium—an arboreal menagerie of wintergreen and ferns and checkered lumps of moss—when a chill ran through me.

At first I thought another eclipse had occurred. That August, the whole United States had paused to witness the celestial anomaly: a cosmic wink in the swill of the everyday. Crowds gathered in public parks, sports games were suspended, work sites stalled. In Washington, the president stood on the White House balcony and stared into the sun with unprotected eyes. There were photos of him doing this, his family standing stoically by. These images subsequently accompanied the news stories detailing the president's permanent eye damage: his vision destroyed. The images were later banned, but not before reaching most corners of the globe. The president—enraged—demanded the reporters be punished for making him look bad. That the mass media be punished for sending the images outward. That the deep state be punished for orchestrating it all. That punishment be meted out swiftly and widely for his misfortune.

Sunlight beamed unbroken through the open hatch of the survival bunker; there was no second eclipse. No sky-obscuring ash from an explosion either—a plausible possibility, given the president's follow-up threats to bomb unsympathetic U.S. states into oblivion.

All was quiet. But I noticed, for the first time, that the wooden ladder leading out of the survival bunker had rotted at its base. My parents had never put in the metal steps they'd once discussed. They hadn't done a lot of things. Over the year prior, they had gone from anxious yet functional, to paralyzed by fear. When they looked at me, it was with bleary-eyed sorrow. Then they stopped looking at me much at all. They stopped leaving our property as well as the house, overwhelmed by bad news, factual and otherwise: the reports of carbon sinks, crypto crime, government mind control, the crisis of automation, the ego-jockeying of nations. Anthrax. Illuminati. Electromagnetic pulse attacks. Mountain lions.

My parents hadn't left the house in part because they did not need to. We had an enormous stockpile of canned food. New were the medications that materialized around the cabin: pills for anxiety, injectables for depression, patches for pain. I found them in the back of cupboards and under couch cushions and once in the brackish water of the toilet tank. My parents must have had the medications delivered, though I never saw this happen. Perhaps I would have noticed if I'd tried harder. I did not think I needed to. My parents had gone through low periods before; this didn't seem any different. Though I had been subjected to dogmatic fearfulness my whole life, I had also been sheltered. There was so much talk of imminent catastrophe, I couldn't see the catastrophe already occurring.

Down in the bunker, the chill in my body persisted: my blood transfused by a cold electrical current. I ignored it—I wanted to finish the terrarium. Rather than using a mason jar, I'd found an old cider jug, and through the jug's narrow glass neck I'd inserted plant specimens like pieces of a model ship. I was pleased with the way a fern bent over a row of oak saplings: the uncanny shift in scale. Though my terrariums had never drawn much interest from my parents, I believed this one might be different. The cider jug, with its delicate miniature forest, might fill their haggard faces with light, remind them that pockets of perfection still existed: worlds untouched by human horrors.

I tinkered with the terrarium until sunlight faded from the bunker's open hatchway. Maybe, on some level, I knew what awaited me above ground. Maybe I was stalling for time, holding on to my near-happiness a little longer.

I could only stall so long. After finishing the terrarium, I sealed the jug, carried it out of the bunker into a thin purple dusk. Across the lawn, the cabin's lights were off. This was odd because my parents had—in addition to weighty adult fears— a childish fear of the dark. The chill in my limbs mounted into a tremble. I became aware that if I dropped the terrarium, the glass would shatter. I was very much on the verge of dropping it. Full of sand and soil and stones, the jug was heavy. Holding on tight became important. Not dropping what I had made: this became my main concern, even as I entered the dark confines of the cabin. Even as I saw what I saw. I concentrated on protecting the jug and the little world within it. I pressed the glass sides so hard that, the following day, my arms ached with the echoes of the squeeze. I felt the terrarium's phantom edges all the next week, during which time strangers—police officers, family members I'd never met—came tramping through my life. I concentrated on the soreness in my muscles while these strangers expressed their limp, waterless condolences for my parents' passing, reiterating "the situation" as if I needed everything explained again: what an overdose meant, why I needed to leave the house, why no one was sure where I would go. Time moved around me in distended shadows. Sunshine speared through the row of terrariums set on the kitchen windowsill, mornings and afternoons oozing past in slow beams of light. It is possible I said nothing that whole week. My silence made my new family members act kinder toward me than they might have—though I also overheard snatches of unkind conversations about my parents, along with rumors of gold buried in the yard. This accounted for the arrival of my father's knuckly brothers and their spray-tanned wives. Had I ever seen my parents digging? Did I know about any hidden compartments, safety deposit boxes, vaults? When I shook my head, my relatives' disappointment flared like a bad smell.

It was strange watching the faces of my family members and seeing traces of my own—the same stubborn chin, snub nose, straw hair—like fragments of a broken mirror.

Put together, we might have formed something whole.

In the end, it was arranged I would live with my cousins, Victoria and Jeanette, in Boston's South End.

That'll be a shock, my aunts muttered when they thought I couldn't hear.

When they thought I could: The girls live in a cute little walk-up, right down the street from a sushi restaurant. You'll love it, Willa. You'll get to try out having sisters—and sushi.

I had never eaten raw fish. My parents' fears had included mercury, scombroid, salmonella. In recent years, my diet had largely consisted of selections from the doomsday stockpile: beans with a canned vegetable du jour. Mandarin oranges in syrup for dessert.

Stick with this kind of food now, my mother had once said. *You won't miss regular meals when society collapses.*

What I missed, though, were my parents. I missed the touch of my mother's hand, her skin papery from incessant soap-scrubbing. I missed my father's rants, the gelatin-jiggle of his neck as he said: *You think AI is wreaking havoc now—just wait.*

Not that I had felt that touch or heard those rants in a while. My parents had been lost in the placating grip of Vicodin, Oxy, fentanyl: chemicals, I now understood, that kept the outside world out, myself included. I should be used to my parents' absence, I told myself on the lonely bus ride from New Hampshire into Boston, dense forests giving way to small towns, then tumbledown suburbs, then a howling metropolitan tangle: the city's roadways looping so loud with traffic I felt I'd been swallowed by the inside of a clock.

In South Station, I hugged my duffle bag close. My aunts had instructed me to meet my cousins under a large electronic timetable—but I struggled to hold my place against the relentless shoulder-bump of passing travelers, the knee-capping swing of their briefcases. The sheer volume of them stunned me. There were so many people with so many different agendas. I'd known they were out there, these people—I'd spent plenty of time perusing the Internet—but the teeming crush of them had been abstract, scentless, far away. After years in the woods, Boston was a sensory punch in the face.

Victoria and Jeanette materialized. They would have stood out even if my aunts hadn't shown me a photo. Dressed in identical red cloaks, ringleted hair bouncing around their faces, their approach felt split screen—the convergence of two Little Red Riding Hoods—as they rushed up and spoke in unison.

Oh you poor thing, they said, their faces pressing close to mine, as if to sniff me. You poor little doll.

A dexterous set of fingers unpeeled my hand from my duffle bag, while another set crept around my waist. My cousins adhered themselves to either side of me in a horizontal embrace. The stream of travelers gave us a wide berth as Jeanette produced, from the sleeve of her cloak, a phone attached to a stick.

Our long-lost cousin, she sang out. Wilhelmina!

The phone stick slid back into Jeanette's sleeve. She took one of my hands and Victoria took the other, their grips firm, their long nails pressing into my skin.

This way, Wilhelmina! Victoria said. We'll show you—

Neither cousin had picked up my duffle bag. I looked over my shoulder as they tugged me toward the exit. The bag grew smaller, obscured behind the legs of travelers. I tried to form the words to tell my cousins. The bag contained the few possessions I'd taken from the cabin in the woods. It was a link to my parents. When they were alive, the duffle had been earmarked as a go bag for when SHTF.

But the fan had been hit—the worst had happened.

I followed my cousins onto the street, my impulse to protest subsumed by shrieking traffic and exhaust-plumed air. Easier to let the bag go, I thought. Even telling my cousins that my name was not Wilhelmina felt too difficult. I stumbled along between them, buffeted by their giggling, first into a waiting vehicle, then out of it, then up the stairs to their apartment. As my cousins chattered at me, my mind wandered back to my terrariums—their mossy luxury, the arc of feather-soft ferns—so that when I returned to the present, I found I was naked, sitting knee-to-chest in a bathtub, the water so hot it scalded my skin pink.

Good girl, said Jeanette. Hold still.

My cousins had changed into silky black jumpsuits. Jeanette cupped her hands in the bathwater, raised them over my head. My hair swished over my eyes in a wet veil.

Chin up, little Wilhelmina.

Victoria squirted a long string of shampoo on my head. The bottle squeaked as she squeezed, which made my cousins giggle. Soap oozed between my shoulder blades in a long cold curl.

You're almost whistle-clean, said Jeanette. Shiny-clean. Ready for—

A musical jingle sounded from the other end of the apartment. My cousins leapt up, flapping their arms. In their black jumpsuits, they looked like a pair of excited crows. They flew out of the room.

I remained in the bathtub, my head half-shampooed. Soap slimed down my back. The bathroom walls rose up around me, bare beige except for freckles of mildew. A nub of sunlight poked through a small stained-glass window, projecting diamonds of red and green and gold onto the peeling linoleum floor. Traffic gurgled outside. A man's voice yelled: You can't put it in there. How many times have I told you?

Then quiet. Then, a rushing wave of grief so intense, so vicious, it stole the breath from my lungs. My parents were dead. The life I'd known had disappeared. I was in a terrifying city with cousins I'd only just met.

Maybe I would wake up, I thought; maybe Victoria and Jeanette were sprites of my imagination.

Real or unreal, my cousins did not return. The bathwater cooled. Light from the stained-glass window slid from the floor to the side of the tub, then onto my skin, turning me jewel-toned, quilt-patterned. I pinched these patches with pruned fingers—but I did not wake up in my bed in New Hampshire.

It took a long time for me to think what to do. The bathroom contained no towels; it also did not contain my clothes.

After rinsing the shampoo from my hair, I stepped from the tub and dripped out of the bathroom into a narrow corridor that led to my cousins' bedroom, as well as to the kitchen. My cousins' red cloaks lay pooled on the floor by their bedroom door. I wrapped myself in a cloak, crept down the corridor, my cousins' giggling reaching me before I saw them: perched on the kitchen countertop, their hands buried in twin jars of strawberry jelly.

Oh, it's you, said Jeanette as she licked her index finger.

How cute, said Victoria. She's trying on your cloak.

We've already taken the cloak photos, said Jeanette, hopping down from the countertop and holding out her phone. Look.

In the image, my cousins' mirrored faces squeezed on either side of a messy-haired girl. A caption read: *Two little reds capture the wolf.* It was me in the picture, caught between my cousins—but also not me. The wolf-girl's gaze glinted thrillingly, her incisors peeping between blood-bit lips.

Pretty, isn't it? said Jeanette.

I touched my lips—chapped and inflamed—and looked at the photo again. Here was a different Willa than the one I believed myself to be: an unbereaved Willa, an unconfused Willa. A better one.

Wait until you see this pic, said Victoria as she held out her phone.

Rub-a-dub-dub, read the caption. In the image, my cousins' long-nailed fingers stretch into the frame, Jeanette's hand cupping water, Victoria's gripping the shampoo bottle. The bathtub isn't lime-stained—it's lovely as a seashell—and it's presenting me: my face and neck and shoulders, soaped up and gleaming.

A new Willa, born in this other sparkling dimension, her head thrown back, laughing.

I lived, for two years, inside my cousins' photographs. The images were a new kind of terrarium: portals into which I could mentally escape. I was installed in fur kaftans and Daisy Duck kiddie pools and beside pyramids of cannoli and on tartan picnic blankets spread over the gravelly sand of Constitution Beach. In the photos, I smile wistfully. I bare my teeth and stick out my tongue. I curl with my cousins in their four-poster bed, all of us wearing the same striped paja-mas. My cousins returned the pajamas the next day, like we did most clothes, but that did not matter. The image lasted forever.

When my cousins showed me the photos after posting them online, I stared at them the way I'd once stared into mason jars full of moss and saplings: losing myself to perfect, parallel realities. In the images, I appeared to be having a good time, or at least an interesting time. This sustained me, even when my fixation prompted teasing from my cousins.

It's awfully vain, said Jeanette in a falsely scolding tone.

You'll rot your brain, added Victoria.

Poor little Wilhelmina—

Jeanette plucked the phone from my fingers, tossed it to her sister. I smiled and reached to take the phone back, but my cousins played a game of keep-away, arcing the phone past my outstretched hands, lunging over futon cushions to snatch it before I could.

Then they grew bored. They merrily returned the device.

Despite their mocking admonishments, my obsession clearly pleased them.

I was glad to please my cousins—glad to amuse them, to be a little pet. I saw no reason to tell Victoria and Jeanette that the photos served a deeper need than vanity. I saw no reason to tell them much of anything. Residual survivalist instincts compelled me to reveal as little as possible: to blend in, keep my head down, hang on. For a long time, I never contradicted my cousins or questioned them. They seemed to me impressively worldly, as evidenced by their employment at an art gallery in the South End, where they turned off their baby-voiced teasing and stared unblinking at the wealthy patrons who came to purchase paintings. My cousins' elaborate matching outfits and dramatic silences made at least a few patrons insecure enough to shell out for the overpriced canvases.

If a customer asks too many questions, Jeanette explained to me once, we just say the painting is "about war."

No one asks follow-ups, said Victoria. Works every time.

My cousins giggled; like a pair of loving bandits, they clutched one another's arms. This bond dazzled me as much as their ostensible savvy. Though born a year apart—Victoria was twenty-five, Jeanette twenty-six—my cousins had grown up as intertwined as identical twins. In elementary school, Jeanette purposely performed poorly so she would be held back and put in class with her sister. And Victoria, after Jeanette had her appendix removed in middle school, knifed a scar into her own belly—to the horror of their parents. My cousins didn't care. They normalized the oddest of one another's notions. When one decided to eat orange foods, for instance, the other would too. Over time, these behaviors isolated my cousins from others, but deepened their connection. Their unflagging loyalty gave them the confidence to pursue whims with impunity. Sometimes, I'd return to the apartment and find them lovingly brushing one another's hair, both dressed as ballerinas. Or mermaids. Or polar explorers. And while Victoria and Jeanette occasionally had boyfriends, these beaus were invited into their lives primarily as ephemeral props for photos. For my cousins, the true partnership was with one another.

I admired this partnership, even when I felt excluded. I was grateful to my cousins for taking me in, grateful for their photos, which were the only way I knew how to cope with my new situation. *You're happy*, I murmured, while I searched an image for a conflation, a connection, an entry point between the person pictured and the person who was me. *You're having a good time.* This Willa had not been abandoned by her parents. This Willa was loved. She knew how to navigate the city and speak to its citizens; she had cash and cachet, a future as bright as her eyes.

In reality, I had a makeshift bed on my cousins' futon. A minimum-wage job at a café called The Hole Story, which specialized in gourmet doughnut holes. And a boss who called me "Bunker Girl," after I mentioned my experience baking hardtack in preparation for the apocalypse—a mistake I did not make again.

In reality, Boston overwhelmed me. The brick-built topography felt like a giant fireplace poised to burn me alive. I missed New Hampshire's mountain forests, its clean air and lichensnug boulders and frigid streams. The city parks were scalped to dirt. They were marred by dog poop, overrun with runners. Without my cousins' photos as an escape hatch, I would have felt unbearably lonely yet relentlessly hassled, exhausted by grief yet jittery with anxiety, my energy scattering uselessly into the *ba-rings* of cash registers.

In reality, my cousins' photos were no charitable gift. And my cousins themselves weren't savvy fairy godmothers. To most people—including their own parents—Victoria and Jeanette were extraordinarily odd. Their father owned a mold remediation business: a small but successful six-man operation in southern New Hampshire. I only saw him once. From what I understood, he was pleased to have "city girls" as daughters, or else pleased to keep my cousins out of the small town where he lived, so they no longer caused a stir among neighbors. He couldn't afford to put my cousins up at Boston's prices, but he had anyway. He also helped Victoria and Jeanette get part-time jobs at the gallery, which suffered numerous fungal issues. My cousins' eccentric outfits and self-documentation was tolerated by the absent-minded gallerist who employed them.

Money was tight, though. If I'd been more alert, I might have noticed the worry brewing beneath Victoria and Jeanette's giggly whimsy. I might have noticed we'd started pursuing riskier images—hanging off bridges, standing on the edges of skyscraper roofs—as my cousins tried to get noticed in the whirlpool churn of the Internet, believing that with the right photo they'd be plucked by an unseen hand, offered a reality show or a product sponsorship or a news anchor gig. My cousins had heard about this happening to others; they believed it could happen to them. They also knew, on some level, that it had to happen—or something did.

But I was too drugged on images of my own happiness to notice. So when Victoria and Jeanette told me their plan to sneak into a fundraising party at the home of a Massachusetts congressman, I assumed the photo expedition would be like any other.

It wasn't. It changed the course of my life.

We showed up to the party late, a doorman ushering us in with an autumnal swirl of fallen leaves. The congressman's home was a brick titan in Beacon Hill, grand with chandeliers and unblemished sofas and windows dressed like wedding cakes. Though my cousins' preening had delayed us, they dragged me through the foyer and in among the guests as if I'd been the one to hold them back.

Hurry, said Jeanette. We have to be quick—

My cousins pushed past caterers palming trays of hors d'oeuvres, nearly knocking over an enormous arrangement of Thanksgiving gourds, which rose up on a pedestal in the crowded solarium. The house smelled like clam chowder and cologne. Guests talked about long-distance cycling; acquaintances they mutually knew; their concern over the upcoming election—though they did not look concerned at all, nibbling their canapés. Someone, somewhere, was making a speech. My cousins and I were the only ones wearing satin gowns and white gloves, but we moved too fast for anyone to comment.

This way, called Victoria as she pointed down a hall. Looks empty.

My cousins had met the congressman at the gallery. Though he'd told them abstraction wasn't his aesthetic—and declined to purchase a painting—they'd overheard him talking to a semi-famous sculptor also visiting the gallery that day. More specifically, they'd heard the congressman extend an invitation to this party.

The congressman, I'd later learn, was in the process of rebranding his image. Old party lines were crumbling under the weight of a president with no ideological compass and a disdain for codified law. After his eclipse injury, the president had formed an unlikely alliance with the disability rights movement. The alliance hadn't lasted, but political patterns were shaken. The two-party system started to splinter. Politicians clung to single-issue platforms like life rafts, their reconfigurations eventually including Global Constitutionalists, Singularitarians, Separatist Feminists, Green Republicans, Buddhist Libertarians, Astro-Conservatives, and even a high-profile band of self-identifying Modern Monarchists who advocated for the United States to relinquish itself to the UK, hat in hand.

The congressman whose party we'd crashed was at the forefront of this shift. He'd started calling himself a Techno-Progressive, his new platform promising prosperity and equality through algorithmic salvation. But he'd also gotten his start developing software that predicted, within a week's range, when its users were likely to die. To soften his image, he cultivated relationships with "creative types"—large-earringed poets, stiff-browed intellectuals, paint-sniffing muralists—who, though not necessarily supportive of him, liked getting grants for their work. They showed up at his occasional parties, their presence a moral balm against the congressman's compromises.

Victoria and Jeanette had little interest in the congressman, less in morality. What they wanted was to take photographs inside his house—endeavoring to capture a "classy, upper-crust location" unlike anywhere they'd photographed before.

My cousins tugged me from one room to the next, until we arrived in a study that was empty of people yet crowded with objects: a mahogany desk, a taxidermied bear, a tightly upholstered divan, an elegant coffee table, a crystalline lamp, shelves of leather-bound books and cartographic instruments, an antique globe missing several continents. The walls were painted navy blue, hung with portraits of dour people wearing large black hats and white collars. The windows were draped like Grecian queens.

We'll start here, said Jeanette—her face pinked with anticipation.

Look this way, Wilhelmina, said Victoria.

I tried to do as my cousins instructed. I sprawled on the divan, my feet propped up on a pillow. The position was awkward, though. My cousins' anxiety made me anxious too. My gown was ill-fitting and one strap kept sliding off my shoulder. The tag made me itch. When I tried to readjust, one of my heels sliced the pillow fabric.

Across the room, a portrait of a colonial governor frowned. Victoria fretted about lighting; Jeanette picked up a sextant and snapped off one of the lenses.

Just leave it, said Victoria—before turning to me to say: Okay, now do ours.

She shoved the phone into my hands. My cousins positioned themselves by the windows, their arms stroking the drapes. I snapped photos; my cousins relaxed.

Now stand over there, Jeanette told me. Get another angle—

Footsteps interrupted, along with the chirp of an approaching voice.

—And this we confirmed was a genuine Turner last April. Not his finest work, but nice to have. What I really want to show you, though, is in here—

Two women entered the study. One had honey-blond hair

swooped into a perfect updo. Her silk blouse fluttered as she gestured to a bookshelf. That she was the congressman's wife—the party's hostess—was unmistakable. She progressed through her home as if it were a showroom, her heels clacking like hammer strikes trying to secure the other woman's interest.

The other woman appeared to be a patient, though reluctant, participant in the hostess's tour. Her steps were unhurried as she studied objects other than what the hostess presented. She was dressed in all black—a loose shift, a shawl, flat shoes—as if for a funeral. Her hair was dark as well, severely bobbed at her chin. She held a wineglass pinched in her fingers like a talisman against inanity.

—We're both *Mayflower* descendants, so we have an interest in colonial artifacts—

The hostess had not noticed my cousins and me standing stiff as the taxidermied bear. She was too intent on showing the woman-in-black a sheet of old parchment.

—I thought you, in particular, might like to see this seventeenth-century broadside advertising a utopian community in the Bahamas—

The woman-in-black did not respond. She stared into a mirror placed above the bookshelf, regarding the tableau of my cousins and me on the other side of the room. Then her gaze focused on me alone. My insides twisted. I had grown up trying to go unnoticed—by my parents, society—lest I cause trouble. Even with my cousins, I tiptoed. I was furniture to them. A prop. A plaything. But this woman saw me and found me worth beholding. I was more interesting to her than anything the hostess had to say—the hostess, who had gone on talking, blithe as ever, pleased to show off the antique broadside, though her scream was coming. Drawing nearer by the millisecond, it altered the taste of the air like the feel of weather changing: a pressure shift before a storm arrives.

—Isn't that fascinating? This sheet of paper compelled people to abandon their lives and sail all the way to the island of—

The hostess was turning, turning, about to see us, about to scream, to call for other partygoers, to call the police, to have us charged with trespassing and destruction of property and who knows what else, when the woman-in-black dropped her wineglass.

The glass shattered. Wine splashed up from the floor in a tiny tidal wave of red. The hostess shrieked, first at the spilled wine and then at me and my cousins as we dashed past her, fleeing the study and rushing back through the party. We ran out of the brick house and down Beacon Hill, until, at last, we slowed to a walk among the fungus-riddled oak trees in Boston Common. My cousins got winded easily.

Oh my god, said Jeanette—half-laughing, half-hugging her sister.

At least we got the photos, said Victoria.

The photos, said Jeanette. Tell me you held on to the phone, Wilhelmina?

I hung my head; in the rush to escape, I'd dropped the precious device. The photos my cousins had coveted were gone.

Victoria moaned, kicked at a rotting tree trunk.

We needed those, said Jeanette.

How could you do this to us? said Victoria. After everything we've done for you?

They both started to cry. I did not understand. The phone was expensive, but they'd lost expensive items in the past. Those losses hadn't caused this kind of reaction. I said we could

get a new phone; I could pay for it. I could get extra shifts at
The Hole Story. At *extra shifts* my cousins cried harder.

We're supposed to be famous, said Jeanette with a sob. We're
supposed to be in a mansion. We're supposed to be on TV.

Now we never will, said Victoria—sobbing louder.

What are you talking about? I said.

It was then I learned they would soon lose their subsidized
rent. Their parents had decided that they—that we—needed
to make our own way. My cousins were being weaned off
funds. That was why they were so desperate to take compelling
photographs; the right image, they believed, would save them.

Later, I would understand that their sorrow stemmed from
more than their dwindling finances. It was about a belief foundational to their bond: they were different, but in a good way.
They were special—destined for big things. Yet if they'd been
wrong about their inevitable Internet-borne stardom, they
might have been wrong about so much else.

In the following weeks, I apologized repeatedly for losing
the phone, but my cousins channeled their frustration with
their situation into frustration with me. Their giggly affection
soured into catty taunts and arbitrary rules around the apartment: *Wilhelmina can only use this plate. Wilhelmina has to
stand on one leg when she speaks. Wilhelmina can only shower
on days starting with T.*

The pair also decided I would no longer be allowed to take
photos with them. Worse, they deleted the online archive in
which I appeared.

But I need the photos, I begged, I—

My cousins wouldn't budge. Though I continued to live
with them, I felt tossed into the cold. Without the photos, I
was vulnerable to despair. My parents' doomsday prophecies

seeped back into my thoughts. Their talk of mass layoffs, mass die-offs, a third world war, secret government prisons was an anti-lullaby that kept me awake at night, brittle with despair in daytime.

The only thing that kept me going—kept me alive—was my memory of the woman-in-black. She'd dropped the wineglass on purpose, of that I was sure. No one had ever taken a risk like that for me. No one had ever looked at me—into me—with such deep understanding. I didn't know it was something people could do.

I'd encountered Sylvia Gill, though I didn't know that yet either. I didn't know she would send me to Eleutheria and back. I didn't know Eleutheria existed: an island caught in the slipstream of idealism and exploitation, the secret crux of the Americas. But what did I know about the Americas? About anything? All I knew was that our meeting had altered me—inexorably—so when my cousins berated me for ruining their shot at celebrity, when my boss at The Hole Story called me a clueless bunker girl, when the affliction of living felt too heavy to bear, I thought of her. The woman's knowing gaze, the pinch of her fingers on the stem of the wineglass—I conjured these affectations in my mind, picturing the congressman's study swirling around us, portraits blurring, books spinning, the antique broadside flapping in a cosmic whirlwind, the two of us wrapped tightly together in the guttural vibrations of the hostess's shriek.

IN A CAVE OPEN WIDE AS A SCREAM, on an island out to sea, the captain's sermons echoed and expired.

Affliction is a bitter root, but it bears the sweetest fruit—

The settlers nodded, though with diminishing conviction. Their captain had promised them a paradise. Eleutheria: a blank slate. A geography of dreaming. On the broadside he'd posted in London—in speeches given in Bermuda—he'd offered them a vision: an island ripe for public works and profit-making and unpolluted prayer. A colony, well beyond the strangling grasp of a backward monarchy, in which any man might find a senate seat, cast a vote for governor. They would right the old world's wrongs. The first settlers would be the forebearers of a just society, their memories immortalized on the hills and roads and towns that bore their names like standards from a bloodless war.

All this the captain had written on a sheet of parchment—his promise sanctified in prose—yet what had he delivered?

Starvation for a start.

With their supplies sunk to the bottom of the sea, the settlers had no tools to till the soil, to plant the seeds they did not have. They filled their bellies by spearing surly iguana. Unripe pineapple stringed their teeth and made their stomachs lurch. At night, they huddled in the cave, stared out at unfamiliar stars. When dawn came, they sweated, dug graves for their companions. They stumbled about in shredded petticoats and pantaloons, their prayers dribbling to muttered discontent. One woman beat her head bloody against a rock. Others spoke longingly of death. All swatted bugs—relentless chigoes, sandflies, gnats—burning brush to keep the biters at bay. The eye-sting of smoke at least gave them excuse enough to weep.

Affliction is a bitter root—but when would come the promised fruit?

The captain roamed the island looking for an answer. Walking among old-growth pine and over sparkling dunes and along wave-battered cliffs, he found mounds of picked-out mussel shells, shards of Palmetto ware. He found bones—thigh bones, rib bones, skulls with eye sockets spilling sand. He found vestiges of the Lucayan people, who had canoed between the island's coves, stalking snapper and snagging spiny lobster, who'd lived on the island and died on the island and who'd had their own vision of paradise—an afterlife among their ancestors of endless celebration—so that when the Spanish arrived with Christopher Columbus and lied to them, stole the gold from their ears, enslaved them to mine for more, set dogs upon them, raped them, forced them to dive for pearls until their skin decayed and their eardrums burst and their lungs filled with ocean water, death may have been an appealing destination: an easy choice.

The captain tossed aside these scraps of the past, distracted by the present. Maybe the society inscribed upon that broadside had been a touch ambitious. Perhaps Eleutheria was not such a blank slate—injustice cloyed the seaside air, festered in his company and his own mortal soul—but what good was introspection when one's stomach raged? To face the days and years and lives ahead, the settlers needed more than unpleasant memories and hollow platitudes.

3

Inaction is the course of cowards.

—Roy Adams

The text rippled above me like skywriting, like a message from heaven, like a series of crisp block letters painted on a ceiling beam for those lying below.

I'd awoken in a cot, in a cabin of bare wooden walls—not unlike my childhood home in New Hampshire. This cabin, though, contained shelves of medical supplies. A ceiling fan whisked warm air around the room, stirring a fugue of pine sap and disinfectant. The window shades were drawn, though a sea breeze twitched their edges.

I was at Camp Hope.

The text on the ceiling beam was a quote from *Living the Solution*. My memory—mud-thick—churned through my arrival on the island: the ride from Deron, Camp Hope's eerie emptiness, the discovery of the crewmembers at the boathouse. And then?

I leaned over the side of the cot and vomited.

Severe dehydration, I would learn later. A touch of sunstroke too.

Faces hovered above my own, diaphanous and interchanging, like humanoid clouds. A mass of white polo shirts cohered, disbanded, the conversations of crewmembers too hushed to hear—though even in my delirium I could detect a tenor of tension.

To think I believed the crewmembers were worried I might die.

By the time the Liberal Arts Girls crept into the medical cabin, the whole day had drifted past in a haze of muttering and thermometer sticking. The trio's voices—the first familiar ones I'd heard—pulled me from a muddled doze, sparked a recollection of our encounter at the boathouse.

Clearly we were mistaken, said one of them.

You were the one who believed her—

There was a quorum.

I kept my body motionless, my eyes closed. I recalled having not been entirely honest with the trio.

Adams told us it was necessary.

But it isn't right—

The Liberal Arts Girls sounded less like competent coeds—plucked from a serene campus quad—and more like students who'd failed an exam. I fluttered my eyes half-open: Dorothy stood beside my cot, her arms folded tightly across her chest. Corrine twisted her ponytail in a finger. Eisa peered through a crack in the blinds.

We could make her tell us, said Dorothy. There are techniques.

There's no time for pride-and-ego, said Corrine. And you know the ethics of—

Is she awake?

I squeezed my eyes shut as Dorothy and Corrine leaned over me, their breath warming my cheek. Eisa said something about compost duty. The trio argued for a minute, then hurried away. Their conversation hovered in the room as confounding as a dream.

No other crewmembers appeared—or no one I remembered. My nausea returned instead. In the darkening room, I tried to make sense of what I'd heard. I could recall, with great effort, the stroke of a kayak paddle, sunlight glancing off waves. I squeezed my eyes tighter. I'd been looking for Roy Adams, but I'd seen a monster rising from the ocean. A hallucination, maybe—though in the chaos of memory, I couldn't keep my timelines straight. The kayak journey splintered into images of Boston, so that it wasn't Adams who rose dripping from the coral reef—it was Sylvia. Sylvia mouthed the text of *Living the Solution*, made me cry out, sit up in my cot, as if by opening my eyes I could escape her, as if she weren't already burned into my every synaptic pulse.

```
Human beings are unwilling to relinquish
their grip on the past because they see no
future. They cling to the rails of a sinking
ship because they see no other ships. The
ocean is cold and vast. Only a martyr would
swim into it and drown. And yet conventional
```

ecowisdom asks the masses to do this and is
surprised when they do not.

There must be an alternative. A new ship,
not a life raft: an offer of salvation that
is at once familiar and improved. There must
be the promise of more, not less.

I felt better the next morning.

Though my body ached and a pressure lingered behind my
eyes, I had crossed the invisible threshold between illness and
recovery. My mind had drained clear in the night. I yanked an
IV from my inner elbow and pressed a finger to the crimson
dot. The twinge of pain felt good. I was alive.

Wrapping a sheet around my body, I shuffled to the bathroom. In an oval mirror, my face blazed red with sunburn.
I ran a finger down the bridge of my nose. The island had
touched me, made me like its own landscape: suffering under
the same relentless sun.

Back in the main part of the cabin, I noticed a wooden
crate on the floor beside my cot. I opened the lid tentatively,
then with rushed excitement. Inside were two crisp white polo
shirts, a one-piece Camp Hope swimsuit, khaki shorts with
ample pockets, a towel, a Camp Hope visor, vegan-leather
flip-flops, vegan-leather sneakers, athletic shorts, a Camp
Hope T-shirt, a rain slicker, a small backpack stitched with the
tagline TO PRESERVE AND PROTECT—TO CONSERVE AND COR-
RECT, and a bamboo toothbrush.

My heart thumped, rabbit-racing ahead. At the bottom

of the crate lay a folder of papers: a contract for tenure as a crewmember. My name was printed at the top. Too good to be true—yet true enough to grip in my shaking hands. I flipped through the pages in a flurry of white, skimming over details about *carbon-debt restitution* and *indefinite wage withholdings*, scribbling my signature on the highlighted lines as if a pen alone could pin down a future.

After that, I put on the uniform: the vegan-leather sneakers and khaki shorts and the white polo shirt. I pressed the collar into place.

Would it have shocked Sylvia to see me? A uniform doesn't mean much, she likely would have said. *Barba non facit philosophum*. A beard won't make one a philosopher.

A beard helped, though. Aesthetics were everything at Camp Hope; they were part of the strategy laid out in *Living the Solution*. Dressed in my new uniform, I officially joined a mission larger than myself. I was one step closer to making my life meaningful, to proving every naysaying voice wrong. No more fantasized realities; I was making the fantasy real.

Three times in my life have I felt unadulterated joy. There, in the medical cabin, I experienced one of them.

```
Radical change is best disguised in the Tro-
jan Horse of normality. Morality! Camp Hope
must appear respectable and familiar. Clean-
cut aesthetics are essential. Uniforms are
key. This is where other environmental move-
ments have failed again and again: they've
made themselves into freaks and nutjobs.
They've been perceived as sex weirdos. As
unwashed bimbos and hairy losers.
```

This needs to change. Recycling must become as American as apple pie, wind turbines as patriotic as the American Flag. We will recruit former firefighters, beauty queens, Nobel Prize winners, football stars, decorated veterans. We want admiration from every angle.

Consider how there's a powerful respect in this country for military culture. Let's use that to our advantage. Let's blend these ideologies. We want to see Victory Gardens on every lawn in this country—only this time the gardens won't be about fighting other nations. They will be about fighting Climate Change: enemy number one of this country, of every country.

If the planet were ever attacked by extra-terrestrials, humanity would band together. True solidarity would occur.

It's Jachi-with-an-I, said my orientation guide.

She anointed me with an airy touchless hug, then beckoned me beyond the medical cabin's open doorway—a threshold on which she'd appeared, moments before, as silently and suddenly as the wooden crate of clothes. Outside, the morning sun beamed bright. So did Jachi. Like most crewmembers, she had an athletic physique, her features strikingly symmetrical, though with her shaved head and aviators she also had a distinctly insectoid appearance—like that of a slender praying mantis—the resemblance accentuated by her tendency to clasp her hands while speaking.

We have so much to discuss, said Jachi. So many people to see. Come.

She led me down a pathway of crushed shells that wove through the compound. Around us, solar panels sparkled. A sea breeze sifted through trellised passion fruit, spun the huge blades of the wind turbine overhead. Jachi gestured toward a biodigester, praising their "hyperenzymatic thermophilic bacteria." I couldn't stop smiling.

That reminds me, said Jachi—turning around, so that my face duplicated in the silver sheen of her aviators—wait here.

She swished away into a small garden. Ahead, around a bend on the pathway, a group of crewmembers approached with heads tilted in conversation. They had the fleecy sun-paled hair of people who spend lots of time on boats. Sunglasses dangled from cords around their necks or perched on their heads like tiaras. I waved.

The crewmembers veered down another path, as if to avoid me.

Here we go, said Jachi—returning with a spear of aloe in hand. Smush this up and rub it on your sunburn. That's right, goop it all over your face. It's nature's moisturizer.

Another pair of crewmembers came into view, backtracked when they saw me.

My smile slackened—the first pangs of worry eroding my bliss.

Jachi, I said. Is there something I should know about?

She sighed with delighted resignation, said: Oh, you guessed it. I haven't always gone by Jachi. You've recognized me from my other life, as *Jacquelle de la Rosa.*

She removed her aviators with a flourish; a pair of big brown eyes fluttered.

Actually, I said, what I meant was—

As you must have seen on the news, Jachi continued, the animal rights people gave me a terrible time. How was I supposed to know the cape was made from real feathers, or those birds were endangered? Yup, I got the full red-paint treatment and everything. And on live TV. Yet the whole ordeal was the best thing that ever happened to me. Really. My publicist told me to read up on animal cruelty—for the apology statement and whatnot—and the more I read, well, you know how it is. Once you start digging into this stuff, your whole world does a backflip. I asked myself: what have I been doing with my life? Who am I, really? Not the person I wanted to be, that's for sure. Then Roy Adams reached out. Bless that man. Because here I am. Clean, sober, happily celibate. Feeling better than ever. Camp Hope is far better than rehab, let me tell you.

I nodded, though I could not recall having heard of "Jacquelle de la Rosa." I didn't know much about celebrities. I wished I could call my cousins—they would have known all about her—but that life, along with everything else, was behind me. Jachi had walked us deeper into the grounds, past a towering apiary and into a fragrant orchard. Beaming a movie star smile, she gestured toward a stand of avocado trees, their branches heavy with fruit. Around the trees, six crewmembers raked leaves in synchronized sweeps. Jachi explained that the Agro Team included an award-winning potato farmer, a champion wrestler, and a model who'd specialized in rugged outerwear. She had started describing Camp Hope's low-water, fast-yield farming techniques, when one of the crewmembers looked up, said: What's she doing here?

Just getting oriented, I said. Sorry to—

Interrupt? said the crewmember. A little late for that.

Another crewmember threw down her rake and stalked off into the orchard. Two others chased after her, while those remaining patted the back of the man who'd spoken. A tear streaked his cheek.

I hadn't misread the crewmembers' earlier hostility—they were upset with me, though I hadn't even met them.

I looked to Jachi for an explanation. She gave me the same dreamy smile, clasped her hands as she murmured that we ought to continue. This was her first chance to give a tour; she was committed to staying on schedule.

And so we visited Camp Hope's biodiesel facility, recycling yard, and solar station—the scene from the orchard repeating in new variations of hostility and incrimination—before I sufficiently pleaded with Jachi to tell me what was going on.

I thought you knew, she said.

Knew what?

About Camp Hope's launch, said Jachi. That it's postponed.

I stared at her, appalled.

It's really too bad, Jachi went on wistfully. We were all ready to go. We'd just finished a final team-building kayak trip out to a reef. Adams told everyone he'd make the first phone calls to his media contacts as soon as he got back. Everything was in place. Everyone was trained. The grounds were fully functional. We were ready to reveal ourselves to the world. Finally. We've been working toward this moment for months. Some of us longer. Everyone was over the moon. Over the sun and stars, too. Out on the reef, Adams announced he'd stay behind for some extra snorkeling. He generally does every activity, every exercise, longer and more intensely than anyone else. He's like a great director—

Please, I interrupted. I need you to explain what happened.

Well, you appeared out of nowhere, she said. Given the timing, I mean with the launch on the horizon, it wasn't outrageous that an outsider might arrive. And Corrine, Dorothy, and Eisa told everyone you needed to see him—that you were part of a preparedness test or something—and those three can be so convincing. So we sent you to the reef. If we'd known what would happen, though, we never would have—

Just tell me.

Jachi swallowed, clasped and unclasped her hands, said: It's hard to say, exactly. You and Adams were the only ones out there. All we know is that when he returned, he was towing your kayak. You were slumped over it, passed out from heatstroke. But heatstroke wasn't the problem. The problem was Adams. He seemed—distracted? After dropping you off in the medical cabin, he announced that we needed to pause the launch while he thought through some issues. Then he went into the Command Center. That was three days ago.

Jachi's gaze floated up to an octagonal building set on stilts near the center of the grounds. A corkscrewing staircase led to a balcony that encircled its eight windowed sides.

Do you really not remember what happened on the reef? she asked.

I told her I didn't. I told her none of this made sense. I couldn't remember much from the kayak voyage, but I knew I never would have done anything to delay the launch. Not in a million years.

After my electroshock therapy, said Jachi, my memory was never quite the same, but I still remember things. Bits and pieces. They resurface.

You have to believe me, I said.

Jachi turned away, murmuring about respecting Adams and his decisions, about animal rights activists and aloe and the blessings of celibacy. She took off her aviators, rubbed her eyes. In a voice that was un-airy, as if coming from a different person, she said: Sometimes we do things for reasons we don't understand.

I remembered, then, I had seen one of Jachi's movies: a sepia-drenched drama about a woman who maintains multiple love affairs while stringing along a mobster tyrant. In the film, Jacquelle de la Rosa has long satiny hair and wears a bustier while smoking on balconies. In the penultimate scene, she shoots her lover in the chest with a pearlescent Colt .45. Sylvia had called the film nostalgic propaganda in which violence functioned as a sedative for the oppressed proletariat. But she'd said these words softly, almost sweetly, her mouth by my ear, her breath tingling my skin. I had not felt sedate at all.

```
The launch will occur after Camp Hope's con-
struction phase has finished, after train-
ing is completed, and after the facility is
brought to peak functionality. Kept secret
until the "fertilization" phase of our oper-
ation, journalists, influencers, vloggers,
talk show hosts, select celebrities, will
subsequently be invited to visit the site,
resulting in the dissemination of our mes-
```

```
sage all over the globe. Camp Hope will
offer a problem-solved society. Not just
carbon neutral, but carbon negative. Not
just coexistent with nature, but actively
rehabilitatory. Camp Hope will show an envi-
ronmental future that does not appear puni-
tive, but rather appealingly liberatory. The
"attitude" of Camp Hope, moreover, will cat-
alyze a shift in global values. Environmen-
tal action will become sexy, but not sexual;
it will be cool, but not intimidating. It
will stoke desire and with that, change.

What better export can America offer, if not
desire? If not dreams?
```

I quickly gave up trying to convince Jachi—or anyone—that I hadn't intended to delay Camp Hope's launch, that I was as confused and distraught as the rest of them. Though the seventy crewmembers came from varied backgrounds, professions, locales, they gave a collective credence to cause and effect. And there'd been an effect of which I was cause.

When Jachi's tour concluded, I tried to suggest that I talk to Roy Adams—visit the Command Center—but Jachi shook her head.

Only Lorenzo is allowed up there, she said.

Can I talk to Lorenzo?

Jachi had drifted away, distracted by a solar array.

I would meet Lorenzo that afternoon, though, when Jachi took me to have lunch in the geodesic dome that served as

Camp Hope's mess hall. The structure was awe-inspiring to step inside. Honeycomb panels filtered sunlight in ecclesiastical shafts. Crewmembers funneled through buffet lines, filling their plates with hydroponic greens and slices of protein loaf, before collecting cups of coconut water fizzed with carbon dioxide extracted from the air. Sitting around hexagonal tables, they leaned over their plates, recited environmental prayers for regenerative growth and abundance. When they finished eating, a compost-cleaning station ensured no scrap of the meal went to waste.

Which isn't to say the crewmembers appeared serene. Some crewmembers openly glared in my direction. Others made sharp remarks to their tablemates. When the Liberal Arts Girls saw me, they turned their backs, stabbed forks at their protein loaves.

In a strange way, this behavior pleased me. The crewmembers' frustration revealed their commitment to launching Camp Hope. They'd left behind their careers and loved ones because they believed the compound would save the planet from climatological catastrophe. If everything went as planned, Camp Hope would be up for the Nobel Prize—among other untold honors—but I sensed that these crewmembers hadn't come for the glory. They'd come to do good.

I loved this about them, even if it meant bearing their animosity.

Oh look, said Jachi. There's Lorenzo.

I squinted in the direction she'd pointed—at the mess hall's compost-cleaning station. Despite the midday light streaming through the geodesic panels overhead, Lorenzo had hidden inside a shadow the way fish hover in coral cavities. His uniform was rumpled and untucked, his hair unkempt. A fuzzy mustache rested above his lip. He fidgeted with a clipboard as his eyes ricocheted around the mess hall.

Lorenzo did not look like the Camp Hope type.

He wasn't eye-catching or obviously extraordinary. Yet this was Adams's right-hand man. It was Lorenzo who was allowed into the Command Center and who communicated with the leader I was desperate to meet.

He wasn't even observant: he startled when I stepped into his shadowy nook.

You need your work assignment? he said. Your housing assignment?

No, I said. I mean, I will—

It's almost ready.

Can I talk to Adams?

Lorenzo fidgeted with the clipboard, looked at his feet.

There's a misunderstanding, I said. About the launch and—

There will be an update tomorrow, said Lorenzo. All other information must remain confidential at this time, as per Adams's instructions.

He hurried away before I could ask more.

Across the mess hall, a table of shark scientists scowled at me, gnashing hydroponic greens between their perfect teeth.

DBCS, or Daily Body Conditioning Sessions, will keep crewmembers physically fit, connected to their immediate environment, and diffuse the restlessness that builds in even the best planned celibate societies. They will begin with the following Daily Pledge:

> *To conserve and correct,*
> *To preserve and protect,*
> *I dedicate myself to the Earth,*
> *For each day I give my worth . . .*

Good morning! said Jachi. Are you ready for the best workout of your life?

It was 5:00 A.M. I'd spent the night in the bunk above hers, in one of the shotgun structures that served as crewmember sleeping quarters. I was tired, still weak from sunstroke, but I hurried to dress, eager for the day ahead: a chance to prove myself as a crewmember and to figure out how to get Camp Hope back on track.

Jachi and I joined the others on a beach near the tip of the peninsula. With the sun hovering below the horizon, a dull purple light soaked the grounds. The air felt cool on my skin. Crewmembers milled about, greeting one another. Everyone wore pale green sweat suits.

Lorenzo stood apart, waving his clipboard. When that failed to get anyone's attention, he called out: I have an update regarding the launch.

The crewmembers quieted; their sweat suits crinkled in the breeze. Adams normally made these announcements, I later learned. Lorenzo was merely standing in.

Adams sends his regards, said Lorenzo breathlessly. He says to keep up the good work. He says to welcome our newest crewmember, Willa Marks. He says to remember *self-pity is selfishness and selfishness is at the core of our environmental crisis*, as stated on page fifty-seven of *Living the Solution*. He also says the launch remains indefinitely delayed—

A collective groan. A volley of side-eyes sent my way. Lorenzo had more to add, but crewmembers tore off their sweat suits in a fury of snaps. They cast the garments aside and set off down the beach, galloping around Lorenzo and nearly knocking him down.

I galloped after them. The loose sand made gaining traction difficult, but I pumped my arms, aiming to position myself in the middle of the pack. The Liberal Arts Girls' ponytails swished in front of me. Jachi sprang with leggy effortlessness to my left. Botanists weaved between meteorologists, while the synthetics experts sprinted up to the front. The sun spilled over the horizon, throwing bright feelers across the water. The ocean glowed golden. The sky bloomed pink. An ecstatic charge filled me: I was running across an island paradise, greeting the morning in the most wondrous of ways.

Thirty minutes later, my ecstasy had faded into exhaustion. We had traveled well beyond the Camp Hope grounds onto a rugged stretch of undeveloped coastline. The beach lifted into rocky cliffs—pitted limestone threatening twisted ankles with Swiss cheese holes—which dropped thirty feet into a thrashing sea. The temperature had spiked, yet the other crewmembers ran with sweatless ease. They held full conversations about metallurgy or reverse osmosis or mammalian endocrine systems. Jachi made cheery comments about cloud formations.

I couldn't answer. My breath ripped through my lungs. My whole body hurt, self-doubt rattling loud in my skull. The crewmembers had all been hand-selected and vetted for their roles; I hadn't—and it showed.

Up at the front of the pack, a nutritionist veered toward a rocky outcropping that jutted over the sea. Her stride lengthened, speed increasing. She ran straight over the edge—into open air—and dropped out of sight.

The other crewmembers followed. One after the next, they ran off the cliff as if onto an invisible bridge: a road no one could see.

This I could do.

Running out into the unknown—I'd been doing it my whole life. And so I willed my body faster, leaping over the cliff and flailing my legs into endless air before descending into a smeary wet chaos. Saltwater filled my nose and mouth. I clawed to the surface, then swam, my strokes labored, toward a stony shore a hundred meters away.

Then came fifty push-ups on the edge of the surf, followed by a hundred sit-ups. Sandflies nipped my skin. The sun blazed spitefully bright. By the time I returned to the Camp Hope beach, I was bloody and dirt-covered. I doubled over, wheezing.

The other crewmembers stretched quietly. They pulled their hamstrings back and balanced on one leg like flamingos: a gorgeously uniform flock.

There was no time to dwell—next came a breakfast of bean-based energy nougats and almost-ripe bananas, then I was on to my work assignment. Prior to my arrival, crewmember work teams had shared the task of cleaning bathrooms, shower stalls, and slop buckets. But since no team wanted to take me on, I was appointed the sole member of a one-woman sanitation squad.

The job thrilled me.

Even cleaning toilets contributed to Camp Hope's cause. In the days that followed, I left meals early to get to work sooner. I scrubbed toilet bowls on my hands and knees, wiping every surface with vinegar and sustainably harvested sea sponges. My elbows jabbed the air while sweat rolled down my nose. I had the idea that if the toilets around Camp Hope sparkled, the other crewmembers would recognize my commitment.

Or Adams would.

I imagined turning around to find him. *This is why I brought you on as a crewmember*, he'd say. *I recognized your dedication from the get-go.* We would shake hands, discuss waste-to-resource circuits and the value of "human manure." We'd chuckle about the manure, though we'd also be deeply serious. I'd bring up the delayed launch; we'd address whatever had occurred at the reef. Camp Hope would get back on track. The planet would be saved from imminent climate catastrophe.

Keep up the good work, Adams would tell me. *The world needs people like you—people stronger than doubt.*

Awaiting this encounter, I scrubbed fiercely, pausing only to wipe my brow or swig coconut water. I recited passages from *Living the Solution*. When the other crewmembers passed by—on their way to rehabilitate coral reefs, or maintain photovoltaic cells, or recycle ocean plastics into polo shirts— I waved.

No one waved back.

So I worked harder, as if the cleanliness of a toilet might hold the dream steady, as if by enacting *Living the Solution*, a spell would click into place.

A week came and went like a hot breath. Then another. My waking hours sped past, bleary and often baffling. My gusto began to falter. The daily exercise sessions left me stiff and sore and stupid with tiredness, made it hard to stay cheerful, especially as the other crewmembers remained distant. I berated myself for failing to remember my encounter with Adams—to recall a detail that might help me fix the problem.

Meanwhile, the island offered up hazards. In the tropical heat, even small wounds festered, and there were plenty of ways to be wounded. Jellyfish stung my feet when I stepped into the sea to cool off. A centipede slithered out from under my mattress and bit my neck. While turning a compost pile, an army of fire ants streamed up my leg.

You should apply ice to that, said Corrine when she saw my swollen calf.

Cold reduces inflammation, said Dorothy.

Inflammation, said Eisa, from the Latin *inflammare*—

Quiet, said Corrine. We need to focus.

She and the other Liberal Arts Girls had cornered me in a shower stall. Though in the presence of their fellow crew-members they made a show of distancing themselves, in private they sought me out, seeking to extract information that might resolve the delayed launch.

Do you remember anything now? said Dorothy. Anything at all about what happened on the reef?

Did you have a conversation with Adams? said Corrine. What did you say?

Their interrogation persisted until it became clear I could offer no useful information. Then I served a different function: I became an audience. The Liberal Arts Girls had been brought to Camp Hope to aid its communication efforts during the launch. They had a gift for distillation, as well as a compulsive need to demonstrate what they knew. With no launch on the horizon, they were bursting with pent-up commentary.

You know these shower walls are made from a composite of ocean trash? said Corrine.

Ocean *resources,* said Dorothy.

They glanced at Eisa to see if she'd comment on the word's Latin root—and in the space of that pause I asked if they'd ever wondered about Lorenzo. It surprised me no suspicion had fallen on him. He was the only person who interacted with Adams. Twice a day he journeyed up the Command Center's spiral staircase to visit. He stayed for exactly fifteen minutes each time.

So? said Corrine.

Don't you wonder if he's up to something? I said.

The Liberal Arts Girls found this funny. Dorothy cleared her throat, settled into lecture mode: Lorenzo had worked with Adams since the beginning. He'd helped get Camp Hope started when it was nothing but a dream. Back then, the peninsula was scrubland, junked with trash, the surrounding waters overfished by locals. Lorenzo had helped Adams organize the initial squad of crewmembers who barn-raised Camp Hope's essential infrastructure, working day and night with air-dropped supplies.

But Lorenzo's the only person who talks to Adams, I said. Or even—

That's for our protection, said Dorothy. Lorenzo's not technically a crewmember. He looks at the Internet, for instance, and reads all the bad news about climate change so we don't have to. He deals with the boring administrative tasks. We get to live in a beautiful bubble. Which is so important, because depression was a big issue with past environmental movements. Everyone was hampered by despair—

Or doxxing, said Eisa. Or death threats. Or actual assassinations.

And potential converts, Dorothy went on, can tell if you're

having doubts. Who wants to join a movement that doesn't believe in itself? The public will sense our honest-to-God optimism when we launch.

The mention of the launch made them go quiet. I squeezed my sustainably harvested sponge, dripping the last drops of vinegar-water solution onto the floor. Corrine cleared her throat.

It's Jacquelle de la Rosa who should make you suspicious, she said. Jachi's only here because she donated like twenty million dollars—which is great—but she's not exactly Camp Hope material.

The trio waited for my reaction. I kept my face blank. I knew they didn't think I fit in either. And Jachi was always kind to me, or at least amnesiacly pleasant. During the mandated forty-five minutes of biweekly R & R, she taught me how to free dive, saying that when Adams returned we'd all go on a boat ride around the island—insisting, also, that Camp Hope would soon launch. This place would change the world. We'd all be famous.

And in the end, she was right—just not in the way anyone could have expected.

Most people address climate change through deflection and avoidance. That is, they do not address climate change at all. This includes the masses, as well as the self-styled environmentalists. The masses make their worlds and their lives small. They worship celebrity and work only to keep candles burning at the ragged edges of their own egos. Most modern environmentalists are

corporate sellouts, number worshippers, tie
wearers who ride bikes to office jobs; or
they are social misfits with no social capital. You know what matters to a social movement? Social capital . . .

Though Roy Adams was not physically present around Camp
Hope, he was constantly invoked. Some crewmembers speculated he was busy studying the Food Price Index, stock market
values, gas prices, until the numbers hit the right thresholds.
Mass social change, after all, required the proper context. Others wondered if he was fasting to gain insight and clarity in
advance of the launch—a theory that escalated after a nutritionist reported Lorenzo had stopped delivering meals. Even
the most data-driven scientists, though, were not above lore.
A meteorologist claimed Adams slept upside down for brain
enhancement. An entomologist said she'd heard Adams only
slept two hours a night.

You know, said a hydrobotanist—during a dinnertime
conversation loud enough for me to overhear—I was up late
last night checking the watercress troughs and the Command
Center lights were on at 2:00 A.M.

He's up to something big, said an engineer. No question.

Other crewmembers reminisced about how rare parrots
converged on Adams's shoulders during trips into the island
coppice; how he had embarked on a multi-mile swim after a biodiesel pontoon malfunctioned. A marine biologist—collecting
a crowd around her table—described how Adams had miracu-
lously saved a research venture.

We were trying to tag a whopper female tiger shark, said

the biologist, so we could track rebounding populations. But she'd gotten a longline hook caught in a gill and we couldn't get it out. So the shark is flailing and biting in the water. Then Adams, calm as a summer day, jumps in the water with a bloody hunk of mantis. Feeds it to the shark with his bare hands. The blood attracts two other sharks and he feeds them as well. By then the female tiger has calmed down. He gets the hook out and—I swear this is true—gives the shark a kiss on the nose, slaps it behind the dorsal, and sends it on its merry way.

An absolute legend, said a solar specialist. I'll never forget when Adams showed up at my Phoenix office unannounced. Freaked me out at first. This was a week after the company got its second pipe bomb in the mail. I was at a breaking point. Didn't know what to do, how to keep going. Adams laid everything out: it was going to be hard, he said, not being in contact with my family. It would be like going away to war, or getting on a flight to Mars. But like both of those things, I would be serving the greater good. I'd be pursuing a goal larger than myself. If I loved my family, I'd be able to handle the lack of contact. And I have. Or I had, until recently—

Not discussed was the possibility of visiting the Command Center and checking on Adams. All of Camp Hope was built on rules calibrated to keep the compound smoothly functional. Rules were what realigned society to fix its environmental failings. Break one rule and the whole enterprise could collapse. So if the Command Center was off-limits, if Lorenzo was the only person allowed up there, then that was how things were. When Adams issued an instruction, it was followed. That was why, despite the crewmembers' frustration toward me, they never tried to eject me from the compound. They weren't friendly, but they never impeded my assigned tasks. Adams said I was to be included and so I was; the crew-members respected their leader too much to defy him.

Adams has Camp Hope's best interests in mind, said a marine biologist after another disappointing daily announcement from Lorenzo. The delay is a test of our endurance before the big show.

Yet each day Camp Hope went unlaunched became harder to endure. Even if crewmembers weren't reading the latest bad news about climate change, we all knew things were getting worse. Sunshine seared the island, making every wisp of breeze a miracle. The heat reminded everyone of the species snuffed out by the minute, the coastlines swallowed by rising seas, the forests clear-cut, the methane belched into an atmosphere already thickened with fossil fuel fumes. Another march wouldn't stop it all. Certainly not another petition. Legislation was too little too late. There were too many people with too much money tied up in the scrap-picking of Earth.

```
The Camp Hope launch should be as sensa-
tional as the moon landing. It should have
the grandeur of an inauguration. It should
feel as good as the Fourth of July. Because
Americans will do anything for pride. They
gravitate toward the promise of more, not
less. Camp Hope offers the spark to move
fast, to set the transition in motion. To
do so globally, wholly. Because things can
happen fast. An image or a song can spill
```

through the minds of billions in a day, can
infect those who hear the message. Camp Hope
will move at the speed of a pandemic.

How?

By being both a target and a destination. A
product and a catalyst. Camp Hope is a torch
in the dark: a signal. It is a fire burning
in promise of a harbor. It is also the fuel.

Four weeks after arriving on Eleutheria, I awoke from a dead
sleep to a full moon staring through the bunkroom window. It
was unusual for me to awake in the night. The physical exertion
of each day left me comatose, even on nights that were humid
and sticky, and when bugs snuck in through the screens.

On the bunk below mine, Jachi slept like a corpse, her
hands clasped on her chest. A faint smile hovered around her
mouth.

The other crewmembers who shared the bunkroom were
gone—their beds uncharacteristically mussed. Maybe there
had been an incident: a filter failed in the aquaponics sector, a
cistern leak. But no alarms had sounded.

Outside the bunkroom, the air was filmy and slick, cloyed
with jasmine. Insects trilled. The moon hung low and bulbous,
lending light to the solar lanterns that marked Camp Hope's
web of pathways. At the center of the grounds, the Command
Center rose on its stilts, windows aglow like a second moon,
an octagonal jewel, a beacon in the night.

I walked toward the edge of the compound for a better

view. Maybe, I thought, I'd detect Adams's silhouette: a glimmer of his presence promising better things to come.

I hadn't gone far when I smelled smoke.

With the weather so hot, so dry, brush could have sparked spontaneously. Or there was an electrical issue. The Camp Hope scientists regularly pushed the boundaries of renewable construction.

Fire, I yelled—hoping someone would hear.

Light flickered at the far end of the peninsula; I ran toward it, tripping through shadows, the smoke smell growing stronger. Reaching a row of casuarina trees bordering the beach, I stopped short.

A bonfire blazed on the sand. Made of driftwood stacked in an enormous pile, the flames crackled, spat ash, illuminating the crewmembers who spilled across the beach. Laughter rang out. Calypso music lilted from a solar-powered radio, the sound of steel drums mingling with the slosh of ocean surf. Aluminum cans fizzed open. A rum bottle was passed hand to hand like a baton in a race toward obliteration. An ornithologist wrenched open a package of store-bought chips. An engineer tossed candy into the air, tried to catch it in her mouth, cheered on by a group of tidal power experts. In the shadows, an oceanographer and a marine biologist leaned against a palm tree, their limbs entwined.

For the first time on Eleutheria, a chill rattled through me. The whole point of Camp Hope was to live by specific principles—to live *Living the Solution*—yet here was everyone going against the codes of temperance, celibacy, discipline, which would keep the community at peak efficiency, palatable to a broad audience when we launched.

A solar specialist opened a crate of lanterns for an

impromptu light show. A member of the Agro Team vomited into a stand of sea grapes.

The chill in my limbs intensified—and with it came the familiar anguish I'd known ever since my parents died: their faces openmouthed and frozen in our cabin in the woods. My parents, so hopeless in the face of the world's challenges they'd given up on living. I staggered, caught myself on a casuarina branch. A few crewmembers noticed the rustling foliage and called out to ask who was there. Their shouts attracted Lorenzo's attention. He smiled shyly as a drunken soil analyst ruffled his hair. Then he headed my way to investigate.

How much did it hurt to have my illusion of the other crewmembers peeled back? Disappointment stabbed into me: icy and sharp. I knew I needed to speak with Roy Adams. I needed Camp Hope's leader to assure me that *Living the Solution* was what he'd claimed it to be—that we could still do what we'd all come here to accomplish.

Lorenzo crept closer. He peered into the darkness until he found my face.

Marks—

I was already running. I crashed back through Camp Hope, stumbling around wheelbarrows and carbon capture units and banana plants. Footsteps clattered behind me. The white trunk of the wind turbine loomed like a limbless tree. I dodged around it. My breath shrieked through my lungs. Lorenzo's thin voice called for me to wait.

After a month of DBCSs, I could run faster than I ever had in my life, but Lorenzo was unexpectedly quick. As I dashed up the Command Center steps, he was on my heels. On the balcony, at the top of the corkscrew stairway, he caught a handful of my shirt.

Let go, I said—and wrenched away.

Wait, said Lorenzo. Wait a second.

His small chest heaved, his mustache quivering as we both paused in front of the Command Center door. He pulled out an inhaler.

I'm going to talk to Roy Adams, I said. Right now. I'm going in there.

Even in my flush of righteousness, I hesitated. Despite all the Camp Hope rules I'd just seen broken, it still felt wrong to break one myself.

Listen, said Lorenzo—trying to catch his breath—people needed a release. They were getting demoralized. I thought a party would help.

You thought so? I said. *You?* What about Adams?

Lorenzo shut his eyes; he took another hit from his inhaler.

What have you done to him? I said. Is he a hostage in there?

Without waiting for an answer, I pushed past Lorenzo, grasping for the Command Center door, bracing myself for every answer, for the man I'd come to Eleutheria to find.

Please, said Lorenzo—but I was already inside.

The Command Center opened into a spacious octagonal room. At the center sat a horseshoe-shaped desk, on which was placed Camp Hope's phone and Internet hookup. There were control panels positioned around the desk, along with seashore detritus—conch shells, driftwood, a buoy—which made the Command Center resemble a cross between a beach house and a spaceship. Around the upper edge of the walls ran a digital script, which noted parts per million carbon counts, along with other numbers adding or subtracting from the fate of the planet.

The Command Center did not contain Adams.

I spun back to Lorenzo, said: What did you do to him? Where is he?

Lorenzo had fully deflated; he was clinging to the door-jamb, a shipwrecked survivor hanging on for his life. In a strained whisper, he said: I don't know. Adams said there were problems he had to take care of. He said we couldn't launch Camp Hope until the problems were resolved. He left three weeks ago and hasn't come back.

WORD SWEPT LIKE WILDFIRE through the colonies: the captain had left his post. A man of tattered dress and bruised ego, he had steered a small shallop from Eleutheria to Virginia, drifting through sharks and shoals to beg for intervention. He spoke of lost supplies and interminable starvation, of how—with the beheading of one monarch, the rise of one worse—exiles from Bermuda swelled the settlers' ranks even as their courage dwindled.

Up north in Boston, colonists heard these tidings with sympathetic ears. The Eleutherian settlement was ambitious—but weren't they themselves ambitious to a fault? Though their waterfront was swampish, their streets mud-trenched, they imagined themselves at greater elevation: a city on a hill. They had quarrelless ale houses and touchless dances. Services three days long. They had reformed the polluted practices of their former country; their England was New.

The Boston colonists took up a collection, passed the alms pail three times around their pews. The haul was respectable—robust. To Eleutheria they sent a vessel packed with the essentials: crates of sugar and sacks of oats, axes and spades and shovels, munitions and pewter spoons, beeswax candles, starched white linens, and silver sewing needles. Muslin netting to shield against mosquitoes. Fishing nets. Two downy calves, a flock of chickens. Guinea corn, along with seeds for pumpkins, peas, and wheat.

They sent well-wishes too, as if such sentiments might be planted, depended on for future harvest.

Perhaps they could be. Some months later, the chartered ship returned to Boston, its hold loaded with braziletto. The Eleutherian settlers, gripping their new tools, had recognized the island's towering mahogany, corkwood, Caribbean pine as virginally verdant. They'd sunk the toothy bite of axes into tree trunks thicker than a three-man embrace, leapt back as the timber crackled and crashed down, exploding songbirds into the sky and sending agouti scampering.

Braziletto: a red-grained wood, a rarity. It was good for fabric dyes and violin bows—for crimson gowns and enthralling sonatas—a wood with little use on Eleutheria, but elsewhere, yes. It could be veritably alchemic.

So wrote the settlers' captain in his accompanying letter: ten pages long, effusive. The sale of the wood, he piously suggested, could help the Boston colonists expand their college for clergy.

Harvard, the school was called.

In the city on a hill, markets bloomed and bustled. The braziletto fetched a handsome sum: the largest gift the college had yet seen. The colonists purchased a second printing press, brought in one young clergyman, and then another. Copies echoed, sent out, distributed. More trees cut, pulped, pressed. More young white men—and later other populations—pulped, pressed, presented. All those doctors and dignitaries, those litigators and billionaires and prime ministers and Pulitzer winners and Hollywood performers. So many pupils sent on their way to power. In Boston, they climbed the slope before them, Eleutheria's old-world growth made into a ladder for the New World's impending elite.

4

Harvard University—to think the backwoods daughter of doomsday preppers would ski her feet across those marble-floored halls, strum her fingers along wrought-iron gates, traipse beneath vaulted ceilings and brick-pinched archways. Not in any official capacity. I was never admitted; I never applied. Yet, the university played a significant role in my life after the party at the congressman's house—my first encounter with Sylvia.

It did take some time to get to Harvard. First passed the interminable winter months, when I did little more than lie on my cousins' futon or fry doughnuts at The Hole Story. Victoria and Jeanette remained upset at me for losing their phone, though as they faced the draining digits of their bank account, their fury melted into an ambivalent funk. They ignored me. This was worse than being actively punished; punishment had at least served as a distraction. Without my cousins' attention—or access to the parallel paradise of their photos—my reality became suffocating. I was only myself: the daughter of parents who had found the world unbearable, yet who had abandoned me in it.

What I still had, though, was my memory of the woman-in-black. I daydreamed her often—mostly during my shifts at The Hole Story. I liked to imagine she was observing me as she had at the congressman's party: her gaze so relentless and thorough it stripped me to the bone. The idea made my fingertips flush, even in the icy cavern of the café's walk-in freezer. More than once, I lost track of time. It took a yell from a coworker to snap me awake. Yet the woman-in-black was with me, always. She watched while I mixed batter, fried and decorated the doughnut holes, set them on trays—a sequence I did over and over each shift. My boss, Ruby, had decided early on I wasn't "front-of-house material."

Have you heard yourself talk, Bunker Girl? she'd said. *We don't want to scare the customers.*

So it seemed a dreamed déjà vu, when, four months after the party, I carried a tray of mini Boston Creams to the front display case and saw the woman-in-black by the register.

Cinnamon or Cinnamon sugar? Ruby asked her. Which one do you want?

The woman-in-black was not wearing black, though her outfit remained subdued: a long tweed coat, the collar upturned. Her dark hair had the same bobbed cut, frayed slightly from the dampness of March snow flurries. Her shoulders were loaded with book-bearing tote bags. She looked tired, though her eyes remained sharp. She frowned at the two sample doughnut holes, displeased by Ruby's question.

There's a difference? she said.

Her voice sent a jolt through me—the unexpected British accent—and I bit my tongue to hold back my surprise.

Blood seeped into my mouth; I swallowed the taste of iron. I hadn't yet installed the tray of mini Boston Creams in the display case, and Ruby noticed. She hissed, *Scat*. I clattered the tray into position, retreated back beyond the swinging kitchen door. Even through the wall, the woman's displeasure radiated. I trembled with the terror and exhilaration of our proximity. There was so much I wanted to ask her. To start: Who was she? What made her brave enough to drop that wineglass at the party? What had she seen in me that seemed worth saving?

I hurried to the café's back door, which led to an alleyway running behind the building. If I was quick, I could catch her when she stepped onto the street.

You *just* took your break, called a coworker—but I slipped outside, my apron strings flapping as I dashed around the edge of the building.

The sidewalk in front of The Hole Story swarmed with people. This was unexpected; the crowd had not been there when I had arrived to work, nor had I noticed them through the café's front window. These people had congregated suddenly and from nowhere. They shouted, punched their arms into the air. A snowball arced overhead. A flash protest, I'd realize later; it was the only way people could demonstrate anymore, with the new laws against large gatherings. Such laws held no interest to me—at least not then. I wanted to find the woman. I searched the crowd, pushing through protesters who stood shoulder to shoulder, yelling and chanting, their faces blurred by the powdered-sugar snowfall. In the distance, a siren squealed. I ducked to avoid the square corner of someone's protest sign, straining to spot the woman, the word *wait* rising in my throat—as if she might have known to listen.

Maybe she would have. That she had appeared at The Hole

Story, of all places, was a significant coincidence. There were bakeries all over Boston—better bakeries—and Sylvia was a discerning woman. She had no reason to visit this South End grease factory, not when she lived and worked across the river in Cambridge.

Or there was a reason, but I never would have believed it.

Sirens stormed closer. Red and blue light stained the snowfall. As quickly as the crowd had formed, it dispersed. The sidewalk cleared with the swiftness of a stage curtain, revealing the woman-in-black half a block ahead, her trench coat flaring at its edges as she strode away. I called out—too late. A van pulled into a bus stop and she ducked inside. The door slammed closed. The van disappeared into traffic, though not before a rush of hope filled me. On the vehicle's side blazed a crimson shield even I could identify: the insignia of Harvard University.

Can we talk? I asked my cousins later that day.

They were ensconced in bed, shades drawn, though it was 2:00 P.M. Neither wore makeup—and without the intentional efforts to homogenize themselves, their faces looked less twin-like. Victoria's thicker eyebrows rippled in low-effort acquiescence. Jeanette clamped her long-lashed eyes shut.

I know you're still upset at me for losing the phone, I said. But I think I have an idea for a new location to take pictures. Maybe even a better place? You said you wanted to shoot somewhere classy, so what if we took photos at Harvard?

I held my breath; I wasn't used to making propositions, but the possibility of finding the woman-in-black made me brave—or at least brave enough to ask my cousins for help

accessing an area of the city otherwise as foreign as the moon.
I didn't yet have the courage to explore new terrain on my
own; I wasn't sure if I could be arrested for trespassing. My
cousins, though, had a knack for entering locations to which
they had not been invited.

My proposition percolated. Jeanette fluttered her eyes open;
Victoria cracked her neck—the prospect of a photo endeavor
reanimating them like puppet strings.

Then they both went slack.

Even if we weren't mad at you, said Jeanette, no one liked
our photos enough to give us a reality television show or even
a minor advertising deal.

There's no point anymore, said Victoria.

Maybe this time, I said. I could—

What we need, said Victoria, is to find rich husbands.
Otherwise we'll run out of money in a month.

Even this furniture is leased, said Jeanette morosely. Even
this bed. We'll barely scrape by. And Dad doesn't even care. He
says it's time for us to pull up our bootstraps.

We won't even have any boots, said Victoria.

I asked if they could work more at the gallery. My cousins
rolled their eyes with oligarchic distain.

Come back when you have useful ideas, Wilhelmina, said
Jeanette.

Defeated, I turned to the door—then another thought
occurred to me.

At Harvard, I said, there are probably a lot of potential
husbands.

My cousins squinted at me through the dim light of their
bedroom. For the first time in a long time, they mirrored identical smiles.

————

We went to the campus in April.

My cousins' interpretation of collegiate fashion included cardigans over button-down shirts, tennis shoes, headbands, short skirts, and knee socks. As usual, the tags on the clothes remained hidden so that we could return them later.

Soon we won't have to, said Victoria. Not if the plan works.

My cousins each carried a stack of textbooks that said CHEMISTRY on the spines.

All we have to do, Jeanette explained, is drop these books in a public place. A potential suitor will come and help.

Victoria bobbed her head in agreement, adding: We've seen this tactic work with great success in several movies.

The metal gates to Harvard Yard stood open. We whisked through, my cousins narrating the expedition's inevitable con-clusion: they'd find rich brothers, like the rowing twins who'd given away the idea for Facebook—except they'd counsel these brothers not to sell out. The brothers would be profoundly grateful. They'd all get married, move into a massive duplex mansion with squash courts and cloned lambs wandering the lawns and robot butlers serving their every whim. My cousins would take up quail hunting from hot air balloons. They'd be invited to star on a reality show about rich wives with minor yet emotionally significant problems.

I half-listened, my attention on the streams of people mov-ing between Harvard's stately buildings. The campus sprawled vaster and busier than I'd expected: a city unto itself. With the fever flush of springtime in the air, there were tour groups spooling along pathways, tourists taking pictures, a dignified man talking to a camera crew, workers carrying chairs, students marching past with teeth-gritted determination. I wasn't even entirely sure the woman-in-black was here.

What about them? said Jeanette, pointing toward several marriageable candidates tossing a Frisbee.

Not bad, said Victoria.

They started toward their prospects, but I stayed put. For the first time ever, I had my own agenda. If I found the woman-in-black, she could explain her actions at the congressman's party. I could spend time in proximity to her poise and her power, which might rub off on me. I, too, could face every obstacle with swiftness and bravado.

I'll catch up with you later, I called to my cousins. I'm going to see what's in there.

I pointed to a brick building with massive colonnades marking its entrance. My cousins readjusted their stacks of textbooks.

Whatever, Wilhelmina, said Jeanette. You'll only find nerds going to class.

Good luck, said Victoria. I hope it's a rich nerd.

I waved goodbye, then followed a line of students flowing up a series of shallow steps into a brightly lit entryway. It never occurred to me to tell my cousins why I actually wanted to visit the campus; I wonder sometimes what might have happened if I had. But the tension between us had only recently dissipated, and I was used to keeping my inner life to myself. Unaccompanied, I moved with the students streaming through the building's corridors: traveling up a staircase and along another hallway, so focused on finding the woman-in-black that I walked straight into a classroom.

The door shut behind me. Students sat down at desks. At the front of the room, a mop-haired man regarded me, glowering as if I were an unruly weed.

Another one, he said. My god—

I froze, unable to flee as the man moved in my direction. Sweat prickled my skin. My cousins would never bother to bail me out of prison once I was arrested for trespassing.

What are they thinking? the man said. That's what I want to know. Sending prospies to an upper-level stats class, it's absurd.

Sorry, I—

You might as well take a seat, said the man. Now that you're here.

I slid into the desk he'd motioned toward. The class commenced. After ten panicky minutes, I forgot I didn't belong. The class involved graphs undulating over projected slides. The mop-haired man used the word *exponential* with increasing frequency. Also *variability*. And *interval*. I didn't understand much, but I liked the feeling of the universe shrinking down to this room: an effort to quantify what was otherwise mysterious. When the class was over, I resisted the urge to clap.

Next time, said the mop-haired man as I lingered by the door, have them send you to a first-year course.

I beamed at him, wandered onward, drifting past lecture halls and classrooms. Each room seemed a sacred chamber: walls blinking with slides and dense with scribblings. To think this had been happening my whole time in Boston—happening my whole life. I didn't find the woman-in-black, but my certainty grew that she was somewhere on the Harvard campus; in one of these chambers, she, too, unraveled the enigmas of the universe.

When I eventually found my cousins, they sat slumped on a park bench.

Book-dropping was a bad idea, said Jeanette when she saw me.

The only attention we got, said Victoria, was from a disturbed librarian.

Victoria and Jeanette declared the excursion a failure, but I kept going back to Harvard. I didn't need my cousins, I'd discovered, to explore unfamiliar places. As spring unthawed the city, I explored the campus—wandering through the grand brick buildings and glassy architectural wonders—searching for the woman-in-black. When IDs were needed, I'd say I lost mine. Or I'd wait for a held-open door. No one suspected a tiny white girl, in a preppy crimson sweater, of wrongdoing. And if someone looked at me twice, I said I was a "prospie." It was a magic word. I would be politely shooed away, or casually invited to observe the proceedings.

And I did a lot of observing. Though finding the woman-in-black was my primary aim, I siphoned off a steady stream of knowledge from America's preeminent university. It was relaxing to sit in college lectures, as much for their content as for their atmosphere. I liked watching the other students' pens scribbling simultaneously—like a hundred seismometers, earthquaked with knowledge. I liked the rain-patter of typing fingers. I liked sinking into the lullaby hush of auditoriums, the quiet just before a professor took the podium. I went to classes covering mitochondrial dysfunction and supernovas and Samuel Beckett's more obscure plays, and often I didn't understand the material but I savored the sensation of information pooling into my body, filling me up from my toes.

Then I saw the woman-in-black again and my whole world went haywire.

The world, of course, had been haywire for a while. In the United States, the frequency of flash protests increased by the day. Often a response to a specific event—a jailed journalist, an unjust shooting, a library closure, a restaurant opening, a television episode—these protests could be apolitical too: demonstration for demonstration's sake. Meanwhile, state and local officials thrashed in the seething waters of constituent concerns. Third-party splinterings multiplied as politicians struggled to align themselves with the moving targets of influence. No one was sure if the president's power was waxing or waning; if his unpredictable actions signaled the demise of democracy, or authoritarian death throes preceding his removal. A slew of executive mandates, like the one against large gatherings, had placed a chokehold on citizen rights—for safety, supposedly. This heightened tensions across the country, the prospect of unwitting criminality coursing through the populace like an invisible plague.

Meanwhile, a real plague, unthawed from the Siberian permafrost, wreaked havoc in Russia. The global water shortages had started, along with local water contaminations. Once, Jeanette turned on the shower and was doused in a red spray that city officials couldn't explain. Bad news was heralded with grim constancy—and yet, in Boston at least, such news was forgotten with equal regularity. As difficult as everything had become, people looked ahead. There was an election that fall. The situation was temporary. And there were still good days, too.

The day I found the woman-in-black had started as a good day. Late-April sunshine welcomed an enormous flock of starlings into Boston. The birds descended on the city like a live black cloud. They roiled and undulated in a collective cadence, settled en masse on rooftops and ledges, draped whole buildings in dark plumage before bursting skyward.

Until they didn't.

Around noon, the birds dropped from the sky like feathery rain. Their small bodies thumped onto windshields and sidewalks and park benches, splashed into the Charles. They did not perk up and fly away. Avian flu would later be tested for, though not discovered. The birds had been electrocuted, some people said. Air traffic collision, speculated others. Or skyscraper windows: Had the Hancock Tower been recently cleaned? Asphyxiation was suggested as well, with smoke from Appalachian wildfires blowing up the East Coast, exiting through Cape Cod like an exhaust pipe.

No one knew for sure. No one would know for sure. The deaths would be labeled mysterious: another tragedy to tuck into the corner of our minds. Mass Mortality Events were treated like anomalies—odd as UFO sightings—rather than what they were: a pattern, a series, a sequence leading toward the unspeakable.

I'd seen the live starlings through a window during my shift at The Hole Story. When my shift ended and I caught a bus to Cambridge, I passed cleanup crews tossing the birds into plastic bags. I'd felt a pulse of despair—but it faded as soon as I snuck into the back of a Harvard auditorium. The course was new for me; called The Origin of Movement, it was team-taught by a choreographer, a sociologist, and an astrophysicist. As usual, I fell into the dozy solace of information. The chore-ographer narrated a series of slides—the outside world tamed by numbers and theories and objective correlatives—and my eyes began to close. Then a familiar voice flooded the room.

Sinewy yet clear, inflected by a British accent, the voice belonged to the sociologist, who had taken her turn at the podium.

—You'll recall Durkheim's foundational study correlating broad social forces with rates of suicide—

It was the woman-in-black. I leaned forward, nearly tum-bling over the stacked auditorium seats. There she was: live as a flame, even in her loose colorless clothing. She stood behind a podium made of polished red-grain wood. BRAZILETTO WOOD, a plaque outside the auditorium had said. AN HOM-AGE TO THE ISLAND OF . . . The woman pressed her finger-tips against the edge of the podium as she spoke, as if drawing power from the surface—as if the wood were superheated, tropically hot.

My breath caught. I watched her tuck the curve of her hair behind an ear. Her maroon lips bent and bowed into words. Above her, the projector image read: COLLECTIVE CONSCIOUSNESS.

—Durkheim deemed suicide an expression of collective dysfunction, rather than—

Her eyes roamed the auditorium as she narrated society's underlying machinations. When her gaze passed over me, I wanted to scream and cry and laugh all at once. No wonder

I'd felt so recognized at the congressman's party. This woman could perceive the larger forces that shaped an individual; she could see what was invisible to everyone else.

I must have wondered aloud who she was, because a real student—cardigan-clad, with two laptops open at once— swiveled her head around, like she'd been waiting her whole life to answer.

It's Sylvia Gill, said the student. Who else would it be? She's good, for sure, but for the real deal you've got to take Lombard's course on The Anatomy of Tyranny—

Sylvia Gill.

I rolled the name around in my mouth, my teeth scraping my lower lip with each *via*. When the astrophysicist took the podium and began droning about thermodynamics, I craned my neck to see where the sociologist had taken a seat. Soon, I'd speak to her. I repeated her name under my breath, the last third of the lecture stretching on endlessly, until, at last, the astrophysicist finished. Everyone stood up, putting their belongings away and glancing at their phones. Students poured down the auditorium steps. The space became raucously loud and somehow more crowded and I was trembling.

From my vantage in the back row, I watched Professor Gill gather her innumerable tote bags. Nearby, the choreographer demonstrated tricep stretches. The astrophysicist couldn't find his glasses. Students circled their professors like sharks.

I floated down the auditorium steps. Professor Gill's mouth sharpened at the corners as students praised her lecture. She accepted the flattery like a pleasant smell: took a whiff and moved on, never indulgent, but not ignoring the praise either. She was younger than the other two professors—

midthirties—though she had a weary steadiness that gave her a gravitas, as if she were so full of knowledge she couldn't move quickly.

She was beautiful too; I let myself see that. The full mouth and deep brown eyes, the charmed tilt of her limbs beneath the fabric of her dress. She shifted the tote bags higher onto her shoulders. Maybe, I thought, I could carry the bags for her once we were properly introduced. Because once we were introduced, and the cosmic thread between this moment and the congressman's party on Beacon Hill was pulled tight, our paths would surely remain entwined.

More students wedged themselves in front of me and into her field of vision—students who were mint-breathed, wristwatched—ready to report what they'd absorbed.

The part about class consciousness, said one. Probably the best take I've heard.

Professor Gill frowned, as if entertaining the idea of a better take was offensive. Her gaze flicked toward the exit as if it were a waiting friend.

I was hoping to discuss research opportunities? said another student. Could we—

Professor Gill waved her hand with bored civility, made a remark about office hours. When she moved toward the exit, I stepped into her path.

Professor Gill, I said. It's me.

She jolted. I bashfully extended my hand.

Actually, I said, we haven't *officially* met.

Professor Gill stared at my hand as if I held a grenade. Her eyes darted to the real students observing our exchange, then back to me. Her face hardened. In a disdainful tone, she said:

It's the end of the semester and you're introducing yourself now?

The gallery of students tittered.

You were at that party, I said. You dropped the—

This, said Professor Gill to her admirers, isn't even a well-concealed stab at grade-grubbing. Waiting until the end of term to ingratiate yourself is a waste of my time as well as yours. I implore you all to think twice before making such foolhardy and offensive advances.

The real students smirked. Professor Gill reshouldered her tote bags and strode out of the auditorium, leaving me alone with my bewildered disappointment.

Fresh air was no help.

Even away from the gawking students, outside the auditorium, I felt unmoored. The campus lawns and pathways woozed unsteady. There were bird bodies lying lifeless on the ground: starlings missed in the cleanup efforts. A pair of them nestled on a plastic shopping bag, like twin sleepers. More birds lay on the walkway. Birds on a bench. Birds in the mulch circling shrubbery. How had I ignored them? The starlings were one of my parents' doomsday prophecies come to life: a stepping-stone to apocalypse. A sign the end of times was near.

For weeks, the Harvard campus had seemed a sanctuary. But those classrooms—filled with incantations of literature and math and history—offered no refuge in the face of disaster. My mother had been right all along: *The periodic table won't save you when SHTF.*

I had wanted my life to have meaning. A secret path. A

fated purpose. I wanted a world that wasn't random, chaotic, cruel. I wanted a link between the congressman's party and the present moment, because it would signal there was a larger plan. Someone was in charge. All was not lost.

No one was coming to save me, though. Not Professor Gill, not anyone.

Melancholia had its teeth in me; it bit down and shook. I might have left campus and walked straight into a volcano, a pit of lava, over the edge of a flat earth. Instead, I blundered across Mass Ave and into a crowd chanting in Harvard Square.

A man with red-rimmed eyes swooped in front of me.

Did you know Harvard is really a real estate company? he said. A tax shelter for the rich?

I knew better than to answer questions posed by strangers on the street—questions on the street were a way for a person to lure you into an unwanted situation—but I was in such distress I took the bait.

I'd believe that, I said.

More questions kept coming, shouted over the group's chanting: Did I know that Harvard was founded on a legacy of discrimination and injustice? That their endowment was built in part on the slave trade? That the institution was responsible for the invention of napalm *and* the social media platform eroding our democracy? That they invested in fossil fuel extraction? That they bought up water rights in communities where the locals couldn't even afford to shower? That they exacerbated income inequality? That they graduated individuals who did unspeakable things? That institutionalized education was a means of transmitting power, not liberation? That what mattered now more than ever was a commitment to liberation?

I kept nodding, like I knew where this was heading. The mob of chanting, sign-holding, drum-thumping people was amorphous, absorbing passersby—like me—while chunks of the group also broke away to merge with the throngs moving through Harvard Square. I was in a flash protest; I was in its thrumming core. A dangerous place to be, and yet the chaos of the crowd drowned out the roar in my head. There was a familiar, familial comfort in the crowd's accusatory paranoia. Someone had a police transmitter and listened with their ear pressed to the device. *Time to scram*, he yelled, and then everyone was scramming. *Take this*, someone else said—and a wobbly bicycle was pushed into my hands—and I was riding, pedaling with strangers down one street and then another, traveling beyond my usual routes, even as daylight faded and the transmitter buzzed accusatorily.

We ended up in an alley. Some members of the group ended up in a dumpster. Then I was in the dumpster as well. My feet sank into damp hillocks, inciting an avalanche of slithering cellophane. I caught my balance on the cold metal walls, scabbed with rust, sticky. I didn't care. I was ready to be murdered, sacrificed to a garbage god. The newness of the experience would at least dull the pain of Professor Gill's rejection.

A person rose from amid the refuse, their backpack giving them a turtle-like appearance. Their upper lip glistened as they stretched their hands forward, palms cradling an orange. I must have looked confused, because they retracted the fruit and fingered the peel. Citrus sparked the air. The orange, denuded, hovered between us. When I shook my head, the person wrenched the fruit in half, extracted a single section like a small slice of moon—a glowing crescent—and pressed the lunar flesh between my lips.

Sweetness; a bursting star; a sour-bright brain hit; a mic-drop mouth kiss. Joy.

Then came purple bunches of grapes and packages of romaine lettuce, cases of craft beer from Idaho. A huge wheel of Parmigiano-Reggiano. Canisters of Tabasco-flavored cashews. Nutmeg. Bouquets of carnations dyed blue and yellow. Ham sandwiches cut into triangles. Jars of salsa. Tins of anchovies. Tubs of herbed mayonnaise.

The group gathered it all up, traveled onward, the city remade as a terrain of potential. They moved amoebically, participants adhering and unattaching. My inclusion was unremarkable. Nothing expected of me, nothing asked. I could have left, but I didn't want to. In another alley, trash bags gleamed satin-black and fat as dumplings. A woman in Coke-bottle glasses shuffled forward. Under the streetlamp, her knife glinted like a fin. She slashed. The bag split. Loaves of bread spilled out. Bakery day-olds that hadn't sold. Plastic-wrapped cookies. Bagels. Croissants. A rainbow spill of maca-rons. People nibbled on oat muffins with the seriousness of connoisseurs.

Next came a dumpster packed with cases of string cheese only a day beyond their expiration date. *These things never really go bad*, someone said. *It's all a marketing scam to keep people buying.* Passersby hovered around the perimeter, their homeward trajectory hiccupping as they paused to watch the excavation. *Liberate yourself from social conditioning. There is food right here and it's free.* A mother and her daughter took a loaf of rye bread, handfuls of saltwater taffy. Passersby smiled. Passersby scowled. A bearded man climbed atop a milk crate to make a speech. *The planet bleeds resources!* Then a woman with pink hair was speaking too: *No more wage slav-*

ery! Speeches overlapped, intermingled. *We're doing nothing illegal,* someone told me, and then I was telling people too: *Nothing illegal, nothing wrong, except the vastness of this waste.*

Our strange parade disemboweled, inspected, distributed. Behind a sporting goods store, someone found boxes of baseball caps stitched with the name of a losing Super Bowl contender. The caps must have been made in error ahead of time—a gamble gone wrong. We gathered the hats and put them on like a victorious team: an inverse of reality. History rewritten. Wrongs righted, made good.

My cousins shrieked, their lips purple with wine, their eyes red and misty when I opened the door of their apartment around 2:00 A.M.

Victoria hopped down from the kitchen counter and rushed toward me—stopped a few inches away. She pressed her fingers into her cheeks hard enough to leave white spots.

We didn't know what to do, she said. You never stay out late. We were going to call 911 but Jeanette has that parking ticket thing and—

It's okay, I said. I'm fine.

Where have you been? said Victoria. We were terribly worried—

From a plastic bag, I extracted a clamshell of macarons piled together like rainbow coins. I placed the container on the kitchen counter.

Victoria's eyes expanded; she moved toward the cookies. Jeanette told her sister to wait—we needed to talk—but Victoria already had a pink macaron in her mouth. Then Jeanette took one too. I produced more items: oranges, macrobiotic rice crackers, canisters of toasted pine nuts. Surprise and plea-sure tangled my cousins' faces.

Where did all this come from? whispered Jeanette.

I pushed the pine nuts toward her instead of answering. I had the sense she didn't really want to know. Or didn't need to. Though my wounds stung over what had happened with the woman-in-black—Professor Sylvia Gill—I savored the sensation of contributing to the household of which I'd long been a numb guest. I liked making my cousins happy. I liked, too, the possibility of reconnecting with this mass of people who moved through Boston on their own terms. That they'd absorbed me so naturally had to mean something. These peo-ple who knew how to find value in the most unlikely places: they had seen something in me and pulled me close. Was that something bravery? I hoped so.

Jeanette and Victoria gobbled the pine nuts. Scavenging supplies, I realized, could also help resolve my cousins' finan-cial woes. They'd been at the end of their funds, as well as their ideas for what to do. Their last remaining scheme had been to steal a painting from the gallery and sell it on the black market—but here was a better path forward, no thievery or rich Harvard husbands required. Victoria nuzzled my shoul-der, sighed contentedly. Jeanette gave me a kiss on the cheek.

Little Wilhelmina, she said. We were all worried about you, but we shouldn't have worried at all.

My cousins did care about me. Maybe not the way they cared for one another, and yet: I was someone to them. My wounded heart quivered. We felt like a real family then. Just the three of us. We could survive this strange and difficult world.

The Freegans, I called the group, though if they'd known they would have resisted the label. *Freegans* was only partly right, insufficient—already loaded with history, public derision. Even if it had been accurate, to label something was to brand it, box it up for consumption: caging purpose in parameters. The Freegans never considered themselves a group so much as a grouping. If there was a name for the grouping, everyone had their own. There was no official doctrine, no official leader, no official meeting times. No email list or website. It had to be this way; any efforts resembling activism were too easily infiltrated. Too easily condemned. You couldn't plan a rally or a march ahead of time. Not these days. Not with the way things worked. Gatherings had to just happen. Spontaneity ruled the day. And so the Freegans operated out of instinct: a collective chemical reaction, bubbling up from fomenting unrest. When the moment came, they knew.

In the following months, I started to know. I developed an instinct for where and when the Freegans congregated, cultivating an awareness of the neck tingle that signaled a flash protest or a spontaneous scavenging run. For myself and my cousins, I brought back a bounty of abandoned goods. Slightly soft strawberries. Day-old baguettes. Bars of imported chocolate, broken in pieces but delicious. I brought back abandoned furnishings as well: mismatched dining room chairs, scuffed ottomans, wall hangings, potted plants.

Though I continued to work at The Hole Story, the job was no longer a means to an end. It was a means to many ends, many meanings. I considered myself an infiltrate, a spy. I was a revolutionary in plain sight. While Ruby harrumphed around the cash register, I put café leftovers in clean trash bags, set those bags in the alley for Freegan collection.

Clothing was one of the easiest items to find. Once I started looking, it was everywhere, shed across the city like cast-off snake skins. I found flannel shirts and tie-dye scarves, bowler hats and miniskirts. With a wash, some restorative stitching, the clothes were revived. I liked imagining the bodies that inhabited the clothes before me: former fat bodies, former thin bodies, younger bodies, less fashionable bodies, more ambitious bodies, dead bodies. There was a resurrectionary element to wearing castoffs, though one Freegan warned me to watch out for negative energy. After donning an abandoned pantsuit, she'd been overcome with premonitions so intense she fainted. She'd had to leave the pantsuit draped over a park bench.

Objects store feelings, she'd said. *Those feelings stick around.*

I never knew her name; I never knew any of the Freegans' names. This was intentional. Everyone was anonymous—or they went by random alphabetic monikers like "K" or "O" or "V." No one knew where anyone else lived, or what they did for work, or where they came from. The Freegans accepted me without question. I loved them for this. I loved that we had no personal histories, only possibilities. I did not need to explain that I'd grown up on canned goods and the rhetoric of chemtrail mind control. I did not need to mention how my parents abandoned me in a world they were too scared to face. I could live in the absolute now. I could be more than my past. I could be like the items we salvaged and revived: the goods we made *good*.

———

I might have been happy, but I couldn't forget Professor Gill. The Freegans distracted me—delighted me—but they couldn't disappear her memory. She flitted in the back of my thoughts and appeared in my dreams: her face scowling, maroon lips pursed. Despite all the new people I met, the hidden corners of the city discovered, disappointment over my encounter with Sylvia remained lodged inside me, emitting a dull ache: bad as a bullet.

I decided to look at her trash.

If this sounds absurd, understand that after a summer spent disemboweling dumpsters, trash had become a portal for making sense of a city that had once seemed unfathomable. By scavenging with the Freegans, I'd learn to perceive society's secret subtext: there was more than enough food to feed everyone and yet people went hungry; there was free furniture and clothing everywhere, yet people endlessly purchased new products; we wasted and wasted to keep spinning the wheels of an economy that benefited only a few.

Professor Gill was a woman with secrets. I knew this instinctually. If I peeked at her garbage, I told myself, she might finally make sense. If I knew what she wished hidden, I might find the impetus to move on with my life.

It was mid-September, broiling hot—humid as well—but heat records didn't mean much anymore, even with baseball players passing out mid-inning at Fenway. I was in North Cambridge. It had been easy to follow Professor Gill when she left Harvard for the day; she'd caught the Red Line north and I'd lurked in a neighboring train car, watched her through the window, then trailed her out of the station, sweat greasing the sunglasses I wore as a disguise.

The heat had made me a little manic.

Professor Gill lived in a neighborhood overcrowded with houses, rooflines bumbling into one another, parked cars hugging the curb. Her house was one half of a two-story colonial, clapboards painted blue-gray, trimmed with white. A small porch leaned onto an unremarkable patch of lawn, which was encircled by granite fence posts and wrought-iron bars. A dog walker skimmed past, his face in his phone. Otherwise, the street was empty; Professor Gill had swished into her house without a backward glance.

In the narrow driveway separating Professor Gill's house from her neighbor's sat a set of trash bins. For a moment, the absurdity of my mission loomed large. What did I imagine I'd find in those trash cans? Vodka bottles? Scratch tickets? Matted balls of hair? Creepy dolls? Drafts of insults to pile on students?

Something—anything—that might liberate me from my fixation?

My fingertips tingled. It would have been wiser to wait until dusk, but I scurried across the road and down the narrow driveway. I took hold of a trash bin's plastic lid.

Don't you dare—

One of Professor Gill's neighbors stared down from her porch. The woman wore a Red Sox–themed housecoat and Red Sox–themed slippers. She held her phone between herself and me like a gun.

Sy, she called. Sy, get out here. There's an intruder. I'm film-ing it all.

Other neighbors, upon hearing the shouting, appeared on their own porches, fluttered curtains open to watch. They also held up phones to film. I crouched down, trying to hide my face, but I was trapped. If I ran, I'd only seem more suspicious.

The neighbor's shouting at last drew out Professor Gill. I couldn't see her face from my crouched position, but I could hear the irritation in her voice as she said to her neighbor: Please stop calling me *Sy*. I've made that request on multiple occasions, along with specific instructions to leave me out of your neighborhood-watch cabal.

The neighbor protested, but Professor Gill had no interest in discussion; her front door clicked open as she moved to return inside. If she left, I'd be at the mercy of the neighbors—who did not appear particularly merciful. I sprang up and called for her to wait.

If my appearance disturbed Professor Gill, this time she did not show it. She looked down upon me from her porch, a thousand feet tall. One eyebrow arched. She gestured toward her open door with regal weariness, as if she—in her infinite and extraordinary wisdom—had expected me all along.

How to begin describing the interior of Professor Gill's house? The entryway offered the bright dazzle of candles, wax pooling over candelabras, light splashing into mirrors that refracted Professor Gill and me, splintering our bodies until the house filled with us. The living room had a decadent plushness: an ungainly accretion of velvet pillows and throws and wine-colored sofas. Books splayed open like resting moths. Tapestries sewn with sequins sparkled on the walls. A thick carpet cradled my feet. In the middle of it all stood Professor Gill, who seemed to grow from the floor as if the room had produced her, the drape of her dress made elegant in the candlelit shadows, the maroon tenor of the room highlighting her exquisite mouth.

Why did you follow me here? she said.

Her question surprised me. I assumed she knew why; I assumed she knew everything. My mouth hung open, like a pillaged vault.

Professor Gill's nostrils flared. She must have regretted letting me into her home. She closed her eyes, drew in a scholarly breath. When she spoke again, her voice was softer, slower, though the curt expectation of information simmered beneath it.

What is the purpose of your visit?

She was testing me, I thought. She knew I'd wanted to look at her trash and learn her secrets. And yet, how to begin explaining myself?

I'm—I'm a student, I said.

Professor Gill's expression remained unchanged. She waited for more details.

Trying to conjure the phrases I'd heard real Harvard students use—along with their affect of effortless sophistication and casual self-aggrandizement—I added that I was conducting an independent study with groundbreaking sociological implications. I thought she could help.

It's about trash, I said.

Professor Gill's eyes narrowed and she studied me as she had at the congressman's party: it was the sensation of being read, one's personhood processed. How badly I'd wanted her to look at me that way again—and yet, having lied, her perception felt too intense to bear.

I blurted: Can I use your bathroom?

She frowned but waved me to a rose-colored room smelling of everything lovely. A candle flickered beside the sink, the bathroom mirror catching its light. A claw foot tub sat in the corner, its brass feet perched on the tiles as if poised to scuttle away. I took a long time washing my face. To calm myself, I smelled each of her soaps and lotions in succession, resisting the urge to apply all her hand creams, then giving in to that urge, so when I returned to the living room I smelled like lemon and honeysuckle and cucumber.

Professor Gill had settled into one of the wine-colored sofas, her legs tucked beneath her. I watched from the edge of the room as she paged through a book. She had not noticed my return, and when a small bunny with black fur gamboled over to her, she put down the book and picked up the bunny, stroking its ears. I felt jealous of the animal. I felt both desperate for her attention and wholly unworthy. Professor Gill seemed lost in thought as she petted the bunny, an aura of sorrow imbuing her gestures. I had no right to bother her. I did not belong in this glittering house with this elegant woman. I belonged back at The Hole Story, frying doughnuts. Or scrounging in a dumpster.

Well, thanks so much, I called out. I should probably get going.

Professor Gill's face snapped to mine.

No—

The bunny leapt from her lap.

I mean, she said—her air of regality returning—you're wel-

come to leave. Go right ahead. I have plenty else to do. I suspect, however, that it isn't yet safe with the neighbors out there.
This is the second time this week they've tried to have an
"intruder" arrested. I would have moved by now if the university didn't subsidize my housing.

Her eyes roamed the living room. Though she'd stared at
me with intensity before, now she seemed unable to see me
at all.

Since you're here, she went on, why don't you tell me about
your project. If you'd like, I could make us some tea.

Without waiting for an answer, she stood up and swished
out of the living room. There was the sound of a kettle being
placed on a stove. A burner flared to life.

I remained still. Professor Gill had made the offer so off-
handedly, I had to repeat her words in my head to make sure
I'd heard them correctly. A cabinet door opened and closed in
the kitchen. I moved to a plush sofa, lowered my body onto the
velveteen fabric. I hovered my nose near a pillow, breathing in
a sweet musk. My pulse quickened. I had the faint awareness
that what I was doing was dangerous. I had told Professor Gill
I was a student and I would have to maintain that lie. More
significantly, Professor Gill had wounded me before; she had
the capacity to do so again.

And yet, there was nowhere I wanted to be more than in
her house, ensconced in the soft furniture, even with hazard
lights flashing in my brain.

The bunny shuffled over. His pink nose quivered. I petted
his fur, whispered: *What do I do now?*

If the bunny could have answered, it didn't have time. Professor Gill returned carrying a tray of sugar cookies.

You've met Simone, she said.

She sank into the sofa across from me and rested her face on her hands, as if the weight of her mind needed extra support. Her fingers looked long enough to spider across piano keys, delicate enough to turn the onion-skin pages of books without tearing them. My heart hammered louder and I wondered if I should have left her home after all.

You're interested in trash, she reminded me. For an independent study.

She had a dry, knowing tone—the kind that makes you want to say something interesting. Looking back, her questions may have held traces of sarcasm. There was so much we both weren't saying. Yet if sarcasm lurked in her words, I missed it in the blast of her attention, the candles flickering and her face attentive to mine: gaze steady, fingers strumming her cheek as she propped an elbow on the sofa cushion. A phone on the coffee table buzzed, but she ignored it.

What is it about trash, specifically, that interests you?

It was Professor Gill who interested me; Professor Gill who I wanted to be near. To be near her, though, meant finding something to say. I started telling her about the Freegans because I couldn't think of anything else. I told her about flash protests and scavenging and the miracles of resource reclamation, and when I paused for a breath she was all X-ray vision, her eyes swallowing me.

What do you think? I said.

I think, said Professor Gill, you're a very unusual person.

Oh.

My fragility felt conspicuous; how easy it would be for this woman to cut me to pieces. She'd done it before.

But instead of cutting me apart, she added, in a quieter voice: I like unusual.

A splash of brightness in her eyes. My whole body tensed. I braced for what might be coming, but also to hold steady the tremble of my own excitement. Professor Gill tucked her hair behind one ear, exposing a smooth pillar of neck.

The teakettle began to scream.

Around that time, a string of especially disturbing directives issued from the White House, including the announcement that Boston, along with several other major cities, would be turned over to "interim" federal control after city officials refused to comply with the prior executive orders. The Freegans talked a lot about this when I saw them. The time had come, they said, for revolution. Their ideas for revolution included shredding bank paperwork and dropping it like confetti from rooftops in a citywide party; tearing up pavement and planting gardens in the streets; an anti-consumerist lifestyle deemed the Cult of Inconvenience; and a political scheme called Generational Representative Democracy, in which government representatives were voted on by age groups rather than geographies.

I couldn't wait to describe all this to Professor Gill.

After our initial conversation, she'd told me that we ought to meet again. She wanted to hear more about the Freegans; my insider knowledge interested her, given her ongoing study of social movements.

But you'll need to keep this between us, she'd said. I don't typically mentor undergraduates. For you, however, I'll make an exception.

She added that it would be best if we met at her house, given the need for discretion.

Come back this time next week, she said.

I did. Bouncing along on my walk through North Cambridge, I was so overflowing with details about the Freegans that words spilled from my lips in whispery fragments. I couldn't believe I'd been chosen from among all her students—even if I wasn't actually a student. That I could give Professor Gill insider insights into a burgeoning social phenomenon thrilled me. Maybe she'd study the Freegans for a scholarly paper.

I bounded up her front steps and knocked cheerily on her door.

She took a long time to answer—long enough that I worried the neighbors might appear again. When she opened the door, she opened it only a crack.

You've returned.

Is this a bad time? I said.

Her silence stretched until, in a resigned voice, she said that since I was here, I might as well come in.

The interior was not jauntily lit by candles as it had been before. In the living room, I tripped on the edge of a coffee table before finding a seat on a sofa.

Professor Gill sat down heavily. She coughed, said: I haven't been sleeping well.

I didn't know if I should ask about her health, or if I should talk about the Freegans, so I said nothing. She was a shadowy mass across from me—a mystery. We sat in silence. I felt I was annoying her; I was an intrusion she was putting up with. A confused longing welled up in me. She had wanted me to come back last time we'd met; she could have sent me away if she didn't want me around.

I started to say this—but Professor Gill interrupted.

Let's have a little light, shall we?

A table lamp sprang alive, illuminating Professor Gill's face: the haze of exhaustion around her eyes.

Did something happen? I said.

Professor Gill's eyes sharpened, and she snapped: Of course something happened.

Do you want me to—

The ferocity on her face made me go quiet. I felt like crying. She pressed her lips together, as if sealing in words.

Then her shoulders dropped. Her ferocity eroded into fatigue. In a quiet yet commanding voice, she said: Tell me about your Freegan friends.

And so I told her.

I continued to tell her, for a string of weeks, deep into autumn. Sometimes, Professor Gill was moody, her house darkened. But she could also be radiantly poised, faintly amused in the questions she posed to me. On those days, we ate sugar cookies and drank tea. Her eyes sparkled when she asked questions. And when that happened I felt I might explode with the wonder of the moment: that I was there with her, in that house. Simone snuffled around our feet and she picked up the bunny, stroked its ears. It amazed me to breathe the same air as her, the constellation of her intelligence whirling around the living room, refracting in the play of light on mirrors and jeweled candle holders.

Do Freegans consider themselves anarchists? she asked, an eyebrow raised.

I replied that some Freegans did and some didn't, some wouldn't have cared—going on and on—as if my talking alone kept us airborne: like a hummingbird's frantic wing beats. It was the Freegans who kept me in her proximity, who kept Professor Gill from sinking into a sullenness, distant and snappy. It was the Freegans who bound us close.

Should I have wondered why Professor Gill made time for me? What her interests were, really? Why we only ever met at her house? Likely. Yet with the situation already tenuous—delicate and dreamlike—I didn't dare question anything. It was easier to assume that Professor Gill, like many others, was committed to appearing calm during a chaotic time in the world. Routine: a balm for agitation. And my appearance became a routine.

She called me "L." That's what I told her to call me—borrowing from the Freegan convention of using a random letter in lieu of a name. Perhaps, I thought, she believes my full name is Elle or Elizabeth or Eldorado. Perhaps there's a real student with that name in the Harvard database. I did my best to appear student-like. I asked questions about sociology—*What was the Thomas Theorem again? Did she believe the Davis-Moore thesis?*—and when she answered, I dug my fingernails into my palms because her crisp Britishisms seeped into me like water in an electrical socket.

Then one day, in late October, I arrived at her house, already charged up from a gathering with the Freegans. We'd narrowly escaped a group of undercover police who'd raided the abandoned warehouse where Freegans sometimes stowed scavenged supplies. This I described to Professor Gill in a rush of words, not bothering to sit down. Law enforcement was after us because we endangered the status quo. What we were doing made a difference—would make a difference. Amid immense turmoil, all was not lost.

It only takes protests from 3.5 percent of a population, I said—quoting a favorite Freegan statistic—to reshape a whole society.

Professor Gill stepped close to me, a strange look on her face, like she was both distressed and intrigued. My shirt-sleeve had torn during my escape from the police and she ran her fingers down the tattered scrap, smoothing it. She had never touched me before, yet she made the gesture as if she'd done it a thousand times, her long fingers smoothing, smoothing, smoothing. I kept talking, speaking faster as her fingers lingered on the torn fabric: the thin barrier between her and me.

I do wonder what's going to happen, I said—putting my fingers on hers, the tear in my sleeve momentarily made whole—because the Freegans keep mentioning a coming *moment*. They say it's getting closer. That we should all be ready.

Professor Gill yanked her hand back.

In a brittle voice, she said: Don't be foolish. These Freegan people may seem like comrades-in-arms now, but what will happen in a month or two? That's the thing about social movements. There are early adopters and there are people who show up later, for the party, so to speak. For most people, activism is a hobby. A feel-good diversion. They always fall away when the going gets difficult. And things will get difficult.

After that, she told me I ought to leave; she had work to do.

Halloween. The day was gray, a thin layer of clouds griming the sky. The sidewalk oaks were sticklike, their leaves shed in mildewing mounds: victims to a fungus that had decimated forests throughout New England. The dying trees added a decompositional mustiness to an over-warm October. The air dizzied the brain, scrambled intentions. At MIT, they had already built oxygenated rooms for students concerned about air quality and cognitive impairment.

It had been an odd day, with costumes and witchiness all over the city, as well as the announcement that the interim federal control would be indefinite. Everyone was fearful about the November elections, less than a week away. I'd had a shift at The Hole Story that morning, the café's cash register ringing nonstop from extra foot traffic and the demand for holiday-themed baked goods. Vampiric jelly doughnut holes. Pumpkin flavors. Ubiquitous black and orange sprinkles. In times of unrest—and looking back it was a time of unrest—holidays become everything. Holidays are the stakes that hold a society in place.

But what did I know about holidays? I'd never celebrated Halloween as a child. There was no one to visit in the woods near my family's cabin, or no one from whom a child could expect candy. Even during the brief periods when we'd moved elsewhere—parking the camper in north country ski towns, in Walmart lots—my parents considered Halloween to be comically dangerous. There were drunk drivers. Abductions. Razor blades in candy. Lead poisoning in costumes. Exploding jack-o'-lanterns. Masked serial killers. Illuminati sacrifices. Diabetes. My first taste of Halloween had come with my cousins, who had relished the chance to wear animal ears with lingerie and walk through the city as Coquettish Rabbits or Flirtatious Panthers or Seductive Koalas.

That Halloween, though, my cousins had decided to stay in.

Scary movie marathon, Jeanette explained to me while I paced the apartment.

You sure you don't want to join us? said Victoria. We can make room.

She patted the armrest of the love seat I'd scavenged. I perched beside the pair, tried to settle into the movie. On the television screen, a nightgowned girl ran screaming through the woods, but all I could think about was Professor Gill. I wanted to apologize to her, though for what I wasn't exactly sure. I also wanted to feel her fingers again on my arm. And beyond both of those wants, was the urge to tell her about what was happening with the Freegans. Because something was happening. A roiling energy coursed through them—through me—more powerful than any force that had ever animated a flash protest.

I needed to go to her, I decided. And so I said goodbye to my cousins and headed back out into the city, grabbing a box of Halloween-themed doughnut holes I'd saved from the café. The pastries would be my pretense for visiting on a nonappointed day.

Outside my cousins' apartment, Boston's twilit streets thronged with devils and faux celebrities and dozens of witches: green-faced, broom-holding, pointy-hatted. A smoky haze filled the air, along with a banging that wasn't music, wasn't random either. My vision had a hallucinatory tinge, as if I hadn't fully woken up, even as my blood pounded and I connected, fleetingly, to the magnetism of reinvention: a human effervescence.

I had to get to Professor Gill.

I descended into a light-flickering T station. A train pulled in. The crowd jostled me against an oily, fingerprinted pole. More passengers crammed together. They wriggled and writhed, their laughter merging with screeching brakes, the

They held on to what others forgot, what others refused to see. Pipelines, poisonings. Political corruptions. They transformed what was otherwise unwanted. They converted bad news into movement. And so, on the Congress Street Bridge, Halloween revelers arrived in droves, swept in by the noise and the smoke and a holiday mania mixed with a deeper malaise. They pushed back against law enforcement, drew in bystanders, until the crowd became a churning mass unhinged on the friction of frivolity and frustration, the tinder spark of fear.

The Halloween Riots, the event was later called, though there were also other names. There were other versions of reality echoing out from the official interpretation. One version was that costume-wearing protesters had converged on Fort Point and poured buckets of blood into Boston Harbor because that's what the government was taxing them in. Others claimed the protesters hadn't poured blood, it had spilled from their bodies when the police started shooting; though some said the police never shot a single round, the noise came from homemade bombs that kicked up the yachts and sprayed water onto the docks and the tourists crossing the bridge. No, said others, it was the police who detonated explosives. They'd been trying to keep people from escaping. Police planned to blow up the bridge the whole time; they'd orchestrated everything to justify the federal takeover—wasn't that what was happening in San Francisco, Chicago, Columbus, New York? After all, what followed was a curfew that hovered over Boston for weeks, along with the return of pat-downs and checkpoints, the city surveilled for safety, because the official stance in the end was that the riots were incited by a group of highly secretive decentralized antiestablishment leftist terrorists who were also responsible for other incidents all over the country, and so, though no official connection was established, these shadow figures were blamed: the radicals threatening the fumes of the American Dream.

Hours had passed by the time I reached Professor Gill's house that evening. Those of us in the stalled train car had had to do an emergency exit—navigating a subway tunnel before climbing motionless escalators into a city turned chaotic. By the time I arrived in North Cambridge, I was exhausted, having walked a circuitous route to avoid tear gas and blockaded roads. Helicopters whizzed overhead. All I could think of was getting to Professor Gill. I held the doughnuts pressed against my chest.

When I knocked on her door, no one answered. I tested the doorknob. It opened.

Inside, the lights were off. A TV played at high volume, flashing footage of the riots breaking out across the city. Explosions burst like fireworks. A newscaster was slammed to the ground and trampled live on the air.

Professor Gill? I called.

My skin prickled. I shouldn't have entered the house uninvited—but I needed to deliver the doughnuts, I told myself. That was my reason.

There was water running upstairs; I'd never been on the second floor. I crept up the stairs, softly calling hello. A light was on in the bathroom, the door ajar. The shower was running. I only meant to tap the door, but it swung open at my touch, a cloud of steam billowing outward. Professor Gill sat on the floor.

L—

My false name sounded wet in her throat. Her chest rose and fell beneath the fabric of her dress, which hung limp against her body, damp from the steam and the water splashing beyond the shower curtain. Her eyeliner welled around her eyes.

Sorry, I said. I didn't mean to bother you. The door was open and I—are you okay?

Professor Gill choked out a laugh.

Am I okay? she said. *Am I okay?* I've been sitting here wondering if you were. I saw the news. I was sure you were on the bridge. I was sure you'd been hurt. It would be my fault, after what I said to you—

She kept talking, speaking in theoretical terms about how I might have developed a cavalier attitude toward activist participation after her comment about early versus secondary adopters in social movements. I couldn't follow what she meant. It was hard to concentrate with her on the floor and me standing. I kneeled down beside her. The shower water sprinkled my back.

I brought you these, I said, and presented the doughnuts. Sorry they got smushed.

She looked at the box, looked away. A streak of eyeliner rolled down her cheek.

Sorry, I said again—feeling agitated, a pressure building in my body as if I might burst out of my own skin—Did I do something wrong?

She looked both inconsolable and irate. I had done something. The shower water pounded and pounded, the faint exclamations of the TV rising from downstairs. I slid all the way onto the floor, so that we sat in the same pool of water collecting on the tiles. The folds of her dress scrunched against my legs. She was all face: her pupils huge and her nostrils twitching. The air between us felt elastic and viscous. I was close enough to inhale the desolation reverberating off her. How, I wondered, were you supposed to approach another's pain when you yourself may have caused it? I thought back to when—years before—I'd shot that bullet into the forest and struck a sugar maple. Afterward, I found the tree, the one I'd hurt, with sap leaking from its wound. I'd put my mouth to that hurt place, licked the leaking sweetness, because that was all I could think to do.

I couldn't think of anything else now, either. I put my lips on the corner of one of her eyes and then the other, though her tears were salty not sweet, inky on my tongue. She pulled me against her. And I put my mouth on her mouth, because her tears had leaked all the way there too.

By early November, the Boston skyline filled with the hum of drones, as if they were mosquitoes hatching.

WITH AN INSECT'S INSTINCT for self-immolation, the Spanish galleon sailed toward a fire blazing on the shoreline: a bright glow on a moonless night signaling safe passage, the promise of a haven.

There was no promise. This was no signal, unless taken as a sign of what was to come: a reef as serrated as a knife. Split timber. The cries of dying men.

Meanwhile, on Eleutheria, the settlers stumbled around a driftwood bonfire, raised off-key voices to carol garbled shanties about bonnie lasses and jolly England and a mistress named the sea. Above them, constellations spun, dizzy with their hours: Andromeda, Perseus, Pegasus flying round and round. The settlers downed the last dregs of liquor gifted by the Boston colonists—none saved for tooth-pulling or sterilizing wounds—because after their initial burst of gratitude, their industry had cooled. Each day became the day before the real labor would begin.

Perfection rests easiest, after all, on a faraway horizon.

When morning came, the Eleutherian settlers rose from the sandy beds into which they'd fallen. They scuffed down the beach, their vision blurred, their boots splashing into tide pools. It must have seemed a mirage when they staggered in among the wonders washed up on the shore: pallets of precious wood, chests of silver, caskets crammed with emeralds, a three-foot Madonna statue made of melted Mayan gold. So many treasures gouged

from the continent's interior—once on their way across the sea—
lay strewn across the island's sands, twinkling like fallen stars still
hot with heaven's blessing.

Only a few among them felt uneasy. Nothing of this nature
had been in the company's initial plans. Yet, they couldn't keep
their fellow settlers from what they had all been promised: a land
of opportunity, the chance to rise above the stations bestowed on
them at birth. They couldn't deny a miracle when it sparkled on
the beach before them: a feast for hungry men.

And so, in the breathless hours after, the settlers took the captain's small shallop and paddled around the island's reefs, ecstatic
with discovery. Not long before they'd named those shoals
The Devil's Backbone—they'd called the coral cursed—but the
name had lost its meaning. The shipwrecked treasure, the settlers
decided, had been divinely dispensed. Their God was wrathful,
yes. He wrought vengeance upon the wicked. But that same God
rewarded the righteous, brought bounty to the blessed.

When confronted with the bodies—bloated, shark-nipped—
the settlers looked away. They looked at the sky. At their hands.
Anywhere but each other's eyes. They gathered up their treasure,
retreated to their meager hovels: the flimsy shacks built of brittle
limestone mud and palm fronds thatched for roofs. They took
their scavenged finds and left the bodies to the birds, the stink
to the sea breeze, the truth to the tide—which took back what
it gave, twice a day. Waves curled open like briny hands, scraped
against the island like one who expects repayment for all the gifts
they've given.

5

Visor, vegan leather sneakers, sweat suit, sun hat, khaki shorts, polo shirt, whistle—

My belongings washed across my bunk, strewn among sheets, as I dug through my Camp Hope locker looking for *Living the Solution.*

—T-shirt, swimsuit, swimming goggles, water bottle, backpack.

Smoke from the crewmember bonfire fumed in my hair. Having failed to find Roy Adams in the Command Center—or to extract a decent explanation from Lorenzo—I ripped more items out of the locker, trying to find the book that might speak for Adams, offer solace, show a scenario in which Camp Hope wasn't careening toward collapse.

Jachi leaned over the side of her bunk, watching with serene interest.

What's that?

She pointed to the envelope from Sylvia—yet unopened—

which lay lodged among the other items like a white flag of surrender.

Garbage, I said. I mean, recycling.

It looks like a letter.

Jachi slipped down from her bunk and picked up the envelope. My voice snagged in my throat as if I'd been touched in a tender place.

I used to love letters, Jachi said as she turned the envelope over in her hands. I would get buckets of mail, you know, when I was an actress. People sent me handwritten notes. They wrote poems. They mailed drawings. They told me about their lives and what my films meant to them. I was always so moved. I used to think it was the purest expression of love, sending a letter. You release your adoration into the universe for someone else to find. There's no guarantee you'll get anything back. I know I was on the receiving end, and it's true my assistant did the replies, but I appreciated what these people were doing. Then I started getting the hate mail.

Jachi continued smiling, though her expression clouded. She peered at the envelope as if she'd realized it could be dangerous.

There's something written here—

I snatched the envelope back. Blue markings ran diagonally along one side. Hieroglyphic at first, the markings reorganized into numbers printed in reverse: a phone number.

Not Sylvia's. I knew that number. I had also studied the envelope before leaving Boston and never noticed any writing; these numbers had appeared like invisible ink.

My mind looped back to that first day on Eleutheria, when,

slumped under an elephant ear plant, I'd pressed the envelope between my sweaty palms.

Deron.

What? said Jachi.

He wrote his number on my hand—

Wonderful! said Jachi. Who is Deron?

Someone who might be able to help.

A few hours later, with the sun nudging the horizon, I left Camp Hope. I hurried along the dirt road that led from the compound to the highway, then followed the highway as it hugged the shoreline. My shoelaces dangled and thrashed. I was heading to the nearest local settlement; I was heading there fast. I was going to meet Deron.

I'd called him using the Command Center phone. Though it had been four in the morning, he'd seemed unfazed by my call—at least after he realized it was me and not one of his friends playing a prank.

You wouldn't believe what's happening here, I'd said.

Try me, he replied.

I described the events of the previous month. The ill-fated kayaking trip. The heatstroke. The delayed launch. Crewmember frustration. The ever-intensifying crush of climate change. The fact that Adams was missing and Lorenzo couldn't explain where he'd gone. Deron listened without interruption, as if all this made sense.

So he's gone, Deron repeated. To the mainland.

I don't know, I said. Lorenzo couldn't tell me. I thought you might know someone who'd seen him. Maybe someone at the airport—

Willa, said Deron, don't you ever wonder if there's more to Camp Hope than compost piles and solar panels?

Excuse me?

Look, said Deron. I'm not trying to offend you. I'm actually trying to build something like an alliance, believe it or not. Because there's still time to keep this all from blowing up in everyone's face. If you took a step back, you'd see.

I did not respond, but Deron heard my frustration crackle through the receiver.

I know where Roy Adams is, he said. Or, I have a pretty good idea. If you come by the hotel tomorrow, I'll explain. Right now I need to go to sleep.

Sorry, I said—remembering what time it was—I didn't mean to ruin your night.

Deron replied that it wasn't a big deal, and not to worry, a genuine friendliness in his voice. His kindness made my breath catch. I hadn't felt anything like it in a long time.

See you soon, I said—and hung up.

Now, on my way to the hotel, the ocean hurried alongside me, water winking between casuarina trees. The ocean was everywhere on Eleutheria. Two oceans, really: the island's skinny hundred miles pinned between the indigo turmoil of the Atlantic and the turquoise calm of the Caribbean. I was on the Caribbean side, where sandy off-roads marked the places where local fishermen pulled their boats to the sea. Along the shore, conch shells rose in spiky, sun-bleached piles. All the shells were marked by a machete cut where a mollusk had been severed from its home—a fact I'd heard the Liberal Arts Girls argue about: Corrine calling the consumption of endangered conch an act of tradition and necessity; Dorothy calling Corrine a morally bankrupt cultural relativist; and Eisa noting how when people heard the ocean in a conch shell, they were experiencing the occlusion effect—*It's the frequencies of your own body.*

If I'd held a conch shell to my ear, all I'd have heard were hurricanes.

Despite whatever progress I'd made—whatever information Deron might share—I remained furious at the crewmembers for having a party on the beach. The fate of the planet was at stake, and yet they'd thrown up their hands.

I quickened my pace, as if I could outrun my own disappointment.

The road curved away from the coast and into island coppice, the dense vegetation blocking any view of the sea. The nearest settlement was five miles away, but after a month of DBCSs, I could easily cover the distance. I half-walked, half-ran, a series of telephone poles towering and tilting along beside me. The wires were consumed in orange vines: a tangled electrical chaos. Spider webs stretched between the wires too, their fist-sized creators braced against the breeze.

A rustling sounded from the mass of leafy branches rising on either side of the road. I kept moving. A strip of blue sky extended overhead like an inverse highway.

The rustling continued, as if the coppice itself was waking up.

A bird, maybe. Or a land crab.

What mattered was getting to Deron, finding Adams, launching Camp Hope. I wondered if Adams was injured, or detained, or trapped. I wondered if I'd be the one to rescue him and save the whole endeavor.

Ahead, the coppice thinned into a patchy meadow. Rooflines peeked over a low hill. A crooked wooden sign spelled out the name of the settlement in faded pastel letters.

The rustling intensified and the coppice spat out a dog: shaggy and golden, its fur dirt-dipped. Standing between me and the settlement, the dog lowered its head, growling like a motor sputtering to life.

I slowed, made soothing noises as I edged around it. Then two more dogs emerged from the brush, larger and leaner than the first. Their rib cages heaved as they barked. The first dog lunged, and I leapt out of the way with a yelp.

Go home, I said. Go.

The settlement was only a hundred yards away, but dog after dog slunk from the brush. They formed a circle around me, barked with their jaws stretched wide, the pink of their throats exposed. The golden dog lunged again, nipped at my ankle. A larger dog caught my khaki shorts in its jaws, yanked until the fabric tore. I spun away, tripped on my shoelaces and fell backward, skinning my palms.

Stop, I said. *Please.*

The dogs stopped, as if they'd been waiting for me to ask. Their heads turned in unison, noses in the air. They galloped back into the brush.

I lay on my back, breathing hard.

The sky remained festively blue.

Two children peered down at me, their small figures backlit by the morning sun.

Are you dead? said one.

I wasn't. I'd hit my head hard on the ground, but—looking up at the children—my dizziness swirled into a wide-eyed sense of resurrection.

———————

To be a child roaming. To be a child with a day as big as a year. There had been a time in my own childhood when I'd gone on what I called expeditions. I would walk from my parents' cabin into the forest, staying within sight of the cabin, then within sight of a tree that was in sight of the cabin, then onward. I was a rubber band drawn out from a fixed point; the idea was always to snap back. Once I found another cabin out in the woods, older than ours, with a roof nearly swallowed by moss. Once I found a glacial erratic shaped like a giant fist. And once I took a nap in a buttery pool of sunlight beside a brook; upon waking, I could not remember how to get home. It took hours and hours before I burst into our cabin's small kitchen, startling my mother with my tears.

That's what you get, she'd said, *for wandering into what you don't understand.*

I continued these expeditions into the woods, nevertheless. I was looking for something, though I hadn't known what.

Then one day I saw a person out in the forest. A man wearing tall socks and sports shorts and a sweaty shirt and a bandanna, who carried an enormous backpack. I'd gone on my farthest expedition yet and the man must have been a hiker who'd left a nearby trail. But to me he seemed a cosmonaut dropped down from another galaxy.

I hid in a blueberry bush. The man squatted under a big pine tree, between two roots that rose like knees on either side of him. He pulled down his shorts, his underwear. He looked around. Then he didn't. When he finished, he covered the mess in leaves, stuck a stick in the earth to mark the place. The gesture struck me as remarkably altruistic. When I pooped in the woods, I left the mess where it lay, like a deer.

I burst from the blueberry bush, excited to meet the hiker-cosmonaut. When the man saw me, though, he released a stream of profanities. Holding his shorts up with one hand, he crashed away through the undergrowth. I didn't follow because I didn't want to lose my path back to the cabin, and because shame curdled my core: the soft place that held out hope I might find someone to explore the world alongside me.

I'd never fully given up on such a possibility, though. Not even by the time I'd traveled all the way to Eleutheria.

Are you dead?

I don't think so, I said.

To prove I was not dead, I stood up. I wiped my hands on my shorts, smoothed my polo shirt. The children looked about five and twelve years of age—a boy and a girl with the same cherubic cheeks and citrine eyes that studied me with skepticism.

Are you one of the crazies? said the boy.

His name was Elmer and he was the younger of the two; his sister was Athena. One of Elmer's front teeth was missing. He poked his tongue in the hole, spoke with a slight lisp. Athena wore a pair of round glasses, her hair braided into tiny rows; she pinched Elmer when he asked if I was crazy. Like Elmer, she was dressed in jeans and a T-shirt. Like Elmer, she had plant burrs stuck in her cuffs, which suggested they'd just come out of the coppice. They both carried bulging plastic bags, the tops knotted tight.

Athena took her brother's hand and started walking toward the settlement.

Wait, I said. Where are you going?

In a single swift motion, Athena turned and flung a stone whizzing past my head.

A lone dog, lurking on the road behind us, leapt back into the brush.

Don't hurt it—

You don't have to hurt them, said Athena. You just have to show them you could.

She gave me a stern look, then continued walking. Elmer picked up more stones and hurled them in several directions, making *pow pow* sounds as he heaved his body into a twirling spin, losing his balance before running to catch up to his sister.

Athena scolded him, laughed at him, tugged him onward.

I trailed after the pair. They mostly ignored me as they walked into the settlement, though when I asked Athena questions, she responded with clipped statements of fact. The wild dogs were called potcakes, she told me. They'd gotten meaner since the recent hurricanes, with fewer scraps to scavenge around the settlements, no tourists to toss them half-eaten conch fritters or guava duff. The dogs didn't scare her.

Athena and Elmer were, I learned, born and raised on Eleutheria. They'd been to Nassau twice but no farther—back when Nassau was a place where anyone went, not yet storm-slammed, ruinous. Back before the sea swallowed the Atlantis resort, when the city's pastel streets were tourist-clogged, giddy with music, and the beaches were raked crisp, not strewn with the remnants of dismembered cruise ships.

I asked if they were on their way to school—it was Tuesday—but Athena replied that there wasn't any school anymore.

All the teachers left, she said.

And they didn't come back, Elmer said—then sang: Didn't come back, didn't come back. Didn't come back!

We passed a roofless cement structure filled with soda bottles, bits of newspaper, and investigative bromeliads. Farther on were wooden houses skirted by sagging porches, as well as one-story cinder-block homes. We passed a goat tied to a long rope on which it enthusiastically chewed. A tamarind tree shaded a clearing beside the highway.

A man leaned out of a doorway, called hello. Elmer picked up a stick and waved it. The man said more, looking at me. Athena yelled a reply too quick to catch.

Shyness overtook me. I wished for these children to like me. I wanted to step out of my grown-up body and wander away with them, throwing rocks and picking up sticks. The crewmembers' bonfire had enraged me because it veered from the Camp Hope mission, but beneath that anger lay a long-term loneliness. I'd thought I was part of a team at Camp Hope—that we were all striving toward the same ideals—but I wasn't and we weren't. This realization made my throat tight. All those weeks of trying to fit in, trying to do right—and for what? For the crewmembers to give up on their commitment? I had not opened the envelope from Sylvia, but I knew it contained a letter that said: *I told you so.*

I missed Sylvia—but she had never been a friend to me either.

Rather than asking the children how to get a ride from the settlement to the hotel, I asked them what they'd been doing in the coppice.

Athena shook her head, but Elmer bounced on his feet until his answer exploded: Treasure!

They had a map, he told me—and pestered his sister until she pulled a scroll from a plastic bag, the damp paper revealing an ink-smudged rendering of a coastline. Dotted lines marked a trail leading to an *X*. Athena gravely explained they were trying to determine where, exactly, this was on Eleutheria.

We're going along the coast, she said. Cove by cove.

Elmer tugged at my leg so we could look at the map together. He traced a little finger over the dots. I asked what they expected to find.

A giant golden lady, said Elmer. With emeralds for eyes. And a crown covered in jewels. And she's holding a baby.

A golden Ma-don-na, corrected Athena. Worth a million dollars.

Fifty million! said Elmer.

From a Spanish ship, said Athena. That crashed onto the island, a long time ago. Nobody ever found this treasure, though.

Our uncle told us about it, said Elmer.

Did your uncle draw this map? I said.

Elmer crinkled his brow, looked at Athena. She pressed her lips together, grabbed the map from me, and rerolled it into a scroll.

I'm sure the treasure is there, I said. If you keep looking—

We have to go, said Athena, and she took Elmer's hand, leading him away.

I remained where they'd left me on the side of the road. My head started to throb from my earlier fall, pain spiking my thoughts. Farther down the road sat a weathered gas station with a hand-painted 7-11 on its side. The sound of a radio trickled through a window. Perhaps this was where Lorenzo had gotten the store-bought food and drinks for the crewmember bonfire. Maybe he'd been right to do so. The struggle against climate change was over. Humanity had failed. There was nothing left except to party into the sunset—to drink beer on the beach until the rising ocean overtook us, or the air filled with so many pollutants we asphyxiated.

Might as well invite Deron to such a party—might as well invite everyone.

I turned to look for Athena and Elmer so that I could ask about getting a ride to the hotel. The pair, by that point, had met up with several other children, all of whom sat in a circle beneath the tamarind tree. Athena had unrolled the map again. She made a presentation to the others, gesturing toward the paper like a coach narrating plays.

And I might have asked—might have set off for the hotel and found Deron, had a difficult yet important conversation about local sovereignty on an island where, for centuries, idealism had inverted into exploitation, and paradisal possibility never kept its promise—if a sound hadn't broken the morning quiet. Until then, the settlement had been marked only by the voices of the children, a rooster's melancholic crow, a muted radio. Into this quiet, a roar grumbled—growing closer—exploding into the snarl of an algae-fueled engine. A white van bombed down the highway in a flurry of dust and stones. Over the steering wheel hunched a huge man, his aviators glinting. The van screamed to a stop just past the gas station. Roy Adams leaned out the open window and asked if I planned to stand there all day like a goddamn sundial.

What one could condemn about Adams was also what made me believe in him.

Launched out of West Point, he'd shot up through army ranks all the way to lieutenant general. He'd buried cities under sulfuric rain, sent uranium oxide into the air and shrapnel into human flesh, spilled blood into waterways already polluted with the hemorrhaging of Humvees. He'd blown up art museums and old-growth forests and wedding processions, left nothing for people but their own misery. He'd been a man who did these things and slept sated on steaks and potatoes, a wife in curlers at his side.

Then he'd changed.

After taking a cruise through the Caribbean, he'd returned a different man. He'd been born again—baptized by the turquoise waters—as moved by the beauty of the region as he was by its endangerment. And if Adams could change, if he could drop to his knees on a trash-strewn beach, if he could scoop up a limp pelican—its belly bloated with plastic bottle caps—if he could hold that bird and weep the fat tears of the repentant, then all things were possible. Even Camp Hope.

The van kicked into drive before I'd shut the door. I crashed back against my seat, my journey to the settlement reversing in a streaky blur. Adams leaned forward over the wheel, a toothpick twitching in his teeth. The open placket of his polo shirt stretched across his chest, exposing a sun-bronzed triangle of skin. A shark-tooth necklace dangled from his neck. He radiated heat. He smelled like cedar woodchips and aftershave and a plan.

I can't believe it, I said. It's you.

Expecting someone else, Marks? said Adams—his voice seismically loud.

I can't believe we're meeting, I said. I was looking for you. Your MO.

And now you're here.

Second time's the charm.

I began to ask where he'd been, what was going on, but Adams plowed forward.

You got a goddamn knack for timing, you know that, Marks? Some people just know when to show up. And I swear to God, you know when to show up.

If Adams was condemning me or complimenting me, I wasn't sure. My face felt tense enough to shatter. It was hard to think with him beside me and the van careening down the highway. Outside the windows, the island whirred past. Adams chomped down on his toothpick. The wood snapped and a piece pinged against my cheek.

Meeting you, I said, it's such an honor.

Speaking of meetings, let's get you introduced, said Adams—and turned to call over his shoulder: Say hi to Willa Marks, everyone.

I spun around; to my surprise, there were twelve teenagers sitting quietly in the back seats, their hands in their laps. All wore blindfolds.

Don't be shy, said Adams. Say hello. And speak up.

Hello-Willa-Marks, the teenagers replied in a road-bumped chorus.

Adams gunned the engine, his aviators glinting, his big hands on the wheel. To the teenagers, he added: Marks is going to show you the ropes, get you into the swing of things. She's a fighter. Tough as a hyena—isn't that right, Marks?

I guess so, I said.

You guess so?

Yes. Absolutely.

That's more like it, said Adams. That's what I want to hear.

Behind us, the teenagers swayed in their seats. In a low voice, I asked who they were. Adams yelled that there was no need to whisper. These were recruits, though I could also think of them as "reinforcements" or "the last piece of this goddamn puzzle."

The launch is back on?

Before you can blink, said Adams, Camp Hope will be on the tongue-tips of everyone, from politicians to pizza delivery guys. We are going to win some hearts and minds, baby—and these kids are going to help.

He thumped a huge paw onto my shoulder, squeezed to the bone. Pain shot down my arm, white-hot, yet wonderful. I tried to find the words to respond, but my brain was scrambled with the pleasure of the touch. Adams had let me know I was a part of the operation; I mattered.

I concentrated on breathing, keeping my posture straight. Adams pulled the van up to Camp Hope's bougainvillea wall. He jammed the stick shift, turned to me. His huge face loomed close: his leather skin pitted, his hair razor-cut, blue eyes rising over his aviators.

Now let me ask you something, he said, before everyone shows up and raises a hullabaloo. Can I count on you, Marks? Are you ready to do whatever it takes?

We both already knew my response, so it was a recruit who broke the space between question and answer. A blond boy in the back—his voice as worming as an eel—called: Can we take these blindfolds off?

———

The recruits—who were they? They were the sons and daughters of Wall Street brokers and high-end lawyers and elite plastic surgeons and CFOs and, in one case, a well-respected U.S. senator. They were all about sixteen years old. All, according to Adams, born and bred for big things. They would be the finishing touch on Camp Hope's preparations, sharpen its optics one final degree.

Kids get people fired up, said Adams in the speech he made to crewmembers later that day. Kids are cute. Kids remind people what's at stake. And as you all know, there's a hell of a lot at stake right now, isn't there?

Crewmembers nodded with solemn enthusiasm, grins breaking onto their faces even as they collectively visualized oceans full of dead fish, and oil rigs suckling the earth, and chemical-laced tornadoes sweeping the country. They beamed at the recruits. While *Living the Solution* hadn't specifically mentioned including young people, their addition fit into the overall premise. If Camp Hope was going to be a cultural touchstone—an eco fever dream—it wouldn't hurt to have young people in addition to other inspiring figures. Youth could be the kindling that set the global consciousness ablaze.

Now I know, said Adams, that my absence has caused confusion. Understand, though, that I didn't want to make promises I couldn't keep. Understand that every move I make is to ensure that when we take this show on the road, we make our one shot count. We've had a minor pause in our operation, sure, but this is going to pay off big time. It's a military strategy: Retrograde Movement. I won't go into the specifics right now, because I think there's something even more significant at work here. Something I want to explain, though it may sound a little woo-woo to some of you—

Adams nodded toward two solar engineers. They waved back good-naturedly.

—Understand that several weeks ago, when I was out on that reef, I had a vision. It was the vision of a child. A child, clinging to a coral outcropping. Seeing the child struggle gutted this old man. Nothing moves people more than children. I took my vision as a sign that we needed to add one more ingredient to Camp Hope to captivate our future audience. Something even more extraordinary than what we've already accomplished—

A breeze whisked the beach, tousling crewmembers' hair and shivering the palm fronds. All was quiet. Even the gulls had paused to listen.

—Of course, said Adams, we all know now it wasn't a child I saw out on the reef. It was our fellow ecowarrior, Willa Marks, blitzed out of her mind on sunsickness.

The crewmembers chuckled happily. They glanced at me fondly, as if they'd never felt anything except camaraderie. I wasn't sure whether to feel embarrassed or exhilarated. People started clapping. A crewmember hooted. Adams gestured for quiet.

The fundamentals of Camp Hope remain the same, he said. We've just got these kids here now: young as they'd come without getting parents too involved. And once we get these kids trained, up to speed, we'll launch this son-of-a-gun and save the world—

Cheering broke out in earnest, scattering seabirds into the air and crabs across the sand. Herpetologists and hydrologists and compostologists pumped their arms. The Agro Team wept. The Liberal Arts Girls gleefully pontificated at one another. Jachi clasped her hands with the serenity of a soothsayer, stared into the sun. The launch was again imminent, all prospects possible. Though twelve crewmembers were displaced from their bunks to make room for the recruits, no one complained. Those displaced were glad to sling hammocks in the boathouse until more living quarters could be erected. Everyone was ready to forget the despair-driven debauchery of the night before. The aluminum cans and plastic food wrappers from the party had been quickly hidden amid ocean flotsam when Adams wasn't looking. Everyone was ready to move ahead.

Only Lorenzo seemed uncertain. Throughout Adams's speech, he stared at me, his mustache twitching. When the other crewmembers set off for their assigned tasks, he plucked at my elbow.

You didn't tell on me? he said.

No.

You didn't mention the party, even a little bit?

I didn't.

Gratitude soothed his anxious face. Solemnly, he said: I owe you one, Willa Marks. I'll pay you back for this, you'll see.

I shrugged. Making a big deal of the party would have only slowed down progress, I replied, but Lorenzo repeated his promise.

This meant nothing to me at the time; I waved Lorenzo away, set off through the compound. My problem, the problem that twisted my insides then—and incriminates me now—is that the recruits gave me a sinking feeling. Against my better impulses, I did not like the girl-recruits with their honey-gold hair and unchewed nails. I did not like the boy-recruits with their peachy soft skin, their natural athleticism. These children named Cameron or Thatcher or Blair, as if they were all British prime ministers. These children who had grown up with cheer squads and soccer teams and hoverboards and best friends and sleepovers and swimming pools and birthday cakes and summer homes and trust funds. It made my stomach turn, seeing the money on them: the thick pelt of privilege.

That first day, the recruits gazed warily at Camp Hope's solar panels and gardens, while the Liberal Arts Girls tripped over themselves to describe the ecospatial designs. A few of the recruits looked bored by this lecturing; some wore breezy looks of satisfaction, as if they owned the place. The twelve youths did not strike me as individuals who might be interested in the fate of the planet. They did not strike me as prepared for what Camp Hope would demand: the physical grind of the lifestyle. The mental grind of it, too. They would not be able to communicate with the outside world until the launch; they would need to live as crewmembers lived.

Their decision to join Camp Hope made little sense.

I didn't want my jealousy to get in the way of the mission, though. I wanted to impress Roy Adams—to do right by Adams—because already he was everything I'd wished for from Camp Hope's founder. I kept thinking about the way he'd squeezed my shoulder in the van. It had felt like a fatherly gesture—like the touch of a father who believed in the future. Who believed in *me*.

As the recruits filed into their bunkrooms after dinner, I approached the Liberal Arts Girls—who stood watching the procession with oozing self-satisfaction—and made a comment about how the recruits must have been kidnapped.

I mean, I said, why else would they come here?

Corrine raised her eyebrows, said: You never attended college, correct?

I went to Harvard—

Corrine laughed, said: That's funny. You almost got me.

I opened my mouth to explain my scavenged college courses, then laughed along instead. Explaining Harvard would also require explaining Sylvia.

It's nothing to be ashamed of, said Corrine. Not with the structural boundaries to higher education and the economic paralysis of student debt—

She wasn't asking for a status update on higher ed, interrupted Dorothy—before turning to say: All you need to know is that these days you can't get into top-tier colleges as an A-student with a bunch of extracurriculars and high test scores. You can't even be all those things and rich. You need to be wildly unusual.

Right, said Corrine. My guess is Adams promised a bunch of prep school parents a summer immersion program in an exotic location with heart-of-gold initiatives and *real research* with bona fide scientists. Not to mention impending international stardom. Colleges want doers, not just dreamers. Innovators, not just valedictorians—

Martyrs, not just millionaires? said Eisa.

Corrine side-eyed the other Liberal Arts Girl, then added: Climate change is hot, no pun intended.

You totally intended that, said Dorothy.

The point is, said Corrine, when the launch happens, these kids will get famous. They'll be youth pioneers. Given the framework of the attention economy, they'll be fast-tracked for—

Dorothy interrupted with another semantic critique; while she and Corrine argued, Eisa leaned in.

I used to work part-time in an admissions office, she said.

You wouldn't believe the things I heard. Thousands spent on coaches with Ivy League insight. Bribery attempts, death threats, sexual favors—all so that these parents got *their* kids the best chance of success. They must see Camp Hope as part of that effort. Which is good for us. I mean, not only will these kids look great when the media arrives for the launch, I wouldn't be surprised if their parents refilled Camp Hope's coffers several times over.

Her eye twitched in the approximation of a wink.

As the last of the recruits disappeared into their respective bunkrooms, I wondered how rustic Camp Hope's living quarters seemed to them. Their potential discomfort, though, did not make me feel any better. Instead, it brought to mind my scattershot upbringing, the hours I'd spent alone in the survival bunker making terrarium after terrarium, as if I might have constructed an alternative reality perfect enough to convince my parents to go on living—as if I could have saved them.

I thought, too, about the local children on Eleutheria. Could they get to college—to anywhere? Did they have paths to follow beyond those outlined on a hand-drawn treasure map: a promise scrawled on a damp scroll of paper, with no clear compass, unlikely odds? The recruits had a well-groomed trail charted for them. Their maps were fastidiously rendered, time-tested, unfairly acquired.

So, it's true, I was secretly pleased by the challenges the recruits faced at Camp Hope, especially at first. They sweated through the brutal morning exercise sessions, hurried to take thirty-second showers and complete their many chores—aquarium cleaning, recycling sorting, compost turning—all of which I doubted they'd ever done before.

Though most recruits were boarding school veterans, hardened to parental separation, a few became homesick, if not for home than for familiar mainland comforts. Some cried at night in their bunks. One or two cried openly during the day, pink-faced, sleep deprived, and exhausted. Such displays were short-lived. The recruits were skilled at self-soothing. They had a knack for settling into a bland, polite attention whenever a situation demanded it. None of the other crewmembers found this off-putting. At mealtimes, the crewmembers talked admiringly about the recruits' large vocabularies and polished manners. They called the recruits cute. And if one did become upset, there would be a coral reef to rehabilitate, a batch of biodiesel to make. Consolation arrived via cheery instruction.

Before I go any further, let me add that despite my misgivings, I never wanted the recruits to get hurt. I never wanted anything truly bad to happen to them. I just didn't like having them around. I didn't think Camp Hope needed them. For all their compliance, their prep school articulateness, they did not seem to care about protecting the environment, about making a better world for everyone, except in the most superficial way. They had come to Camp Hope to buoy their college applications; they had come for themselves.

I trusted Roy Adams, though. If he considered the recruits essential, I'd do everything I could to get them ready for the launch. I wanted Camp Hope to make a difference in the world and if it meant working with the recruits, I was going to do that. I would do it for him.

That was why, to fulfill his directive that I give the recruits "guts," I took them into the coppice.

The trip was a way to enter into the unknown, to press against risk: sinkholes, poisonwood, spiders. It's true, I also

had the wild dogs in mind. Maybe I imagined the dogs fright-
ening the recruits before I demonstrated how a stone's throw
could save us. Maybe I wanted the recruits to grasp the full
power of nature, to respect it. To feel a brush of fear in lives
that seemed, from the outside, decadent with plenty and love.

I parked the van on a sandy off-road that disappeared into the
coppice. I'd seen the road during my walk to the local settlement two weeks before. One of the geologists had given me a
compass, promised that if we kept due west, we would reach
the coast. A marine team conducting mangrove research
would pick us up when we arrived.

The geologist, like the other crewmembers, was newly
friendly toward me. Though I had been previously perceived
as the reason Adams absented himself from Camp Hope, I was
now seen as the reason he returned: bringing with him essential reinforcements. I was the reason why—very soon—we'd
launch.

The recruits were in high spirits as we set off, chatting
among themselves about the locations of their families' second
homes and their favorite international airlines. The sandy off-
road transformed into a path naturally paved with planes of
limestone. Stands of buttonwood and cottonwood filtered sunlight. Birds warbled, spirited out of the brush.

As we traveled deeper into the coppice, though, the brush
thickened and poisonwood pressed close. Birds became secretive; insects, more active. We passed a dead snake, split open
and partially eaten. The recruits fell into a restless quiet.

Are we going the right way?

The question came from Lillian McClatchy, the yellow-haired daughter of a beverage corporation's CEO. She was one of four recruits who insisted on wearing pearl earrings with her Camp Hope uniform.

Where are we even going? said Thatcher Craven III.

I repeated we were going to the island's other side; we'd get picked up by boat.

Why, though? said Cameron Espinoza.

I put a finger on my lips, listened for rustling, hoping the wild dogs would appear. With my free hand, I dipped my fingers into my pocket, caressed a clutch of smooth stones. I'd wait until the recruits were adequately frightened before I scared the dogs away.

The island remained quiet. We marched on, the sun high and sweaty in the sky. The geologist had mentioned we'd climb a ridge before reaching the shore, but we seemed to be losing elevation. We'd been walking for over an hour. We had not packed much water.

Could I try the compass? said Lillian.

I gave it to her, my interest in the excursion waning. I wanted to be back at Camp Hope, not giving rich kids anecdotes for their college applications.

But there was Adams to think of—Adams to impress. I wanted to again feel his hand on my shoulder, hear his booming praise. *Marks,* I imagined him saying. *Your commitment has always stood out. You're willing to do what it takes to get these recruits fully trained. To train them right.*

We should go that way, said Lillian—she pointed down the path by which we'd come—If we backtrack a bit, we can take one of the side trails.

The world needs people like you. People who see the mission all the way through.

The recruits set off and I slugged after them, lost in my imaginary conversation with Adams. When the recruits stopped short, I startled.

We'd come to a cave.

The stony mouth yawned wide, opening into a spacious hollow. The floor was flat and sandy. The cave seemed like a place people could live—and likely had.

What is this? said Cameron. I thought we were walking to the ocean.

Do you have any idea where we are? said Margaret Lu with a frown.

To maintain a shred of authority, I forced a smile. I told the recruits the mission had actually been to find this cave. Now they were free to explore.

The recruits glanced at their watches like time-pressed executives-in-training. Thatcher raised the topic of dinner. I continued smiling—fiercely—until they reluctantly wandered the cave, dipping into its shadows, kicking the sandy floors.

I watched with fleeting interest. Let the recruits craft application essays about this hole in a cliff; they would all end up at places like Harvard anyway.

Instead of watching them, I imagined how I could use the excursion as a reason to speak to Adams, gain his approval. *You're something else, Marks. Truly dedicated and—*

A recruit sidled up beside me.

His name was Fitz Albemarle. He had a beaky nose, pouting lips, his face otherwise obscured by a wide-brimmed hat—a necessity given his complexion: rice-paper pale. Though only fifteen, he had the sneering demeanor of someone already steadfast in an attitude of general contempt. He looked like a kid who played lacrosse just to hit people with sticks; a kid who would grow up to be a banker so he could foreclose on homes; a kid-turned-recruit who made comments to a crew-member just to get under her skin.

If those idiots fall from up there, he said, they'll break their necks.

He gestured toward the cave wall, which several recruits had started to climb.

They'll be fine, I said.

Are there any sinkholes around here?

Could be.

Do you have any idea what you're doing? said Fitz. I mean, are there even rules here? How is any of this legal?

I gritted my teeth; I did not want to bother with Fitz's questions. I wanted to be left alone with my imaginary conversation with Adams, or better yet: I wanted to get back to Camp Hope so that I could talk to Adams in person. But I needed to respond, so I made a few bland remarks about the importance of immersing oneself in local ecology while thinking about climate change on a global scale.

Fitz was grumpily turning away, when he noticed something by my foot.

How often do those spiders bite?

A silver-dollar-sized arachnid picked its way over my toes.

I'd made the unwise decision to hike in strappy sports sandals. The bare skin of my foot prickled. Without moving the lower half of my body, I shrugged and replied that the spider wasn't an issue.

Fitz lifted his chin. His hat slid back, revealing eyes turned pink around the edges. His mouth twitched scornfully. The prickling sensation crept up my calf. I willed myself not to look at the spider. I would not give this weaselly rich kid the satisfaction of my panic. I stayed motionless, even as I braced for a bite.

Whoa, said Lillian—too nosy not to notice—Look at the size of that thing.

More recruits gathered around me. Those who'd been climbing the cave wall came over to watch the spider as it crawled up my thigh, over my hip, my torso, all the way to my neck. I closed my eyes as the recruits squealed delightedly.

I thought of Adams—his proclamation that I was "a fighter" and "tough as a hyena." He had said that in front of the recruits; I didn't want him to be proven wrong. This wasn't about protecting my pride, or even my safety. It was about showing the recruits that Adams meant what he said: Camp Hope and its crewmembers were the real deal.

It is commitment, your full-on commitment, that will change the world—

The recruits squealed louder as the spider crawled along my jaw. They jumped up and down, covered their eyes as it reached my chin, its long legs testing my lips. I waited for the spider to move toward my hair, before I said, in a calm voice: There's no reason to be afraid. When you stop worrying about losing everything, that's when you can accomplish anything.

It was a line from *Living the Solution*. I felt as strong as I sounded. The recruits nodded, marveling as I guided the spider onto my hand and then onto the ground.

All of them except Fitz. He had melted back into the shadows of the cave with all the carelessness, the inexplicability of a ghost.

ANOTHER BODY: sun-bloated, salt-streaked, left to rot upon the rocks. It may have been an accident, the first time the settlers burned a fire near a jagged stretch of reef—the light luring a passing ship toward an illusionary harbor, the wooden hull soon lacerated, sailors crying for salvation—but it was not an accident the next time, or the next.

It was no accident when a shipwrecked survivor crawled onto the island's fine white sand, spitting blood and seawater, begging for assistance, only to receive, instead, a boot to the temple: a swift death the closest thing to a hospitable reception.

There were no laws on Eleutheria—no officials to enforce them. There were no magistrates, no courts. There were no taxes. No banking systems. No tutors and no seminaries to seed enlightenment. There were no decent blacksmiths. No dentists, even bad ones. There were no churches at which to prostrate, unless one counted the cave—a dim dent in a cliff, with only a boulder for a pulpit—and even then, there were no clergy.

Those living on Eleutheria were luckless, wayward. Too stubborn to leave. Too stubborn to live elsewhere. Their numbers grew in fits and starts. From other colonies were sent unrepentant Quakers, adulterers, pickpockets, misfits—all those the New World did not want among its numbers. To Eleutheria were sent the free Black people who made white colonists uneasy; the enslaved

Black people who made white colonists afraid—plots of rebellion enflaming paranoia in so-called masters' rotted souls.

The island: an unofficial penitentiary—though not particularly penitent—could be a site of freedom if one could survive. Poison spiders in the foliage; sharks cruising through the shallows; sting-rays laid out like stepping stones to the bottom of the sea. The island was an otherworld. The doomed thrived and the blessed expired. The island was an afterlife: a heaven or a hell, no one was sure. A woman, once shamed and banished, could pick her way along the shoreline, search ropes of seaweed for shipwrecked trea-sures or lumps of ambergris to make a wealthy person's perfume reek. When the day grew long and endless, boredom her cruel-est warden, she could look for other items too. Pretty shells and smooth stones. The heart-shaped beans that floated across the Atlantic like missives from a lover.

The sea washed up what it chose—for all its unknowns, that much was certain—what crashed ashore, crawled out, stuck or did not.

Lived or did not.

At night, the settlers held lanterns against the darkness, the light a winking eye—a diamond nestled against velvet, a grain of salt on the tongue—the brightness beckoning, *come closer.*

6

Sylvia's face hovered close, her eyes hazing into shadows, her mouth glinting wet. We were on the floor of her upstairs bathroom and I could still feel the press of her lips on mine, taste her sea-salt tears. The electricity had gone out and it was as if the kiss had summoned the surprise darkness. Then the shower water turned off too—no more spray misting the room—and all stood motionless. Except I was trembling. I wasn't motionless at all—or quiet: my breath short and fast. If it was the shiver of damp clothing, or a vibrating anticipation, I did not know. I felt I would die if I did not get what I wanted. I felt almost as if I *had* died and dropped into an otherworld, everything upside down: a riot roaring outside, and me, somehow, sitting on a tiled floor with Professor Sylvia Gill.

She started to speak, so I kissed her again.

This time she responded with lips that were pillow-soft, then urgent, her hands—those long elegant fingers—lacing up the base of my neck and into my hair. When her eyes met mine, they were wild. Her voice rasped, *Not here.*

Out into the hallway, arms entangled, her mouth meeting mine in the doorway to her bedroom. A stack of books tumbled invisibly in the dark. Her bed: a sea of blankets, swelling around us. My trembling intensified. In the chilled air, my skin goose-bumped, muscles tense. I peeled off my damp layers. Sylvia peeled away hers. Then her body pressed close, her warmth seeping into me, and the tension in my limbs melted into a helpless want. I went limp. I was lost. She wrapped her legs around mine, bit my shoulder, my neck. Her perfume whisked up into my skull—that humid, too-sweet musk of ambergris—along with the scent of wet skin, wet hair. A tangy womanness. I buried my face in her. I was breathing her in. I was swimming in her.

She pulled away.

Was that wrong? I said—my words whisper small—Am I doing it wrong?

I felt cold again. What did I know, except the excruciating vastness of my desire for Sylvia? A desire that left me vulnerable, that had put me in danger before. Back in September, I'd walked out of Sylvia's lecture and found starlings dropped dead all over campus. Starlings on the pathways. Starlings on the steps of the library. All those feathered sleepers, no longer flexing and undulating, skidding across the sky in a singular million. After Sylvia's rejection, I'd felt dropped down too: broken from the heights of expectation.

Wrong, Sylvia echoed, you're all wrong.

My belly felt full of starlings: a roiling, chirping mass. They'd ended up inside me, and I'd ended up in this otherworld. Darkness draped us; we might have been anywhere. Anywhen. Birds in my belly, shrieking, rioting. Except that Sylvia was drawing close again, her hands on my face, elegant fingers catching my lips. Hands sliding down my body—*wrong, wrong, wrong.* I slipped into the ocean of a moan, all ache, unsure if it was mine or hers, or the whole world's. Out beyond Sylvia's bedroom lay the metropolitan sprawl—spiky with sirens and the roar of a protest not yet suppressed—but I heard only Sylvia's shallow breathing, felt only the tourniqueting twist of sheets, the chill of a Massachusetts autumn absolved in her radiator warmth. It didn't matter if we were in an otherworld, because all I wanted was her wet mouth, soft hips, the dig of fingers into flesh, a paradise of feelings, starlings set soaring free.

She was gone in the morning.

If I hadn't woken up in her bed, I might have thought what happened was a dream.

There were sirens ringing through the city, the whine of an alarm. I'd almost forgotten about the riots. The power was back and the TV had reawoken downstairs. I wandered down to the living room wrapped in a blanket. On the TV, footage unspooled from the day before. It dawned on me that the Freegans had been involved—this may have been the "moment" they had talked so much about. After all, the previous evening, I'd felt the pull of their gathering, the tug of a collective consciousness. If it hadn't been for Sylvia, I would have been with them. I'd be out in the city now.

But I was thinking about her body against mine. The sweet terror of that touch. The ache between my legs that had rippled into pleasure almost too good to bear.

It had been my first time. That was supposed to mean something. For some reason I had always assumed my first time would be with a man, though I'd never been especially drawn to one, and could only visualize the act happening in an abstract way. My cousins had talked at me about men all the time. They'd teased me about which ones I thought were cute. I'd answer at random; Victoria and Jeanette giggled regardless. Sometimes they would round up men to be in our photos, back when we'd taken photos. Once they'd told me to kiss a guy we'd collected outside a bar—and the guy had grabbed me before I could say no. It shocked me, having his tongue shoved into my mouth, his beard scratching my face. Made me feel like I was drowning. Even my cousins had been able to tell the kiss upset me. They hadn't bothered me so much about boyfriends after that.

It hadn't felt like drowning with Sylvia.

I was still on her sofa, swathed in blankets and absently watching TV, when her front door clicked open that afternoon. Simone the bunny sat beside me. I'd eaten the doughnuts I'd brought the previous night, and the sugar made me feel light-headed even before she appeared. I knew I was supposed to leave. I didn't want to, though—and so I had made up a story in my head about how she would be glad to find me there when she returned.

However, when she entered the living room—with a swish of a long wool coat, the snap of boots—her eyes flashed, irritation accumulating on her face like a thunderhead. She was towering and elegant. Formidably beautiful. My blood pooled, sugar-thickened. A want billowed through me.

As you might imagine, said Sylvia, I have a lot to take care of right now.

She started going through a folder on a table at the edge of the living room. I waited as she kept shuffling, papers flying, the TV playing footage from the riots over and over: explosions and people running, the federally appointed mayor decrying citizen behavior.

I uncocooned myself from the blankets on the sofa, went to her. My bare skin smiled with my own courage; I'd never gotten dressed.

She ignored me, so I slid a hand to her waist. Her hand lashed out, grabbed me tight. The grip almost hurt. Then it did hurt. But I felt peeled open by the sensation: her nearness and all the possibility of it.

Why, she said, are you still here?

To see you, I said.

You're a fool.

So? I said—feeling insolent with my own lust, the sugar rushing to my head—You want me here too.

You should stay away from me.

I don't want to.

I'm not a good person.

This made me laugh—which made Sylvia step back, surprised. I replied that she was the best person: my favorite person. I said she was bewitching and brilliant and daringly righteous, and the more I said, the more stricken she seemed.

Oh, she exclaimed—as if wounded. Stop.

I didn't; I kept talking, listing her every lovely quality until she couldn't stand it any longer. She pulled me close against her and back into her life.

Early December. Five weeks since the Halloween Riots. The city tense, curfew kept. Drones zipping through the dark. All government elections would be postponed, people were told, until the citizenry stabilized. Officials warned of a radical decentralized terrorist network stalking the nation—the implication being that anyone could be indicted for suspicious activity. Among my coworkers at The Hole Story, speculation circulated about shadow prisons, secret interrogations, people "disappeared" by a branch of extrajudicial law enforcement. I hadn't seen the Freegans since before the riots; scavenging wasn't safe. It felt like a risk even to go beyond the path between my cousins' apartment and my job. It was a risk to go to Sylvia's house.

But I did.

We'd fallen into a new pattern in which I went to her house and we ended up in her bedroom. No more talking about social movements, or sitting on the sofa drinking tea. It was only sex. Our encounters were intense, ephemeral, which felt good and then terrible—but the good was good enough. Even though Sylvia always disappeared afterward.

Then, one morning, I woke while she was getting dressed. It was dark outside, more night than morning. Sylvia sat on the edge of the bed, pulling on a black stocking. A muted lamp illuminated a wardrobe, wood-carved, one door draped with scarves. Piles of books sat stacked on the nightstand. A vanity, pressed against a wall, was dusted with rouge.

Sylvia stooped to collect an errant earring and deposited books from the nightstand into a tote bag. She had put on a black dress, her waist cinched by a belt. Her hair was coiffed and her eyes outlined with dark liner. She looked like a preoccupied queen.

Very busy, she said when she noticed me watching. You'll let yourself out?

She was always busy, always unable to talk. I realized I missed the way we'd once sat in her living room, and I'd gone on and on about the Freegans. I wished I could tell her about how I hadn't seen them in so long. I worried about them. I wondered if they were hiding out, or if they were camouflaged, or if they'd been taken away to secret prisons.

Sylvia hunted around the bedroom for her reading glasses.

What's so important today? I said.

Sylvia kept searching as she explained that a news program had asked her to comment on the third-party du jour: Green Republicans. They were another newborn political faction trying to get a foothold amid the political chaos. The news outlet wanted her academic perspective to balance out the inane commentary of nutjob pundits, though it was likely those pundits would get the bulk of the speaking time. She didn't love these appearances, but they raised her academic profile. And she needed to keep her profile raised, what with dozens of the nation's universities collapsing, and the cutthroat mentality of her colleagues. They were wolves in tweed blazers. They wouldn't let a particular incident go.

What incident? I said.

Nothing important.

Sounds like it wasn't.

Never mind, said Sylvia—forcefully flipping a pillow to peer under it.

I didn't mind; all I minded was Sylvia leaving again. The only thing keeping her near was that she hadn't yet located her glasses.

Whatever your colleagues think, I said, I know you're smarter than them all.

Sylvia turned, so I wouldn't see her enjoy the compliment. I spotted her tortoiseshell glasses in a fold of the comforter. I slid them out and perched them on the bridge of my nose.

You may need these, though—

Sylvia tried to take the glasses, but I dodged away.

L, she said. I don't have time for this.

I reluctantly handed over the glasses. I still didn't want her to go, and I had the sense a part of her didn't want to leave either.

Can we have tea again sometime? I said.

Sylvia sat on the bed. She traced a finger around my bare ankle, then let it drift along my calf. Her eyes snapped to mine and my whole body came alive. I felt like an interesting specimen in the woods. A little flower. A sapling. I wanted to be plucked, looked at—loved. I wanted to be pinched out of my normal life and flattened in a book for preservation.

Sylvia's phone buzzed, returning her to the business at hand.

This producer keeps calling, she said. As if I've never done an appearance before—

I leapt off the bed. An idea had shivered into me, and I threw on my shirt and sweater and pants, trying to hold it in my mind. The idea made my skin hot; not yet fully formed, I didn't want to lose it. My coat lay on the hallway floor. I dashed out of the bedroom to retrieve it, Sylvia trailing behind.

What is going on with you? she said.

I punched my arms through the coat sleeves. I couldn't explain myself to her, not yet; the idea was getting louder and I wanted to hear it all the way through. I kissed her cheek, then hurried out of the house into the predawn darkness, the idea waiting for me like a ship hidden in a harbor—our voyage imminent.

———

Freezing rain overnight. Sidewalks slick with ice, parking meters and stop signs glinting in their frozen casings. Lamp-posts hardened into icy yellow lumps. Even so, my limbs swung light and tireless as I walked through the frozen city. I slid my feet forward as if skiing. I huffed smoke-breath like a train. I hummed.

Sylvia's mention of speaking on television had stirred up the makings of a plan, and that plan—though coalescing—made me invincible. I could walk for miles and no temperature would touch me. I walked through the dark part of the morning, all the way across Cambridge, and over Harvard Bridge, and down to the South End. The sun came up pale pink as I neared my cousins' apartment. Light prismed through the iced-over landscape, jeweling it, making everything appear infinitely precious. If I hadn't had to work at The Hole Story, I might have walked for hours more, watched the city come to life as Bostonians emerged from their homes to throw salt on sidewalks and chop at the ice sealing car doors.

The plan was that Sylvia could help the Freegans. In a way, they could help her too. The obviousness of this arrangement beamed through me: that Sylvia gave lectures, wrote articles, appeared on the news, made her the most powerful person I knew. She was a merchant of perspective. People listened to her; they believed what she said. If she advocated for the Freegans and people like them—for a movement in the making—she could sway public opinion. She could explain how the Freegans weren't a danger to society, but a chance for salvation. They weren't a radical decentralized terrorist network; they were an amassing of individuals awakened to what civilization could be.

The facts of my existence began to align. We meant something, Sylvia and I. The universe had pushed us together for a reason: we were cosmically called upon to serve the greater good.

All day, I daydreamed future scenarios. At The Hole Story, I distractedly overmixed the batter, producing a batch of doughnut holes as hard as musket balls. No matter. I disposed of them quickly, made more. I whistled all the way through my second shift as well. I'd taken on extra hours; my cousins and I needed the money with scavenging made difficult. Victoria and Jeanette had started applying for new jobs, since their work at the gallery was part-time and low-paying. The odds of them finding anything were low, however, given their strangeness, their sparse résumés, and the atrophied job market.

Every worry faded under the glow of the plan I'd soon share with Sylvia. That night, the cold weather turned colder and a polar vortex twisted through Boston, ushering seawater into highway tunnels and freezing them like pipes, before dumping four feet of snow on the city. Tree branches snapped onto power lines and smashed the cars not lost in snowdrifts. Public transportation ground to a halt. And yet, I imagined a wondrous life ahead—harmonious with cooperative potential—so that, four days later, I rat-a-tat-tatted on Sylvia's door, buzzing with as much anticipation as when I'd left.

No one answered. I wiggled inside my coat to stay warm. Sylvia's neighbor emerged on her opposite porch wearing a Red Sox beanie. She poked at the ice on her steps, making a show of coincidence, before she said: You're the student.

Sure, I said.

School's out of session?

I shrugged, not caring to explain. I shifted my feet; knocked again.

Strange, said the neighbor, students coming all the way out here.

To keep my fingers warm, I blew on them.

You all look the same, the neighbor went on. It's like you're carbon-copied. Or cloned, like they did with those babies in—

I knocked again, loud as I could without damaging the door, and this time I heard footsteps on the other side. I shivered, ready to share my plan for helping the Freegans, ready to make the world better, but then the door opened and I was swallowed by the perfumed home—by Sylvia—and everything turned inside out, myself included.

That was the problem: I could never find the right moment to explain to Sylvia my idea. She had to be in the right mood—receptive—but her moods were hard to track. The window of her attention was limited before other matters consumed her mind. When she was focused on me, I could not resist the deluge of her desire. I liked feeling needed, even if only for a short while. I wanted to be what diverted her from her work. I wanted to be wanted. I wanted my mind scrambled by hours in bed, so that when I stumbled out of her house, dazed, and remembered what I'd intended to ask, it was already too late.

The distracting, decadent clutter of her home didn't help my sense of focus, either. But her home was the only place we could meet. Sylvia had told me to stop sneaking into Harvard.

They've upgraded their security, she said. It's not worth the risk. And I certainly cannot deal with the responsibility of liberating you. I've got too much else going on.

How to ask her about the Freegans? How to ask for more when she already gave me more than she wanted to give? In her house, papers piled everywhere. Books splayed open on the living room floor, sticky notes tagging their pages like yellow fins. Sometimes books nestled into the bedcovers too; their spines dug into my own as if to insist they deserved Sylvia more than me.

I didn't want to lose her. I didn't dare lose her. Sylvia was the life raft keeping me afloat.

The whole winter passed like that; her bedroom became the only real place in the city. Everything else faded, went out of focus, even as pundits decried the deteriorating state of society, and religious leaders praised the pleasures of the afterlife—a consolation prize for those struggling with the present—and American leadership stoked nationalism over the hot coals of prejudice. Borders rose everywhere. The U.S.-Mexican border, electrified and land-mined, was patrolled by drones with even less sympathy than their human predecessors. Denmark, Sweden, Norway, Finland—abandoning the limping EU—sealed others out. China and Spain sealed citizens in. The ultrawealthy fortified their doomsday hideaways in New Zealand. All over the world, protesters could barely lift signs before law enforcement swept through in the name of public safety and private property. Yet every time I found the courage to tell Sylvia my idea, the moment failed and my plan floated out of reach, around the corner of the next minute, hour, day.

Which isn't to say there weren't times when—standing in line at the grocery store rationing counter, passing the paramilitary guarding a corporate office, reading about another natural disaster—I remembered how Freegans had said it only took 3.5 percent of a population to initiate a massive cultural shift; when I recalled their talk about tearing up the city's pavement and planting gardens in the streets; when I remembered I'd meant to ask Sylvia to help communicate the Freegan fight for revolution, to help find where they'd gone, to help them however they needed help, because the world needed something different and the Freegans were as different as they came.

I suppose a part of me, deep down, knew that asking Sylvia for something would change what we had.

And I liked what we had, imperfect as it was.

Spring arrived in a bright glassy burst. Snowdrifts disappeared, their secret contents exposed: the melting archeology of coffee cups and single mittens and lost house keys. Daffodils knifed up from the soil in green blades, donned their yellow bonnets. Rhododendrons blossomed. Azaleas too. Cherries frothed pink along the Charles. There were flowers all over the city—more than usual—and, if I'd been paying attention, I would have connected the blooming to the global spike in CO_2. Such displays were happening in countries all over the world—happening in the sea as well, where coral blazed bright yellow, pink, violet, the colors visible from the air like desperate neon signs begging for attention, for rescue, their gorgeousness pleading with the human eye for help.

Maybe the flowers at least made my eyes open wider, because one afternoon, near an exquisite hump of rhododendrons, I noticed a wanted poster taped to a wall.

There were similar posters all over the city: printed like movie posters or presented on massive video displays. The U.S. government, courting public solidarity, had begun an *Enemies Among US* campaign. The messaging used Wild West aesthetics to highlight lawbreakers, undocumented people, algorithmically suspected terrorists. *The only thing between US and Law and Order . . . Is Them,* the signs said. I usually ignored such images, but walking down the street, I recognized the face of a Freegan: a woman with pink hair I'd met at my first scavenging run.

I ripped the poster from the wall, hurried toward Harvard. Though I had a shift scheduled at The Hole Story—and though Sylvia had told me not to sneak onto campus—I couldn't delay another second.

Sylvia's office was at the end of a corridor, past glass-walled meeting rooms, a scowling administrative assistant, and a group of graduate students reverently encircling a copy machine.

Walking onto the campus had been easier than expected, though I knew security measures weren't always visible. I used the campus directory to find the sociology department, located the office labeled *Sylvia Gill.*

Her door, blessedly ajar.

I barreled in, relieved to see Sylvia behind her desk. With her hair coiffed, eyes rimmed in black liner, scarf swept around her shoulders, she looked as stately as ever, radiating the potential to effect so much good.

I rushed to her side, held out the crumpled wanted poster. My words tumbled over one another as I said: It's the Freegans—

Sylvia did not look at the poster or at me. In a low, cold voice, she replied: I told you not to come here.

There were two other people in the room—men, sitting across the desk: academics with rumpled button-downs and thick owlish glasses. They squinted at me, muttered to one another. One raised his eyebrows at Sylvia.

Really, Sy? he said. After what happened before?

We talked about this, said the other man. Students are off-limits.

Sylvia's mouth tightened. She was exquisite and terrifying: her scarves shifting about her. I wanted to touch her—to be touched by her—but she wouldn't look at me.

You're jeopardizing the whole department, one of the men went on. You know we're a hair's breadth from being merged with Poli Sci.

There was a glee in the man's scolding, in the other man's headshake. They peered at me like a zoo animal. I hated them both; I willed Sylvia to look at me, if only for a second, to con-firm their unworthiness.

And she's the spitting image—

Sylvia shot up from her desk chair in a rush of fabric. She told the men they had no right to make such statements; their inferences were ill-informed and sensationalist. But when her eyes finally met mine, there was fear on her face.

Sy, I would have thought you'd know better by now.

At least be discreet—

She opened her mouth to reply; but no sound came out. This, more than anything, disturbed me; Sylvia had always known what to say. She could pluck the thread of any conver-sation out of the air, twist commentary into neat little bows. Except she couldn't this time. Her speechlessness must have disturbed her as well, because she fled her office in a streak of scarves and the red rip of an angry mouth.

———

I was an hour late to my shift at The Hole Story.

While I sullenly operated the fry station, my boss, Ruby, went on a rant about punctuality—*Is that what you learned in your bunker? Were there no clocks down there?* I barely listened. My mind churned with the episode at Harvard. I'd left after Sylvia—feeling angry at the owlish men, if only for being present. I was upset with Sylvia too, though as time passed—and I mixed batter and fried endless doughnut holes—I felt only sorry and sad. Maybe I was defective: I didn't understand relationships. What was expected. The rules. Sylvia had told me not to go to the campus and I hadn't listened. But then again, I had had to tell her about the Freegans and there'd seemed no other way.

I needed someone to explain to me who was in the right. But who could I ask? Not my colleagues—they already considered me an oddball, and made a point of further avoiding me after Ruby's tirade.

When my shift ended that afternoon, I returned to the apartment, hoping my cousins could offer insight. The apartment was empty. An assortment of tasteful blazers sat piled on the kitchen counter. I remembered that Victoria had secured a full-time job the week before. The job was a miracle, really—a dental practice had hired her to run their social media. There'd been an influx of well-off clients seeking substantive dental work in case of total societal collapse. This was good for the dental practice—and for Victoria—though not so great for her sister. The practice had only hired one person for the position. Jeanette was stuck working part-time at the gallery. Both cousins had cried on Victoria's first day of work; they were unused to separation. But given their financial situation, there wasn't a choice. All Jeanette could do was put in her hours at the gallery, then hang around the dental practice afterward so that she and her sister could reunite as soon as Victoria's workday concluded. Jeanette was likely there that afternoon.

A headache skewered my temples. I wasn't sure when my cousins would be back, or if they'd even be able to parse my relationship. I'd never told them anything about it, just like I'd never told them about the Freegans. Though my cousins and I had grown closer, they still saw me as their *little Wilhelmina*. If I explained the true contours of my life, they'd be too shocked to offer useful input.

My temples throbbed. Feeling faint, I stumbled to the apartment window and flung it open, gulping lungfuls of the damp spring air.

On the sidewalk below stood Sylvia.

Hands pressed neatly together, she glanced at passersby as if expecting someone to stop and question her presence.

I closed the window carefully. Then I went to the sink and splashed water on my face. My headache, along with the riot of my thoughts, had cleared into numb blankness.

I went downstairs to see her.

L—

Sylvia's face brightened when she saw me step onto the sidewalk, but I kept my own face neutral. I asked how she'd found my apartment.

I followed you, she replied. After you left your workplace. I called out to you several times, actually. But you were, well, preoccupied.

You know where I work? I said.

This revelation caught me off-guard. Then I remembered

how, many months ago, Sylvia had appeared at The Hole Story.
She hadn't seemed to notice me at the time. I'd assumed the
visit had been a fortuitous coincidence.

Listen, said Sylvia—a faint crimson rising in her face—there
are some things I need to talk to you about. There are things I
need to explain.

Around us, people bustled by on the sidewalk. Vehicles
raced between stoplights, clanking over potholes, honking.
Despite the noisiness, the busyness, Sylvia seemed more present than she'd ever been—her eyes fixed on me—like she was
there with only me, not everyone else in the city. Like there
was nothing else on her mind.

What were those men talking about in your office? I said.

Sylvia set her jaw, took my hands in her own. It was the first
time she'd ever touched me outside her home. The visibility of
the touch—the fact that anyone could see us—sent a warmth
through my limbs, even as worry brewed in my gut.

You look like someone, L.

Sylvia winced at her own words, but kept going.

You look like someone I used to know, she said. A young
woman with whom I was once involved. When you appeared
in my office today, my colleagues noticed.

I don't understand, I said.

Car horns blared. People trudged past, giving us side-eyed
looks, or no looks at all. Sylvia barreled forward, saying what
neither of us wanted to hear.

Your likeness was unsettling when I first saw you, she said.
It made me feel unhinged. You made me feel unhinged. And
then even more so when you kept appearing in my life. You
haunted me. You reminded me of my mistakes. You kept
wedging yourself closer to me. I tried to hold you at a distance,

I really did. You have to understand that. I tried. But you were so persistent. You were—

Someone else? I said. You thought I was someone else?

Sorrow slammed into me. I pulled away. Breathing had become difficult; the city block spun.

I'm so sorry, Sylvia was saying, as she went on with her explanation that the person had been a student and it had been a huge mistake. Easy and natural at first, almost an academic tradition, but a mistake in the end. A series of incidents occurred and the girl had to leave school. The whole ordeal almost cost Sylvia a job, and maybe should have cost her a job, but the timing was such that she'd just made strides in her career, and then the dean owed her a favor. It was a complicated situation and—

I don't think it's complicated, I said. You thought I was someone else. You were pretending I was someone else.

Sylvia's cheeks turned a deeper crimson. She was not a woman who wore shame easily. It wouldn't stick to her. She wouldn't let it. I almost admired the way she flung the feeling off: a burden she refused to carry.

No, she said. Maybe it started that way, but I fell for you, L. You have to understand that. I couldn't stop seeing you, as hard as I tried.

You don't even know me.

I do, I—

You don't even know my real name, I said. Which is Willa. Willa Marks.

Sylvia hesitated, and I got the sense that this information wasn't new. Maybe she'd already known—maybe she'd known a long time.

Well, she said, I *want* to know you, Willa Marks. I thought us not knowing one another would protect us both. I was wrong. And I don't want that anymore. I want to know everything about you. I want to know how a creature as unusual and miraculous as you found her way into this city—this century.

A drone was watching us. Hovering near, like an eavesdropping insect, it hummed as it observed us. We both ignored it. We ignored, too, the quietness that had overtaken the street: the sign of an impromptu curfew. We could be fined if we didn't clear out.

A weariness washed over me. I wasn't sure if I believed Sylvia. I wasn't sure of anything. I wanted to dig a hole and lie down in it and go to sleep. I wished the Freegans would appear—that I'd feel the neck tingle of a flash protest and get carried away in the mindless ecstasy of human effervescence—that I wouldn't have to think at all.

Sylvia was saying she wanted to make this right. She wanted to fix things. Don't you ever wish you could redo some aspect of your life? she said. Repair what you got wrong? Understand that I was, if anything, trying to revise my own history in a way that felt morally right, to unmake my mistakes—

I thought about what it would mean to revise my own past. Could I have saved my parents? What if, at seventeen, I'd stopped fiddling with that terrarium and left the survival bunker sooner—found them before they died? Maybe I could have saved them.

Sylvia was saying she wanted to have a real relationship. Everything out in the open. It had been her own issues—her need to hide things—that had been the problem. But that was done. She was thinking we could take a trip together. We could start over. Her friend had offered to let her stay in a family cottage in Martha's Vineyard; she could call the friend and make the arrangements. Wouldn't that be nice? Going on a trip? What did I think? Could I answer instead of staring into space? Was there something I wanted? Was there something she could do?

Yes.

From my pocket, I extracted the crumpled poster and showed her.

I want you to help the Freegans, I said.

Sylvia narrowed her eyes, glancing at the drone hovering overhead, as I explained how the Freegans needed help. They were being scapegoated, suppressed; they might be in secret prisons. It wasn't right. And anyway, their ideas for reinventing society were too important to disregard. They needed an advocate. They needed someone like Sylvia to stand up for them.

You could go on TV, I said. Share their proposals. People listen to you.

The drone buzzed closer and Sylvia seemed to be trying hard not to look at it; she reached out and lightly touched my cheek.

You're such a believer, she said. It inspires me the way you hope on things.

So you'll help them?

She cupped my face in both hands, and my breath hiccupped—because her touch undid me. Her touch remained the most powerful force I knew.

Darling, of course.

She pulled me into an embrace, her arms looping all the way around me, the wanted poster disappearing between our bodies. I had more to say, but my words floated away and a drowsiness dropped over me. I wanted to fall asleep right there against her. I closed my eyes and the musk of her perfume enveloped me, soothed me, overtook all bad feelings.

First, she murmured, let's get away from here. Let's go on a trip. Just us.

We bundled off, nine days later. Sylvia arranged a bunnysitter for Simone. I left a note for my cousins pinned to the futon.

Having revealed her secret about the former student, Sylvia seemed looser, lighter. As we stood on the deck of a ferry churning away from the mainland, she gripped the railing with sailorly élan, her scarves aflutter.

A two-week vacation, she declared. I don't think I've ever taken so much time off.

She smiled—a knock-you-flat smile—and I tried to feel happy rather than nervous. Sylvia nibbled on chips she'd purchased from the ferry snack bar. She tossed one up to a hovering seagull. The bird caught it midair, which should have been funny, but I kept looking over my shoulder at the disappearing mainland.

Sylvia didn't know me; I didn't know her either, not really.

There on the ferry deck, she stood proud and windswept, watching me. She called out that she was so glad we were doing this.

Have you ever been out to any of these little islands? she said.

I've never been on a boat, I said.

Not even a rowboat? said Sylvia. Or a canoe?

Her curiosity startled me. When we'd had long conversations before, the subject matter was never personal. We'd only discussed Freeganism, or the content of her lectures, or Sim-one, or different types of tea. Our histories we'd left untouched.

Not even a little paddleboat with your family? said Sylvia.

My real answer rose in my throat like bile: growing up, my parents did not trust boats—they considered them dangerous, susceptible to storms, sinking, pirate abductions, murders. *Easiest way to hide a homicide*, my father had said. *Dumping a body in the ocean. Government does it all the time. Do you think that many people fall out of their rowboats and drown? Lean too far over the sides of cruise ships? Do you really believe all those duck boats just "disappeared"?* Boats, to my parents, had been one among an infinite number of potential threats.

How to explain this to Sylvia?

In a sickly lurch of perspective, I realized that I had felt so known by her—so recognized—because she was seeing me as someone else: her former student. That girl had been a ris-ing academic star, born to a normal family in suburban Con-necticut; I came from an embarrassing mess of a family who'd hidden themselves in the New Hampshire woods. The more Sylvia knew about me, the more her interest might fade as the distance grew between me and my uncanny archetype.

I shuddered at this—that my past might drive Sylvia away—a new nervousness born inside me as the ferry churned farther from the mainland.

So you must have grown up somewhere landlocked? said Sylvia.

I grew up in the circus, I said.

I'd hoped she'd laugh and we would move on, but she waited for a real answer. She was trying hard to be patient. My stomach roiled; I announced a seasickness that warranted going inside the ferry's cabin.

Sylvia's questions, though, followed me onto Martha's Vineyard. They were lodged in the diesel fumes of the harbor, in the sunburned tourists swarming the shoreline, and the reek of fried fish that staggered around corners from seafood restaurants. The questions curled along the island's cliffside roads, lurked in the cotton-candy blue hydrangeas encircling the borrowed cottage—which wasn't a cottage at all, but a mansion dressed in salt-weathered shingles, a breezy wraparound porch skirting its base. The questions sunned down from the sky. They rose up in the damp mist of coastal mornings, while Sylvia and I sat on the porch clutching hot cups of tea.

Do you have a favorite place? she said.

When I shook my head, she added that the Vineyard made her nostalgic for the English seaside.

And I never miss home, she added, except when I eat American chocolate.

She took another sip of her tea. She asked what I missed from my childhood.

Why would I miss something, I said, when I have all of this?

I leaned over to kiss my way out of further interrogations, but Sylvia tilted out of reach. Time had slowed on the island. While in Boston there'd been a frenetic forward urgency, on Martha's Vineyard, minutes lasted longer. Days moved in slow motion. We seemed to be outside of time; no bad news or grim world events could reach us.

I couldn't escape Sylvia's questions. She treated me like a geode—like she believed something glittering waited inside me, if only she could find the right place to strike.

Tell me, she said. What do you miss?

I miss five minutes ago, I said. I miss tomorrow. I miss now.

I began to talk about the weather, if only to fill the air. It did not occur to me to ask Sylvia about herself and swing the conversation the other way. I saw no need for the facts of our pasts to flood the space between us. Knowing about Sylvia's romance with a former student only clouded the present. And I wanted to think about the present, or, better yet, a future where Sylvia and I worked together to save the Freegans. I wanted Sylvia as I'd first known her—as the woman-in-black, who'd rescued me through sheer impulsive bravado.

Perhaps I also recognized, on some level, that knowing too much about a person's past would only lead to pain.

To reach the geode center of someone, you have to break them first.

The island was so lovely, though, when it was lovely. Sylvia and I watched vivid pink sunsets. We made love in the mansion's many rooms, surrounded by nautical décor: old rigging, buoys and barometers, dead eyes and glass bulbs. We wandered among shops where Sylvia bought seafoam-scented soaps. We swam in the cold kelpy Atlantic, bobbing over waves as ferries belched back and forth from the mainland.

We even rode the old island carousel, its lacquered wooden horses rising up and down, both of us laughing as a brass ring whizzed past.

We were only supposed to stay for two weeks, but Sylvia's friend called to say her family had decided to go to Nantucket instead that summer. The mansion remained ours to inhabit. Two weeks stretched into three.

You know, I said one afternoon. I should probably make a few phone calls.

Sun-drunk, stretched out on a blanket spread on the sand, I rolled over to Sylvia, who sat upright, wearing large sunglasses and paging through a sociology journal as if it were a fashion magazine. An outdoor orchestra played through a thicket of picnickers.

I should probably call my boss, I went on.

Sylvia snapped her text shut, said: Did you not request time off?

I laughed and said I hadn't—my boss wouldn't have given it anyway—and when Sylvia didn't reply, I added that maybe I ought to call my cousins as well, since I hadn't been home in a while.

What's it like to live with your cousins?

I went quiet. Sylvia, trying to coax forth more information, talked about her own cousins; she had lots back in the UK. Compared to siblings, she mused, cousins were a hybrid of the known and the unknown. She appreciated their accessible mystery.

Do you get along with yours? Which side of the family are they from?

I shrugged and started getting to my feet as if I'd suddenly decided to swim. I did not want Sylvia to know about my cousins. To discuss my cousins, my reason for living with them, seemed too close to an explanation of my parents. The way they'd lived—then died—lay in wait like a swampy nauseous fog, poised to poison Sylvia's sense of me.

See you in a bit, I said—wobbling as I stood up.

Sylvia's fingers encircled my ankle.

Stay, she said softly.

I sat down. Around us, kids darted from beach towels to the water's edge. Sylvia began to narrate her own childhood. She paused periodically for me to echo back my own life. When I didn't, she continued. I wanted to run away from the story, even as it engrossed me, because the more she said, the more unbalanced our personal histories became.

She had grown up in London, she told me, the daughter of an immigrant textile manufacturer and a self-styled Christian communist. She was a middle child in a gaggle of siblings. They'd all shared a two-bedroom flat in the southwest part of the city.

In school, she said, I wore a uniform that included a pleated plaid skirt, a white blouse, and a navy-blue sweater with a patch in the shape of a shield. Early on, the teachers assumed I had a developmental issue because of my shyness and a minor speech impediment, as well as my poor handwriting—which ranged large and illegible over pages—and so I was nearly eleven before anyone discovered I could not only read and do maths, but that I could do those subjects extraordinarily well. Sometimes I wonder if I could do those subjects so well *because* I'd been placed with the special needs children in a room with dull scissors and pipe cleaners and empty time. My mind was hungry to move in those years. I did algebra problems in my head. I read the encyclopedia page by page—a habit the teachers mistook for play-acted compulsion—and then I read books after school as well, because I'd been so bored all day. My placement wasn't helped, either, by the fact that my father was foreign-born. The teachers held that against me, though of course they never would have admitted to it.

Growing up, I knew on some level I was keeping a secret— that secrets were wrong. I did not aspire toward immorality. Yet I also knew I would lose something if I was found out. For the most part, students with special needs were treated kindly, not made to repeat grammar, sit for hours, and navigate the cliques and bullies of secondary school.

Eventually one of the teachers—or she may have been a parent volunteer—stumbled upon my secret. I'd been reading medieval poetry at home. My mother had an eclectic selection of books around the house, and several passages had gotten lodged in my head. Among them was a poem called "The Land of Cockaigne." I'd read it over and over at home, while my siblings garbled and giggled around me, hitting our toy xylophone or creating forts out of sofa cushions. The rhyming in the poem delighted me, as did the imagery. At school, on a piece of construction paper, I scrawled out the beginning of the poem to consider its meaning more deeply. *Out beyond the west of Spain,* it starts, *lies a land they call Cockaigne. No place on Earth compares to this, for sheer delightfulness and bliss.* At eleven, my handwriting was better, though persistently oversized and backward-leaning—as if windblown—in a manner an analyst would later characterize as a sign of selfishness and imminent carpal tunnel. In any case, the teaching aide saw this fragment of poem and asked me about it. At the time, she seemed to me a harmless woman—soft-bodied, soft-spoken, a lover of fuzzy wool sweaters—and I trusted her enough to recite the whole poem from memory. But the teaching aide did not give me the sweet, sheepish look of approval she gave the other children. She balked. It was the first time I recognized the effect one's intelligence can have on other people. People see it as dangerous, especially when it comes from a source they do not expect.

Anyway, a gauntlet of adults ruminated over whether I exhibited latent signs of Asperger's or early signs of schizophrenia. Their various theories were conveyed to my parents in a solemn meeting. My parents, distracted by my other siblings until that point—my eldest brother had issues with the law—laughed when presented with this information.

All Sylvia does is read, my mother replied. *There's nothing wrong with her. She's just shy.*

I was promptly deposited in the school's regular classes, my seat sticky with residual chewing gum, my presence met with the bovine curiosity of my classmates. I knew right away that I'd made a terrible mistake by exposing my capabilities. I much preferred the freedom to read and think as I pleased. But there was nothing to be done except make the best of the situation. I finished secondary school with a pristine record and went on to Oxford. Later I had the idea to go to Stanford, though California ultimately did not suit me. And now I'm here.

Sylvia paused her story and turned to me.

Yes, I said. You're a famous sociologist.

A weight settled on Sylvia, and her limbs flattened against her beach towel. I had likely reminded her of all the work she had not done—work she was putting off by being with me—or else it was the fact that I had not answered with my own story.

I mean, I said, you're my favorite sociologist.

Like many people, she said. I wanted to be something else first.

What?

Sylvia gave me a look of reproach, as if I'd missed a crucial aspect of her lecture.

A poet, she said—and her face became mournful, before cracking into a sharp birdlike laugh—I was obsessed with the notion of a poem as a kind of social grenade: a tightly packed ball of emotion and human experience tossed into the populace. It's arrogant and melodramatic to say that now. It's much more efficient to study real grenades and real social conflict. People say I got lucky with my doctoral research. I was way out ahead of everyone in my fieldwork on the Occupy movement. But from a sociological perspective, it was not luck at all. It was context. Social physics.

I don't think it's silly, I said. About the poetry.

Sylvia crinkled her eyes in a gesture of mature affection. The orchestra had finished playing. Everyone was clapping.

Later, Sylvia told me her father was retired and bored in Leeds, that her mother had dementia and lived in a care facility. Her siblings had scattered everywhere, though only one also lived in the States: her eldest brother, the one who'd once had trouble with the law. Now he was an orthopedic surgeon who worked at a hospital in Milwaukee.

You'll have to meet him sometime, Sylvia said. You'd like Thomas. He collects vintage bicycles and rides them in parades.

She paused as she always did for me to share details from my own history and when I didn't—because I never did—she sighed deeper than usual. When she spoke, her voice was calm but firm; she was trying her best to be gentle.

The mystique was charming at first, she said. But it's become frustrating, Willa.

We were on the porch, in the cottage-mansion. We were ensconced in big wicker chairs, sunk in soft cushions. We were in the part of a summer afternoon that seems end-less, too hot to move, when you start to believe the day, the earth, is stuck in place. Insects trilled a single long note. Sylvia was smoking one of the aromatic cigarettes she'd found stashed in a kitchen cupboard. She wore a gingham dress, indigo-dyed—the airy cotton unusual for her—she'd bought it in a shop on a whim. It was like a costume. We were pretending, the pair of us. She wasn't her and I wasn't me. Maybe, I thought, we would remain suspended like this: forever not quite ourselves. So while I felt the impulse to deflect Sylvia's request—to joke about having grown up in witness protection or with wolves—I instead asked, slowly—my words dripping out, sunlight a truth serum—if she had ever thought about the end of the world.

What if, I said, you had hypothetically spent your whole life trying to outrun a despair you learned as a little girl? A bad feeling that ran so deep it threatened to split you open? A feeling that there was nothing a person could do with her life except wait for the world's end, that the only proactive act was to meet that end earlier?

I closed my eyes. Amid the heavy heat and the sluggish buzz of crickets and the slow drag of the tides and the late-day light winking on the moisture beading our cups of iced tea, I told her. I told Sylvia about my parents' doomsday prophecies and the survival bunker and my terrariums. I told her about their overdose and my move to Boston and taking photos with my cousins. I told her about how, at the congressman's party, she—Sylvia—had saved me. She had made me believe that I was worth saving, that a person could be brave instead of fearful. Brave was a way to be. You could help people for no reason except that it was right.

I told Sylvia that I loved her.

She leaned forward in her wicker chair, the fibers crunching against one another. She exhaled a long breath of tobacco. The smoke hovered and swirled.

I love you too, Willa.

POWER GRAB was too delicate a phrase, for the Lords Proprietors had a *power grip*. The men wore wigs of flowing curls, strutted palace halls in silken justacorps, their pointy shoes flouncing with ribbons. They were flatulent from cream puffs, intoxicated on sparkling wine and their new elevated stations; they were powdered and empowered, appointed and anointed. The winds of rebellion foiled: *God Save the King*. Only two Lords had glimpsed the New World, but all eight controlled massive tracts of land. The Carolinas concerned them the most, though the Bahamas had potential.

Tobacco, said one.

Indigo, said a second.

Cotton, said a third, kept in production by thousands of hands on plots designated by our king and taxed on a scheduled basis.

The Lords Proprietors signed decrees, their feather quills twitching like a flock of tiny peacocks. They etched lines across maps, caging up the continent, neo-feudal fantasies thumping in their hearts. Beside them, on a table made of mahogany—the wood polished and demure—a bowl offered up the latest colonial sensation: spiky and strange, a "pineapple," people called it. The Lords Proprietors had not yet tried the fruit—the flesh yet too valuable for their bloating bellies—but they hovered their noses near: the aroma growing sweeter as it rotted.

Baron, Viscount, Earl, Marquess, Duke—the notes of aristocracy tolled constant in their minds. If only the Bahamas could be made to sit up straight and behave. If only the settlers would take up farming or fishing or saw-milling their forests—or at least speak politely to their assigned administrators. Those reckless fools. Those feckless scoundrels. They were unwilling to desist their harassment of Spanish ships, tempting the fury of a war they were not prepared to fight. Worse: they savaged shorelines for wolf-seals, as if Jamaican sugar mills did not need the oil. They burned braziletto, mahogany, pine, as if the trees hadn't market value.

And, oh God, the turtles. They killed the creatures constantly; there were hardly any left for crafting the little combs the Lords used to groom their wigs.

There would be a turtle tax. The settlers would have their shallops monitored for secreted doubloons and ambergris scavenged from the islands' capricious beaches. Tithes collected, the crown respected, democracy would be stamped out—a pestilence—or else made merely a pageant to keep the more outspoken settlers subdued.

Parchment shuffled, feathered quills twitched. Empire was built on order—or perhaps an ordering: whose life was worth the most, whose life could be expended; who could own and who was owned, who had a right to profit from his labor. A turtle wasn't only an ungainly reptile, but a resource to be roll-called. The islands could yet turn profitable if one knew how to wring them for every shilling.

Baron. Viscount. Earl. Marquess. Duke.

The Lords Proprietors daydreamed their titles rising—normalizing—bestowed on sons, and sons of sons, their names surfacing like wheat from chaff in history's brutal thrashings.

7

Wind smashed the side of the biodiesel van, the invisible punch rippling onward across Eleutheria. I steadied the steering wheel, called over my shoulder to the twelve recruits sitting snugly in the back: Almost there—are you ready?

The recruits ignored me, their attention fixed on the seaside vistas blurring beyond the van. Over a month had passed since the trip to the cave—a trip deemed a success by the other crewmembers—and since then, the recruits and I had explored more around Camp Hope. This trip, though, took us the farthest they'd ever been from the compound. And this time we had an objective beyond exploration.

We were on our way to rescue a sea turtle.

Do you remember what to do? I said. We have to move fast.

The recruits murmured in affirmation, leaned closer to the windows as we slowed to drive through a settlement. On one side of the road, locals filed into a steepled church for a service, though the windows were boarded up. Against the wind, the women held tight to their hats. Men's ties snaked out from their necks.

Fitz's voice buzzed forward from the back seat like a biting fly: Will it rain? We don't have any rain gear with us.

I met twelve sets of eyes in the van mirror. The recruits were rangier than they had been when they arrived, their bodies burnished by salt and sun. They had developed hard little biceps, like stone dinner rolls, and calves that could propel them through ocean currents. A month in and they had swallowed Camp Hope lingo like a series of pills—"photovoltaics," "anthropogenic emissions," "Hadley cell circulation," "sediment starvation," "Bazhenov shale," "solastalgia"—and could recite from memory the passages from *Living the Solution* that crewmembers read to them like bedtime stories. They did their chores and their training sessions, ate their protein loaf with minimal complaint. They had, by almost all respects, been integrated into Camp Hope's systemology. Most crewmembers believed the recruits were ready for the launch—that we were all ready. And anyway, how much longer could we wait? How many species disappeared every day? How many antelope, starfish, starlings, coyotes, dragonflies lay down and died for every second Camp Hope spent in its purgatory of anonymity?

How many people?

Yet Roy Adams refrained from setting a launch date. In the rallies he held weekly—often at night, palm-leaf torches burning in the dark—he'd declare: We can't be ninety-nine percent ready. We need one-hundred percent functionality. We need one-hundred-and-ten percent commitment. We need one-thousand percent belief. And you know what? We're going to get it. We're going to show people a reality beyond their wildest dreams. When we launch, we're going to rock the goddamn world.

I believed him. We all did. There seemed no reason not to, when Adams lived up to his hype. During the day, he strode through the grounds on tree-trunk thighs, his shark-tooth necklace swinging, his aviators glinting. When a wind turbine malfunctioned, he shimmied up the pole with a wrench in his teeth. To help the meteorologists recapture a lost weather balloon, he kite-surfed one-handed through turbulent waves.

He was an action hero come to life—an action hero with a tender respect for nature. Once during dinner, he'd thundered into the mess hall, red-faced with the news that a marine-waste influx had surged onto one of Camp Hope's beaches. He carried a piece of debris over his shoulders: a storm-tossed carousel horse, legs frozen in a prance. To the startled crewmembers and recruits, he said: Looks like a whole seaside resort strewn in the sand in sector four. Probably a storm-surge casualty. Debris must've washed south. We'll need a cleanup squad to hit the beach stat, and do a maintenance check on that SeaVac—

A gasp sounded. Crewmembers leaned closer to the carousel horse, which Adams had set down on a table. From a hole in the horse's belly, a milky-white limb appeared, followed by another, and then another. A tiny octopus oozed forth.

Would you look at that, said Adams, we've got an unexpected guest.

He held out his palm. The octopus wrapped one finger in a tentacle handshake.

If this isn't a sign, Adams said, I don't know what is. This right here is a miracle incarnate. This is proof we've got Mother Nature on our side. She's here with us and she wants us to win.

He held the octopus aloft for everyone in the mess hall to see. Crewmembers cheered, pounded their tables, and I cheered too, because I—like all the crewmembers—believed in Adams. Because Adams made us believe in us. Because if Adams wanted to get the recruits to 110 percent commitment, 1,000 percent belief, then I was going to help get them there for the launch—which is why we were going to rescue a sea turtle.

It would be a small eco-victory in the grand scheme of things. What was one saved turtle when thousands choked on plastic bags, got strangled by fishing lines and mowed down by motors? The mission, though, was more about the recruits' internal transformation than external impact; the recruits would recognize their own capacity for creating change.

To Fitz, to all of them in the van, I said: We'll deal with the rain when it rains. For now, remember your roles. Remember the steps we talked about.

I pulled the van onto a potholed side road. The vehicle bounced along until we reached a dirt clearing beside an ocean hole. This was a renowned site, I'd been told, but I found the pool of inland ocean unassuming. Rock-rimmed and wide as the base of a circus tent, the water mirrored the sky in a silver disk. A rusty ladder led down the side.

Move quickly, I said to the recruits. Get in position.

They filed out of the van. In the distance: run-down houses, the ragged edge of coppice. Most local people were at church. Only a lone stray dog—copper-bodied with white paws—observed us from beside a crooked palm tree.

Fitz glanced at his watch. The other recruits stared skyward, hair rippling around their faces. Nets and dive masks hung limp in their hands.

Let's go, I said. Get into formation.

Half the recruits stripped to the wet suits they'd worn under their uniforms. They looked good: like an environmental SWAT team. Led by Lillian, they climbed down the ladder into the ocean hole, pulling on their goggles before they plopped into the water.

The other half of the group circled the rim, their polo shirts fluttering in the breeze as they squinted at their fellow recruits.

Fitz rocked on his feet. The area around the ocean hole remained quiet. The stray dog had disappeared.

From the rim, I called: See anything?

The recruits reported three minnows, a shred of kelp, and a plastic milk jug. They did not see any turtles. The plan had been to return the endangered creatures to a stretch of conservation land owned by Camp Hope—a plan that seemed straightforward enough. Adams had assured me there'd be at least one turtle trapped in the ocean hole, maybe more.

Ripe for rescuing, he'd said. *That'll get the recruits' blood pumping. Make them feel useful. If I learned one thing in the military, it's that a guy will do just about anything to be a hero, once he gets a taste of how good it feels.*

Fitz peered at the gathering clouds, at the palm fronds and elephant ear plants harassed by wind. The coast was not in view—there was no way to see the ocean kicked up, waves thrashing—though on an island like Eleutheria, you could always sense the nearness of an edge.

Make 'em feel like heroes, Adams had said. *You can do that, right, Marks? I can count on you?*

Keep looking, I called to the recruits. Don't give up.

Down in the ocean hole, Lillian treaded water, no turtle in

sight. She was likely getting cold, as were the others. On the rim, Fitz whispered mutinously with another boy.

Five more minutes, I said.

The recruits no longer looked like a sun-kissed environmental SWAT team; they looked like a group of bored teenagers. Clouds bulged, the wind intensifying. Cameron complained about missing lunch: that day's menu included algae burgers and mycelium-carob cookies—a recruit favorite. A tree branch skittered across the dirt lot. A coconut thumped to the ground from a palm tree's bulbous clutches. The recruits in the ocean hole had drifted closer to the ladder, poised to leave. The recruits on the rim bunched up as well.

Thatcher pulled his hands out of his pockets and pointed to the water, yelled: Look.

A tiny head periscoped the surface of the ocean hole.

The recruits stared for several seconds, then remembered what they were supposed to do. They swam into action: paddling into a circle around the turtle and drifting a net under its belly. The turtle, listless and sluggish, was easily captured. The recruits on the rim lowered a second net by ropes. Together, the two teams raised the turtle from the ocean hole, faces reddening as they made sure to keep the net from swinging against the rocky sides. Cameron trembled, her eyes shiny as beetle backs. Margaret bit her lip. Blair flared his nostrils. Geoffrey breathed in panting bursts. Even Fitz seemed intrigued.

The next steps happened quickly. Once the turtle was onshore, the recruits lifted it collectively as if conducting a séance, making the turtle appear light, though it must have weighed over one hundred pounds. They carried the turtle to the van, loaded her into a nest of blankets.

Let's name her Patty, said Lillian as she and the others inhaled the first fumes of success.

It's easy to imagine how the trip might have unfolded from there. In another reality, we drove straight to the conservation land, released the turtle, returned to Camp Hope. In that reality, the recruits later left the island and penned self-aggrandizing college application essays about their time rescuing wildlife—and went on with their lives.

Instead, as we pulled away from the ocean hole, a pickup truck rumbled toward us from the other direction. The truck belonged to Deron.

He and I paused, driver's-side window to driver's-side window. The wind hissed through the canyon between our vehicles. Deron rolled down his window and I rolled down mine. Deron quieted his radio. I told the recruits this would only take a minute.

Sorry I haven't been in touch, I yelled over the wind. Sorry I never made it to the hotel to meet you—

Deron draped an arm out the truck window, eyes half-closed as he studied me, the van of recruits, the purpling sky overhead.

—I did try and find you, I said. It's just that Adams came back. And things have been nonstop since then. But I was on my way to meet you, really.

Sure you were, said Deron. Sure, Willa.

The wind stilled, the landscape quieting. I lowered my voice, added: Also, I'm sorry for calling you in the middle of the night. It seemed like an emergency at the time.

Deron drummed his hand against the side of the truck, his head tilted as if listening to faraway music. A smile hovered on his lips. One of the recruits waved at me in the van mirror, pointed to her watch. I mouthed *just a minute.*

Willa, said Deron. You owe me a favor.

Anything, I said.

Anything?

Anything. Of course.

You need to put that turtle back.

Deron's faint smile persisted; I stammered that I didn't know what turtle he meant.

The one in your van, said Deron. From the ocean hole. The one you took.

The wind returned, rattling between our vehicles; the sky darkened, the air cotton-ball thick. I opened my mouth, closed it. I said I didn't know what he was talking about, but I knew sea turtles were critically endangered and that an ocean hole wasn't their proper habitat; in one they wouldn't survive.

Willaaaa, said Deron—nonchalant, even as the wind intensified—if you're so worried about survival, let me tell you something, because I know about survival. All of us on Eleutheria do. Because after the most recent hurricane, no one brought over any supplies. In the past, some countries sent food, water, medicine, but now we're on our own. We aren't responsible for creating these superstorms or the rising seas, but we have to bear them. After the recent hurricanes, the only supplies came from other Bahamians who came by boat from other islands. The only place to go was the other islands, or what was left of other islands, because we couldn't leave. Too much of a security risk. No room in America—sorry. No room in the UK either. Even for kids. Even for grandmothers and grandfathers. All we have is ourselves. All we have, Willa, is this island. And we have survived. We have hung on and rebuilt in our own way. If you don't want to help us, that's fine, but don't make everything harder. The hotel I tried to tell you about, it's locally built, locally owned, because we are trying to get back on our feet. And this turtle, she's for hotel guests—or future hotel guests. Because we need more activities. We don't have Jet Skis and we don't have shopping malls, but we can offer this place. This turtle is for tourists to visit. They can swim with a real, live sea turtle in a natural inland pool.

The first drops of rain plopped onto the van's windshield like small wet fists.

So let's drive over to the ocean hole now, said Deron. Let's put that turtle back before the weather gets ugly. Because it looks like it's going to get ugly.

Behind me, the recruits had turned to statues, stiff and straight in their seats. All those young minds, young bodies, needed for Camp Hope's launch—what choice did I have with their gazes fixed upon me, waiting to see what I would do?

I shook my head, told Deron I couldn't go back anywhere: I had somewhere to be.

Eleutheria had been a vacation hot spot not so long before—that is, before hurricane after hurricane ripped across its shores, smashing infrastructure and touristic interest. The island had attracted rock stars and honeymooning royalty, tennis icons and banking executives, the sailboat set and swimsuited families of four. These visitors descended on Eleutheria to enjoy its ocean views and palm frond cabanas. Beachside massages. Beachside reads. Breaded spiny lobster. Piña coladas made with pineapple picked just outside resort walls, the fruit lingering from plantation cultivars introduced decades before.

Eleutheria also attracted divers—that's what one of Camp Hope's marine biologists had told me. The island was famous in the diving world and even Jacques Cousteau had visited. Among other things, Cousteau wanted to find the bottom of Eleutheria's famous ocean hole. So he put on his diving gear, the best equipment of his day, and slipped down as deep as he could go. He and others tried. They dove and dove but never found the bottom. They knew the ocean hole connected to the larger ocean somehow; tides made the water level rise and fall. There had to be a passageway linking that inland pool to something so much larger.

Isn't that interesting? the marine biologist had said. *There's a path to the ocean if only you could swim deep enough?*

To think there are ways of escaping our circumstances, if only we could swim deep enough. If only we could hold our breath long enough and dive.

To think we might not escape, even with doors as wide open as the ocean.

By the time the recruits and I arrived at the stretch of beachside conservation land to release the turtle, the sky was knotted with clouds, a gray-purple pall cast over the landscape. Rain splattered across the sand, heckled by wind. I didn't have to tell the recruits to hurry. They lifted the turtle from its nest of blankets and carried her toward the water. On the cusp of sand and foam, the recruits slid the turtle into the sea. It did not move. It seemed stunned, or else exhausted. The recruits urged the turtle forward. They walked out into the surf to stand alongside it.

Go, Patty, said Lillian. You're free.

Swim, said Thatcher.

Another recruit called to give the turtle space. They all stepped back. Perhaps they'd had pets and considered themselves equipped with expertise in animal psychology. Space and quiet, these were important for an animal's well-being.

Surf struck the turtle. The wind picked up, thrashing the nearby casuarina trees, harassing sea grapes, our hair. The turtle remained motionless. She could have been a stone if we hadn't known what to see: her shell a dark spot, like a stain in the water. Larger waves crashed forward, foaming white. Clouds pressed close. Over the roar of the surf, the rush of wind and rain: the first peal of thunder. Thatcher shrieked. Margaret and Cameron cowered together. Fitz sprinted toward the van.

We aren't done, I called—but the others followed him, running with their arms over their heads as the rain gushed down in a sweeping curtain, soaking everyone in seconds. The rain worsened on the journey back to Camp Hope. The drive seemed submarine: windshield wipers frantically etching out a path. I was glad for the difficulty, though, because it meant the recruits couldn't ask questions about what had happened, what we'd done—and also because I couldn't ask myself.

In a storm, anything can become a projectile. A conch shell. A piece of driftwood. A tree. A microscope. A bicycle. A biodiesel pontoon. A bunkroom roof. Back at Camp Hope, crewmembers rushed around the grounds. They boarded up windows, strapped down solar panels. They yelled to one another through rain pelting down in dense sheets. Or, in the case of one meteorologist, complained miserably that she'd been saying this all along—the storm would strike us straight on.

The sea raged. Palm trunks bent back like slingshots. Lightning shattered the sky. The wheel of an upturned wheelbarrow spun uselessly in the air, as if trying to escape with the foliage whipping across the grounds. Crewmembers' shouts tangled, blew away. The recruits tripped into one another, knocked sideways. Then they were scrambling—we were all scrambling—toward the storage barn: its second floor turned into a makeshift shelter. We ran with the tops of our heads pushed forward against the wind, stretching our arms toward the barn doorway, grasping for a handhold, for what we hoped would keep us safe.

Time distorts in a storm. The plywood on the storage barn's windows blocked out any view of Eleutheria—not that a view would have helped: daylight had disappeared. The universe shrank to seventy crewmembers and twelve recruits. Most people slept during the first day. The shelter had been hastily stocked with blankets, cots, and the almost-soft corners of sacks of rice. Everyone discovered a bone-deep exhaustion. Everyone submitted to the big emptiness of waiting. Everyone except me.

I needed to talk to Adams about the turtle mission. I needed to ask if what I'd done was right. Adams, though, had not taken shelter in the storage barn. In fact, no one could remember seeing him all day. Everyone had been caught up in storm preparations.

When I suggested sending out a search party, however, the other crewmembers dismissed the idea.

He's probably holed up in the Command Center, said a bio-diesel specialist.

And it's not safe to look for him, anyway, added a mycologist. Not in this weather. That's against protocol.

He's always fine, said a solar technician. He's Roy Adams.

A clap of thunder shuddered the storage barn, as loud as the earth splitting open: tectonic plates shifting, old gods upset. Most crewmembers and recruits kept sleeping. They lay strewn across the storage barn floor like licks of seaweed, flotsam. Jachi sat cross-legged in a dim corner, her eyes closed, her face serene as she meditated. I tried to sit with her for a while, but I became claustrophobic with my own thoughts.

The same marine biologist who'd told me about the ocean hole also described how the ocean keeps a record of all our actions. The water, he told me, absorbs the heat of human industry and holds it in a vast liquid memory. The intense storms we experience now are manifestations of decisions made decades before. And the storms of the future—ever more violent, ever more devastating—will be this present resurging as the past.

Isn't that interesting? he'd said. *The ocean never forgets.*

By the second day, with the constant grinding assault of rain and the thump of projectiles striking our shelter, everyone became restless.

To pass the time, the ecologists—who had long ago developed skills for emotional resiliency—started telling jokes.

Hey Gertie, said one. What did one hurricane say to the other hurricane?

Gertie, a meteorologist, did not respond.

I've got my eye on you!

Another ecologist attempted a comedic monologue about sand dunes, until one of the geologists made a neck-cutting motion with her finger.

The recruits began to ask questions: How long would the storm last? Would we run out of water and unripe bananas and cold oatmeal and bean-based energy nougats? Would an ocean swell reach the second floor of the storage barn? Would saltwater contaminate the cisterns? Would the laboratories be ruined, along with all the crewmembers' research? Would everyone be sent home? How would they get home if the roads and the airport were destroyed? Would Roy Adams send in a rescue team? Where was Roy Adams? Why wasn't he with us? Was he on-island? Was he off-island? Was he lost? Was he injured? Was he dead? Would he be able to write their letters of recommendations? Could someone forge his signature? How would Camp Hope's failure impact their college applications? Their personal livelihoods? The inevitability of their future success?

Still the storm pounded the shelter. The huge swath of unscheduled time—the nothingness of our togetherness—made the air murky, made people anxious and exhausted. My head felt like a balloon on a string. It wasn't until the second day that anyone noticed Lorenzo was missing as well. Or else, we noticed how Lorenzo had served as a buffer between us and reality, when Adams was last absent. Without Lorenzo, nothing protected us from truths we preferred not to inhabit.

I understood better, then, why Lorenzo had organized the

crewmember party: the necessity of distraction, the preservation of morale, the need to do *something*. At a certain point, human beings require more than ideals to keep going.

There could be no parties in the storage barn. We barely had sufficient supplies to stay fed. In her dim corner, Jachi meditated with more forceful intensity. The Liberal Arts Girls bickered over three sheets of construction paper as they tried to devise an educational activity—eventually settling on climate trivia—which they hustled the recruits into groups to play.

Q: *What was the increase in category 5 tropical storms over the past three years?*
A: *25 percent.*

Q: *Which country experienced an unprecedented 15 consecutive days above 110 degrees?*
A: *France.*

Q: *How many inches is the sea expected to rise over the next decade?*
A: *5.*

A: *No, it's 11.*

A: *Excuse me? 5.*

A: *11.*

A: *I looked this up last week and it's 28.*

*Q: Moving on: How many Mass Mortality Events have
occurred so far this year?*
Q: Anyone?
Q: Anyone?
Q: Where are you all going? We're not finished—

Some crewmembers did jumping jacks and push-ups,
gnawed on protein sticks. Some stared at the dark squares
where windows would have been, if the windows hadn't been
boarded up. Scientists split into discipline-centric cliques—
analyzing, hypothesizing in a language of numbers and ratios
and precedents—ever struggling with absolutes, grasping for
verifiable evidence.

The recruits chewed their nails, their hair, bad habits
emerging through the veneer of good breeding.

I paced. It was easy to imagine a swollen ocean submerging
our shelter, washing us away. In *Living the Solution*, Adams
described the necessity of encountering danger—of facing the
screaming pressure of climate change head on—and yet here
we were, facing that danger, with no leader to lead us.

Fear is a slimy sensation; it oozes into your limbs like a
chilled eel. Our makeshift shelter began to resemble the survival bunker of my childhood. Except this time, there were no
terrariums into which I could pour my attention. This time, I
knew the shelter would not protect me from what waited outside. I'd leave and suffer from what I found. Because in that
storm shelter, on that island, I shuddered with the memory of
my family's cabin gone dark, my parents reaching rigor mor-
tis in the living room, their faces frozen in fear. I'd come to
Camp Hope because I'd believed Adams embodied my par-

ents' inverse: he was relentlessly optimistic, a pioneer of eco-actualization, a believer in futures beyond apocalypse.

Yet for all I knew, he was dead too.

A popping sound broke through the gush of rain. Several crewmembers sprang up, looking for a leak, a broken pipe, a problem. There was none. The sound came from Fitz, who crouched beside sacks of rice, his face specter-like in the candlelight. He had a finger in his mouth, which he dragged against the inside of his cheek until it burst spittle-slick from the side of his lips.

The other crewmembers shook their heads, said nothing. Fitz continued dragging the finger, his expression glassy-eyed and haughty.

Cut that out, I said.

Fitz plunged his finger into his mouth again, produced another pop.

I marched across the shelter, nearly stepping on the sprawled forms of crewmembers and recruits. Once in front of Fitz, I said: Stop. Making. That. Noise.

Fitz's eyes crawled toward me, red-rimmed and mirthless. He raised his hand to his mouth, his fleshy lips open, his finger poised threateningly.

You can't expect us to stay here, he said.

We're staying here.

I want to call my parents.

Don't we all.

Fitz hunched over, dry heaving. When I asked if he was sick, he bounced upright, as if spring-loaded. A clown grin stretched across his mouth. The pink tip of his tongue slimed his lower lip.

I'll sue you, he said. I'll sue you and everyone here—

Sit down, I said.

Fitz's breath grew jagged. In fragments, he ranted: This isn't fair—unacceptable—for us to keep—to be shitting in buckets—do you know how much my parents are paying—this stupid place—I want—you people are crazy—so pointless—a joke—

I grabbed Fitz's shirt collar. I hadn't consciously decided to do it; I wasn't trying to hurt him. The fabric bunched in my hands. I was only vaguely aware of Fitz's shriek, the alarm raised by crewmembers and recruits. In my head, I was trying to protect them from him, from his bad attitude. I was trying to protect myself. People must have asked what I was doing, but I couldn't hear them. I was in my own head. I was in my own head with Adams, because if Adams wasn't present, what could I do but conjure the passages from *Living the Solution* I'd memorized?

Self-pity is selfishness, I thought as I pulled Fitz by his collar to the door. *And selfishness is at the core of our environmental crisis*—

You want to leave? I said.

As soon as I unbolted the door, the wind flung it the rest of the way open. Water sprayed into the storage barn. I pushed Fitz onto the howling threshold: a dark wet chaos.

He was shaking his head, shaking his whole body. He squirmed away to get back inside. Tears burbled out of his eyes, while snot ran from his nose in long viscous threads.

It took the whole weight of my body to pull the door closed against the wind. The ensuing silence was stark, the air vacuum-sucked from the room. I was drenched, dripping a puddle on the floor, but my skin felt hot enough to steam the water away.

What's the matter, Fitz? I said. Did I hurt your feelings? Did I scare you? I did, didn't I? Well, you need to feel scared. Because it's just us and this storm, Fitz. No one is going to save you. Your parents aren't going to come here and save you. You can't just keep feeling sorry for yourself. You can't cry for your parents because they're not coming, Fitz. They can't help you.

I wiped the water blurring my vision: stormwater, saltwater, tear water. The other crewmembers had gotten to their feet. The recruits huddled together.

None of your parents are coming, I said to all the recruits. Because your parents are the problem. Your parents have abandoned you. They've abandoned all of us. They're bad people and they've let everyone down. They're going to keep letting us down. They are robber barons and hyperconsumers and emissions mercenaries. They are liars. They are the reason so many people on this planet are suffering. And you are too. You are the problem. Because this is your legacy. This storm: it's your inheritance.

I said other things, of which I'm sure multiple people have gone on the record about by now. That speech is likely considered a turning point—given what happened with the recruits later on—but I want to clarify that for those twelve young people, I was merely one small piece of a much larger story.

The Liberal Arts Girls crept around Fitz, all holding out flat palms, as if to prove they had no weapons. Fitz wept. Other recruits started to cry as well; Lillian was red-nosed and bawling. Margaret pressed her face into Thatcher's shoulder. The Liberal Arts Girls jerked Fitz into the center of their protec-

tive triangle. Dorothy muttered about professional conduct
and boundary crossing. I snorted in response: as if boundaries
meant anything now?

The other crewmembers wouldn't look at me.

In the corner of the storage barn, Jachi continued meditat-
ing, her face serene.

After three days in the storage barn, everyone woke to the
shushing sprinkle of unremarkable rain, the first chirps of
birds, and, finally, a pounding and a metallic screech. Roy
Adams knocked the plywood off the storage barn windows,
hollered *rise and shine* as he blinded us with dewy brightness.

Adams grinned, big-toothed and broad-shouldered as ever.
He was fresh and clean, his polo shirt unwrinkled. A sunbeam
pulsed his face.

Everyone accounted for? he boomed. Everyone here?

Crewmembers staggered onto the balcony, squinting in the
brightness.

What's the matter? said Adams. Tree branch hit you all on
the head? Let's move!

No one moved. An agronomist asked where he'd been.

I'll explain later, said Adams. Right now, we've got work
to do. Hop to. Cleanup time. Because I've got capital-N news.
The launch is official. August fifteenth. Five weeks from now,
we light up the goddamn world.

He waited for a cheer.

He received murmured consternation. A permaculturalist
asked if he was joking. Beyond the storage barn's balcony, the
Camp Hope grounds were battered and confused. Seaweed
lay strewn across pathways. Trees were snapped. Windows

smashed. Gardens mangled. Hydroponic beans flung far and wide.

Fixing this place up will take months, said an engineer. Maybe longer.

Adams bared his teeth, said: What happened to you all in there? Catch a little cabin fever? What you're seeing is our best opportunity yet. This is a chance to show our resilience. Show what we're made of. Come on, where's your fighting spirit?

Crewmembers—wan and reeking and exhausted—shifted uncomfortably. Their gazes goaded me like knifepoints. They believed I'd damaged the recruits beyond repair; that even if the storm hadn't trashed the grounds, the whole enterprise was ruined.

It was true, after the incident with Fitz, the recruits gathered together and barricaded themselves behind sacks of rice—Fitz at the center. It was true they'd refused to speak to anyone. The crewmembers believed the recruits would demand to be sent home, and, once home, they would speak ill of Camp Hope—destroy public perception before we had a chance to make our case.

The Liberal Arts Girls fake-coughed into their shoulders, one after the next, deciding who would speak first.

There was an incident, said Corrine.

A highly problematic incident, added Dorothy. Between a recruit and a crewmember.

It was Marks, said Eisa—unable to hold back. And for the record, the three of us had nothing to do with her actions this time. We did not sanction her behavior and are wholly opposed to her faulty decision-making.

Adams folded his arms across his chest. The usual flintiness in his eyes dimmed.

This true, Marks?

I wanted to scream. I wanted to tear my hair and say that I'd needed Adams and he hadn't been there; I'd only done what seemed right; I'd done what *Living the Solution* advised.

A botanist ran out of the storage barn, yelling: Has anyone seen the recruits? Did they go out a back entrance? I can't find them—

Probably already hitchhiking to the airport, said a member of the Agro Team.

In a growling voice, Adams said: Marks, you better get explaining.

Lorenzo inserted himself between us, clipboard tucked under one skinny arm. Where Lorenzo had come from was unclear. He looked skinnier and more disheveled than before the storm. With his free hand, he gestured over the balcony railing, said: She didn't do anything wrong.

'Renzo, not now, said Adams.

Marks always puts the mission first, Lorenzo insisted.

Adams reddened, his biceps bulging—but several crew-members leaned up against the railing, shading their eyes to look where Lorenzo had pointed.

The hell? said an ecologist.

The recruits had scattered around the Camp Hope grounds; like a flock of sky-flung birds, they'd burst into action. They dashed from cleaning supply closet to hydrology lab to bunk-room to mess hall. They had sponges in hand, wheelbarrows, rags.

They've gone mad, said an aquaponics specialist.

They're doing what they should do, said Lorenzo. They're getting the cleanup started. If Marks did something to the recruits, she did something right.

Did something right, repeated Adams, testing the concept, the redness draining from his face. She sure did. Look at this. This is commitment. This is what we want. Let's hear it for Marks.

Jachi—who'd just emerged from her meditation—fluttered her palms into a clap. A smattering of crewmember applause followed. The Liberal Arts Girls stared at me, stunned.

Adams thumped my back, boomed: Time to lend our recruits a hand. Let's move.

Crewmembers hesitated, but only briefly. They hurried down the balcony stairs, spreading out across the grounds to get supplies of their own. It was then that Lorenzo approached me, his cheeks as round and loyal as the moon. He asked if he'd done a good job; if he'd helped me in the way I had once helped him.

Yeah, thanks—

I was distracted by my efforts to spot Fitz among the other recruits. It didn't take long: he sprinted across the grounds, towels in hand, his tongue lolling, his pale face pinked by exertion. He dropped supplies in the arms of other recruits. He dashed back for more.

And so, we had an official launch date. A leader. We had a band of youths fired up to save the world. Despite the hurricane damage, Camp Hope began to resemble its former self in the weeks following the hurricane, progress occurring faster than one might have anticipated upon first beholding the wreckage. Crewmembers and recruits worked in shifts to haul debris and repair broken windows and replant vegetation. Everyone talked about resilience; about cooperative recuperation in the face of climate challenges; about how Camp Hope's speedy recovery proved we had what it took.

In his speeches to crewmembers, Adams said things like: Now, I didn't want to tell you *I told you so,* but I damn well told you challenges would only make us stronger.

When pressed about his absence during the storm, he laughed.

You should all know, he said—tapping his forehead—that I was here with you, mentally, the whole time. Problem was that when the storm hit, I got stranded down island where I'd been scouting more conservation land to buy. I couldn't get back, couldn't get that information through to you all because Lorenzo was holed up in the Command Center.

Crewmembers accepted this story. I accepted it. Optimism abounded, especially with the recruits having become genuinely inspiring. Their whole demeanor had shifted, their posture, their speech. They chatted with me during meals as if nothing had happened during the storm. Like everything was going to work out as planned. Before meals even officially ended, they leapt up to do volunteer dish duty, compost brigade. Lillian no longer wore pearl earrings—she'd thrown them into the sea. Cameron had cut off her long, shiny ponytail—it got in the way during DBCS, she explained. And Fitz stayed up reading and rereading *Living the Solution* late into the night.

Adams's reasoning for including recruits made more and more sense: the vigor and earnestness of youth were awe-inspiring. Their commitment to change was different from that of adults. It was purer, more intimately tied to the future.

These kids are going to look great on camera, said a biologist during lunch. And the subsequent surge of media attention—a blitzkrieg of feel-good stories—will fast-track Camp Hope's recognition on a global scale.

Mind bombs, said a nutritionist. That's what Greenpeace called their photos of bloody Russian whaling ships. And those images exploded in the public consciousness. They literally blew up.

Right, replied a soil specialist. But Greenpeace didn't have the organizational savvy to harness that attention and make substantive structural change.

When Camp Hope explodes, said the biologist, we'll be ready to use that energy, catapult forward. We'll actually have a strategic follow-through.

We don't have any whales, I said. I mean, no bloody ones.

The biologist winked and said: We may have something better.

Was there, in fact, something a little off about the recruits? No crewmembers would have admitted so, but the recruits' gazes did go unfocused at times. They were sleeping fewer hours. When not otherwise engaged, they whispered to one another in hushed, fervent voices. For all their diligence and enthusiasm around Camp Hope, they also seemed possessed by a parallel dimension from which crewmembers were excluded.

Nothing, certainly, was said to the recruits' parents, who contacted Roy Adams in the wake of the storm. The Liberal Arts Girls were temporarily installed in the Command Center to field the inquiries: a role they relished.

Was your child in danger? I overheard Corrine say. Absolutely!

That's what makes this whole experience so valuable, said Dorothy. Imagine this tropical storm anecdote in a college admissions essay.

Eisa: It's application gold.

I overheard these conversations while lurking around the Command Center, trying to catch a word with Adams. I still wanted to ask about the turtle mission—to get Adams's confirmation that I'd made the right choice in my encounter with Deron. I carried my copy of *Living the Solution* around with me. The book felt important to have when Adams and I did talk. He might cite a passage I could return to later. Also, another question nagged me—a question I'd long avoided—relating to how I'd found the book, back in Boston. I wanted to understand the book's connection to Sylvia. If *Living the Solution* had not yet been distributed to the media—to anyone—why did she have a copy?

Asking this question, however, would have meant talking about Sylvia. And anyway, Adams was heroically busy: carrying whole trees on his back and lifting solar panels onto roofs. During meals, admirers engulfed him. When he did see me around Camp Hope, he gave me a thumbs up or a hearty shoulder thump. He even distributed fatherly pieces of advice. Once, during dinner, he leaned in to tell me to add more protein loaf to my plate—to keep muscle mass up. I never wanted to shift the mood of those moments. It felt so good to be noticed by him, to have my contributions celebrated. In my wildest fantasies, Adams was more than a parental figure—he outright adopted me. The other crewmembers, meanwhile, had started treating me like a full-fledged comrade-in-arms. The marine biologists took me out on their boat for a shark-tagging mission. The solar team invited me to sunbathe on a roof with them during our mandated forty-five minutes of R & R. My concerns about the turtle mission and Deron, about *Living the Solution* and Sylvia, seemed small enough to push to the side, again and again, until there was no need to ask about Deron because Deron appeared at Camp Hope, along with a dozen other locals, two weeks before the launch.

They parked their vehicles outside the bougainvillea wall and called out that they wanted to talk.

Adams went to meet them—Lorenzo trailing with his clipboard. They all spent fifteen minutes out of view behind a parked pickup truck. When Adams returned, he was red-faced. Veins rose ropily in his arms. As he explained, the locals had presented a dossier of legal material essentially amounting to a cease and desist order. They wanted Camp Hope's current occupants to leave the compound, as well as Eleutheria. Any remaining property would be turned over to local island governance.

It's just a big hoo-ha for show, said Adams. No real legal backing. All scare tactics.

But why? said an entomologist. Why are they bringing this up now?

Adams reddened more as he replied: They're questioning Camp Hope's right to operate on Bahamian soil—as if there could be any other industry here. I've actually spent time at the second-rate motel they call the "new resort." It's half-built, stuck on the edge of a lagoon. Didn't look like business was going too well. Why would it? My guess is they're looking to extort money. But you know what? I don't negotiate with extortionists—

While Adams continued with his defense, the Liberal Arts Girls whispered among themselves.

It's true, said Dorothy, Camp Hope is one-hundred percent colonialist.

I'd argue eight-five percent, said Corrine.

Doesn't necessarily make it wrong, said Eisa. Given the larger scope.

I consider the operation a manifestation of post-postcolonialism, said Corrine.

Like post-postmodernism? said Dorothy.

That's not a thing, said Corrine.

If it's not a thing, asked Eisa, then technically none of us exist? And are therefore absolved?

Adams frowned at the Liberal Arts Girls, made his voice louder as he announced Camp Hope was moving full steam ahead no matter what.

I feel for the locals, said Adams. I really do. I'm sure the recent hurricane hit their communities hard, after a lot of other hard hits. So, you know what, we're going to send over a couple of crates of solar chargers and water filters and energy nougats. They're trying to get the island back on its feet and I respect that. But Camp Hope is trying to get this planet back on its feet. Camp Hope is here for everyone, not just one tiny island. The planet needs us. Think about the glaciers melting like ice sculptures in the Sahara. Think about the forests clear-cut just to make more goddamn toilet paper. Think about how many lives are lost every second to air pollution, water pollution, mind pollution. Think about the fact that this island will be underwater soon anyway, unless we act. We've got to get Camp Hope launched ASAP. I'm sending *Living the Solution* to our media contacts today. What do y'all think of that?

Crewmembers hooted, clapped in agreement. Adams kept his gaze steely. He lifted his palm upward while looking at me—as if he sensed my indecision, the squirreliness in my gut. I wondered if Deron had brought up the missing turtle.

A crewmember nudged me, said: Raise it up, Marks.

She meant *Living the Solution*, which was tucked under my arm. I lifted the book over my head. Crewmembers cheered louder and Adams bared his big white teeth, his shark smile confident as a hundred million years. He asked if we were ready to save the one and only planet we had. We were. He asked if we were ready to live the future we wanted. We were ready for that too. Adams kept talking, booming out his plan for moving forward, his huge voice stoppering the hollowness inside me—a crater left by my parents' despair—made bigger by Sylvia. I felt the blast of Adams's belief in me, his brightness blowing away doubt, my own cheering filling my ears as I raised *Living the Solution* higher, the sound ringing out over Eleutheria, through its stands of casuarina trees and overgrown pineapple fields, its seaside cliffs and tide pools and pink-sand beaches, its underground caverns and an ocean hole plunging deep into the island's secret heart.

Never mind that Sylvia's home office had been where I'd found *Living the Solution*. Never mind the clean blade of that connection.

Everyone returned to their tasks as if the locals had never arrived. The launch was only two weeks away. We couldn't wait.

MOONLIGHT GLINTED ON THEIR MUSKETS—the two hundred Spanish soldiers sailing silent from Havana, they held their weapons at the ready. Having wearied of the Bahamas' toothy waters swallowing their galleons, they'd come to exact revenge. First traveling to New Providence—not under God's protection after all—they took the encampment by surprise. Their foes, barely dressed, half-drunk, defended themselves with screams alone as their thatch-roof hovels and tawdry alehouse and miserable gardens were burned and broken into bits, stomped with boot heels into submission.

The soldiers extracted loot, extracted prisoners. Then they sailed onward to Eleutheria, hurried by a sea breeze flecked with embers as bright as bugle notes.

The settlers on Eleutheria had no means, no will to fight. Nothing, really, to fight for besides their lives. They fled into the brush, hid in sinkholes, climbed up trees, waded into the murk of mangrove swamps—believing the island would hide them. It would not. Those settlers cowering among the mangroves found their ankles frisked by unsympathetic lemon sharks, moray eels, the stinging waft of jellies. The settlers hiding in sinkholes were pinched by land crabs, bitten by spiders until they yelped their positions along with the wild dogs circling their refuge. Up in tree branches, settlers tried not to scare the birds and give themselves away, but the birds had no reason to see the settlers as their allies.

The wood stars, warblers, rose-throated parrots burst skyward like winged flares, flashing their feathers amid the smoke of the settlers' meager possessions vanishing.

Exposed, the settlers tried to pray, but those words had also vanished—they'd been gone for years.

Violence rose like a tidal wave shadowing Eleutheria. Across the sea, the Lords Proprietors bickered and bemoaned the cost of sending military aid. Some still hoped to squeeze a profit from the Bahamas—the word *plantation* on their lips—believing land could learn a purpose through written declaration, that parchment signed could sway the turning of the earth.

War would slap Eleutheria, leave rubble in its wake. The Bahamas were at times forgotten, at times coveted, as European nations clawed for their claim to profit: the British, French, Spanish, Dutch all elbowing for empire. Having brutalized native peoples, they enslaved Africans to toil on stolen land, as if one sin could exonerate another, as if the birth of the Americas wouldn't be forever cursed—profiteers and their ancestors forever haunted—the fever-dream of opportunity feeding into madness.

No matter.

Kings and queens shifted their subjects like pawns on the checkered map of the New World. They fought with their official fleets, or—when the rules of engagement did not suit them—they set loose scores of privateers. A letter of marque was quick enough to write: the envelope's thin lips sealed with drips of crimson wax as bitter red as the blood the letters would bring.

Then: cannon fire and musket bursts.

Air thickened with ash.

8

Back in smog-grizzled Boston, I asked Sylvia again about helping the Freegans.

Maybe you could write an article, I said. Or go on a talk show? Or could the university help?

She waved her hand, mind elsewhere, and said: Of course, darling.

We were in a car, driving to her house. We passed a food bank with a line of exhausted, sweat-drenched people stretching around the building's side. August temperatures in Boston held steady in the triple digits. While we'd been away in Martha's Vineyard, power outages rolled daily through the city, the grid overtaxed. Another water shortage prompted a wave of price gouging. Though the evening curfew had been lifted, most people had gotten into the habit of going home and staying home, where one could pretend all things were fine, that we hadn't entered the twilight of environmental livability, alongside the golden age of the surveillance state: a time when mailboxes snapped photos of our faces and refrigerators recorded our whispers and mercenary "peace" patrols kept dissent subdued.

What if you started with the Freegan proposal for Generational Democracy? I said. That's where political representatives are voted on by age groups, rather than by geographies, so that decision-making has long-term—

Yes, said Sylvia. You've described this all to me on multiple occasions.

She smiled reassuringly, added that we would figure something out. It would take time, though, to get the messaging right. And she had so much work to catch up on.

I love you, she said—the words bursting like fireworks in my ears—and I loved spending these past weeks with you. But I'm terribly behind. I meant to get back earlier.

What she meant was that she'd stayed on the Vineyard longer than planned because of me; because of my reticence to speak about my life, I had consumed her summer.

Right, I said. I understand.

And, truly, Sylvia did become busy when her fall semester started, her face ever pressed into a book or blued by a computer screen. Even so, I was glad to be ensconced in Sylvia's universe: a bug in amber. Never had I felt closer to someone. Sylvia had listened to descriptions of my childhood, my parents, my cousins, and she hadn't run away. When we shared meals, or curled together on her sofa, she continued to listen, unflinching, through descriptions of the survivalist drills invented by my parents for apocalyptic scenarios: flash floods, earthquakes, a nuclear winter, infectious cannibalism.

More than once, I told her, my parents had me practice shooting a human being.

Sounds useful, said Sylvia—unperturbed.

I put my trust in her. Though I was eager to move forward with helping the Freegans, I could wait for someone I trusted. Sylvia, her work within the university—the university itself—these were things I trusted largely because I did not understand them. The university was a black box: a place one entered and then left, transformed on the way out. Freegans had called college a pyramid scheme built on student debt, the indentured servitude of adjunct professors, the corporatization of the mind—but after Sylvia got me a temporary Harvard ID, this was easy to forget inside the grand old buildings with their spacious auditoriums, their lights dimming low. Easy to forget in the presence of Sylvia, the lovely-voiced professor. *Next image please. Next. Next. Hush now and listen—the world is yours to know.*

Be patient, she told me.

Time moved elliptically. I felt I was making progress, though in reality everything was moving around me while I stayed still. I became part of the furniture of Sylvia's life, mixed in among her clutter of books and candles and sarcastic fridge magnets. She had a claw foot tub perfect for luxurious soaking. She had a pantry stocked with artisanal herbs, glass jars of saffron and cinnamon, and endless bottles of cabernet sauvignon. I wasn't so unlike the house-trained bunny, Simone.

When Sylvia was working—and she was mostly working—I wandered from room to room in her house, creaking upstairs and down, poking into her basement, which was filled with abandoned exercise equipment and mildewed suitcases. I did chores in erratic bursts of industry: organizing her bookshelves, repainting a ceiling. Or, I nested in blankets, absorbed a steady pulse of information as I read from her personal library. I did not go to work. Even if I hadn't been fired from The Hole Story for disappearing over the summer, the café shut down that fall. It had been one of the last brick-and-mortar businesses remaining on its street; now vacant store-fronts lined up in a cavernous row.

I hardly ever saw my cousins.

This was because I visited the apartment infrequently, but also because my cousins were harder to be around. A tension emerged between them after Victoria asked Jeanette to stop hanging around the dental practice. It confused Victoria's coworkers, who would see her at her cubicle and then do a double take when they passed Jeanette in the lobby.

You're the most important person to me in the world, Victoria told her sister, but maybe we shouldn't be together 24-7. It's not normal.

This request wounded Jeanette, her feelings crushed by the insinuation that *she* was the weird one. My cousins had always been weird together. They'd supported one another's choices, validated the strangest of one another's notions. They'd served as mutual reflections: each a reassuring mirror image. But that reassurance had fractured. Jeanette was lonely at the gallery, lonely in general. She was disturbed, too, by Victoria's acquiescence to employment norms—such as dressing in unobtrusive cardigans and slacks. Victoria also went out with her coworkers to get after-work drinks. She talked in a conventional manner, her speech unpunctuated by giggles and breathy ominous pauses. She had realistic goals, like running a 5K.

What next? yelled Jeanette in one of their fights. Are you going to save for retirement? Are you going to start a blog about cooking healthy yet affordable meals? Date some bozo who thinks sports are important?

What if I am? Victoria shouted back. Sounds better than living in a delusion.

I left the apartment whenever these arguments started, which was whenever my cousins were near one another. I preferred to hang around Sylvia, despite her busyness, and despite her campaign to get me to attend college for actual credit.

You could earn a degree in digital forensics, Sylvia had said. Or in computer repair. You like refurbishing things. You'd be good at it. Here, take a look at this brochure—

She also started making suggestions about my appearance.

Your outfits are so *interesting*, she said. And I know you love wearing clothes you scavenged, but don't you think it might be worth sprucing up your wardrobe?

So I wore the new clothes she purchased. I studied the vocabulary sheets she brought me, under the pretense of applying to college for real. I wanted to show Sylvia I was trying. I made a point of sprinkling the vocabulary words into our conversations: *abscond, acrimonious, adminicular.* I stood up straight instead of slouching. I didn't eat with my mouth open. I brushed my hair. I listed to the music Sylvia liked: operas, mostly, in languages I did not know. I tried to learn those languages. I tried not to peer into dumpsters and trash cans when I passed them. I did all these things as if they might inspire Sylvia, in her own way, to take action on behalf of the Freegans. As if my gestures might strengthen our love.

For all my efforts, Sylvia became more distracted. She was working closely with a group of graduate students that fall. There was one student, in particular, who absorbed much of her time: a talented young scholar named Gretchen Locke, who was writing a dissertation on Dutch clicktivists.

You'd like her, Sylvia told me—over a dinner I'd had to

reheat, because she'd returned home so late—Gretchen has done a deep dive into these online communities. She does her research in a spirit of complete immersion.

What do you think of the potatoes? I said.

I'd been trying to learn how to cook, thinking that would impress Sylvia. I'd struggled, though, to get the hang of anything. Plus, the food shortages made getting many ingredients difficult. I'd wanted to make potatoes au gratin, but I hadn't been able to find any cheese.

The potatoes are fine, said Sylvia—and then, recognizing my dismay, added: it's so thoughtful of you to make dinner.

She took another bite from her plate in demonstration.

How are your college applications coming? she said.

I told her they were going great; I'd submitted everything. This wasn't true—but I didn't think that would matter, because soon the pair of us would be dedicated to supporting the Freegan cause. This wasn't the time for more school. Because by then a "radical-decentralized-leftist-terrorist network" was blamed for everything from car crashes to sinkholes to mass shootings. Radicals were blamed, too, for the death of the sitting president earlier that summer—though the man's ill health, unscrupulous associates, and the unhinged state of U.S. politics seemed equally suspect. The federal elections still hadn't happened. There was a rumor they'd take place later that spring, but so many factions had branched from the traditional two parties that organizational momentum had stalled. Crises bore crises. The system was sunk. Revolutionary thinking was urgently needed, and—though I knew there was a risk in attaching oneself to perceived criminals—I believed Sylvia was brave enough to ignore the risks. To me, she remained the

woman-in-black: courageous and infinitely capable. I imagined
her going on talk shows to defend the Freegans, along with
people like them: people trying to live differently, think differently, struggling toward alternate future realities. I imagined
Sylvia explaining in her crisp and confident way how Freegans
were heroes, visionaries—how they could show everyone a
path forward.

I'm sorry to run off, said Sylvia—though she had barely
eaten anything—but I have a phone call scheduled for this
evening.

She headed for her office; I slumped in my seat. I wondered if she was going to talk to Gretchen. They would discuss
Dutch clicktivists, their conversation purportedly about the
subject at hand, though really they'd be discussing something
else—desire underpinning the exchange—just as Sylvia and I
once talked.

Willa?

I looked up. Sylvia leaned back into the dining room.

I forgot to tell you, she said. I have a surprise planned for
this weekend. It involves a work party. I meant to tell you
sooner, but I'm all over the place these days. Also, don't worry
about the dishes. I'll take care of them later. Go take a nice
bath or something.

Then she was gone again. I sat up straight. A surprise could
only mean one thing, because there was only one thing I really
wanted. This was the start of our pro-Freegan operation. That
we were going to a party seemed extra auspicious. I'd first
known Sylvia as the woman-in-black at the congressman's
party—three years prior—and now I was her official compan-
ion. This trajectory proved there'd been a fated aspect to our
relationship. The universe had pushed us together: there was

a larger plan, a purpose, a rationale behind what we would accomplish.

I was so excited I did the dishes anyway.

The work party turned out to be fancy enough for Sylvia to insist she buy me more new clothes. Expensive ones.

They're a gift, she said when I protested.

I fingered the smooth fabric of a beige shift. The dress came wrapped in tissue paper that smelled like sandalwood. It had a simple elegance, clean lines. I'd worn expensive clothes before—back when my cousins put me in their photos—but always with the tags preserved for their return. Sylvia insisted I keep this dress. Also the matching pumps and a glossy white handbag and a pair of gold earrings. She said it was okay to look nice. I agreed to get my hair cut too. Newly shorn, I stood in front of the bedroom mirror; Sylvia came up behind me, drifted her fingers along my neck.

What? I said.

She paused, as if deciding what to say, before responding: You have such lovely ears—like little seashells.

Sylvia wasn't one to give out compliments, even about scented soaps and theorists she admired. Happiness melted through me. How silly I'd been to worry about Sylvia's new favorite student. Sylvia loved me. She was ready to help the Freegans. My certainty swelled when she mentioned there'd be someone at the party she wanted me to meet.

Yes, I thought. There will be a politician, or an important journalist, or someone with the power to get things rolling.

The plan was for Sylvia to pick me up from my cousins' apartment that evening. While I waited, Jeanette slumped out of her bedroom. I felt self-conscious in my new outfit, but Jeanette seemed not to notice. Her eyes were puffy from crying, or sleeplessness, or both. She had swaddled herself in a white bedsheet, like a disheveled Greek goddess.

Have you seen Victoria? she asked.

I replied that I hadn't. Jeanette belched noxiously, dragged herself to the refrigerator. She extracted a bottle of wine, took a swig. Then she slugged back to the bedroom, wine bottle in tow—though she paused in the doorway, muttered: You look nice.

A car honked outside.

I wanted to thank Jeanette—to say something—but she disappeared before I could. I grabbed my new purse, hurried out to where a sedan idled by the curb. Sylvia waited in the backseat. We beamed at one another, neither of us needing to speak. This beautiful, formidable woman: she had come to collect me.

As the driver pulled into the flow of traffic, a violin concerto lilted through the vehicle's speakers. I felt wrapped in a fairy tale, riding through the city in a modern-day carriage—as long as I didn't stare out the windows at the smogged city, the glum faces of the unemployed, unhoused, unwell. The sedan zipped onto the newly privatized Mass Pike. The road was sleek and smooth and safe, unlike so much infrastructure in the city. A tunnel in East Boston had collapsed the day before, killing ten people. Flood damage and poor maintenance were the likely culprits. But as usual, blame was piled onto a "radical-decentralized-leftist-terrorist network." More Freegan faces floated though the news, the word *WANTED* above their heads.

The sedan pulled up to the party's location and Sylvia pressed her lips to my cheek. Her perfume engulfed me. Desire unfurled along my spine and I leaned closer to tell her, my fingers sliding up the length of her thigh.

Sylvia clamped my hand down.

People at this party may be boring, she said. That's not their fault, though. Try not to hold that against them.

I wiggled my fingers to free them, but Sylvia held them fast.

Also, she went on, remember not to eat too many cheese cubes.

I tried to laugh, tried to stay cheerful as we left the vehicle and walked into the party. To enter, guests had to pass through a weapon-detecting security system, followed by an antimicrobial tube filled with UV light. After that, the problems of the world disappeared. Everywhere: shiny shoes, expensive watches, cigar smoke, throat-clearing, hand-shaking, exclamatory greetings. Sylvia laughed in a trilling manner at a man's unfunny joke about the collapsed tunnel. I drifted around an appetizer table decked with extravagant pyramids of food. Little flags impaled the cheese cubes, identifying their origins. Everything was labeled. We were in a special Harvard museum that exhibited glass botanical specimens. Hibiscus, banana plants, lilies—they all sat in display cases, frozen in growth. Party guests peered at the glass plants, commenting on their likenesses to the real specimens, their astonishing delicacy and longevity.

Marvelous, said a woman with a face so poreless it looked plastic. Makes you want to crush one in your hand just to feel the stamens snap.

A man in a bow tie raised an eyebrow.

Don't let the docent hear you, he said.

The woman made a show of talking louder, which attracted another bow-tied man, brimming with chummy irritation.

You two talking security? he said. Because I can't get a straight answer from anyone on the best personal security firm for hire.

The woman tried to offer a consolatory pout, but her too-taut face thwarted the expression.

How do you buy loyalty? the second man continued. That's what I want to know. Or, more realistically, how do you test for it? Because you want people who will get into your helicopter and go to your safe house, no questions asked, no special requests. The last thing you want in an emergency is to have to make an unexpected detour to pick up your bodyguard's wife, mother, niece, nephew, and mailman, because your guy is having an emotional meltdown.

An announcement was made about an auction. I floated among the display cases of glass flowers, all blooming for over a century. There was a sea anemone too: tasseled and tubular, exquisitely alien. I wondered if I'd ever get to see one in real life. I wondered how many of the species in the museum had since gone extinct.

Disturbed by this thought, I drifted back to Sylvia. I slipped my hand in hers as she nodded pleasantly in front of a mustached man who wore cowboy boots with his tuxedo.

What a handsome couple, he said—appraising us like a pair of attractive cows.

Sylvia's expression remained immutable. The man droned on. When he finally left, I asked her who he was—who all these people were.

Donors mostly, said Sylvia. That gentleman owns the

world's second-largest media conglomerate. Might be the single largest by next week.

Is this the surprise? I said—getting excited. Are we going to tell him about the Freegans? Maybe he can run a special series to correct public misunderstandings?

Sylvia waved to someone across the room. Into my ear, she murmured: I'll be right back, my raucous little anarchist.

I was alone again. Though the museum likely had a high-end air filtration system, the indoor atmosphere thickened, hazy with cigar smoke and cologne. A woman's laughter jangled like dropped coins. Party guests compared engine brands on their sports cars. They discussed their vaccine stockpiles, traded stock tips, praised the genome edits on one another's designer children. I wobbled in my heels as I pushed through partygoers to find where Sylvia had gone. In the museum of so much preserved preciousness, the passing of time felt conspicuous. How long had I waited for Sylvia to help the Freegans? I caught the edge of a display case, woozy with the gut punch of the answer.

She was never going to help. Not if she was happy to hobnob with people like this.

A woman noticed me leaning on the display case.

No touching, she hissed.

Gazes turned toward me—the dead-fish interest of the rich—all those eyes, laser-fixed, computer-chipped. My father had once ranted about the billionaires getting precautionary surgery in case civilization collapsed and optometry became inaccessible. *Lasered to twenty-twenty,* he'd said. *They all want to see the apocalypse—see it clearly. I read all about it. Those Silicon Valley people. Wall Streeters. Billionaire hotshots. They're the canaries. Bellwethers. They have info the rest of us can't access. They don't care about anyone but themselves. They've got helicopter pads for when SHTF. They're all buying citizenship in New Zealand. They're building fortresses with armed guards—*

My father, he'd lolled like a stalk of grass, his feet planted on the ragged braided rug in front of our TV. On the screen: images of palm trees ripped horizontal by hurricane winds. His eyelids fluttered, almost coquettish.

—We'll get a fortress too, he said, catching himself on the back of the armchair where my mother had sprawled in a chemical haze. *Don't you worry—*

Two months later, my parents would be dead.

The memory made the museum spin. When a caterer offered me a tray of beverages, I took two glasses of wine and downed them one after the other in long, gulping swigs. The room spun faster, faces whirling carousel-quick. How close despair lurked: always waiting. Always ready. I wanted Sylvia. I needed her—needed her to keep the promises she'd made.

She was in a back corner of the museum when I found her. She leaned in to embrace a slender woman with smooth dark hair. A woman who wore a cardigan and heels, who held an elegant clutch. I couldn't see the woman's face, but I could see that Sylvia did not release the woman's arms when she stepped back. She held onto them, her face affection-lit. She loved this person. Perhaps this was the brilliant Gretchen. This was Sylvia's ideal partner: a disciple who did not wobble in heels, or look longingly at the cheese cubes, or demand—over and over—that Sylvia support an amorphous anarchist collective wanted by the law.

Sylvia noticed me staring. She released the woman's arms and approached.

What's the matter?

When are you going to help the Freegans? I said. When are you going to get them donations or write newspaper articles or go on TV? When are you going to do anything?

Sylvia regarded me coolly. In measured lines of jargon, she spoke about risk assessment and public perception and the necessity of discretion and professional consequences in a time of employment scarcity.

What kind of sociologist of social movements, I interrupted—my voice louder than intended—distances herself from a social movement?

Willa—

Also, is that your new girlfriend? Is she more tolerable? Does she do as she's told?

I might have caused a full-blown scene if the auctioneer hadn't stepped up to a microphone at the other end of the museum. Sylvia spoke in curt whispers, but I didn't listen. I backed away, wanting only to escape. For this reason, I didn't notice the tall man beside the elegant woman I'd believed was Gretchen. The man was Sylvia's brother, Thomas. The woman was his wife. Sylvia had wanted me to meet them both; that was the surprise she'd mentioned. She had wanted to welcome me into her family.

But I was beyond rational thinking—beyond basic observation—my anguish mounting on the pyre of my own inaction. I'd let the Freegans down. The people who'd accepted me for *me*, back when I'd been flailing in the ocean of my own loneliness; the people who'd made me feel alive with possibility, at a time when I was choking on my parents' despair. They'd shown me everything and I'd done absolutely nothing. I'd wasted so much time.

I retreated to the appetizer table. Sylvia did not follow, which made me both relieved and angry. Across the museum, the auctioneer called for bids on an exclusive excursion to see a glacier chunk recently calved from a beleaguered Arctic ice sheet.

See it before they're gone! he called. Do I hear a starting bid?

I grabbed a handful of cheese cubes and stuffed them into my mouth. Then I used my forearm to bulldoze a whole pile into my patent leather handbag.

On my way to the exit, I thumped a fist against one of the glass display cases of botanical replicas. Nothing happened. I slammed the display case harder, pain spiking through my wrist. A fissure appeared in the glass. Thin as a spider's leg, the crack stretched and split and spread.

I tried to find the Freegans. I staked out old haunts, dodging security guards and police Humvees and drones to pace around dumpsters, back alleys, and street corners. I strained to feel the neck-tingle of a collective consciousness.

Nothing.

I kept looking. Once I caught sight of a person with a turtle-like backpack—who resembled the Freegan who'd fed me my first dumpster-dived orange—but the person scuttled onto a bus before I reached them. And once, on a park bench, I saw the pink-haired woman who'd attended flash protests—but she turned out to be an old lady in a wig.

If the Freegans were gone, or imprisoned, or hiding, I could not be sure. What was clear was that the U.S. government—clinging to the supposed objective of Law and Order—produced only regulations and no regularity. As winter melted away, so began a series of calamities pundits called "The Ten Plagues." There was the resurgence of a virulent swine flu, which escalated already skyrocketing food prices. Toxic algae bloomed in Boston Harbor. Mass Mortality Events increased; one weekend, thousands of mice crawled into the streets to die; the next, ninety-three bottlenose dolphins washed up in Plymouth. Meanwhile, the tick population exploded—and with that came tens of thousands of cases of Lyme disease, which resulted in even inner-city parks being doused in chemicals. Then there was the pollen. A great veil of golden dust wafted into Boston from western Massachusetts. Ragweed and pine trees, dizzy with unprecedented CO_2, sent a million-trillion microscopic invaders drifting over cars and windowsills, settling into gutters and people's hair, rendering the whole city sneezy, red-eyed, and weepy.

I was red-eyed, weepy, in part from the pollen, but also from the text messages Sylvia sent. On the phone she'd gifted me, her texts arrived in neatly punctuated sentences.

I see you are determined to avoid me.

It would be worth having a discussion.

Willa, I worry about you.

I did not respond. My mind felt distant and floaty. I'd wasted so much time because of her, and for what? Sylvia texted that we could visit the Vineyard again: a vacation might help us reset. Even if I'd agreed, the following week a hurricane trashed the island's entire north coast. The cottage-mansion, along with the seafood restaurants, the little shops, the island carousel with its old wooden horses, was swept into ocean currents.

Whereas time had once seemed infinite, now it rushed

away too fast. Spring rainstorms arrived, the downpours
flooding roads, acidifying waterways, bursting dams. The
water swallowed the yellow shroud of pollen, swirled gold
rivers into storm drains, and I felt sucked into the drains as
well. I sold the clothing and jewelry Sylvia had bought me;
I sold my plasma, bags of blood, a skin graft from my calf. I
tried to get short-term work doing people's chores. I stood in
line for hours at the food bank with a thousand others, waiting
to collect my corn stix and packets of soy drink mix.

My phone buzzed. *Please, Willa. Can we simply have a
conversation?*

I typed: *u r a coward.*

Then I pawned the phone too.

The phone was hardest to relinquish. Not for what it could
do, but because it had been a birthday gift from Sylvia. That
September, she set aside time to present me with an exquisite
cake: bakery-made and covered in dark chocolate, fresh rasp-
berries. She had even sung me the birthday song, her voice
terribly off-key and endearingly embarrassed. I'd thrown my
arms around her neck and kissed her so she could stop.

That had been the first time I'd celebrated a birthday in
years. My cousins had never asked about the date. My coworkers at The Hole Story had no reason to know. And when my
parents were alive, they'd only occasionally remembered.

Tell me more about them, Sylvia had said—after we licked
the last of the chocolate cake from our forks.

I told her there were times that almost felt like good memories. When I turned nine, my mother let me eat as much
astronaut ice cream as I wanted. The powdery candy was my

favorite survival food, though my father deemed the label misleading.

Humans have never been to space, he'd said. *The moon landing was all camera tricks and costumes—which isn't to say there aren't extraterrestrials among us.*

You would know, my mother chirped in reply.

The three of us giggled. A rare occurrence, yet it happened. We lived in a state of suspended animation—anticipating doom—but we'd also laughed together. At least once in a while.

Then there was a birthday near the end, when my parents set off emergency flares against a pitch-black sky. The three of us watched the orange beacons rise over treetops, arc down like falling meteors.

Should that have been a warning? I said to Sylvia. My parents shot those flares into the night and nothing happened, no one came. It was a celebration, but they'd been begging, begging for help.

Sylvia's brow pinched. I'd thought she understood, then, why I needed to be a part of making the world better—why I needed her to help me. If I wasn't part of such an effort, I'd succumb to what took my parents away. Because without a vision of a better world, it was despair all the way down.

Victoria, of all people, brought Sylvia's op-ed to my attention. Though Jeanette continued to struggle with their growing distance, Victoria thrived. She'd been promoted at work. Her social calendar bustled. And she was in the midst of dating a dentist from her workplace—genuinely dating him—even going out to eat at one of the few sit-down Italian restaurants still operating in the North End.

For Jeanette, Victoria's newfound romance was the final transgression upon their sisterly bond. At first, she tried to sabotage the relationship. When that failed, she dated a dentist as well—thinking the sameness might rekindle their twinship—but the relationship didn't stick.

The worst thing, Jeanette said to me after Victoria left for another date, is that she keeps telling me to floss.

What's wrong with that? I said.

Jeanette kicked over a chair.

The morning of the op-ed, my cousins screamed at one another until neighbors complained. Then the pair whisper-shrieked, which was worse to be around—like getting carved into tiny pieces by feathers. I had nowhere else to go, though. No job and nothing to do. There'd been an ozone alert issued on the air outside.

The door buzzed and Jeanette glaringly ushered in one of the lovers she courted online. Her guest hadn't even pulled off his safety mask before she hustled him into the bedroom she shared with Victoria, snapping the door shut behind her.

Victoria appeared unmoved. Seated primly on a kitchenette barstool, she peered between a phone and tablet laid out on the counter in front of her. Though I felt sorry for Jeanette, I liked Victoria more now that she was seeing the dentist. I hopped onto a stool beside her. The way she peered at the screens reminded me of the way she and Jeanette had once curated photos of themselves, beamed the images into the Internet as they awaited the rising star of celebrity. I picked up a tablet, expecting to see a series of photographs featuring her and the dentist: a well-groomed couple delighting in each other's company across various backdrops.

Victoria had newspaper apps open.

Ronny doesn't like taking pictures, she said—guessing at my surprise. Having spent so much time studying the before and after photos of mouths, he hates how every photo of us is a *before*, so to speak. A photo initiates a comparison and comparisons create tension between the past and the present. He's very against tension. That's why he made me a custom mouth guard for nighttime grinding. He can make you one too, if you want. I've heard you grinding at night on the futon.

Victoria looked at me philanthropically; in the bedroom, Jeanette released a series of acrobatic moans.

Do you want to know a secret? said Victoria.

She leaned closer and I leaned in as well, glad to be given a secret: the first promising offer I'd gotten in months. Wasn't this what I'd always wanted? A close friend—a confidante? I imagined stepping into Jeanette's former role in Victoria's life: the pair of us spending long afternoons gossiping about our love interests. I would tell her everything about Sylvia, and Victoria would commiserate, saying there were lots of fish in the sea. The true partnership, though, would be us.

The secret, said Victoria, is that sometimes I take photos of Ronny when he's not looking. Do you think that's bad?

I thought for a moment. Then I said: If I've learned one thing, it's that everyone has a secret agenda in romantic relationships. That's part of being a pair.

Victoria wrinkled her nose—unimpressed by my hard-earned wisdom. She politely added: I'm trying to read the news before our date tonight. Ronny likes to talk about current events.

On the screens in front of her, headlines scrolled past, one noting that the world population had crossed another billion-person threshold. The U.S. had expanded its military presence in the Gulf Coast to block migrants fleeing the storm-beaten Caribbean. There was a massive oil spill in the Arctic.

My despair deepened. I slipped off the stool, intending to make myself a soy-mix drink as a distraction, when the name *Sylvia Gill* rose from a screen like a viper. Her face and body followed. She wore thick makeup and an uncharacteristically colorful blouse. As a video clip, she was miniaturized—flattened into a rectangle of light—and yet she might as well have filled the room. She was on a talk show that billed itself as intellectualism for the mainstream. She was there to debrief the op-ed she'd written, currently making a splash on social media.

Victoria made a move to click to another screen, but I snatched the device. The text of Sylvia's op-ed swam on the screen. *Of Pirates & Progressives*, read the title, *the many ineptitudes of the modern left.*

In the bedroom, Jeanette crescendoed.

The op-ed still makes me angry. In her piece, Sylvia argued that contemporary social movements were mere ritual, conducted with the flimsiness of spell-work to ward off a sense of complicity in the ethical transgressions necessitated by industrialized nations to maintain power and relevance in late capitalism.

> Take "Freegans," whose random demonstrations of dissent have included consuming municipal waste to draw attention to inefficiency and excess. Beyond the fact that this is not a particularly new idea, the group's primary critique is also its fuel, a paradox predictive of the group's downfall. When asked how they might transform society, if given the

opportunity, my source offered solutions such as "open-access dumpsters," a system of living called "The Cult of Inconvenience," a political scheme called "Generational Democracy," and three-day workweeks for all. These are no hardened guerrilla warriors poised to tear down our infra-structure, our economy, our sense of self. These are lotus eaters. Desperate dreamers. Hotheaded kids, yes, but not heroes. If anything, they are mere pests to the powers that control our global order. Could a band of pirates create a progressive new civilization? I think not. To believe soci-ety might be rescued by Freegans or any similar groups is fantasy. To believe in these so-called modern leftist outlaws is to believe in unicorns. There are no magical people, no miraculous movements, that will save us . . .

I went immediately to Sylvia's house. Through the kitchen win-dow, I could see several drab university people sitting around her dining room table, their soft hands clutching crystal tum-blers turned citrine with whiskey. Someone raised a glass.

I used my key to enter through the front door, then walked straight to the dining room. Several people shrieked, includ-ing the two owlish academics I'd encountered in Sylvia's office. One of them spilled his whiskey on his button-down shirt.

Only Sylvia looked undisturbed; a tender relief washed over her.

Willa—

Is she dangerous? interrupted the whiskey-spiller.

Sylvia gave the man a glare so sharp it shut him up. Against my better judgment, I felt whiplashed by longing. Here was the person I'd always wanted her to be: the woman-in-black, effortlessly brave, fiercely decisive. When she beckoned me into the living room, I followed.

In our semiprivacy, Sylvia said: I hoped you would come here. I know my op-ed did not perhaps contain the precise message you wanted me to convey, but you must understand I was trying to help.

Help? I said, choking on the word.

Darling, said Sylvia as she took my face in her hands. Your friends are in trouble because they are perceived as a threat. I was trying to neutralize public opinion.

You were what? I said—twisting away. Why would I want that? Also, why are those people here?

My colleagues and I are celebrating the fact that I've—

Sold out? I said, my words sounding overwrought even to me.

I said more things, not nice things. In the other room, the guests rustled, ice clinking in their glasses. Sylvia stepped back, studied me. Her tender relief soured.

Do you really think you're such a revolutionary? she said. When we were living together, whose food did you eat? Whose bath did you use? Whose bed? Whose books? Was that part of a Freegan model? Living like a parasite off someone else? How is that sustainable? How does that serve society? I wish it was different, but this is reality. It's embarrassing, Willa, the sheer depth of your naiveté. This is what I initially found so fascinating about you. You live in fantasyland. And people like the Freegans—they live there too. The ideals you adore, the talk of "revolution," it's all self-soothing gibberish.

I dug my fingernails into my palms. I'd thought Sylvia understood why I needed those ideals: the possibility for radical transformation. I thought she understood that I grew up so

close to the abyss, its gravity never left me. I needed something
to hope on, if only to hold me back from the edge.

Darling, said Sylvia as her expression softened, I know this
is all hard for you to process, but it's the truth. It's something
you have to understand. Compromise is a part of growing up.
It's also part of being in a relationship.

She took my limp hand in her own. Simone peeked over
the side of a sofa cushion.

I miss you so much, she said—her eyes sorrow-soaked,
pleading—Willa, you have to understand. You had a difficult upbringing and that has distorted so much for you. You
try hard to be good, but there's no such thing as good. There
is only scarcity and plenty, our fear of the former. It took
me a while to learn this, but even the most robust and well-
organized social movements are inevitably swallowed by the
mainstream. At most, they gain millimeters, not miles. And
they do so at great cost.

Something broke loose inside me: denial, refusal,
resistance—call it what you will. I shook myself free from the
cashmere softness of Sylvia's sweatered grasp, the aroma of
lavender soaps and the musk of old books and the vinegar lilt
of wine. I couldn't stay, but I couldn't bear to leave either. I
ran to Sylvia's office, locked the door. She followed, rattled the
handle and called for me to come out.

I pushed over a stack of books, which thumped and splayed
onto the floor. I threw papers fluttering into the air. Tipped a
recycling bin. The gestures felt futile. I slumped into Sylvia's
desk chair, laid my arms on the armrests. A book sat waiting
in front of me. Perhaps, I thought, it would be satisfying to tear
this book up page by page.

The office door had stopped rattling. A desk light sizzled.

To think I would end up sitting in that chair all night, consumed by what I read—my despair relieved by a text that showed how massive change was possible, how it was essential, and how I could take part.

To think that what I read would lead me to Eleutheria.

I turned my attention to the first page of *Living the Solution*.

You have a reason you think you're reading this book. But already this book knows more about the future than you. Because the reason you're reading this book is not the reason you think you are. Because what you need to do is not what you think either. Not even close.

Which is why I'm going to tell you.

CALL THEM PARASITES, pests, a plague on civilization. Scum to squash and smear. Call them fools for thinking there would always be more blood to suck—ships to pillage, rum to rinse their minds of cares—that they might have a fate beyond the gallows, anything but their bodies dangling, heads lollipopped on spikes.

They'd be vulture-picked until their sun-bleached skulls stood only for defeat.

And yet, by the hundreds, by the thousands, pirates circled the Bahamas. They flew their Jolly Rogers high. Trading cannon fire for terror, terror for ingress, they walked with sea-legged swagger, their belts clattering with pistols and the swish of human hair. They smelled like rotting seaweed. Their skin was scabbed with ink. The port at Nassau they preferred the most: its women briny-mouthed, its liquor barrels bullet-bled. But Eleutheria offered refuge.

On that narrow island, with beaches warm and pink, pirates could stash unspent treasures in limestone sinkholes or stalactitic caverns. Their doubloons, their jeweled daggers, a golden Madonna statue said to be unlucky—emeralds twinkling in her eyes—all this they saved for later, as if later might someday come. Because, after rising from sun-blessed sand, they stretched their limbs and strode down to the island's docks to find another crew. On a roll of parchment, they inked their given name or nom de guerre, or signed an X marking their spot.

Here find: Liberation from conscription, from boredom and from bondage, from despair and desperation, from a society some called civil and the demands of domestic life. Here find more than you could have ever hoped—

Sharking round the archipelago in stolen ships and swift schooners that could outpace a man-o'-war, the pirates plundered the English, Spanish, French, and Dutch: those nations whose coffers grew fatter on the new continent, on the labors of those they had enslaved. The pirates pillaged slave ships too. They set the captives free. Or ransomed them. Or they offered up the tattered parchments inscribed with their pirate codes—the promise of equal shares, equal votes, equal fortunes upon the sea—and pressed a quill into the palms of new pirate recruits.

Thus, a ship might comprise men of different races, men both aristocratic and impoverished, escaped or just eccentric, and sometimes, even, a woman with a dagger in her teeth and bloodlust burning in her eyes. A ship might have a crew, however multitudinous, kept leveled by the same need to stay afloat—bound by something more than money—even with an entire Royal Navy swarming the horizon in their scopes.

Call that wishful thinking, a romanticization, an exaggeration, lore. Call it what you will—because for all the carousing, the grog-drinking and the weevil-ridden biscuits, the tar-black flags and decks spackled with blood, those ships meant something in their moment: circling the archipelago, they hovered in the netherworld between possibility and pain, criminality and correctives to injustice. They were another grasp at freedom. Those ships—black-flagged, dream-driven—they orbited Eleutheria as if it were a sun.

9

Bright light, sharp on the peaks of ocean swells. The biodiesel yacht skipped like a stone across the water. From its deck, Eleutheria's shoreline was a green smear of sea grapes and casuarina trees. The island, so low to the horizon it might have been a mirage.

Roy Adams stood bare-chested in the yacht cockpit, one hand on the steering wheel. He wore an unwet wet suit on the lower half of his body, the top half swaying from his waist. With his aviators mirroring the landscape, his square jaw set, he eased the yacht's path toward a natural island harbor.

On the seat behind him: a clutch of spear guns.

Jachi was on the yacht as well. Coconut-oiled and perched on the bow, she looked glamorous even in a standard-issue Camp Hope swimsuit. She let a hand drift over the boat's side as it slowed, her fingertips skimming the frothy tourmaline water.

I flopped onto my belly beside her. The wind wisped our hair.

We're really launching tomorrow? she said.

We're really launching tomorrow, I said.

Jachi flashed her movie-star smile. She sighed and rolled onto her back. I rolled onto my back as well, feeling sun-warm, satisfied. Though the launch, long-awaited and longed for, was at last at hand—and with it the expectation of unprecedented global transformation—a calm had come over Camp Hope. Crewmembers believed we were ready: our every gesture, every machination, practiced and perfected. We believed nothing could go wrong.

That afternoon, crewmembers needed only to prepare a spectacular sustainable feast for the media's arrival. Journalists and talk show hosts and influencers and vloggers and select celebrities—they would all be collected from the airport, brought to Camp Hope the following morning. They would be presented with cutting-edge ecotechnology, shown research on hyperaccelerated biome rehabilitation. They would be immersed in a compound that wasn't just carbon neutral, it was carbon negative—offered a lifestyle as innovative as it was enthralling—so that when they shared their experience in photos and videos and articles and VR-experiential tours, Camp Hope would spark the imagination of people all over the world.

Adams steered the yacht into a cove, yelled: Marks. Hop to.

I scrambled over to the anchor, lowered it carefully into the water.

That's right, boomed Adams. That's my girl.

I bit my tongue to keep a smile from breaking open my face. Adams's approval glowed across me like a second sun. He was proud of me, yet pushing me to be better—believing better was possible. No one else in my life had ever done that. Not my parents. Not Sylvia.

Got those nets ready?

We'd cruised into an undeveloped cove to fish. For the welcome feast there would be aquaponic salads and cricket-based
protein loaf and fungi-grown-on-ocean-plastics and edible
blossoms and coconut on everything. As a centerpiece, we'd
serve lionfish: the invasive species killed and grilled, topped
with a pineapple-rosemary purée.

Crewmembers had rehabilitated the fisheries around Camp
Hope, so the lionfish had to be caught far down the coast.
Adams wanted to hunt them himself. *You all trying to make
me soft?* he'd boomed when a marine biologist suggested letting crewmembers take care of the fishing. He invited me to
come along. The offer felt like the culmination of so much
struggle. Months ago, arriving at Camp Hope, I'd fantasized
about this moment—and here it was. Adams and I were working closely together, because he recognized my commitment
and potential. *You and I need to touch base on some plans,* he'd
told me before we left Camp Hope. *Big plans, important plans.*
Then he said to bring Jachi, too—*For scenery.*

You gals ready to hunt some lions? said Adams.

He'd already pulled his wet suit up over his shoulders, fitted
the spear gun to his chest, put on goggles, a snorkel, flippers.
Before Jachi or I could answer, he tipped backward off the
side of the boat, splashing into the cove with the unshakable
confidence of a man who believes he knows what awaits him.

Crossing the threshold between air and ocean means changing universes. Sound elongates, splinters into light. Everywhere: champagne bubbles, the flick of fins and the crackle of
plankton, the blood rush of a dive taken too deep. Underwater,

one is on borrowed time. The sea is a place a person can only visit in glimpses.

I glimpsed.

Sunlight filtered through the water, illuminating a silver school of minnows. The fish glittered, parted to reveal the waft of a sea fan, the ribboned bulges of brain coral, and the sculptural fingers of a tube sponge. A starfish feasted on a crab, its stomach distended. More fish—pink, orange, teal—flickered past like living confetti, their celebrations interrupted by a barracuda, many-fanged and slender, as well as jellies dragging their tentacles like a starlet's endless gown.

Back on the surface, I gulped air. Jachi waved from the boat deck; she wanted a deeper tan before the media arrived. Adams remained submerged: a man of iron lungs.

I filled my own lungs and pushed back underwater. Further on, beyond the boat, the reef gave way to a stretch of sand disturbed by ocean currents. A dark mass rose from amid seagrass and debris. I swam closer. A pile of cylinders materialized: sand-coated and cannon-shaped. I dared to think, *shipwreck*.

A sunbeam stung the water. Two emerald eyes sparkled.

Two emerald eyes set in a pious golden face—a woman's face—not unlike the lost Madonna once described to me by local children: Athena and Elmer, with their hand-drawn treasure map, their search along the coast.

Had it always been there, then—this possibility?

Out of breath, I surged to the surface, the question following me even as sand billowed, enveloping the treasure, and I hacked up the water I'd swallowed. Adams undulated to the surface beside me like a buff merman, a spear gun in his fist.

Did you see that? I said. The statue?

What? said Adams.

A statue—

Stay focused, Marks. This isn't a pleasure cruise.

I know, I—

Adams dived again. He'd spotted a lionfish beside a rocky outcropping, the creature's spines flared in a venomous armature. Adams aimed the spear gun, kicking his legs to steady himself and releasing bubbles to regulate buoyancy. The lionfish hovered, unflustered: floating dumbly, decadently. What did it have to fear, this florid species from elsewhere—this invader—a creature of another realm with an appetite so huge and no predators to speak of? The fish had laid eggs by the millions from the Bahamas to Boston Harbor, its offspring carried north on warming waters.

The spear ripped through the water and pierced the lionfish below its pectoral fin—Adams's aim as precise as when he'd struck targets in Fallujah.

The lionfish twitched. Blood plumed into the water. The creature began its slow-motion free fall. I dove after the carcass and grabbed hold of the spear—careful not to let a spine graze my skin. I deposited the fish into the mesh sack I'd clipped to my wet suit.

Adams had already spotted another lionfish. Again he took aim, fired.

So went the afternoon: Adams shot and I retrieved. When the mesh sack was crammed with fish, I swam it to the boat, got another one.

For the media's welcome feast, many lionfish were needed— there was little meat on a single specimen—yet even after we'd collected dozens, Adams continued hunting. Daylight dwindled. There was always another fish, another reason to continue. This species: an enemy distilled. The death of each fish rendered the sea a little closer to its earlier state, and us to the environmental future we wanted.

Also, Adams liked to kill.

The sun sank lower, daylight bruising purple. Without dive lights, it became impossible to see. The hunt had to end. I slurped my exhausted limbs out of the water and onto the yacht's deck. The dead lionfish, crammed together in the netted sacks, were a slick spiny mass, fins twitching their last, vacant eyes leering.

Jachi was no longer on the deck. Likely, she had gone down into the hold to nap on a bed of orange life preservers and dream of the impending launch: her redemption in flashbulbs. Soon her name would again be spoken with reverence, her lost career, her lost friends, her lost loves returning to her like a castaway's deliverance.

Over the side of the boat, Adams bubbled below the water before bursting to the surface with a spear held aloft. He had skewered two lionfish at once. He raised the spear over his head like a triumphant, gruesome kabob.

Watch those spines, I said. They might slide and—

Adams tossed the spear onto the boat deck, climbed in after it. In the semidarkness, his body towered monstrous and unfamiliar.

What was that you were saying earlier? he said. About a statue?

It was nothing, I said.

I hadn't meant to lie. My words, more than anything, were an expression of desire: I wanted the golden Madonna to mean nothing. Because despite everything else happening—the lionfish hunt, the launch—the statue surfaced in my mind, and with it came Athena and Elmer; with it came all the local communities on Eleutheria; with it came Deron. I did not want to think about them. Without them, everything was simple. Right and wrong were simple. But here was this statue I'd assumed hadn't existed. Here was this lost artifact from the past—thrust forward by the sea—demanding consideration. If only it could have stayed submerged for a little while longer. Or forever.

You have a good time, Marks? Adams said—true curiosity in his voice.

The best time, I said. I wish we could've kept going.

Adams shook his body like a dog, grabbed a towel and rubbed down vigorously. A nervousness crawled across my skin. To soothe my nerves, I kept talking.

We sure got a lot of fish. More than enough for—

Marks, interrupted Adams, we're going to need to put most of these fish on ice.

Through the growing darkness, he fixed me with night-visioned attention. What he meant about the fish, I wasn't sure—all I knew was that it felt good to hear the word "we." I let this goodness chase away the sparks of alarm. Adams loomed closer: a mountain of a man. He was the author of *Living the Solution*, the book I'd stayed up all night reading in Sylvia's office, carried away on the reverie of its promises. The book was an antidote to despair: the cure-all I'd sought my whole life. Though its aims were monumental, its methods were pragmatic. After I'd finished reading, I'd climbed out of Sylvia's office window and gone home, where I read the book over again, and again, until I was sure I had to go to Eleutheria. I had to go to Roy Adams, whose vision for the future was unlike any I'd ever heard. I had to join Camp Hope: my life depended on it, everyone's did.

Positive thinking, Adams was saying, that's where progress comes from. And we have a hell of a lot to be positive about, because Camp Hope is about to get a bigger boost than anyone could've imagined. We're going to get extra support—allies you could say. Because you know what wins wars? Alliances win wars.

Right, I said. So, we're going to save the fish for day two of the launch?

Adams paced the yacht deck, making the boat sway in the cove's calm waters. I picked up the spear gun he'd tossed on the deck to make sure he didn't step on it.

Marks, said Adams—waving his hand in the air, as if the hugeness of his palm could clear away logical concerns—we need to get to the meat of the issue. Because I've got a proposition for you. And I'm asking you because you get it. You get what it takes. I knew that from the beginning, when I saw you hacking through the ocean in your kayak. I knew when I saw you hit that coral reef head-on, delirious as a drunk at an open bar. You had a goal and you were going to do whatever it took to get there. I thought to myself: Here's a born soldier. Here's a person who would die for the cause. And you almost did. Near-drowning aside, I was damn glad you showed up that day, because—and don't take this the wrong way—I needed an alibi for delaying the launch that wouldn't break morale. Anger keeps people fired up. You took the fall, which was a hell of a sacrifice. Someday we'll get you a medal.

What are you talking about?

Money, said Adams. Mistakes were made regarding the

budget. We needed Camp Hope to be sustainable finan-
cially, not just environmentally. You think all this ecotech is
cheap? We'd torched our runway. If journalists unpacked our
finances, we would've been toast: a debt-chewed pie in the sky.
I had to fundraise before we launched. Luckily, with the extra
time, I got the recruit scheme going. Worked like a charm. We
got donations by the bucketful, along with connections that
opened up more opportunities, the ones I want to talk about
now.

He grabbed my shoulders, his face eclipsing my vision. He
gave me a little shake.

Picture this, Marks, he said. Camp Hope: a global phenomenon. *Living the Solution,* a bestseller. World leaders doing
what they need to do to save the planet. Imagine that's only
the beginning—

Adams, over the past months, had been in secret meetings.
He'd met power brokers on the mainland, as well as at Eleutheria's sole hotel. This information, it would occur to me later,
was what Deron likely would have shared, had I ever been
willing to listen. Deron must have overheard these meetings,
or at least been aware of them. He'd been trying to convey this
to me—what Adams was really doing. What Adams was now
telling me on that boat spinning slowly in a cove: that he'd
devised a plan to merge Camp Hope's debut into the public
consciousness with a burgeoning third-party faction that, with
U.S. elections on the horizon, could recalibrate governance all
the way to the White House.

Green Republicans, the faction called themselves, though
pundits called them *Teddies*. They were bear-hunting, boot-

wearing billionaires. Businessmen, really, styled in the spirit of a certain Roosevelt cousin; *Conservatives* in more than one sense of the word. Once marginal in the political sphere, they'd gained momentum. The Right's embrace of climate science, after decades of denial, had left opponents speechless—Libertarian crowds pledged allegiance, swayed by the stench of authenticity—giving the Teddies easy access to voters made fearful in the face of wildfires, fracking earthquakes, a corn blight, disasters arising one after the next. Climate change had become a new bogeyman—or, rather, a bogeywoman. The terror of Mother Earth, her kamikaze revenges, made the public pliable. Religious rhetoric hustled the Bible belt into compliance: *We will prepare the USA like an ark for the impending floods. We will protect the chosen. Everyone else can go to hell.* The Teddies' presidential pick, though unexpected, was not unwelcome to the old-school GOP, most of whom were willing to buy into whatever would keep them in control. "Green Business" was booming. Everyone was talking about geoengineering. Cap and trade. Smog futures. Undergirding the platform, the same old principles applied: consolidation of power, resources for the elite. A dead planet, after all, wouldn't keep anyone in bratwurst and brandy and sixty-foot sailboats.

Adams, in his secret meetings, had tapped into these political tides; in fact, he'd gone ahead and surfed them. While wrangling donations in D.C., he'd connected with old military buddies. The Pentagon had long tracked climate change. A single crop failure could destabilize nations. Pressure points had to be managed, all threats considered—and there was nothing more threatening than an inhospitable planet. Sure, they'd obscured their reports when politics demanded silence, but when the Teddies took power this would no longer be necessary. Camp Hope could fit neatly into their objectives for U.S. border protection, resource aggregation, "displaced persons defense." Camp Hope would be one facet in the large-scale changes initiated by the new regime; specifically, Camp Hope would be its face.

Here's what I need from you, said Adams. And I'm asking you because you've done so well. Because I trust you, Marks. I've seen what you're capable of and I'm proud of your commitment. Proud of what you've done here—

His huge hands remained on my shoulders. Thumbs and forefingers massaged my neck, exploring the tense flesh between tendon and bone.

—I want you to step up as my second in command, Adams went on. I want you to help get all of this implemented. It's going to take a little finesse, as you might have guessed. Because we want the Teddies to be here when the media comes.

Wait, I said—extracting myself from his grasp—what?

Adams laughed, said: Don't tell me you're surprised. You're a natural.

I'm honored, I said. I'm just trying to understand.

You've got to know I've taken a shine to you.

Submerged in shadows, Adams was invisible except where his teeth caught the light from the illuminated yacht cabin. The pearly set grinned.

The Teddies, I said—trying to steer the conversation back— Nothing about them is described in *Living the Solution*. Nothing even close.

Sure it's there.

I could still feel Adams's hands kneading my shoulders, as if flesh could be molded into form. The yacht, tethered by its anchor, spun in circles in the cove. My stomach spun too. My reply came out in a whisper: There isn't anything about launching with political alliances. Camp Hope is supposed to inspire a groundswell movement, which will result in a recalibration of social value systems. Otherwise corruption takes root. It says so in chapter three.

I knew this to be true. That's what I'd loved about *Living the Solution*—that's what kept me reading all night in Sylvia's office. The book promised a plan at once ethical and effective. That's what made me pack my belongings, travel to Camp Hope. That's what made me leave Sylvia, my cousins, my life in Boston—however imperfect—behind.

This part of the plan is in there, said Adams. It's a note at the end.

I've read *Living the Solution* six times, I said.

Adams boomed out a too-loud laugh, made a joke about me needing to get a hobby.

You know what, Marks? he said. I'm going to let you in on a secret, because we're going to be working together and I want to be transparent. I want us to be close. So let me tell you: if connecting with the Teddies wasn't in the book's final form, it should've been. But you can't control everything. Especially when you're not exactly the literary type. You've heard of ghostwriters, haven't you?

Out in the cove's dark waters, a fish jumped, the splash loud as a slap in the face.

Adams took my silence as understanding. He moved toward me, while I backed away, his huge figure rippling in and out of shadows as he explained that, to maximize Camp

Hope's public debut in a way that helped the Teddies capitalize on our political currency, we'd need to delay the launch again.

I just got off the phone with their chief strategist in DC, he said. They're thinking maybe four or five months from now will be the peak strategic opportunity to unveil Camp Hope with the Teddies present. We'll have to cancel the media visit tomorrow, though that'll be good in its own way: It'll build hype. Anticipation.

But what about—

Adams steamrolled on, his voice echoing across the cove as he explained how the real challenge, once again, would be maintaining crewmember morale. It would be hard to explain the nuances of this latest delay to the more hotheaded crewmembers. The Agro Team, especially, had a thing about timing. Plus he, Roy Adams, needed to maintain trust. That was leadership objective number one. A strategic imperative. So, he needed a fall guy.

The thing is, Marks, said Adams. You've already taken one for the team. And you're too valuable elsewhere. What needs to happen is this: Lorenzo takes the fall and you replace Lorenzo as my right-hand man. Might not be pretty, but the kid needed to bow out anyway. He's just not cut out for this. A major disappointment, really. For me more than anyone. None of the other crewmembers know this, but Lorenzo's actually my son. Surprises me too sometimes. Met his mom in Okinawa thirty-odd years ago. I'd hoped having him around Camp Hope would get him off his video games. Give him some direction. He's just not going to fit in, though. He can take the fall. He'll understand—

A spear sailed through the darkness and struck Adams in his chest.

He stared at the protruding stem. Then he fell like old-growth timber, crashing onto the deck with his arms at his sides. The lionfish venom that had coated the spear swam into his bloodstream—the pain immediate—and he thrashed in the darkness, his limbs spasming, until he slammed his head against the deck railing and went still.

I stood holding the spear gun. The shot had been reflexive and for several minutes I didn't feel anything. Out in the cove, dark water sloshed. It lapped at the blood dripping down the yacht deck, before swirling back around coral reefs and sea grasses, the barracuda and a green-eyed Madonna statue clinging tight to her child as she had for centuries.

Shoot the bad man dead, my parents had urged me, years earlier, pointing a rifle toward a straw-stuffed figure dressed in the clothes of my father. *Don't be afraid, baby, don't be afraid.*

To think I ever believed I could outrun my own history—any history.

A rustling sounded from belowdecks. I dropped the spear gun as Jachi emerged on the top of the stairs, yawning.

What a wonderful nap, she said. Though I had the strangest dream.

The Camp Hope grounds were dark when we motored up to the boathouse. Everyone had opted for early bedtimes in preparation for the following day. The aroma of rice protein lingered in the air. Palm trees stood frozen, fronds jagged in the light of solar lanterns.

Jachi and I each put one of Adams's huge arms over our shoulders. We dragged his body from the boat onto the dock and then through the grounds, his feet grooving the gravel pathways in twin tracks. We hauled him all the way to the medical cabin, lifted his body onto a cot. His limbs splayed limp, as if all his bones had been removed. His breath rasped. The skin around his shoulder had turned purple, though the bleeding had stopped. He convulsed when we poured disinfectant onto the wound but did not regain consciousness.

I'd been the one to yank the spear out. Back on the boat, I'd told Jachi the attack had been perpetrated by masked assailants who subsequently disappeared into the night. Jachi accepted this story without question. *They were probably trying to stall the launch*, she'd said. Her eyes released a stream of perfect tears as she recounted a film she'd starred in that involved a pair of masked mobsters. In one scene, handcuffed to a chair, she'd escaped using a pin from her hair. This recollection gave her strength, and, in the medical cabin, she spoke with a heroine's steady concentration as she outlined the situation.

The media was coming tomorrow.

Adams was alive but gravely injured.

There were no hospitals on Eleutheria.

Having Camp Hope's leader airlifted off the island would not look good. In fact, it would look very, very bad.

I rubbed my face; I could not quite believe what I had done—what, moreover, I had heard Adams say. I tilted my head back, as if an answer might shake loose from my own stretched flesh.

Inaction is the course of cowards, read the quote from *Living the Solution* inscribed on the medical cabin's ceiling beams. A quote, I now knew, that didn't belong to Adams at all.

The launch must go on, said Jachi—fluttering her eyelashes determinedly—It simply must. This is our *moment.*

Everyone's expecting Adams, I said.

Jachi clasped her hands prudently, said: Adams always disappears at crucial times.

She was right. Crewmembers would be disappointed, but not entirely shocked if Adams was absent. And because the medical cabin wasn't on the visiting media's itinerary, there was a chance no one—crewmember or visitor—would notice we'd stowed him there. The details of the situation could be dealt with later. For now, what mattered was launching Camp Hope. The planet couldn't wait any longer.

Someone will need to stay here with him, I said. To make sure—

Jachi held a finger to her lips. Her whole time at Camp Hope, she told me, she'd been waiting to really, truly, have a role in the compound—a role that mattered. Also, she'd once played a nurse in a short-lived hospital sitcom. As she spoke, her eyes shone with a different kind of dreaminess. For the first time, she didn't look like a movie star at all.

Back outside, I crept through the compound, listening for the voices of crewmembers.

Only the shushing of surf sounded, the wind turbine whispering through the night.

Exhaustion deluged me. I wanted to sleep, to lose myself to blankness. But, remembering the lionfish, I detoured back to the biodiesel yacht; I was too well trained to let any resources go to waste.

The netted lionfish remained where they'd been left on the boat deck. I dragged them onto the dock. I was readjusting my grip, preparing to drag the mesh sacks all the way to the kitchen, when a pale face materialized in the darkness.

Hello, Willa.

I swallowed my scream—it was Fitz.

Have you been here the whole time? I said.

Yes, he replied. Fifteen years and five months and three days, I've been here on this earth.

If I'd hit the hallucinatory point of exhaustion, I wasn't sure. I squeezed my eyes shut, then opened them wide; Fitz remained on the dock beside me.

In all the time I've been here, he went on, I never saw a sky like this before.

His gaze turned heavenward. He seemed pensive, not like someone who'd witnessed two crewmembers dragging their wounded leader across the compound. I looked up at the sky as well.

Above: a wash of pinprick stars, the gauzy glow of interstellar light.

After a minute more of contemplation, Fitz moved to the edge of the dock, sat on its edge with his legs dangling in the water. His body swayed to an inaudible tune.

Spread out in the oil-dark water were the rest of the recruits. They floated on their backs, quiet as manatees, all gazing at the sky.

There were Lillian and Cameron and Thatcher and Margaret and all the others. They paddled their limbs gently to stay afloat, their movements trailing a bioluminescent echo, so that the cove glowed blue-green with celestial reflections.

My throat tightened. Something was happening. Something, perhaps, that required action. I stayed frozen, trying to think of what action to take, but the recruits remained caught up in their own reverie, and I didn't have the energy for anything except a vague admonishment about not staying up too late.

We're launching tomorrow, I said. Remember.

Fitz slipped splashlessly from the dock into the water.

What else could I do? I dragged the netted lionfish to the mess hall kitchen, installed them in the walk-in fridge. My eyelids fluttered, trying to shutter closed. I forced them open. I went next to the Command Center, my limbs leaden as I hauled my body up the wraparound staircase. A part of me believed Adams would be up there. A new Adams, a better Adams. An Adams who had written *Living the Solution*. An Adams who believed in the original plan, who believed in a better future, who believed in me.

Not a fraud, a creep, another disappointment.

Inside the Command Center, a computer monitor glowed ecstatically with a system update. The ticker tape of CO_2 measurements and eco-headlines scrolled silently along the upper edge of the ceiling.

I was alone.

My body descended, my legs stretching out in front of me on the floor. I leaned against a wall, intending to rest only for a few minutes. Through an open window, a breeze arrived, carrying the usual marine aromas, along with the acrid char of garbage burned in a local settlement. Trash lit aflame because there was nowhere to put what was unwanted except into the sky.

My dream came swiftly. I was back in Boston, the city almost as I remembered, with the vertiginous thrust of skyscrapers and the sooty air and the impossible roadways. The envelope from Sylvia blew past me like a fallen leaf. I chased it, but garbage lay strewn everywhere. It flooded the streets—a tide of black trash bags and coffee cups and busted cardboard—sloshing against buildings, pushing up against itself, rising.

Eat the rich, Freegans used to say, meaning their waste.

I ate. Without discretion, I gobbled floppy heads of lettuce and unwanted pizza crusts, licked out old yogurt containers, sucked down the muddy dregs of coffee, then chewed the Styrofoam cups. In the distance, I saw Freegans eating as fast as they could. I tried to wade through the garbage to reach them. When that failed, I tried to eat a path. I mashed up cardboard boxes, empty soda bottles, stained mattresses, broken windows, crunching it all up and swallowing the scraping bits down.

My eating wasn't enough. The tide of garbage rose, lifting me with it. I could see into skyscraper windows as I moved upward. Secondhand furniture turned into particleboard minimalism, into catalog sofas, into the furry puddles of bear skin rugs. Posed beside a row of Grecian statuary, the powdered faces of my cousins blew kisses.

The tide of garbage overwhelmed them too. The floors became empty, hollowed out and dimly lit, except for one. In it stood Sylvia, her face turned away. She held an arm outstretched, the envelope she'd given me fluttering in her fist.

The garbage lifted me to her. I tried to speak, but my mouth was too full, my words choked by all I had stuffed down my throat.

———

The Command Center glowed amber. Morning sun filtered through the tinted windows, turning my body orange—as it had been my first day on Eleutheria—except this time no monarch butterflies burst into the air.

I rubbed my face, stood up slowly. I had spent the night sitting against the wall. I should have been stiff and sore. Instead, I felt immaterial, as if all light and matter might pass right through me, as if I were as delicate as an idea.

There were voices outside. I smoothed my polo shirt, combed my hair with my fingers. It was 5:45 A.M. In four hours, the first chartered plane full of media insiders would touch down on the island.

A gentle wind stumbled through an open window, beckoning the sweet rot of overripe fruit. Papaya, maybe. The charred smell had vanished. Around me, the Command Center held its breath: the desk, the computers, a pile of seashells that looked like bones if you squinted your eyes. And everywhere, the grit of sand.

There was a knock on the door—Lorenzo peered into the Command Center with friendly nervousness. His mustache quivered.

Everyone's ready, he said.

He did not ask why I was there instead of Adams, though the question hovered between us. I tried to find evidence of Adams in Lorenzo's features. Maybe in the flare of Lorenzo's mouth? For all his nervousness, his mouth was resolute.

There was no time for speculation; I told Lorenzo that Adams had asked me to step into a leadership role while he took care of something else.

Okay, said Lorenzo—glancing at his clipboard as if to seek confirmation. Adams mentioned he was meeting with you. I was actually worried that—

Adams told me you might be worried, I said. But he also wanted me to tell you that he believes in you. He knows you'll do everything you can to get Camp Hope launched.

Happiness walloped Lorenzo; his eyes widened.

And, I added, he said that you've done so well and that he's proud of you.

Lorenzo looked as if he might weep, which hurt to see because I understood what he had longed for. I understood it well.

Too well—I couldn't stick around. I grabbed a copy of *Living the Solution* on Adams's desk, held the book tight against my chest as I walked onto the Command Center's wraparound balcony. From that vantage, the grounds spread out like an eco-kingdom: the orchards and the gardens, the laboratories, the boathouse, the fleet of biodiesel vans, the solar panels and the wind turbine. Recruits and crewmembers streamed from their bunkrooms in tributaries of white polo shirts, all moving toward the Command Center.

Everyone had questions.

I, Willa Marks, had answers. I explained that Adams would not be present that morning. He would return soon. The launch would otherwise continue as intended. Everyone would maintain their assigned roles. They all knew what to do. Everything was going to go exactly according to plan.

Telling people what they wanted to hear, I discovered, was easy. People wanted confidence more than they wanted truth. And for the few crewmembers for whom confidence wasn't quite enough, I read from *Living the Solution*.

```
There must be an alternative. A new ship,
not a life raft: an offer of salvation that
is at once familiar and improved. There must
be the promise of more, not less . . .
```

Crewmembers had envisioned Adams present because they expected him to be larger than life: to invite a miracle onto the Camp Hope grounds. But we could be our own miracle. With or without Adams, Camp Hope sparkled around us. We sparkled with it. We who had created a community unlike any in the world—a community we were ready to share.

```
Camp Hope is the golden alternative . . . Camp
Hope is innovation and determination . . .
a target and a destination . . . Camp Hope
is a torch in the dark . . .
```

Don't be afraid, I told the crewmembers and recruits. Don't fear what will happen if we act. Think of what will happen if we don't. *Inaction,* after all, *is the course of cowards.*

Thus began the day: a synchronized dance, Camp Hope's most perfect performance. Every crewmember and recruit submitted to their assigned role. They inspected solar panels, harvested hydroponic lettuce, farmed heat-tolerant coral polyps, manufactured shoes from plastic scraps caught in the offshore SeaVac.

An agronomist nodded at me as he carried a basket of hemp stalks to a lab. Recruits and crewmembers sat beneath palm frond cabanas, having boisterous discussions about geothermal energy, photosynthetic infrastructure, worm farms.

Returning to the Command Center balcony, I watched the

road to Camp Hope for a sign of the biodiesel vans the Liberal Arts Girls had driven to the airport. The media, by that point, should have been on their way. It would be a historic moment when the vans pulled up to the bougainvillea wall, and the media beheld Camp Hope for the first time.

```
The Camp Hope launch should be as sensa-
tional as the moon landing . . .
```

Yet, as time passed, I watched the Camp Hope grounds more than I watched the road. Everyone—recruits and crewmembers—performed their roles with vivid, effortless efficacy, the text of *Living the Solution* brought to life in a human-sized terrarium.

For the third time in my life, I felt unadulterated joy. I imagined showing my younger self—a child-Willa—Camp Hope. *Look*, I'd say, *look at what we made real.* Child-Willa had hoped her parents would be healed by peering into a tiny terrarium. Grown-up Willa would show a full-sized terrarium to the world—heal all that was wrong. No more despair. No more pessimism. No more rote survivalism—or worse, no will to survive at all. Because how could a person look upon Camp Hope and not feel the pull of possibility?

Had the launch gone as planned, Camp Hope would have dazzled our media contacts—as well as the world—of that I am sure. We would have catalyzed global transformation the way *Living the Solution* predicted.

But by that time, on Eleutheria, there were other forces at work.

Or perhaps there had always been other forces at work: a whole history of them destined to resurface.

A lone van crept up the road to Camp Hope.

There were no camera crews or news anchors leaning out windows, no influencers or celebrities blowing kisses.

My first thought was that I had misheard Adams on the yacht—he'd already canceled the media's arrival—but when Eisa leapt out of the driver's seat, her expression suggested a worse development.

A man and a woman got out of the van.

If I could go back in time, I'd have kept the grounds sealed. I would have preserved Camp Hope's perfection for as long as I could.

The visitors were in their early thirties, their faces sweaty and—in the case of the woman—dour. The man wore a too-long tank top, board shorts, and thong sandals. He surveyed the bougainvillea wall, then stared at his phone, ignoring Eisa's efforts to usher him inside.

You think this is it, babe? he said to the woman.

No, idiot, she yelled back, it's the Taj Mahal.

She plopped out of the van, her long skirt billowing. Her makeup, applied earlier in the day, had shifted from its original placement, giving her a duplicated, stereoscopic appearance.

Is there a bathroom in there? the woman shrieked. Or do I need to pee in the bushes?

Babe, there's a bathroom, said the man.

I'd descended the Command Center stairs to greet the pair, but they brushed past me into the grounds as if walking into a public park.

Look for signage, said the man.

The woman swatted a honeybee out of her face. I trotted after them, trying to introduce myself. All around the grounds, recruits and crewmembers worked at their allotted tasks, any dismay suppressed beneath a bulwark of cheerful industriousness.

There's a bathroom right there, called Eisa as she also tried to get the pair's attention. It's that cubical structure built of recycled glass and carbon sequestered from—

The woman stormed toward the building, lifting the folds of her skirt as she entered a composting toilet.

Leonida is actually a sweetheart, said the man without looking up from his phone. Love of my life.

Eisa beckoned me over, her pert ponytail gone slack. It took her a minute to start to make sense. The media was on the island, yes. They'd arrived right on time. They weren't here, though. And they weren't coming—at least not for a while.

They wouldn't listen, she said. Even to Corrine. Even to Dorothy—

Eisa seemed disturbed, more than anything, by the trio's rhetorical failings: their inability to convince the media to come to Camp Hope.

We got to the airport too late, she went on. Or else, we got there and weren't ready in the right way. A group of locals were waiting on the tarmac with a caravan of vehicles. They picked everyone up before we could, took them to the hotel. Maybe the media didn't realize that's where they were going, but once at the hotel, they wanted to stay. I know because we followed them and tried to get them to come to Camp Hope. Corrine and Dorothy are still there—trying to convince people to leave—but everyone is a few drinks in. There's a barbecue going. A live band of local musicians. The band is really good.

Eisa's ponytail wilted further.

The only reason Henk and Leonida are here, she went on, is because the others made them come as "representatives." I don't think this pair is well liked.

From inside the composting toilet, Leonida yelled: You have got to be kidding me. Where's the toilet paper?

A crewmember explained through the wall that there was a basket of foliage at Leonida's feet, which helped the composting toilet epitomize cyclical resource use.

Wipe with leaves, called Henk.

A stream of expletives followed about rashes and female anatomy. Henk shook his head, smiling to himself.

So when is the rest of the media coming? said a marine biologist who had ducked away from her assigned post. We have so much research to show—

Several other crewmembers tried to usher the marine biologist away, resulting in a strangely smiley argument. The compost toilet had gone quiet. I asked Henk if he wanted to view the hydroponics labs, or interview young recruits, or go diving around a restored reef, or examine the biofuel production units, or see examples of carbon-negative infrastructure. Henk glanced at the grounds as if just noticing them. He thrust his hands in his pockets, tugging down the fabric of his tank top.

Here's the thing, he said. I wasn't even supposed to come on this trip, but a friend offered me their spot last minute. I'm a sportswriter, see. Content writer, to be specific. Blogger, if you're splitting hairs. For basketball, mostly. Do you guys play basketball? You all look like you're in great shape. Do you surf? The guys at the hotel said they'd drive us out to a surfing spot later, after the rum tasting. That's what Leonida wants to get back for. It's her half birthday. And the hotel people comped us some sick ocean-view suites. Hard to turn down, you know? The only bummer is they're doing construction in the harbor, so you can only swim in the pool. Which is cool, even though I mostly came here to catch some waves. And I liked the idea of taking my girl to the Bahamas. To be honest, I got this island confused with Jamaica—which has, like, more than one functional hotel?

Leonida emerged from the composting toilet like a reanimated corpse. To Henk, she said: You've got ten minutes. I'll start counting now.

She really will count to sixty ten times, said Henk. She's thorough like that.

But where are the others? said a nutritionist who had approached with a platter of seaweed-cricket snacks. Where are the camera crews? Where are the vloggers and the influencers and celebrities and news anchors?

And what was that you said about construction? said a coral scientist who, like many of the other crewmembers and recruits, had abandoned his assigned post.

So yeah, said Henk. You can't surf by the hotel because they're doing construction in the harbor. There's a barge out there and that's affecting the water or something.

Dredging, said an engineer morosely. The media is sitting around at that hotel drinking rum and eating barbecued animal meat and watching them dredge.

You guys certainly take things seriously, said Henk. The hotel guys mentioned you might get weird about this. But you know what: one of them—Derek, or Dee-Man, or De*rone*?—he said to invite you all. He said to say hi. He said to say hi to someone named Willa, specifically. Maybe we could all head back to the hotel and grab a drink?

Henk moved to the shade of the biodigester, where Leonida stood counting.

The kids, he said—with a nod to the recruits—could play in the pool or something.

The recruits stared at him.

Seriously, said Henk as he took Leonida's hand. Open invite—

Do you have any idea what's at stake? said an aquaponics specialist. Do you understand how important this place is?

Don't raise your voice at Henk, said Leonida with a scowl.

We are in a climate emergency, said an ecologist. Only radical intervention—

Look, man, said Henk, I know you guys want me to write something. You want everyone at the hotel to come and film this place—which is, like, what? I don't even know. Something environmental? There are guys back there who report on environmental stuff—disaster stuff, like wildfires and oil leaks—but this place isn't a disaster, as far as I can tell. Maybe those guys will come by later. But let's be honest: there's not much of a story here.

You've got some nerve, said a solar specialist. How dare you.

More shouting followed—shouting that must have made its way to the medical cabin and penetrated the skull of Camp Hope's semiconscious leader. Because while crewmembers argued with Henk, Adams staggered from the medical cabin, bandages dangling, the purple skin around his wound exposed, his eyes bulging.

The fuck? said Henk.

He tried to pull Leonida close, but she was watching Adams with interest.

Are you all, like, a death cult? she said.

Crewmembers rushed to help Adams, everyone asking what had happened, where he'd come from and what was going on. Was this part of the launch plan?

Henk opened his phone and started taking notes. To no one in particular, he said: Is that Jacquelle de la Rosa over there? This could actually be interesting.

Confusion consumed the compound. There was more yelling, people running back and forth. I hugged *Living the Solution* to my chest, closed my eyes. I thought of wildfires searing ancient sequoia trees and glaciers dripping to puddles and dolphins poisoned by oil spills and cities drowned by rising seas. The book's message tolled in my mind, throbbed through my veins. I did not know who'd written it, but that didn't matter anymore—the words had become mine.

Because I had my eyes closed, though, I did not see the recruits leaving. No one did. All the crewmembers' attention was directed toward Adams, or toward correcting Henk and Leonida's misperceptions—everyone trying to communicate the goodness and necessity of Camp Hope—so no one saw the recruits gathering together, whispering. We didn't see them slip beyond the bougainvillea wall and climb inside a van and drive away. Of course, there are people now who think crewmembers sent the recruits to the hotel on purpose. Understand, though, that had we seen the expressions in the recruits' eyes, if we had understood what was happening, we would have put them under lock and key—I would have, personally. But we didn't. By the time we realized they were missing, they had a good ten minutes on us, and by the time we guessed where they were going, they had another five. And even then, we didn't realize what they were going to do.

IN THE HUSH OF WAITING, the air ran restless, the sea quicksilver-rippled. Here, beauty and pain twined together: like bright red berries, poison-plumped; like fish as venomous as words; like a ship, breeze-blessed, nimble through reefs, arriving from Guinea with three hundred men, women, and children imprisoned in its hold.

Gulls screamed, whirled above the harbor. The ship cast its bowline down. The gangplank groaned, slapped the wharf. Onlookers touched their pockets.

From above, the birds observed the unloading of more human cargo than the islands had ever seen.

More ships would follow: sloops, schooners, merchant vessels with exteriors made swift with copper plating. Ships steered by British Loyalists—pushed out by revolution. Ships carrying many hundreds more of those enslaved. Ships leaving the archipelago, holds loaded with salt and sea cotton, indigo, sugar. Ships triangulating continents, trade routes crossing like corset strings, binding nations tight. Ships loaded with textiles and pekoe tea. Leaving with pineapple. Sugar cane. Sisal. More, more. Faster, faster.

Listen: the whipcrack of progress.

Wind-driven sails give way to steamboats, their smokestacks puffing coal. The British abolish slavery and the Bahamas become a haven for those escaping elsewhere—but segregation stiffens the distance between poverty and power. The first tourists trickle into the archipelago, an annual regatta invented to keep people entertained. The Civil War erupts instead. Confederates run block-ades: England will mill their cotton, the bales floating between shorelines like a thousand compressed clouds. Soon, all-white settlements fixate on genealogy, while young Black boys give up school to dive for sponges. The hook and sculler teams are cut-throat, ill-paying, but there is no other way. Steamers start to skip the out-islands; Eleutherians are marooned. The First World War, at least, demands more labor and then a means to drink the war away. Here come the rumrunners, another spill of tourists steering yachts on the Twenties' diesel roar. Golf courses spring up. Tennis clubs and pigeon-shooting ranges. But also, a devastating sponge blight. A hurricane. A second nation-shaking war, after which the Bahamas' wartime airfield becomes an airstrip for a parade of bikinied bottoms. On Eleutheria, a Black minister calls for true democracy, true representation for the people. This prompts a bloodless sixteen-day strike, though it will take another sixteen years before Majority Rule: the nation's teal-black-yellow flag wind-rippled in the sky. Americans, meanwhile, keep the claw-hold of an empire, accountants flying Pan Am to delight in tax protections: executives can hide their wealth among the palms. The Americans build military bases, too, testing sonar radars and stoking long-range missiles. Why do your dirty work at home? The Americans will leave—on ocean liners and jet planes and helicopters—once circumstances do not suit them. Drug planes follow, turboprops landing lightly on the tarmacs left behind. Fishermen net cocaine from Colombia: square grouper with plastic wrap for fins. Another nightmare hurricane sweeps whole resorts from the shores on which they'd sat. *On Eleutheria, you'll feel the brush of trade winds*, the tourist brochures had promised, as if such breezes weren't traced with blood, the abominable cartography

10

Turn off your lights. Turn off your computers, your printers, your phones, your security systems, your air-conditioning, your robot vacuums, your entertainment consoles, your microwaves, your heat-sensing pillows, and your electric toothbrushes. Pull all other plugs. Drive less, bike more, find alternatives to flying. Plant trees. Plant native trees. Plant flowers and vegetables and then eat the vegetables and some of the flowers. Clean your plate. Compost scraps. Divert gray water for irrigation. Take shorter showers. Use biodegradable soap and make your own cleaning products. Air-dry laundry. Repair the clothes you have. Repair the shoes you have. Repair furniture. Repair houses. Repair friendships and have your friends over for dinner. Speak to strangers. Skill share. Ride share. Babysit. House sit. House share. Reuse, reduce. Work less. Buy nothing. No straws. Pick up litter. Keep bees.

Create bike lanes and pedestrian walkways. Limit tailpipe emissions and institute congestion pricing. Enforce energy-efficient building codes. Promote zero-carbon construction.

Generate electricity from renewable sources. Consider cogeneration, carbon capture, citizen-owned utilities. Promote public transport—better public transport—and make it free to all. Create community gardens. Stormwater gardens. Wastewater gardens. Create community forests and fields and rivers and lakes and marshlands and mountains and subtropical shrubsteppes. Fund environmental education. Make nature easy to love. Add green roofs, green walls, green sidewalks. Make spaces multifunctional. Give artists license to add beauty. Set up free ecolibraries. Seed banks. Time banks. Donation centers. Volunteer networks. Make quality healthcare available to all. Make fresh produce available to all. Make sustainability synonymous with equality.

Set binding international climate treaties. Set ambitious targets—the ones required to avert climate catastrophe—and do what it takes to meet those goals. Tax toxins, or better yet ban them. Prosecute offenders for crimes against the earth. Decouple money from regulation. Decouple money from governance. Close loopholes. Close drill sites and fracking operations and ruinous mines. Decentralize the Internet and energy systems and power structures in every sense of the word. End wars. End the cult of GDP—measure well-being instead. Invest in research that helps everyone. Listen to scientists. Listen to teachers. Listen to poets. Listen to indigenous voices along with those of others silenced over the centuries. Pay reparations. Then pay more. Pursue carbon equality. Restore ecosystems. Prioritize biodiversity. Remove international borders that prevent wildlife from roaming. That keep people from roaming. Offer global natural disaster support. Relocation support. Immigration support. Decolonize countries and economies and thought patterns. Tell the truth. Represent the people. Take responsibility for the past, and for the future. Try.

I'm trying—

For all the cases that can be made against me, know that I'm trying, that I have been trying, that I will continue to try, along with many others. In fact, more people are trying than ever before.

What else can a person say with so little time remaining?

Eight months have passed since I returned from Eleutheria to Boston. After walking into my cousins' apartment, I never left. I couldn't leave. Too dangerous: my face newly famous. Or infamous, I should say.

Instead, I paced, counting my steps. There are six steps between the bedroom and the bathroom sink, ten to the kitchen, three spanning the width of the oriel window—long curtains pulled tight. I walked even more miles in my mind, running through what happened at Camp Hope, and earlier: my whole life on rewind. I thought about my parents, my cousins, about Sylvia. I used Jeanette's computer to watch events unfold: the progression of "a global tragedy" to "an alarming phenomenon" to "a call to action" to "an emergency assembly of world leaders."

I watched with a knot in my throat, but also a heart juddering with expectation.

For all the suffering that has occurred—for all the tragedy—look at where we are: soon we'll know the results of the vote for the UN Treaty for Carbon Mitigation and Emissions Reparations—an emergency mandate designed to keep global temperatures from rising higher, to rehabilitate ecosystems on every continent, and to restore climate justice. That this vote is even happening is a miracle. And if the miracle goes further, if the mandate passes, the reason is Camp Hope. Camp Hope set this all in motion—*Living the Solution,* really—and I helped.

Is it wrong to wish others might see the situation this way?

Earlier this evening, I heard my neighbors in the apartment building's stairwell. They were discussing the mandate, the impending vote. Like much of Boston, they waited with their lights off, their electronics unplugged. The intentional darkness was a vigil. My neighbors—like people all over the world—were newly willing to try anything, everything, to fix what has gone wrong. Through the apartment door, I listened to their voices, whispers scratching the air. Their words hope-tinged, yearning. When their stairwell conversations swelled, my anticipation swelled too: the mandate must have passed.

So I opened the apartment door. I peered beyond its threshold. Eight months I'd stayed hidden; eight months I'd been careful. This evening I showed my face.

Maybe my reason is a sign of insanity, but I wanted to see my neighbors' expressions—to see if they'd connect the UN mandate with me. A part of me hoped they'd recognize me not as a wrongdoer, but as an idealist. A believer. Or even a pipe dreamer—high on the smoldering friction of slim chances and monumental change.

I was wrong on both accounts. The vote hadn't yet happened. My neighbors looked at me with surprise, then recognition, then horror.

I should have known better.

Then again, I should have known better about so many things.

The neighbors have no doubt contacted law enforcement. A SWAT team is likely on its way, if not already here: officers silently circling this building, snipers taking aim from across the street—the apartment's oriel window magnified in their scopes. If they've hesitated to burst through the apartment door, the only reason may be that they're waiting to hear news on the emergency mandate as well.

Is that wishful thinking?

It's true I may have also been allowed to talk through the night because someone, somehow, is recording what they'll call my confession. There are microphones so small they can fit on the backs of flies.

Either way, I don't have much time—so let me go through the last parts of the story, the parts that are hardest to tell. I'll start with my arrival back in Boston: how I've stayed hidden this long. It was luck, really. Or maybe Jeanette's ill luck. Because by the time I returned to Boston, Victoria had fled to Canada with her new dentist-husband, blessed by a visa in a lottery for health professionals. The rest of my cousins' family had been evangelized into estrangement. Jeanette was alone. She was grieving, enraged—which is what ultimately protected me: the shell of her anger wrapped around us both like armor.

There was no reason for her to shelter me. Given what had happened on Eleutheria, there was every reason not to. But, at least at first, Jeanette was too caught up in her own struggles to care where I had been for all those months, or why I had returned. When she answered her apartment door, she wore a too-tight sequined dress, her hair bedraggled and over-glittered. Her nail polish was chipped.

What happened to your face? she said.

She turned away before I answered, not caring to know. I think she was expecting Victoria at her door. It must have been disappointing to find me instead. Even so, I followed her into the apartment, where afternoon light sprawled through the oriel window, illuminating a landscape of takeout boxes, empty wine bottles, dirty dishes, unwashed laundry. Jeanette tottered and tripped around these piles. Her movements lacked the vigor they'd once had, as if she'd needed the orbital energy of Victoria to maintain balance—even if she and her sister had long been at odds. She hardly seemed to realize I was there.

I did my best to keep Jeanette tethered to this earth. I cleaned the apartment. I made her meals and then made sure she went to sleep. When Victoria deposited money in the bank account the sisters had once shared—but did not call—Jeanette cried and I listened, stroking her hair. I was glad to take care of her, glad for something to do. All my life, I'd been looking for someone to take care of me—to be a parent—only to be disappointed. I discovered a solace, though, in being a parent to someone else.

Regardless, I doubt Jeanette has let me stay because I've taken care of her. Or out of any familial loyalty. She has kept me here, kept me hidden—despite the escalation of events with which I am linked—because I've served as a facsimile of her sister, however inadequate.

If I understand anything now, it is the lengths people go to cope when those they love leave them.

When I got back to Boston eight months ago, Camp Hope was everywhere. Beyond the news headlines, the think pieces, the talk show debates, there were the video clips: repeated, refracted, before they were banned—an effort that had no effect on what was in motion. By then, the so-called alarming phenomenon couldn't be stopped.

For a while, though, Camp Hope proliferated. The bougainvillea wall, the wind turbine, the biodiesel vans, the gardens—they filled screens and social media feeds, filled imaginations. There were the photos of crewmembers: everyone mug-shotted and stunned. There were quotes from *Living the Solution*—the text puzzled over, picked apart. There was Roy Adams, his chest dramatically bandaged as he stood in front of microphones on courthouse steps, his attorney proclaiming his innocence.

Most ubiquitous, though, was the camera phone footage of journalists and other members of the media drinking rum punch on the spacious deck of a hotel in the Bahamas. Before the video was banned, you could watch them laughing and having a good time, enjoying the view, the complimentary drinks, a rake-and-scrape band. Looking closely at the footage, you can glimpse Corrine and Dorothy in a corner, pleading with a vlogger to come back to Camp Hope. Deron is there too—high-fiving a newscaster—though he appears for only a second. The camera turns to twelve young people in matching polo shirts and khaki shorts who have appeared on the beach below the deck. *Is this supposed to be a performance?* says a journalist, as the young people run across the sand, dive into the harbor, swim toward a dredging barge. *Damn,* says a B-list celebrity, *those kids must eat their Wheaties—look at them go.*

In later interviews, those same public figures would beg forgiveness. How could they have known what was about to happen? How could they have been expected to go after those kids? They'd been drinking. They had no idea what was coming.

How could anyone have known?

In the video, the twelve young people swim out to a barge at the edge of a harbor. The camera zooms in as they shimmy up the anchor chain and climb into the boat. *What the hell?* someone at the party can be heard saying amid laughter. On the barge deck, a captain appears to be saying the same thing. The dripping-wet recruits gather around him. By the force of many arms, they throw him and his partner overboard. The camera footage gets knocked to the side here. A manager from the hotel is yelling, as are others—maybe Deron, though it's unclear. There is a scuffling commotion, a shout to get help. There won't be time. The recruits have swarmed the barge, some going below to cut fuel lines and punch holes in the diesel tank. Others fling open a fire cabinet, find solvents to splash across the deck. The last bit of footage shows a row of recruits lined up along the barge railing. Fitz, Cameron, Thatcher, Lillian, Margaret, and others. They're waiting for the camera—the many cameras by that point—to steady. They are making sure this image comes out crisp. They look stoic, resolute. A sea breeze tousles their hair. The sun glows golden on their skin. They gaze back upon the island: a swath of green glinting in their eyes. The barge erupts into flames.

A media frenzy followed, with cries of tragedy and child abuse and conspiracy cover-ups and cult sacrifice and teen ecoterrorism coming from every angle. These children of the elite—these beautiful young people, so easy to love—these young lives cut short, they captured the nation's imagination, and with them: Camp Hope. People wanted to know why the recruits had done it. They wanted to know what had been happening on Eleutheria. Crewmembers were taken into custody, slammed with litigation. When the Green Republicans were discovered to have connections to Camp Hope, the scandal tanked their political prospects.

For all that initial attention, the events on Eleutheria might have faded from public view, if not for what happened three weeks later. In Langley, Virginia, a class of sixth graders stood up from their desks during second-period social studies, walked swiftly and silently out of the classroom, then up three floors to the school's roof. From there, they looked down at the administrators and teachers—and later the parents—who gathered below to insist the children step away from the edge. *What on earth are they doing? Why won't any of them speak?* The children stared impassively back. A professional crisis team had to remove them. All the children were hospitalized, put under surveillance, their behavior deemed an anomaly—until a similar gathering occurred the next day. In the midst of a soccer tournament in Centennial, Colorado, two hundred children walked off their playing fields. Parents and coaches grabbed at the young people's arms, tried to contain them, but the sheer mass of children exceeded anyone's grasp as they all marched in silence toward a highway. Vehicles screeched to a halt. The children flooded the road, blocking traffic until a crisis team removed them as well.

The phenomenon spread. Across the U.S., children walked away from schools and sports fields, from playgrounds and stoops, basements and bedrooms as if hearing an invisible call. In dozens and hundreds, they gathered on roofs, on bridges, at the edges of lakes, in parking lots, in roundabouts, outside prisons, outside power plants, in the middle of construction sites.

They never spoke. Their expressions stayed stoic—though one reporter described them as "dead-eyed," giving voice to what so many wondered: was this linked to Camp Hope? Was it some kind of copycat thing?

Panic fomented, fueled by the possibility that these children might act upon whatever impulse had compelled those at Camp Hope—that these children were threatening their own self-destruction.

Of course, children were already dying everywhere; at borders, in sweatshops, in shantytowns, in wars. Dying of poisoned water. Gun violence. State violence. Overwork. Hunger. Neglect. It was just that these children—the ones gathering— they were supposed to be healthy and happy and free to pursue success as they someday saw fit.

The gatherings persisted. The numbers of participants grew. Children poured from their homes without warning, walked away from birthday parties and bat mitzvahs, from the grocery aisle where a parent was shopping. Children collected on overpasses, stared down at drivers. They stood in the middle of parking lots. They congregated at bus stops.

By Columbus Day—two months after the explosion on Eleutheria—the issue was declared a national emergency akin to a pandemic.

And for a time, people did speculate that an illness had infected the children, compelled them toward mania. *Doesn't that happen to certain animal species? Like when dolphin pods beach themselves?* But out of everyone, the children were calmest: steady and stoic and ever deliberate. And the travel bans and quarantines had no effect when the gatherings went international. Nor did the cocktail of feel-good pharmaceuticals many young people were prescribed. People's children and grandchildren, nieces and nephews, godchildren and stepchildren, students and scouts, piano protégés and neighborhood menaces continued to gather in silent assemblies.

Adults, meanwhile, swarmed city halls and government offices. They banged on doors, demanding action be taken. Lawmakers, though, sat stock-still at their desks—groups of children stood silent outside their offices watching them work. The same thing happened outside corporate campuses. Beside the New York Stock Exchange. The appearances unsettled all who observed them, implicated observers as well. Because if it wasn't your child, it was often a child you recognized—a child you loved—who stood in an intersection with twenty other young people, watching stalled traffic with the grim solemnity of a jury.

Newscasters read reports with jaws clenched. *Another gathering, this time in Dallas* . . . What could be said of the sheer eeriness of it all? . . . *Three hundred children, outside the airport* . . . The stares of those children seared into your brain. Their gazes twisted your gut, gave you a sickly sensation: the cold sweat of culpability, a fever haze of complicity. It was worse, in some ways, that these children threatened an act without acting. The persistent possibility wrung even the toughest hearts raw. Some parents stopped leaving their homes, stayed fixed to their kids' sides. There was an effort to restrain children, to restrict their movements to padded safe rooms, but the ramifications of these prisons became too heavy to bear. People begged their children to explain what needed to happen for them to go on with their lives.

The answer, though, had been there the whole time. It only grew louder amid the children's ongoing quiet. There could be no more school. No more soccer practice. No more chess club. No more babysitting. No more video game playing while a whole day drifted past. There could be no return to the psychosis of denial: business as usual in the midst of a crisis. Not so long as the whole world steamed along with no regard for the burdens to come: the oceans overboiled and the soil blowing away and species pushed off the edge of existence.

If adults wanted children to act as if a future awaited them, then perhaps they ought not to destroy it.

Meanwhile, I was dead—or presumed to be. That's one reason why, in their testimonies, interviews, apology statements, crewmembers invoked my supposed secret agenda. *She came here to destroy us*, a solar specialist claimed. *She brainwashed the recruits*, an ecologist insisted. *She was part of a highly secretive decentralized leftist organization intent on assassinating the elite to create a new world order*, said a Liberal Arts Girl.

Someone had to be the scapegoat. That's why, once again, Roy Adams and others pinned blame to my body.

My body: never discovered, despite thorough searches of the hotel's marina and beyond. I was deemed lost at sea. I had been in the water when the barge exploded. Having realized the recruits had gone to the hotel, I'd driven after them at top speed. I'd arrived before any of the other crewmembers, leapt out of the van just as the recruits were climbing aboard the barge. I swam toward them as fast as I could. In one of the videos, my head bobs into view on the edge of the frame. Investigators assumed my body burned up in the explosion, or that I'd been struck by debris. There was shark activity in the area. My watch may have been found, a scrap of my shirt.

I don't think anyone wanted me to be alive anyway. Dead, I could be the scapegoat they needed.

I am not dead, though.

I am here.

To make a long story short, after the explosion I became flotsam—tossed out into a current that washed me up on a beach farther down the island. When I crawled onto the sand, I was bleeding, in shock. If a more substantial law enforcement unit had surveyed the island sooner, officials might have found me, but all attention was on the hotel. And so, in that interval—before the helicopters touched down, along with investigators, more reporters, curious onlookers, grieving parents—I walked all the way back to Camp Hope, crossing through the island coppice and the outskirts of settlements. It took all night and the next morning. If this sounds implausible, know that, in the wake of what happened, I became only my body: a body that elbowed and clawed through the brush—pushing through spiderwebs, the slice of saw grass— a body that felt nothing except the tugging need to return to Camp Hope. I stumbled through palmetto and gumbo-limbo, into groves of poisonwood, twisting my ankle in sinkholes that slammed me to the ground. I got up, hobbled onward, the pain a welcome distraction from the desolation lacerating my insides.

By the time I made it to Camp Hope, I was bleeding in a dozen places. My tongue was fat with dehydration. My skin, especially my face, was puffed with rashy welts from poison-wood and insect bites.

Camp Hope looked no better. The grounds were police-taped, roughed up, empty of people. Crewmembers who had not gone to the hotel had, by then, been taken into custody. Local law enforcement would return—along with the FBI—but I did not care. What mattered to me was that the passion fruit trellises had been knocked over, the carrots needed watering, the compost needed turning, the aquaponics filtration system needed cleaning. I went around the grounds, righting all that I could.

I might have stayed at Camp Hope—tended the grounds until I was dragged away—but while neatening my bunkroom, I found the backpack I'd brought with me to Eleutheria.

The envelope from Sylvia remained inside.

That envelope: impossible to discard, impossible to open. I'd held on to it ever since Sylvia slipped it under the door of my cousins' apartment, days before I caught a standby flight to Eleutheria. At that time, I'd been reading—rereading—*Living the Solution*, obsessed with the promise of a compound at the edge of the Caribbean, where a team of eco-revolutionaries came together to save the planet. Sylvia's gesture had always seemed like a taunt: she didn't think I had what it took to make a difference in the world. The envelope was an escape hatch to a comfortable life kept buoyant on compromise.

So I left Boston. To prove to Sylvia—and to myself—I was willing to walk my own talk, I went to Eleutheria.

Yet I didn't leave the envelope behind, did I? I couldn't discard that pathway back.

There at Camp Hope, at the end of everything, I had nothing left to lose—least of all my pride.

I opened the envelope.

There's not enough time to get into my journey back to Boston, but know this: there are Bahamian islands located less than fifty miles from the U.S. mainland. It was easy to steer one of Camp Hope's biodiesel yachts into a Floridian port recently mangled by a hurricane, to sink the boat in the harbor where other yachts and schooners and sailboats had sunk. On the U.S. mainland, the poisonwood welts on my face—blistering red—provoked disgust in people, made them look away, or take pity on me. The welts also confused the facial recognition technology installed in every city. A certain amount of naiveté protected me as well. I wouldn't glimpse my televised face—my unblemished face—until I reached North Carolina. And I wouldn't understand that I'd been cast as a villain until Rhode Island.

I kept going, though. Once back in Boston, I went straight to Sylvia's house.

Those front steps, so familiar; the same scattershot yard. It was September by then. Burning hot. Dripping hot. Sweat making my blistered body burn.

I stood on that porch with Sylvia's letter pressed against my chest as if it might staunch all the hurt in the world.

Of course I have the letter with me now. It hasn't left my person since.

Dearest Willa—

If you are reading this, then perhaps you have not quite given up on me, as I fear.
    This is one of many fears. Much has frightened me in this life. There was the possibility of not becoming

*the scholar I sought to be, then of not finding employ-
ment, then of losing that employment and not having
the opportunity to pursue the life of the mind. There
were the banal fears: spiders and heights. Also the fear
of losing my memory, like my mother, and becoming a
husk of myself—or of remembering some things too well,
and becoming paralyzed by my own failings. But nothing
frightened me more than you.*

*Willa, you were the molten lava into which I longed
to thrust my hand. You were the tiger waiting in the
dark. You were the poison I longed to sip.*

*Forgive these clumsy analogies. I do not know how
else to say this.*

*Willa, when I first saw you—frozen like a wax
figurine, in that house on Beacon Hill—I believed I was
hallucinating. You were wearing an old-fashioned gown;
more significantly, your face reminded me of the face of
someone I had once known—someone I had hurt. My
first thoughts were, <u>Get away! Escape! Flee!</u> And so I
dropped the glass of wine. As I later came to understand,
you believed I dropped the glass to save you. Really, I
was trying to save myself. I never told you this because I
did not want to disappoint you. I have never wanted to
disappoint you, Willa.*

*It seems, though, that I have. I have disappointed you
in ways I cannot take back.*

*There are other things I never told you, which I
may as well tell you now. To start: you tend to wear
this expression—of which I doubt you are aware—that
brims with expectation. You look at people and places*

*like they have infinite potential. There is the way you tilt
your neck to one side, then the other, and crack it. You
have this innocent recklessness. There is a sense of fate in
your steps.* ~~*You look hungry, as if ready for*~~ *I have always
believed that in another life you might have been a wandering prophet.*

*Returning to that first encounter: After you and
your companions fled, and after the hostess had been
calmed down, the spilled wine attended to, I locked
myself in a bathroom to catch my breath. I was gasping
like a fish because I'd felt how thin the membrane was
between us. It was only air; nothing else. I knew that you
were <u>not</u> the person I'd once known—that you were a
stranger—and yet a part of me believed you embodied
her. I was experiencing a great deal of guilt at the time. I
was not sleeping well. And when you appeared—staring
back at me with all the expectation in the world—it
made me afraid.*

*However, after doing breathing exercises and splash-
ing my face with water, I began to doubt my paranoia.
You were a stranger and you were gone. I chided myself
for ruining the hostess's carpet.*

*I should have left it at that. I should have disregarded
the encounter, but I have a researcher's need for explanation. I had the phone you dropped at the house analyzed
by a friend in Harvard's IT department. This was for my
protection, I told myself. Your appearance had the aura
of the uncanny; I needed to confirm you had not been
sent by a right-wing think tank to sabotage me. Wilder
things have happened to academics in our ongoing*

*culture wars—and, in a recent interview, I'd made a few
thoughtless remarks about conservative hypocrisy that
had drawn ire. I had to be careful.*

*So I learned where you worked, where you lived. I
learned your name. There was a lot missing. No records
of schooling. Almost as if you had stepped into a false
identity. Yet, there was no sign of pernicious activity,
either. <u>Let it go</u>, I told myself. But I couldn't. I visited
your workplace, The Hole Story, to "double-check." To
check what? As I have said, I wasn't sleeping well. Memories of what I had done—damaging a vulnerable young
woman's life—gnawed at my mind. For some reason,
studying you seemed logical.*

*Then you recognized me. I was sure of it. I upbraided
myself all the way back to Cambridge, certain I had lost
my grip on reality. I committed to forgetting you existed.*

*But how could I, Willa, when you turned up in my
class?*

*I know my reaction hurt you. Understand, though,
that it was as if my former student had waltzed in and
announced herself—right there, in the most public of
places. I was terrified a colleague, or another student,
would recognize the similarity. I was terrified of you,
even as I felt your pull. It was all I could do to push you
away and escape.*

*You haunted me, Willa. Then and now. You ended up
at my house. There's no escaping this, I told myself. And I
wanted it. Wanted you. I wanted to know who you were.
In my home I was also more comfortable. No spying colleagues or meddlesome students.*

What I remember most about that first conversa-

tion were the bruises on your arms. You had this purple undertone that came to the surface easily, and chapped lips that bled at the corners—perhaps a sign of vitamin deficiency? Your hair, that afternoon, was always falling into your face. Rather than brushing the hair away, you peered past and around it, as if through a grate.

I kept waiting for you to reveal that you weren't a real Harvard student—you struck me as a fundamentally honest person—but you admitted nothing. You seemed at home in my house, as if you'd been there before. And while in many ways you weren't like the student with whom I'd had the disastrous romantic entanglement, the resemblance made me uneasy. It also soothed a complicated grief I had yet to untangle.

Against my better judgment, I invited you back. It's true, I do not have many close friends. I have many associates—colleagues and fellow scholars—but their cynicism can become tiresome. You were so easily enchanted. Your wonderment washed over the clutter of my home. You were delighted by the simplest things, like petting Simone or eating a sugar cookie. After that first meeting, I missed your wonderment when you left.

I liked being with you, though you tormented me. I experienced a series of depressive episodes while wrestling with my own motivations, my guilt. Even so, it also pleased me when we continued meeting in the guise of student and teacher; at times, I could convince myself I'd repaired my past mistakes by maintaining professional boundaries. But what was motivating you? You sat before me: a spritely Rubik's Cube. Always, I have been able to ascertain explanations for uncommon

*phenomena. As a sociologist, I bridge the general with
the particular, connecting individual realities with larger
forces. (To quote Bertrand Russell: "While economics is
about how people make choices, sociology is about how
they don't have any choice to make.") Yet I could not
identify the forces guiding you, Willa. You were ready
to give a stranger everything in your pockets, but you
wouldn't reveal where you were from. You sometimes
added or dropped Rs to words—I found it sweet how
you said "idea" like "idear," as if you personally loved
the notion—and this tendency made me think northern
New England, maybe Maine. But you could be eccentric
as well. You would have made the Puritans blush. Once
I spilled tea on myself and—in a flash—you pulled the
scarf from your neck and began dabbing my collarbone.
You did it without asking. You offered to let me keep
the scarf—blinking at me with your face so earnest. I
declined because the scarf represented a temptation I
was determined to avoid. Your scarf would be too full of
your sweaty, powdered-sugar smell. If I wasn't careful,
when you were telling me all your idears, I'd let my eyes
wander along the curve of your seashell ears, your thin
wrists, the bruises running along your arms. Then I'd
chastise myself. I had many arguments in my head while
you talked, one voice in particular saying: "Well, she isn't
really a student. She's something else."*

*I was also afraid of what that something else
might be.*

*You wanted, with such fervor, for me to find the
Freegans compelling. They were mildly interesting, if only
for the extremity of their beliefs, as well as the subcon-*

*scious animus undergirding their collective actions. My
work, though, focuses on social movements with specific
and deliberate strategic goals. These people seemed too
chaotic to accomplish anything. There were times I wondered if you had made them up. I took a pitying stance.
Poor girl, I thought, she doesn't even know her compatri-
ots' names. She has no understanding of the long-term
investment true social change requires.*

*Meanwhile, I congratulated myself on maintaining
our stalemated charade of professor and student. I had
revised my poor behavior from the previous relationship.
I looked ahead. In academia, we become amnesiac from
one semester to another: we are always starting fresh. I
was on the path to tenure—the culmination of a lifetime
of study—but I lived, too, in repetition, every term washing away the last.*

*To think I believed you could be washed away. When
the Halloween riots happened, my fear became one of
culpability. The Freegans were <u>not</u> without impact, and
I might have compelled you to get too involved. I might
have ruined another young woman's life.*

*How relieved I was when you appeared that night.
It was as if a spell had been broken—or cast. When you
kissed me, it was as if I had been forgiven for all wrongs.
This was irresistible, understand. I was helpless to it. In
past relationships, I tended to take control; other women
have called me "highly communicative." But with you, I
felt wordless. I felt language sucked from my body and
with it, all my strength, like having all the blood leeched
from my muscles. ~~In bed, I became only feelings.~~ Maybe
that had to do with being around someone like you:*

*seemingly without inhibitions or shame. Again, you had
that uncanniness, a familiarity, like you already knew
me—my body—knew how to touch me. After that first
time, I wanted to get away from you, if only to process the event, to return some blood to my limbs, find
words. You had gotten into me, though. I shouldn't have
expected to extract myself easily.*

*This is only physical, I told myself. That's all. That's
not so bad. I was terrified of you. Terrified of hurting
you. To keep the relationship purely physical seemed saf-
est for both of us. There would be no expectations. Our
relationship could be a mere transaction.*

*And so, that first winter, I tried to keep you at a
distance. I tried to keep the relationship inside a set of
parameters. I tried to protect us both.*

*As if a relationship could be an island. In the end,
I had to tell you about the former student. This was
not welcome information, I know. And to be fair, nor
was your request that I help your Freegan friends.
You seemed fundamentally unaware of the danger of
such associations. You wanted me to work with them,
as if such a liaison would not have had profound
repercussions.*

*Am I making excuses? Admittedly, I suggested we
go to the Vineyard in part to hide away, in case you
were under suspicion by the authorities. You must have
noticed, at least, the escalations of high-profile arrests
that spring?*

*Regardless, those days on the Vineyard were won-
derful. You had mermaid hair from the saltwater, and
you seemed so amazed by everything. It was like tak-*

ing a puppy outside for the first time. Your joy became mine. I began to believe that a full relationship—a life together—was possible, if only you would open up to me. When you didn't, some of my old concerns resurfaced. It was my brother, Thomas, who first suggested you were using me for money. I told him about you over the phone. At first, to Thomas, I scoffed. I said that he didn't know you—to which my brother replied: "Well, neither do you." This was a fair point. Though then you did open up to me and I realized how fragile you were. This new understanding also coincided with worried emails from my department chair. I won't go into how things became strained. I don't think you realized I stayed up at night while we were at the Vineyard, working on the laptop I kept tucked away. This was not ideal for a number of reasons, but it brings me to what I most want to tell you—one of my reasons for writing this letter.

After I read what came next, I sank onto the bunkroom floor, my gasp ricocheting across the grounds of Camp Hope.

There is something I need you to know. I've been writing this letter to explain myself, but the more I write, the more I am unsure whether I even know my own story.

Willa, I was drawn to the field of sociology because I was, at first, delighted by the great collective expressions of human intention through history—how we are not solely defined by our individual choices so much as the warp and weft of society. I studied social movements, specifically, because I was interested in the ways a group might push back against the mainstream: how a

small group might divert or direct the shape of civilization. ~~My mother was a Communist, you'll remember~~
It is through such study, though, that the inevitability
of human fallibility is raised again and again. That can
make a person cynical, when the study of social movements is your life's work. There has been so much good-
will throughout human history, but so much corruption
and violence and failure as well.

You still believed in change, Willa. You believed with
such ferocity. Of course you loved <u>Living the Solution</u>. I
wrote it with you in mind.

You won't accept this, I know. You are telling yourself
now that this is impossible. But who better to write the
path to a perfect society than someone who, for a career,
has studied the rise and fall of social movements?

Suffice to say, around the time we became romanti-
cally involved, I was approached by a law firm—a first
for me—and offered the chance to ghostwrite a manual
according to general goals laid out by an anonymous
organization. I was also given audio recordings of a
military man who rambled pompously on and on. My
understanding was that several other individuals were
also offered this opportunity and one of our texts would
be selected, the winner receiving a large payout. The
organization did not specify what they would use the
text for. I did not ask.

The offer struck me as bizarre, and too large a task to
take on with all my other work. But you had put these
notions in my head: the utopian spirit, one might say.
And I knew, moreover, that I could not do what you

wanted me to do: put my career on the line to advocate
for your criminally suspect Freegan friends. Writing this
manuscript was something I could do for you instead—
I could give you this text, even if I couldn't undertake the
radical actions you wanted me to pursue in real life.

Understand, Willa, that Living the Solution *is a*
response to the Freegan theories and dreamscapes you
brought to my attention. I would revise their flawed
premises in my head, align possibility with pragmatism.
Crafting the text was an act of pure problem-solving.
How, I asked myself, might a small group of people
realistically influence the global imagination for environ-
mental ends? Utopias have always existed most com-
fortably in prose, ever since Thomas More invented the
word.

It was on the Vineyard, when you finally told me
about your childhood, your parents, their beliefs, that I
was able to fully stitch the idea together. Living the Solu-
tion was, at its core, a book for you: a fairy tale that cor-
rected your every hardship. Here was a society beyond
the constraints and hindrances of family. Without the
tumult of biological or romantic love, participants could
stoke true loyalty to a collective cause. Here, too, was an
endeavor born from your cousins' obsession with image
as a catalyst for fame. Here was a closed system, akin to
a terrarium. As an academic, this careful distillation of
your life was the best I believed I could give you.

Writing in the rambling military man's "voice," I
should add, was not difficult—if anything, it was too
easy. How horrifying to discover one has internalized the

*overconfident declarations of all those fathers and patri-
archs echoing through the centuries? Yet, I channeled this
voice without a second thought.*

*When my text was selected, the prize money added
a layer of financial security to my life—and your life
indirectly. I felt, for a while, that I owed you some of
the payout when it arrived. I hoped the money made a
difference to you, since you had—if unwittingly—aided
in its creation. I had the idea that I would tell you about
it when I received a printed copy. Then we had our
disagreement.*

*I did not regret writing <u>Living the Solution</u> at the
time; I would have, had I known it would take you
from me.*

*Was it irresponsible to create a blueprint for utopia,
set it free? I never expected anything to come of <u>Living
the Solution</u>. When my copy arrived in the mail, the
attorney mentioned that "it" was well underway, and
that my text had helped fine-tune "its" final stages. I was
under contract to keep what I knew a secret. This did not
matter to me because I did not think "it" would concern
me. I was worried about you, what you were doing, and
this was interfering with my scholarly work. You were
angry with me. You felt I'd betrayed you by not supporting the Freegans the way you wanted. I had always
hoped your interest in them would fade—that you would
recognize the danger of associating with them, the use-
lessness too. I hoped you would take up watercoloring or
kickboxing or online gambling, or anything. I knew I'd
lose everything if I did what you wanted me to do—and
it all might be for nothing. I'd lose my job and my house*

and all my nice things. Those things, I believed, were the reason you loved me, even if you didn't know it.

My material security wasn't what you wanted, though, was it? You had decided, for some reason, that there was something brave in me. I wasn't a wheel-spinning coward to you. ~~You seemed to think this, even when~~

I was sure you were wrong.

Then you found <u>Living the Solution</u> in my office. I thought I would lose you if I told you the truth, but it seems I will lose you anyway. So, I am trying to do the brave thing—the Willa thing, as I think of it—and I'm starting by writing this all out. It's 2:00 P.M. and my class has begun and I'm not there. But I need you to know that I am trying to be braver. I will keep trying.

With all the love in the world,
Sylvia

I pounded on Sylvia's door for a long time. Maybe she was taking a nap, I thought. Maybe she would open the door, half-asleep, and my appearance would seem like the welcome turn of a dream.

I imagined putting my hands on the soft sides of her face and whispering that I was here. Everything was okay. We had both been wrong about many things—we were both awfully imperfect—but we were bound together, she and I, by a cosmic thread. Her letter had made me cry and gasp and laugh aloud with wonder. Neither of us was the person the other had originally thought, but we loved one another—of that I was sure. *Living the Solution* made me sure, now that I knew why it was written and by whom.

If she would only open her door, I could hold her tighter than I ever had. I could tuck my neck against hers, inhale the universe of her perfume, describe how much I'd missed her. I could tell her I loved her. We'd each made mistakes, but everything was honest now. We'd start anew.

I'm here, I called through the door. I've come back.

Sylvia's neighbor emerged on her porch and did not bother to make a show of pretending to do something else. The woman had a cane and did not look well. She stood with both hands on the top of the cane, leaned forward.

Were you born that way? said the neighbor. With a face like that?

Where's Sylvia? I said. Where's Professor Gill?

I don't like the looks of you, said the neighbor.

Please, I said.

I always knew Sy was trouble, said the woman. Consorting with terrorists and anarchists. You should have seen the people she'd invite over. This respectable lady, quits her job at Harvard to—

Is she here? I said. Will she be back soon?

That's the question, said the neighbor.

She lifted her cane and jiggled it at me. On cue, a police car rolled past on the street. I remembered my vulnerability; I was supposed to be dead. My face was all over the news, and—now that I was back in Boston—someone might recognize me despite my blemished features. If I was caught, I might never see Sylvia.

I told myself I'd return to her house another time. I'd search for her in the days to come. I hadn't fully grasped the extent of my infamy—though later, at Jeanette's apartment, it would become clear that I couldn't venture out into the city again. To do so was to be apprehended at once, especially after my face healed. I would realize I had been lucky to make it to the apartment at all. And I needed to look after Jeanette.

Before I knew all that, though, I hovered on Sylvia's doorstep, willing her to appear.

The neighbor kept talking, saying: I've been collecting Sy's mail all this time. And taking care of her rabbit. She hasn't been here in weeks—

A second police car rolled past; the hair on my arms prickled.

If she comes back, I said to the neighbor, will you tell her I was here? Will you tell her I'm looking for her?

And who are you?

L.

L?

L as in lonely. *L* as in lost. *L* as in liar. *L* as in loony. *L* as in libertine. *L* as in love.

My parents had never been sure how the world would end. They had been sure, though, that it would.

Life, they told me—then only five years old—was a series of small apocalypses leading to a big one. To believe otherwise was to engage in delusion. So much of modern civilization, they said, was built on delusion: the belief that water will always pour through pipes onto our awaiting hands, that air will whisk comfortably through our lungs, that civilization is civil, that life can offer anything beyond disappointment and pain.

Delusions, my mother said, are why people get hurt.

I understand, now, she was trying to protect me. Both of my parents were trying to protect me in the only way they knew how, until they couldn't anymore.

Even so, I think delusions may be all we have.

Delusions are how things start to change.

The sun has come up. Out in the city, people are trying to set things right. They have torn up parking lots to plant gardens. There are bee boxes on rooftops, along with new solar panels. In the harbor, the power plant is being retrofitted to run on tidal energy. Volunteer crews work day and night on these projects. Governments at all levels have reoriented toward sustainability. It will take centuries to fully undo what has been done, but we have started that undoing. We have to and we are.

The mass mobilizations of silent children, according to some news outlets, are decreasing in frequency—though it's too early to know for sure. So people keep trying to do better.

Jeanette will be back soon; she will be tired, but she will have a light in her eyes. She will have been riding my old bike all over the city. She has been going out every day on these missions, often at night, to take photos of renovation crews and planting crews and other volunteer efforts.

It's the only thing I've ever been good at, Jeanette said when I asked about her photo-taking.

She didn't say anything else. Though when she goes on her computer—once a day now, to save electricity—and beams the images outward, she seems more at peace than she has been in a long time.

———

Peace hasn't come for me. At night—the nights I sleep, of which there are not many—I dream of them. The recruits, I mean. Fitz and Lillian and Thatcher and Cameron and all the others. I dream of them as they were the last night at Camp Hope: all floating gently in the cove, their strokes sweeping bioluminescence through the water like starlight, galaxies blinking awake.

I dream of Athena and Elmer on some nights as well. I see them pulling the golden Madonna statue from the sea; history righting itself, wrongs made good.

It's not impossible. It never was.

I dream of all the other children, too—the ones I've never met. All those children wishing toward a future.

I choose to believe in the future. That's what I've been trying to tell you—because that's all I ever wanted someone to tell me. I want you to know I believe in a future for you.

I haven't forgotten how I participated in creating tragedy. Maybe I don't deserve my own life anymore, though I wouldn't call hiding out like this living. Regardless, I know there are other people who will not forget. I will be held accountable when the time comes—and that time is rushing up fast.

I would do it all again, though.

There, I said it.

We were going to suffer one way or another. Better to suffer on the way to making something new.

————

There's a commotion in the corridor—footsteps on the stairwell. Doors opening. A rush of voices. The UN mandate has passed: that's what I'll choose to believe. The commotion is a celebration. International leaders have come together, their cooperation unprecedented, their goals for planetary preservation aligned. Soon, this work will be a global effort: humanity a unified front.

The voices are louder now, the footsteps just outside the apartment door. A SWAT team, maybe—come for me at last—come to take me away for a crime so much bigger than one person, bigger than one country, even one generation.

Or else, maybe it is Sylvia outside with her hand on the handle? It's Sylvia who's there—come to sweep me into her arms. There are only eight steps from here to the front door and I'm going to take them. I'm going to fling that door open and embrace what's coming. Because I believe it will be good.

ACKNOWLEDGMENTS

This book was written in six states and five different countries; it had a lot of help along the way. Thank you to the Elizabeth George Foundation for a life-changing grant. Thank you to the Jentel Foundation and to the Montalvo Arts Center for the time, space, and clarity to write. Thank you to the Bread Loaf Writers' Conference for all the inspiration. Thank you to the many individuals and organizations whose time and support made *Eleutheria* possible.

Thank you to my incomparable agent, Erin Harris, for believing in me and for making dreams into realities. Thank you to Caitlin Landuyt for giving the novel an incredible home, and for her expert editorial eye. Thank you to the amazing team of people who helped put this book into the world, especially Carla Benton, Edward Allen, Maddie Partner, Nick Alguire, Angie Venezia, James Meader, Sarah Nisbet, Jessica Deitcher, Annie Locke, Alexa Thompson, Beth Lamb, and Suzanne Herz.

Thank you to all my teachers and mentors over the years.

Thank you to my earliest manuscript readers at Arizona State University and at the Writing Workshops in Greece. Thank you to Pete Turchi for always pushing me to step up my game. Thank you to Matt Bell for the late-stage manuscript read and the encouragement to hang in there.

Thank you to the loved ones who have made me laugh and helped me grow. Special shout-out to the Oberlin crew for helping me land on my feet. Thank you to Nora, Kyle, Daniel, Eva, Kirstin, María, Bryan, Jennifer, Adrienne, Dennis, and Thirii for your thoughtfulness during a difficult time. Thank you to my family for not asking too often when this book would be done. Thank you to my parents for the writing residencies, and also for everything.

Thank you to the activists—especially the youth activists—who continue to inspire, and who lead the fight for a just and equitable world.